The Crossroads

ELIZABETH CORBETT

The Crossroads

APPLETON-CENTURY   NEW YORK

APPLETON-CENTURY
AFFILIATE OF
MEREDITH PRESS

Library of Congress Catalog Card Number: 65-23022

MANUFACTURED IN THE UNITED STATES OF AMERICA FOR MEREDITH PRESS

To Robert Earl Jones

The Crossroads

WAVERLEY BOOK SHOP WAS SITUATED AT THE CROSSROADS OF The Village. When you said "The Village" like that, with the article as well as the noun capitalized, it could mean only one locality: Greenwich Village, that famous district in downtown New York. The Village, so royally condescended to by the provincial press as "New York's shabby 'Bohemian' Quarter," so regularly pointed out by the barker of the sight-seeing bus as "the home of curious Bohemians," with curious in this context serving as a synonym for "shady." It was all in the course of their day's business. Harry Martin, proprietor of the shop, was inclined to laugh at such aspersions. They sometimes made Alice Martin indignant.

Alice and Harry were joint owners of the shop. They had been married even longer than they had been in business together. Their commercial undertaking not only earned them an excellent living; it gave them an absorbing interest in common. It kept them, too, from missing their children, who were now grown up and out in the wide world. In 1928, their first grandchild was born away out on the West Coast, and remained unseen, though dearly loved.

Waverley Book Shop was situated on the east side of Seventh Avenue—of Seventh Avenue South, to be precise. Only a few years before the Martins set up shop here, the thoroughfare had been extended through a mass of old buildings, at an angle which left many of the remaining structures of a very odd shape. Oh, well, people expected "quaintness" in The Village! It was an excellent location for business. An excellent location for other purposes, too; it all worked together to make the Martins' enterprise the institution that it was.

All sorts and conditions of men came into Waverley Book Shop. Steady customers. Drop-in customers. Friends who wanted to pass the time of day with Alice and Harry Martin. Friends who wished to meet other friends and used the shop as a rendezvous; its location made it a very convenient "See you at—"

Then there were people with time to kill. New York swarmed with such characters anyhow. One of the things that struck Alice most forcibly when as "young Miss Frederickson" she moved here from upstate New York was the number of people who gathered to watch the steam shovel work. Harry Martin, a Main Streeter from Indiana, had noted it too, and with decided approval. Since they had had the shop they realized that Greenwich Village had more than its share of such leisured inhabitants.

Resent as they might the implication that all residents or habitués of Greenwich Village were spongers and drunkards, the Martins realized that some very odd specimens did show up at one time or another. So long as they behaved themselves they couldn't very well be asked to leave. Harry Martin laughed off their oddities, or blamed poverty, plain old-fashioned laziness, and Prohibition, two of which were here to stay, the third, which had made itself uneasily welcome, was

[4]

probably on its way out. Alice often laughed with him; but she sometimes gave way to concern or disgust. Sometimes she was simply bewildered.

People who wanted to ask a direction came into the shop, too. Or if they were lost and happened to meet her in the street, they stopped to ask her. The answer required an amount of gesticulation that made obvious to all passersby what was going on. Even a human semaphore was up against limitations, however, and sometimes had to wind up on the installment plan. "That will take you to Sixth Avenue," Alice Martin had been known to say. "When you get there, ask again for directions."

It was indeed "a goodly place," this shop of the Martins. They had now reached "a goodly time," too, though not the golden prime of great Harun-al-Rashid, that fabled monarch who belonged back in fairyland with the rest of the *Arabian Nights*. This was the good old U.S.A., and the head of the government was the personification of Yankee shrewdness and common sense.

Calvin Coolidge had originally succeeded to the presidency on the sudden death of Warren Harding. But he had been chosen for a second term on his own merits. He had proved to be a highly successful and popular President. "Stay cool with Coolidge," his campaign slogan had run. For almost four years now the nation had continued to do exactly that. The country had been prosperous and at peace. He believed that the government should mind its own business and let other governments mind theirs. Business was good; the stock market continued to rise. Coolidge was as heartily against entangling alliances as George Washington himself had been. He was blessed with an exceptionally gracious and charming wife, who, like him, believed in minding her own business. The tragic death of their younger son (like the Martins, the Coolidges had had only two children) attracted universal sympathy. There was a large fund of "Coolidge stories." A good many of them had actually happened. Even when they were apocryphal, they showed him to be an extremely likable character. Coolidge himself enjoyed them; he was one of those enlightened souls who can laugh at their own peculiarities.

In 1928 the country had been faced with another Presidential election. But Coolidge, whose reputation was that of never having made a political mistake, had once made a slip of the tongue and alluded to one of his colleagues as "President Hoover." The result was indeed a foregone conclusion. Now here they were in 1929, and Herbert Hoover was indeed President. "Nothing is too good to be true," Mrs. Martin said one night to her husband. "But some things are just too good to last."

They were on their way home to Brooklyn, where they still lived in the old "railroad flat" that had been their residence for many years. They changed trains at the Battery. The long subway trip to Manhattan and back, which they usually made together, was time consuming; but they were used to it. Going to work, Harry read his newspaper while Alice observed their fellow travelers and more or less planned the day ahead. On their return, which generally took place along toward midnight, they both relaxed, and Harry sometimes dozed.

Alice was leading up to something. As was his habit, Harry Martin played along. "Then we might as well enjoy them while they do last, shouldn't you say?"

"We generally do that. We really ought to go a step further and take advantage of them."

"Meaning—?"

Alice showed her dimples. "People never can let other people alone, can they? Always with the best intentions, they have to mind your business for you."

"Coming from you, that is an extraordinary statement. You are a confirmed matchmaker. The fact that you've had reasonably good luck with your interference is all to your credit, I suppose. But now you are simply the pot calling the kettle black."

"To which the kettle could reasonably agree."

"That sort of household aphorism—where could it possibly have originated?" Harry wondered. "A thing gets put into such a shape, and handed down from one generation to another. But it has to start somewhere."

"Does it have to start in any one place?" countered Alice. "After all, a great many people must have had the same experience. In the days of old open-hearth cooking, both the pot and the kettle must have got frightfully black. So much of a woman's time went into drudgery in 'the good old days'— 'good' when they became old."

"Men did a lot of drudgery, too," Harry reminded her.

"Sure. All they couldn't get out of. A very popular jingle used to be:

> Man works from sun to sun,
> But woman's work is never done."

"Out of date, Mrs. Martin, out of date! Largely forgotten by younger people these days, I should think. Nowadays a woman pushes a few buttons, and the work is done for her. Gives her more time to play cards and gossip about the neighbors."

"As if a woman couldn't gossip while she got the family darning done! But I suppose you're right. For tradition we'll have to fall back on 'Thirty days hath September. . . .' A useful production, though disfigured by a false rhyme."

That started Harry on calendar reform. He'd have to look up more about it when he got home. He was great on looking things up. He thought of a lot of things to look up, too. That was a habit which he sometimes urged on his customers. It was advice in their own best interests, of course; but it wasn't

[7]

at all bad for business. The Martins stocked an excellent line of one-volume dictionaries as well as other medium-priced reference books; and these were items that never bounced back for display on the "Used Books" tables.

Harry had sidetracked himself so successfully that he forgot Alice might be leading up to something. He went on and on, first about aphorisms, then about calendar reform, then wound up, "I wonder if Jean ever talks to her classes about such things."

Jean was their daughter. She taught in a high school in Minneapolis, and was married to an instructor at the University of Minnesota. She and Earl Crawford had been at home for the Christmas holidays, as usual, but had left for the Middle West again just before the New Year rolled around. The Crawfords were childless as yet. Jean said there was no hurry about beginning a family. Presumably the couple settled such things in a private discussion; but Harry had a sneaking suspicion that Jean announced the important decisions and Earl replied, "Just as you say, dear." On this matter of having children, indeed, the wife was entitled to her say-so. The husband's cooperation, while essential, was by far the easier and pleasanter part of the task.

"You might write and ask her," said Alice with a hint of wifely irony. Harry regularly left the family correspondence up to her, and contented himself with sending a message. Alice had threatened indeed to have a rubber stamp made. But she typed so fluently that she would write a message in less time than it would have taken her to get out the stamp and ink pad. This way, too, she could ring in slight changes of phrase.

The Martins' railroad flat dated from before it had become the fashion to call multiple dwellings "apartment houses." "Railroad flats" were so dubbed because many of the rooms were strung out one behind another like the cars on a railroad train. Such a building was cheap to build and to main-tain. Its disadvantages were that the majority of the rooms got light and air from small courtyards, if indeed they got them at all; and a long hall with a row of doors opening off it gave access to those same surrounded rooms.

Left to itself as a simple passageway, this long narrow hall could be very bleak. The Martins had not left it like that. It was lined on both sides with bookshelves reaching from the floor almost to the ceiling. These shelves held hundreds and hundreds of books, most of them volumes that would be in less immediate demand than those housed in Waverley Book Shop itself, but choicer in quality than those in the Martins' warehouse, which was also in Brooklyn. The bedroom that had once belonged to Jim was long since abandoned to stacks of books, too; but Jean's room could still be used as a guest room. It always was when the young Crawfords came for the holidays. There too Alice sometimes read late at night in order not to disturb Harry, who was an inveterate sleepy-head.

This was one of Alice's evenings to open a can. It did not occur too often. Customarily on Sundays she let Mr. Martin precede her to the shop, while she prepared a casserole or a stew or even set a capon or a turkey to roast. The Martins dined about once a week at a local restaurant to which they were devoted, or were the guests of Village neighbors. But the can opener, though it did not rank with the typewriter as the means of Woman's Emancipation, certainly gave both practicing housekeepers and businesswomen a great lift with their cooking. Oh, a man could probably wield a can opener too! Alice was not so much of a feminist that she grudged the masculine sex their kitchen privileges.

She used the can opener and made a salad while Harry set the table. He had helped put himself through college by working as a waiter in a student boardinghouse; he had never lost the dexterity thus acquired. Then he arranged a small table in the living room with a plate of crackers and two glasses of chilled white wine. Alice laid aside her apron and joined him there. He made a flourishing bow and waited for her to be seated before he sank into his own chair. They lifted their glasses to each other.

"Sometimes I think that this is the best hour of the day," Harry said meditatively.

"Sometimes I think your talent is wasted in the book business," retorted Alice. "You really should have been an actor. You are the biggest ham!"

"Ham!" He affected injured dignity. "I want you to know that if I had chosen to tread the boards, I'd have been at least as good an actor as—"

"As any of those who come into the shop and try to 'borrow' five dollars until they get their next engagement?"

Harry grinned. "That is one of the occasions when H. Martin, Esquire, can take refuge behind his wife's petticoats. A bachelor has to come right out and say, 'Sorry, old man, I'm broke myself.' "

"You say, 'I'd like to, you know, if I had only myself to consider. But Mrs. Martin keeps such a close eye on the cash drawer that I have to watch my step.' "

"That's the general idea, though there are variations. Ready for a refill, Mrs. M.?" Harry helped them both to seconds, relaxed again, and repeated, "This is the best hour of the day."

"You think that any hour is a good hour except the one when you have to get up."

"Isn't it? If I ever make a great deal of money, this is what I'm going to do: I'm going to buy twelve alarm clocks, and set them for twelve successive hours. Then every time an alarm goes off, I'll say to myself, 'Hell, I don't have to get up yet!' "

Alice shook her head in mock despair. He never got up to the sound of an alarm. When she came to, she glanced at the clock; then she either settled herself for another nap or rose and took first turn at the bathroom. After that she would raise the window shades and call him, then fall back on the old, "Do you realize how long it takes you to bathe and shave?" or perhaps, "How do you want your eggs this morning?" or, "Would you rather have ham or bacon? I'm giving you your choice." This dream of Harry's must go back to his undergraduate days. Strange that he had never mentioned it to her before.

"Am I supposed to sleep through all those alarms?" she demanded. "Or is all this supposed to take place after I've gone to the Happy Hunting Ground?"

"I'll keep my clocks on my side of the bed, and turn off each alarm as soon as it begins to sound."

"Were you ever without an answer, Harry Martin?"

"You ask such intriguing questions, Alice Martin. Care for another drink?"

"I haven't finished this one. Help yourself if you like." Alice took a sip of wine, then went back to an earlier conversation. "You haven't yet looked anything up. Are you going to do so while I get the dinner on the table?"

Harry did just that. But when he had taken the edge off his appetite, he said, "All that about the alarm clocks was just one of those ideas I throw off from time to time."

"Rehearsing it now, so that you can gladden all hearers the next time we have dinner with our gang at Hotel Romano?"

"You like everything to be put to some use, don't you, Alice? It's the feminine instinct for thrift, like using the outside stalks of celery in the weekly stew."

"I was thinking more of eating the hearts of celery at Sunday dinner, or on the rare occasions when we have guests over here and really let go."

"At a Carrie party or a Carrie-cum-Phyllis party," Harry agreed. Carrie had been the Martin's help-by-the-day for years and years now. Phyllis was the daughter whom she sometimes sent in her stead. If the two of them were hired for the same function, it was really a gilt-edged affair.

[11]

"We've already eased up some in the shop," Alice went on. "Since we took on William Thayer as full-time assistant, we've really had a little leisure."

"Now I'm the one who has put it to use," Harry interrupted not perhaps her actual speech, but certainly the trend of her argument. "Doubtful use, you may think. My translations from the Latin, all neatly typed, are gathering dust in a drawer in the shop, while the carbon copy reposes here in the apartment, just in case either place should have a disastrous fire."

"You mean you want to publish them at your own expense?" demanded Alice.

"At *our* expense, Mrs. Martin? They're not all that bad. It's just that so far I haven't been able to think of any market for them."

"So far? You mean you think that eventually you'll find a market for them?"

"I'll find a use for them. I've a beautiful new idea. Here you and I have been reading all these years, partly for pleasure, partly in the line of business. You've always done the lion's share of the business reading, covering the new books the way you do."

"That was fair enough. You handled the mail order end of things; that is our backlog."

Alice knew all this quite as well as Harry did. But of course he was leading up to something. Perhaps he was trying to convince himself as well as her.

"This is strictly confidential," he went on.

Alice smiled. "Any communication between husband and wife always is. She cannot even be called on to testify against him in court. You weren't planning to kill anybody, were you?"

"Has Don Burgess used that dodge in any of his books?" Donald Burgess was their close friend: a writer of detective stories who had recently married another close friend of theirs, Virginia Daly, who wrote biographies. Alice Martin had patted herself on the back for having made that match. Matchmaking, according to her creed, wasn't the same thing as mischief-making. It was just giving people a chance at greater happiness. She had never put a pistol to anybody's head.

"He probably has. We have autographed copies of every whodunit he's ever written; but offhand I couldn't say whether he has included that particular trick. If he hasn't, he will. But you're enjoining secrecy on me?"

"I certainly am. If nothing comes of this, I don't want it known. Much as I love our Village, I must admit that Greenwich Village contains a lot too many people who spend a lot too much time talking about the writing that they're going to do."

"You're not thinking of *writing* a book, Harry Martin?"

"Not that bad. I'm thinking of compiling one."

It took a minute for that to sink in. Then Alice said slowly, "An anthology? Is there room for another anthology?"

"I feel that there is. I'd include the things I've liked best over the years: the ones I want to reread. I'd like to introduce them to a fresh audience. They might like my book well enough to go on from the samples I've given them."

"It sounds promising. It will entail a lot of work; but that will all be work toward an end."

"Bless you for your auxiliary verbs, darling! You said 'will,' not 'would.'"

"So I did! That was quite unconscious. You're starting off with my blessing, then."

"It's a long road," said Harry. But he said it complacently.

"We know the market. We know the publishing field," Alice went on to encourage.

That was all Harry Martin needed. He punished a second

helping of the lamb stew, canned though it was. He drank two cups of coffee, and cleaned up his fruit and cheese like a good one.

Alice was happy in his happiness. Harry Martin was a trial in some ways, but he had his strong points. Single-mindedness was one of them. To call it selfishness was a little bit too strong; he was always at the mercy of his latest enthusiasm. So completely was he overcome by his idea for an anthology that he had completely forgotten Alice's remarks about taking advantage of their good times while they lasted. If Alice was leading up to something, that something would have to wait.

2

ALICE MARTIN WAS ONE OF THOSE WOMEN WHO KEEP THEIR good looks indefinitely. Actually she had not reached her best until she was in her middle thirties, a wife, a mother, and a businesswoman. The wistfulness which had been hers as "young Miss Frederickson" had then given way to mature charm. She had realized her full potentialities, indeed, only when she began to crowd forty on the wrong side.

She had, of course, followed in the lines of the Latin aphorism which Harry found it easiest to translate, but which sounded almost better in English than it did in the original. Times changed, and Alice changed with them. A small blonde to begin with, she had never put on any excess weight. When her fair hair darkened to brown, she dressed more demurely. She was a living refutation of the old superstition that blondes age faster than brunettes. A good deal depended on the particular blonde, in her estimation.

As for that other ancient notion, that women aged faster than men, she found that here too times had changed: in this case, vastly for the better. You needn't talk to her about "the good old days" of household drudgery and incessant child-bearing, when a reasonably vigorous male could wear out one wife after another, and when so many babies were born only to die. Any visit to an ancient cemetery would tell the tale on that score.

Harry Martin, indeed, looked older than Alice did in one respect: his hair was not only receding at the temples but also getting thin on the crown. He did not take the pains with his appearance that Alice did with hers, either. So long as his clothes were clean, he didn't mind their being shabby; he had a nice little business of his own, he would argue, and he didn't have to put up a front like a fool of a floorwalker in a department store or a business executive behind a three-hundred-dollar desk. He hated to shop, and Alice sometimes had to take a very high hand with him on the score of buying new clothes. There were times, indeed, when she felt that something might be said for wives condemned as "nagging." After all, we have never been favored with Xanthippe's side of the story.

Doubtless there was a book in that. There was a book in almost everything, Alice supposed; the difficulty was to get it out. Thank goodness Harry Martin hadn't fancied himself a writer. That trade looked so much simpler than it was. Of the books published every year, Alice read perhaps a hundred of the more promising specimens. Even there she had to do considerable wading. As for the mass of manuscripts which never reached publication—well, she would sooner be in her business and sell books than be a publisher and try to decide what was worth printing.

"Worth printing" meant of course what would show a profit. A lot of guesswork there. According to Don Burgess, a lot of big talk, too, to cover a publisher's essential ignorance. Donald Burgess and Virginia Daly were the two authors whom the Martins knew best. Virginia did not growl about publishers the way Don did. She did not growl about anything the way Don did. He could outdistance her almost as often as Harry Martin outdistanced Alice. The "strong silent man" of Victorian fiction, if he had ever existed in fact, must have become extinct along about the time that the Dear Queen died.

"The publishers must be right at least part of the time," Alice had once remarked to Harry after a session when Don Burgess had been especially voluble and sarcastic. "If they weren't, how would they ever manage to stay in business?"

"In the palmy days some of them even left the parent firm and branched out for themselves," Harry recollected. "I suppose it isn't quite as much of a gamble as betting on the races."

"Aren't you drawing a false analogy?" aksed Alice. "The proprietors of racetracks thrive; it's the horse players who lose."

"You have a point there, Mrs. Martin. You're as intelligent as you are beautiful—almost."

"You're even more intelligent than you are hand—" Alice broke off in the middle of the word and clapped her hand over her mouth.

"That remark is deservedly ignored. To be sure anybody who goes into business for himself takes a chance. Not nearly such a chance, in my opinion, as anybody who gets married. Still, we take the biggest chance of all when we get born; and most of us aren't given much say-so about being shot into this wicked but interesting world."

"Not so many people go into monasteries," Alice pointed out. "Even there they go in provisionally, don't they? They are given a chance to change their minds."

Harry was no expert on that subject; but he believed they were. Abelard and Eloise were an instance which sprang to mind. Harry promptly went to look them up. That was one way to end an argument, even if Alice couldn't convince him: switch to a subject which he would want to look up.

[17]

Harry Martin was a handsome man, but he was beginning to have a worn look. That showed up especially when his face was in repose. His face was almost never in repose, however, except when he was reading or writing or sound asleep.

Virginia Daly was a writer who had married another writer. She had known in advance that he would have to remain silent while he was working; yes, and while she was. During their research, too. She had to do a great deal more of that than he did. Donald Burgess wrote detective stories, and must be sure of many facts in his backgrounds; but Virginia wrote biographies, and the longer, if not the more difficult, part of her job was assembling the necessary facts.

She had got the jump on him at the very beginning. He had preceded her to the Long Island house which was to be their joint home, and had settled in there before they were married, had even hired and broken in the very capable married couple who were to look after their house and garden and the car which was practically a necessity for commuters. Virginia had kept her old Village apartment as a *pied-à-terre*. She and Donald could always sleep there if they planned to spend a night on the town. If they wearied of each other's exclusive society, too, they could always go there and spend a crowded week revisiting their old haunts and investigating new ones.

Now here, early in her married life, Virginia Daly, barely used to being Mrs. Burgess in purely social circles, burned with all the zeal of a convert. She couldn't very well preach marriage to Alice Martin, who was a veteran of that state, and had done her share toward inveigling Virginia into it. Blind Chance had done its share, too; but there are times when Chance needs at least a nudge, if not an out-and-out shove in the right direction.

Perhaps Virginia thought she was simply repaying a favor. At any rate she had put a new idea up to Alice; had elaborated on it, indeed, with a thoroughness which showed not

[18]

only her kind intentions but also the fact that she must have devoted a great deal of thought to the matter.

"You and Harry love that old Brooklyn flat of yours," she conceded. "I don't blame you a particle. It has been home to you for so many years, it must have wonderful associations. Don has told me how he used to take refuge there when things got too much for him. I've been entertained there myself, and loved it. But—"

She hesitated, and Alice said crisply, "Brooklyn is as good a dormitory for New York as New Jersey is. The transportation is simpler, too. I'm not thinking of moving."

"Oh, I wouldn't dream of suggesting that! But you and Harry have reached the stage where you can afford to spread out a bit. You owe it to yourselves, too."

Virginia had asked Alice out for coffee, at an hour in the afternoon when business was slack. Harry was putting up the mail order packages, and Bill Thayer was there to help wait on customers. Alice had been sorting, and dusting as she went. Virginia had chosen the hour wisely; Alice was glad of a little change.

Now she took a bite of her doughnut and waited for her hostess to go on. Advice was a strange commodity, Alice reflected: it was the only article anywhere around that everybody wished to give and nobody desired to take.

"You and Harry could get yourselves a little place on Long Island. A place right in our neighborhood. I know you'd love it; and Don and I would love having you there."

Alice shook her head. "Perhaps we could stretch to the added expense. But it would be time consuming; we're both very busy people."

"You have your own shop. You could arrange the hours to suit your convenience. Think of all the fresh air you'd breathe. These torrid summers you would enjoy a little garden, too."

"There would be not only transportation to consider, there

[19]

would be the help problem. We'd need a car, too, and neither of us has ever driven one."

"Oh, but there'd be taxi service from the station! You wouldn't need to use it often, though; we could have our man meet your train when you arrived. We'd love to."

"Gardening is one of the least of Harry's hobbies. For him, it's strictly something between the covers of a book."

"There are neighborhood gardeners. Or maybe our George could do for you too. He'd probably be glad of the extra money."

"It's an extremely interesting idea." Alice finished her doughnut and took another sip of coffee. "I'll need time to think it over, though. You haven't said anything to Harry about this, have you?"

Virginia shook her head; for the first time her gray-green eyes gleamed. She was a good-looking redhead, with all the energy, and occasional rashness, commonly associated with her coloring. "I thought I'd better put it up to you first. If I convinced you, it would be your job to land Harry."

"I have confidence in my persuasive powers, thank you. But I'm not yet certain that our gig needs a third wheel. Between home and the shop, we manage to keep pretty busy." *Harry is just starting a huge new enterprise, too,* Alice thought. But of course his project for an anthology was nothing she could mention even to a close friend.

Virginia looked disappointed. "Of course this is just a suggestion."

"For which I thank you very much," Alice said heartily. She finished her coffee. "Are you starting a new book soon?"

"When I do, you'll be the first to hear of it." Virginia always bought her source books from Waverley. "Right now it's Don's turn to grunt. After all, I let him set up housekeeping for the two of us while I finished a book. It isn't every man who would do that for a woman. But of course a fellow craftsman could see my side of it."

"You and Don have so awfully much in common."

"Just the way that you and Harry have."

Alice nodded. "That is what counts in the long run, I'm sure. In fact I've seen it happen in many other cases: with my schoolteacher daughter and her professor husband, for instance."

There was a brief digression while Virginia inquired about Jean and Earl Crawford. Then Alice went on, "Love is important, of course. You might say it's fundamental. But it is by no means the whole of marriage."

Virginia smiled. "The poet puts it elegantly: 'What of life was left, I wonder, when the kissing had to stop?' "

Alice wondered in passing whether Harry would put that "Toccata" into his anthology: Browning offered such a vast rich field that it would be hard to make a selection. "You could put it less elegantly?"

"Yes indeed. I'd say, 'Things are going to look very different after the slush has dried up a little.' "

Alice laughed. "It's much easier walking, if you ask me."

Virginia returned to Waverley Book Shop with her and selected two novels, one to read on the train going home, the other to show Don that she liked buying things for him, too. He paid the running expenses of their household; Virginia had now taken over most of the active management. It was fun, however, to buy him presents with money which she had herself earned. Her choice was somewhat limited by his vocation. She could not buy a detective story for either of them. Don sometimes bought the products of his rivals, in "Used Books," and for the purpose of tearing them to pieces. But that was part of his job just as much as working with source material was part of Virginia's.

Harry, with his packages for the post office under his arm, paused to say to Virginia, "I don't know what you two girls had your heads together about. But if it's anything that involves me, the answer is 'No.' "

[21]

Virginia gave a barely audible gasp. Alice said sweetly, "Mrs. Burgess came in here to buy something, dear. That is no way to talk to a customer." As a red herring, that might do. But Harry had chanced on the answer which, in more roundabout terms, Alice had been trying to give Virginia.

When the Martins had settled down at home that evening, Alice confided, "Virginia Daly was trying to talk me into something. She thinks that you and I ought to get ourselves a place on Long Island."

"And commute from business instead of to it? I hope you discouraged any such idiotic notion." Harry began to chant:

"The longer I long for I long for Long Island,
 The longer I can stay away.

Hand that to some of your poetizing friends," he wound up. "It's strictly non-commercial, and should go big in certain circles. Don't try it on the Long Island Chamber of Commerce, though."

"Virginia thinks we owe something to ourselves," Alice pressed.

"What we owe ourselves is the least of my worries. We don't have to pay interest on that debt."

There the matter rested for the present. But Virginia had put an idea into Alice's head. The Long Island scheme was out. Suppose, however, that they picked up the idea from the other end: instead of making things harder for themselves, made them easier? Waverley Book Shop was a going concern. It had done proportionately more business since Bill Thayer worked there full time. Their children were off their hands. The country was enjoying boom times. The Martins were not growing any younger. They were getting into a rut. The time might have come for a change; but the change must be of their own choosing. There was all the difference in the world between adopting an idea and adapting it, even if the two words did sound so much alike.

Their old Brooklyn flat was home to the Martins: a plain place, but they loved it. With the help of their Carrie, who had been with them for more years than either she or Mrs. Martin cared to count, the place practically ran itself. Carrie, or her daughter Phyllis, those two could never be expected to commute to Long Island. But commuting to Manhattan would be vastly different; they might even brag to their friends about that.

So far Alice had settled things in her own mind. It remained to consult Harry before she started house hunting in the vicinity of the shop. That project would consume so much time that she would have to account for her repeated and prolonged absences from their shop. She'd better sell him the idea before she had anything more tangible to offer.

The idea was already half sold, however, thanks to that Virginia woman. "We don't really have to come back here every night of our lives," Harry said uneasily. "If we both kept dressing cases in the shop, we could spend the night at a neighborhood hotel any time we didn't care to face the long journey home."

"That's what telephones are for," Alice agreed. "There was something to be said for the old days when people lived in a few rooms behind the shop. We've agreed to forget about the good old days, though, haven't we? It's the future you and I are planning for."

The future was creeping up on them at that very moment. This was a Saturday evening. On Sunday Alice stayed behind to get a lavish dinner started. That was one of her reasons for maintaining the old home; she loved cooking and household management just as much as she loved working in the shop, though in a totally different way.

She arrived in the shop just as Thomas Carroll had completed one of his purchases. A dandiacal man in his early fifties, he worked in an art gallery up on Fifty-seventh Street. It was a well-known gallery, and he always had money to spend. He lived in the immediate neighborhood of the shop.

On her entry today Carroll sketched a salute, picked up the package which Harry had just finished wrapping, and went off without his change. Alice, still in her outdoor wraps, picked up the change and followed him.

He crossed Seventh Avenue with considerable agility. Alice, just beating a change of traffic lights, followed him across the street. He had turned into a cross street just south of them, and was headed for a four-story building three doors along.

Alice caught up with him just in time to keep the door from closing in her face. At the sound of his name he turned halfway up the first flight of stairs and came back down.

"You really shouldn't have bothered," he protested. Then, after a perceptible pause, he added, "Now that you are here, won't you come up and pay me a little visit? I live on the third floor, but the steps are easy."

"Some other time, thank you," she said cordially. "I'm late at the shop as it is."

Outdoors again, however, she resumed her westward way. This was a dead-end street only two blocks long. It was called "Commerce Street" in the face of the fact that there wasn't any commerce on it; originally it had been "Cherry Lane," Alice remembered. It was picturesque; it was tidy; for Manhattan, it was quiet. On her return trip Alice noticed something that had escaped her attention while she was chasing Thomas Carroll: the building where he lived displayed a "Vacancy" sign. Alice stepped up to the doorway and rang the bell marked "Superintendent."

She had the good luck to find him at home: a very neat

[24]

colored man in his forties. He said it was a fourth-floor apartment; he'd be glad to show it.

He did. It was what in New York they call "a two-and-a-half-room apartment." There was a good-sized living room with a skylight, a bedroom that would do nicely for two, and a bathroom which was of the latest convenience and boasted its own skylight. When Alice demurred about the small size of the kitchenette, the superintendent, John, informed her, "The landlord will convert to alternating current for a good tenant, and put in an electric refrigerator."

That all but settled it. Alice smiled and said, "Easy to get to the roof from here, isn't it?"

"Oh yes, ma'am!" he assured her, and led the way up.

The flat roof was covered with gravel and surrounded by a waist-high brick parapet. It sloped slightly upward toward the front. Alice walked to the edge and looked across to where on the other side of Seventh Avenue Waverley Book Shop displayed its afternoon awning and its tables of used books. As she did so, a breeze from the Hudson ruffled the sides of her hair. The sunshine today had a delusive hint of spring.

Alice pointed out the shop and said, "I'll send my husband over to see the apartment. Be on the lookout for him."

Harry teased her about Carroll. "I was getting a little anxious. I was afraid you were spending all this time with him." But when he heard about the top-floor apartment, he was intensely interested. "We could have a second establishment here so handy to the shop? That would give us a chance to get a few new furnishings, wouldn't it, and save a lot of hours in the subway. Is this Greenwich Village's answer to Long Island?"

"Go ahead and see for yourself," advised Alice.

He did more than that. He inquired about the rent, a detail which Alice had neglected, and noted the landlord's phone number. Then he had the superintendent take down the "Vacancy" sign.

They closed the shop early and went back to their new apartment to size up its potentialities. This was a *pied-à-terre*, and much more to their advantage than a country estate would have been. The Martins were in a jubilant mood for their dinner that Sunday evening.

"We have paid our debt to ourselves the cheap way," Harry summed up.

3

THAT WAS ONE WAY OF LOOKING AT IT. COMPARED TO A
"place" on Long Island, indeed, a small apartment in the
heart of the Village was cheap enough. But even this was
spreading out. There was no sense in acquiring a second
home unless you had it pretty much as you liked it. The
Martins had entered on a new program. It would absorb a
good part of Mrs. Martin's energies for some time.

The pleasure of shopping for a new household was hers
once more. She brought to it considerable experience, mature
taste, and the comfortable knowledge that the money was
there to spend. Woe betide those unlucky couples who
bought things on the installment plan. Their rose-colored
glasses would very likely turn a pallid hue before those hope-
fully ordered items were half paid for.

Alice sympathized even where she could not approve. "A
home of her own" was what a lot of women got married for:
that, and financial support, and a chance to show the world
that they could catch themselves husbands. Alice had helped
more than one couple toward the entrance of the "honorable

estate." She was of a managerial turn of mind. She did not go so far, however, as to think that, like St. Peter, she held the keys of Paradise. Even in her most sanguine moments she never envied St. Peter his job. In times of discouragement she could even fall back on the stale adage, "Misery loves company."

The furnishings of the old Brooklyn flat had been modified or replaced over the years as times changed, the children grew, and Waverley Book Shop continued to show a profit. On her daughter Jean's marriage Mrs. Martin had had some say-so about the properties for the new ménage. More recently, she had helped their sculptor friend Emil Koenig, when after the poverty of his early days he reached the place where he could set up a decent apartment in addition to the working studio which had so long served him as living quarters too.

Alice had gone with Emil to Wanamaker's, that landmark of downtown New York. Their housefurnishing and housewares departments could not be beat; and at Wanamaker's, if you paid for what you got, you also got what you paid for. But for tables and rugs she led him to the secondhand stores along University Place, where good values were often to be had, and sometimes real bargains for a man who was handy with a paint brush or a pot of varnish. When Kitty West married Emil Koenig, she had also married a ready-made apartment. But that was in itself a step up for a girl who had gone there from a furnished room and "housekeeping privileges," and who before that had lived in a residential club for girls, with its institutional air and meals cooked in quantities.

Now Alice went to Wanamaker's on her own hook, and bought a brown mahogany double bed with the latest thing in box springs and mattress. After short hesitation she bought a dresser and chiffonier to match. They would crowd the new bedroom; but if worse came to worst, she could move Harry's chiffonier into the living room and dignify it as "a chest of

[28]

drawers." After all these married years, a little extravagance was surely justified.

She made the move without consulting Harry, and told him about it afterward. "Would you like to go and see the sample before they have a chance to deliver from the warehouse?" she demanded. "There would still be time to change our minds."

"If I'd wanted a say-so I could have gone with you in the first place," he pointed out.

"You will come with me when I explore the secondhand shops, won't you?"

Harry did, and lasted just one session. At the end thereof he proclaimed, "It all looks awfully disheartening to me. Why don't you just go back to Wanamaker's and get what you need? There's no sense in having a charge account if you don't use it."

"This just isn't your cup of tea, I gather?"

"I might much better be putting in my time at my own business. I realize that it's your business too, and you handle your half of it fully as well as I handle mine. Shall we say, then, that I trust your judgment more than I do my own? I prefer coffee to tea anyhow. What say we stop in somewhere and have some on our way back to the salt mines?"

The new apartment had a set of painted bookshelves over the radiator. It was a legacy from a previous tenant; and although the heat must be bad for the books, it made good use of what would otherwise be waste space. Alice found matching sets of low bookshelves which would fit in under the windows. A room-size rug in a neutral tone would do very well after a trip to the cleaner's; two scatter rugs would serve in the bedroom. Alice would rather have liked a bare floor there; but the feelings of the third-floor tenants should be considered, and the Martins did keep odd hours.

A solid table with drop leaves. Four floor chairs, an armchair, and a davenport with good springs, though the upholstery had seen better days. They could throw a plaid blanket over it at first; later on they might stretch to reupholstering.

But there for the first time Mr. Martin set his foot down. "Have it reupholstered right away, and get a good job while you're about it," he commanded.

Alice showed her dimples. "That skylight does throw an unmerciful glare on it. I suppose my idea was silly. In books, the shabby furniture looks so comfortable and homelike. In my house, it never looks anything but shabby."

At the Brooklyn apartment Alice sorted out dishes and household linen, enough to make a beginning in the Village place. Those things could be added to from time to time; buying them was a pleasure, not a responsibility.

Then all at once they came up against a consideration which had not occurred to either of them. They might want to stay in the Commerce Street place not only overnight, but for days and even weeks at a time. With a little planning, the matter of supplies could be managed; but who on earth was going to attend to the chore which had been Harry's for so many years? The Martins' Brooklyn flat still had an old-fashioned refrigerator, serviced by Louis, the iceman on the corner. In their absence, who was going to empty the pan under the refrigerator?

The answer was simple enough, now that the question had brought itself up. The Brooklyn building had had alternating current right along. Harry Martin would buy himself an electric refrigerator. It was what he should have done the day the new-fangled contraption came on the market.

"Why didn't I think of that sooner?" he exclaimed in self-derision. To which query Alice made the obvious retort, "How could you possibly think of it before you thought of it?"

As for the wine they had been buying for years from Louis-on-the-corner, who all during Prohibition had found that commodity more profitable than ice, the Martins could no doubt have found a purveyor of "dago red" closer to their New York home. But they liked Louis's product. They liked Louis himself; in fact, Alice had yet to meet an Italian whom she could not like, which was vastly more than could be said for persons of British-Isles descent. So, because the gallon jugs in which their wine was delivered were heavy and would have been conspicuous in the subway, Harry now transported to their new home wine which had been poured into old gin bottles.

"A husband's work is never done!" he lamented. "I have simply exchanged one form of slavery for another."

"This particular job will last only until we get Repeal," Alice pointed out.

"I won't hold my breath until we do. I'm already a little curious, though. If and when we do—I suppose I can drop the 'if' and say 'when'—"

"Where did anybody ever get the idea that women talk more than men do?"

"People used to call President Coolidge 'Silent Cal,' didn't they?"

"Did they? Well, maybe; but we have yet to hear Mrs. Coolidge's side of the story. Anyhow I happen to be married to a man who believes in never using one word where he can make ten do."

"I happen to be married to a woman who generally succeeds in throwing me off the track when I start to say something."

"I could do something worse, I suppose, such as not listening. I do listen, you know, even if it's only for a chance to get a word in edgewise. I remember, too. You were expressing curiosity about what may happen when we get Repeal."

"Prohibition made drinking fashionable. I wonder whether with Repeal drinking will go out of style."

"A person will have more choice in the matter, that's certain. Virginia Daly used to make awfully good wine right at home, didn't she? That's an art I never learned; and it would be a little late now to begin."

"It would save my carrying those bottles. But you're right, it would be a little late to begin. Besides, it would take up space in our new home. I'll continue to tote bottles until further notice."

"I wonder what free-love couples talk about in their spare moments," Alice said suddenly. "There probably are some in our Commerce Street building. Greenwich Village does harbor a lot of them, I believe. In that way it lives up to its reputation."

"There may be some right here in our old building in Brooklyn. The East River doesn't make such a distinction as all that," Harry assured her. "Even the marriage service makes allowance for that sort of thing: 'and forsaking all others.' "

"That judge out in Denver has been all for legalizing such unions so long as children are not involved. 'Companionate marriage,' he calls it."

"The prospect of children might hang over that one." Harry yawned luxuriously. "I wouldn't mind one more glass of chilled wine before I slumber, Mrs. Martin. I can tote in earnest for a few days and stock up there."

He had bought two new fans for the new place. Both at the old flat and the shop, Harry Martin had a system for setting two fans at such an angle that they not only kept the air circulating but actually cooled the place. His engineer son had started him on that track. The new fans were practically noiseless; such devices were improving right along.

"Fanning oneself the old way by hand," he pointed out, "heated a person almost as much as it cooled, though the air did smell a little better when it was stirred up."

"Slaves did it for monarchs. Cleopatra and such really had it cool in their day. But those big fans served another purpose, didn't they? Besides creating an artificial breeze they chased insects away. Harry! There were insects in ancient Egypt, no doubt. Weren't there also insects in old Troy?"

"There's no mention of them in the Greek dramatists, so far as I know. Such things are left for modern 'realists' and 'naturalists.' Some of them dwell constantly on the mosquito side of life, and look down on writers who don't emphasize it. 'Escapist' is the word, I believe. It's a term of contempt."

"We're escaping ourselves when we turn our backs on the business and come up here," Harry decided. "There is very little insect pest in New York, by the way. When I was a boy out in Indiana, screens were a summer necessity. People who could afford it screened in their porches, too."

"Oh, the good old days that people long for!" Alice sighed gustily.

"Oh, the better new days that are still to come!" Harry sighed even louder. "A hundred years from now, things will be fantastically improved; but I won't be here to see it."

"Neither will I. Even if it were possible, I'm sure I wouldn't want to be. A hundred years wouldn't be too long if I could stay my present age. But a hundred years more on top of those I've piled up . . ." Even a sigh was insufficient for such a prospect; Alice groaned.

Harry bought a folding card table and collapsible canvas chairs for use on the roof when they chose to dine there on summer evenings. Away from the heat of the sidewalks and pavements, and catching whatever breeze there was, they found this graveled space delightful; they could see the closed shop across Seventh Avenue, or if it was Bill Thayer's turn to shut up shop for the night, could see him waiting on a few late customers and then putting the Waverley business to bed. This was getting perspective, both physical and spiritual.

Other tenants made scant use of the roof. When they appeared, the Martins passed the time of day with them, then kept to the space over their own apartment. They generally outlasted the others; that was one advantage of keeping book-shop hours instead of having to show up at an office. Week-ends, too, the Martins practically had the place to themselves. Everybody who was anybody got out of the city on summer weekends. Went farther and fared worse, in the Martins' opinion; the roof on Commerce Street offered no traffic jams or auto accidents.

When she realized that their privacy was assured them, Alice went a step farther and bought bathing suits for both of them. She had retained her bathing-suit figure. It was only a few years back, indeed, that her sculptor friend Emil Koenig had confessed something which startled her more than it need have. To his artist's eye she might just as well not have worn clothes at all; he saw right through them to her beautiful body.

Harry had not been so lucky. He had long since acquired "a scholar's stoop"; Alice was used to it and found it not unbecoming. But she now realized with something of a shock that, although he was by no means getting fat, he was devel-oping a small paunch. "The middle-age spread" got itself tacked onto many women who spent long hours in office chairs, or alternatively at the bridge table. When men were concerned, the "spread" was commonly worn in front.

Did Harry Martin realize the way that time was taking its toll of him? If so, did he resent it? Alice couldn't very well bring up the subject; but she was glad the thought had oc-curred to her. One of these days he might turn to her for reassurance.

Right now he began to reminisce. "Remember when we were newlyweds, Alice? We were poor in those days, but we enjoyed ourselves. Oh, how we enjoyed ourselves! The bath-ing suits of those days were less revealing than they are now. We made ours last. We used to go down to Coney Island for a cheap swim. We devoured hot dogs there. We learned to put tomato catsup on French fried potatoes; that pepped them up and made them quite a treat."

"Beer was legal in those days," Alice remembered. "What a sport I used to feel like when you treated me to a glass! I didn't care much for the beer; you generally had to finish mine for me. We used to lie down in the shade of the board-walk, and read and dream. Often you took a nap."

"Sometimes I sang," said Harry. "That was one way to chase you into the surf without my having to go along." He tuned up then, and Alice covered her ears. She had a reason-ably good parlor voice; in an earlier day she might have been impressed into the village choir, or even have sung an occasional solo at an evening party. Harry was not quite tone deaf; but he had a poor ear for pitch; he could sing with greater cheerfulness and enthusiasm at least a quarter of a note flat.

He shook his head sadly. "Nobody really cares for my singing. Some day though I'm really going to let loose. I'll go off by myself to a cabin in the wilds. There I'll feel free to let go. I may even sing all through 'Forty-Nine Bottles.' "

"What on earth are you talking about?"

Harry chuckled. "Didn't they teach you that classic in New England?" He rose, struck an attitude, and began to intone,

> "Forty-nine bottles hanging on the wall!
> Forty-nine bottles hanging on the wall!
> If one bottle sh'd happen to take a fall,
> Forty-eight bottles hanging on the wall.
>
> "Forty-eight bottles hanging on the wall!
> Forty-eight bottles hanging on the wall!
> If one bottle sh'd happen to take a fall,
> Forty-seven bottles hanging on the wall."

[35]

He was trying to break her down, of course. Alice was determined not to let him. After the thirty-fifth bottle Harry yielded. "I don't think I'll go on right now. You get the idea, don't you?"

"Well no, I don't. Why a lot of bottles should be hanging on the wall in the first place I don't see. It can't be a counting game for children, either, or it wouldn't start with forty-nine and go backwards."

"Forty-nine may be a mystic number. It's the square of seven, you know; and seven has always been held in high esteem by necromancers as well as by prophets."

"Next thing we know you'll be tracing your ballad back to the Druids. It's all right if you do, too, so long as you refrain from any more singing."

They were silent for a few minutes. Then Alice said softly, "Those cheap swims and cheap lunches! Long trips on an open-deck bus, when we weren't the only couple who were holding hands. We could ride all evening on the Staten Island ferry for the one fare. There is something to be said for the Good Old Days, though I don't often say it."

"Go ahead and work it up into a legend," Harry advised. You may even want to write it down some day."

"Not I! Writing is low-down labor if a person takes it seriously."

"Work the bygone days into an oral legend, then. It will be something to tell your grandchildren."

"Tell them long distance?" said Alice sharply. Jim's little boy was well toward a year old now, and the West Coast was a long way off.

The mood of the moment had been broken. Harry hastended to retrieve their spirits. "Jean and Earl will be here now in no time at all. They will pay us a good visit."

Alice agreed somewhat forlornly, "It's better to love grown children and miss them, I suppose, than to have them live next door and quarrel with them."

"We'll have a lot to show them this time. Our new place here, and a close-up view of the Village."

"We might lend them this place, so far as that goes. Let them take over and see for themselves, while we go back to Brooklyn."

"Are they planning to visit us, or are they simply saving hotel bills?" Harry asked sharply. "The Crawfords are not a honeymoon couple. Last year they took a big trip to the West instead of coming back to New York."

"They have their own lives to live," Alice reminded him. Then she laughed, and the tension passed. "You can sing 'Forty-Nine Bottles' for them. It will be as much a blow to them as it was to me.—Oh, sorry! Did I say 'blow'? Of course I meant 'novelty.' "

"Earl may have picked it up in Minneapolis. He may even have known it from way back. You never can tell where a thing like that will recur."

"Any more than you can tell how it occurred in the first place," Mrs. Martin agreed. "I can't much blame the Druids, though. That prolific author, Anonymous, has a lot to answer for."

" 'That prolific author Anonymous' is good. I may want to use that in my anthology."

"You're welcome to it, I'm sure. Ben Johnson used some of your cracks in one of his plays, didn't he?"

"He did. They weren't the worst lines in the play, either. That was the play which got produced. We know a produced playwright and two published authors, don't we? They are customers as well as friends."

"There may be other authors among our customers," Alice reminded him. "Some of them may be future friends, too. There's no limits to friendship. Even husbands and wives sometimes stay friends."

"Even after 'Forty-Nine Bottles'?"

"Even after that, if the husband is the man who put new

[37]

wine into old bottles. Old gin bottles, in this case. I declare, all this about bottles has made me thirsty. What say we go inside and treat ourselves to a cold drink?"

Harry sprang to his feet and began to fold up his chair. "We could leave these on the landing if they had our name on them," he remarked. But he made his two trips cheerfully and quickly. Harry Martin was a handy thing to have around the house. Sometimes he was even amusing.

4

How important money was! Its far-flung tentacles reached even into remote corners where a person would certainly never have expected to find them. Harry's decision to have only as many children as he could afford to educate at his own expense, for instance: Alice had agreed with it and had done her best to cooperate. She had been very lucky in her limited family; after Jim and Jean, any more offspring would certainly have been a comedown. But sometimes for a lonesome moment Alice wished that she had had another child, and one who would stay a little closer to home. That was sheer weakness on her part; she was generally too busy, and too sensible, to indulge it.

Important as money was, it must not be allowed to hog the center of the stage. That not only distorted values, it corrupted conduct. *"Auri sacra fames, quid non mortalia pectora cogis?"* ran a Latin tag in Harry's collection. That was a sticky one to translate. Try, "Undue love of money makes people do awful things."

Emphasis of course was on the adjective. Money was a very convenient thing to have, very difficult to do without. As for those old killjoys who whined that "Money cannot buy happiness," Alice could almost find it in her heart to be sorry for them. They had never tasted French fries at Coney Island, or laughed with a partner when the beers were drawn with a collar of foam, so that a sixth of the customer's money went for the air in the bubbles.

There were, on the other hand, people to whom money meant happiness; or, if not precisely that, at least it was an object in itself. As a theme for the great Victorians, miserliness had produced two of the most beloved stories, *A Christmas Carol* and *Silas Marner*. In contemporary American life, however, such characters didn't reform. Every once in a while Alice was fascinated by a newspaper account of "an elderly recluse," generally a woman, who was found dead in a dirty dwelling piled with rubbish, among which were eight or nine bankbooks revealing assets well into the thousands, though there wasn't a decent garment in the place and scarcely a scrap of food.

The pleasure of making money, however, was surely legitimate. To make it by doing something a person thoroughly enjoyed was cause for all-around satisfaction. Waverley Book Shop yielded a tidy profit annually; even Bill Thayer's salary as a full-time assistant didn't cut into it particularly. Besides, employing him gave Harry Martin a chance to turn his attention to his anthology: a project which might be profitable in the end, and which he was deeply enjoying as he went along.

These new arrangements gave Alice more time to herself. Not very much time, really, but she could put it to good use. An hour or two more a day when she didn't have to be in the shop, time saved from subway trips to Brooklyn: a good deal of this she put in exploring the Village, its lanes and byways, its small shops and pushcart markets.

She passed the time of day with people; but strolling alone as she did, pausing to look at whatever struck her fancy and making an occasional small purchase, Alice listened more than she talked. She was increasingly impressed by something which had lately come to her attention in the shop, too. Everybody seemed to be possessed by a fever of speculation.

She heard it in the cobbler's, where she took Harry's shoes as well as her own to have the heels straightened. She heard it in the shoe-shine parlor, when she waited while Harry was being attended to. She heard it in the drugstore when she stopped at the soda fountain for a phosphate or an orangeade, and again across the aisle while she was buying cold cream or facial tissues. She heard it in the beauty parlor. Alice had now shifted to a Village beauty parlor. All her wavy brown hair needed was an occasional cut, but she sometimes had a professional shampoo as well. Books had a natural affinity for dust, and being in a dusty business, Alice was accustomed to washing her hair frequently. Now and then, however, she liked to sit back and let herself be ministered to.

Here in the beauty parlor, too, she was favored with gossip about the other patrons' stock operations. That was all very well in its way, and passed the time better than reading movie magazines. But when the proprietor began to offer tips on the market, Alice ventured to remark, "I hear a lot of this talk nowadays. Sometimes I feel like suggesting that people tell it to the Marines."

The proprietor, a second-generation Italian, like so many others in the neighborhood, grinned amiably. "I was in the Marines myself. I heard a lot there; but I don't remember hearing much about the stock market."

"I heard a lot about buying government bonds during the war. The theme was even set to music." Alice sang softly,

"Every bond that you are buying
   Will help our boys to cross the Rhine.
Buy bonds—buy *bonds*—
   For your boy and mine.

That was one case where patriotism and pocketbook went hand in hand. They don't always."

"You mean you're still holding government bonds? But even those you can sell at a small profit. Put your money into something where it will really make money for you."

Alice and Harry had some other investments, too. Jim had advised them, the year after he had gone to work and begun to have some little savings of his own, "Put your money into basic American industries. The value is there."

The senior Martins had bought some steel, chemical, and electric stocks. Alice allowed Harry to do the selecting; but since some firm names were practically household words and Harry stuck to those, there wasn't much to argue about anyhow. Their dividends had come in, and had been reinvested in stocks of the same firms. But every quarter those dividends bought less; the arithmetic was harder to do, too.

"It's a new economic era," Al Recetti explained to Alice.

"A new game, too, where everybody wins and nobody loses," she retorted.

It happened that on that very evening a strange character came into the shop. Alice knew him by name and reputation. He was Frank McCann, a veteran living on his pension; "shell shock" had affected his wits, which were not powerful to begin with. He never bought anything but the cheapest "used" books, and those very seldom. But Alice was sorry for him and could always spare him a few minutes.

Now, blessed if he didn't favor her with some financial advice. "You don't have to have all the money, you know," he began. "You put up part of it, and wait until your stock goes up, and sell out and buy something else."

That was buying on margin. Alice knew of the procedure, since most of the other speculators were employing it. She disapproved of it heartily. But sooner than try to explain why, she temporized, "But you do have to have part of the money to begin with."

"Oh, you can get that from your bank!" he assured her earnestly. "Just tell them that you have a business of your own, and explain what you want the money for. They'll take your note, or—or something."

This was piling absurdity on absurdity. To end it, Alice thanked him cordially for his advice, and in return bestowed on him as a gift any three books which he might choose to select from the most marked-down table.

But it set her to thinking. Perhaps she had been overlooking something. She had pitted her own judgment against popular opinion; that was something she did not do in the case of Waverley Book Shop, where part of her job was to gauge people's reactions and take advantage of them. "What goes up must come down," the old saw ran. But as for how long it was going to stay up or how high it would go, Alice Martin's guess was as good—or as bad—as the next man's.

She told the whole business to Harry Martin when the two of them sat relaxing after their late dinner. "You might sell out all those odd lots of stocks we have," she wound up, "and use the money to take a flier. That would at least give us some arithmetic without any fractions in it."

Harry grinned. "*You* might do it, if it really needs doing. You're the one who seems to collect all the stock tips."

"You haven't heard me out," Alice insisted. "If you speculate and make money, you're welcome to invest half the profits. The other half I want you to hand me. I'll put it into a special savings account."

Harry shook his head and remained speechless, but his grin widened. Alice broke down and laughed. "All right, then, that second part just occurred to me. But what do you think of the first? The flier part?"

"You've spawned better ideas on other occasions. When we moved in here, for example. Your plan for taking a flier strikes me as like the circus trick of riding three horses bareback and leaping from one to another while they canter around the ring. A lovely thing to watch; but it seems to me a droll way to make a living. I'd make up my mind which horse I'd like to ride and stick to that one."

"The answer is 'No'?"

"Not so fast, my love, not so fast! I'll talk to Earl Crawford when he and Jean come visiting. They're due here very soon now. Are we going to go back to Brooklyn and put them up there in her old bedroom, the way we always have?"

"We might let them have this place, while we do the subway riding. But that wouldn't give us much chance for visiting, would it?"

"Or much chance at Mamma's fabulous cooking. They are coming to visit us," Harry reminded her, "as well as to buy new clothes and see the sights."

Actually they combined both schemes; and one evening, when they were surprised by a sudden downpour, the four of them bivouacked in the Commerce Street apartment. There was some dispute as to who should take the bed; the Martins were entitled to seniority, but they were the hosts.

"If I had thought to buy one of those couches that open out into a double bed—!" Alice apologized.

"On the chance that the young Crawfords would come visiting that next August and get caught in the rain and be too stingy to flag down a taxi for the long ride to Brooklyn!" Jean jeered.

"You wouldn't buy a secondhand open-out any more than you'd buy a secondhand bed," said Earl. "This is a good roomy davenport. It seems a shame to desecrate your new upholstery; but if we put the loose pillows on those three chairs, we can manage a very comfortable bed. I claim it for myself and my wife, too. It was my idea."

Earl fitted in. He had fitted in right from the start. It had taken the senior Martins longer to grow fond of Jim's wife; but after she and Alice came to an agreement, Alice acted as if she had invented Kathleen. Mustn't think about the California kin tonight, however. Mustn't let anything interfere with the pleasure of the present visit.

When Harry got around to consulting his son-in-law about Alice's ideas for small-time speculation, Earl was amused. "You give her half your winnings to put where it will earn a little interest; but your losses you pocket. Does Mrs. M. hedge her bets that way when she lays a wager with you?"

"The only way Alice ever bets is to take four one-dollar bills out of the cash register and bet me two of them on her side of the question. Whoever wins, the money goes right back where it belongs."

"The 'heads I win, tails you lose' type of gambler, isn't she? Go ahead with her scheme if you think you'd care to try it. Just don't get so you enjoy it too much."

"You think it's a silly scheme, don't you?"

Earl grinned. He was a fine-looking, tall fellow with a particularly engaging smile; it must do a lot for him professionally as well as personally. "Look at it for yourself. Waverley Book Shop is a going concern. You're a settled married man. A preference for the four-per-cents is supposed to be characteristic of the breed."

"Poor old Harry Martin! Poor old hide-bound Harry Martin! He could pose for the cartoons in a radical sheet. They would show him alternately reposing on his moneybags and grinding the faces of the poor."

"Don't make me cry. You two have been sensible to get yourselves a second home. It's a saving of time and energy. They are as important to save as money, often more so. There comes a time to spend. —Good Heavens, I sound as if I were delivering a lecture. It's high time for the bell to ring."

"Books are my business," Harry summed up. "Securities aren't. I feel that I've done pretty well so far. But perhaps I ought to change with the changing times. 'A new economic era' finds me still wearing the old economic uniform."

"Which is becoming enough. A conservative cut goes well with the four-per-cents."

Harry thought of mentioning his new undertaking; but he decided not to speak of it even to this sympathetic auditor. The idea was glitteringly new. Best not mention it until he himself had decided on more of its features.

Instead he told Earl of his ambition to sing "Forty-Nine Bottles." Earl had never heard of it before, and thought it immensely entertaining. The idea of forty-nine bottles hanging on a wall and then their "happening" to drop in sequence! He drew a diagram of them; he recognized, as Harry had done, that forty-nine was the square of seven, and arranged his sketch accordingly.

"Now would they drop off in order?" he wondered. "This looks sort of like a game of ticktacktoe, doesn't it? Did you used to play that when you were a kid?"

Harry had not had a particularly happy childhood; he seldom spoke of it, and thought of it as little as possible. It had been different with his own children. "Jim and Jean used to play it," he remembered. "Poor Jean could never win a game. If she managed to get ahead, Jim would take two plays to her one. Brothers are like that."

This time it was Harry who had brought Jim into the conversation. Oh, no sense in trying to keep him out! If you miss your miraculous firstborn, might as well go ahead and acknowledge it.

"Jean still has a younger-sister adoration for Jim," Earl remarked. "He is a very fine fellow. I don't say I married Jean just on account of her family connections—but it all helps."

"I suppose there's a grim truth behind those mother-in-law jokes. I wouldn't know from my own experience; I married an orphan, and Alice has always been on good terms with the younger people."

"Grim truth, I'm afraid," Earl agreed. "Didn't some wise

[46]

man once say there would be no humor in heaven? Nothing to contrast with the state of universal happiness; no bitter from which to extract the morsel of sweet."

"If it hasn't been said, it should be. But I'll take your word for it, sonny. I'm in no hurry to get there and find out."

"If you did, you couldn't come back and tell me. Heaven is a nice idea; but it's curiously vague somehow."

"Like astronomical distances, too big for us to take in. Yet men dream up such things in the first place. Other men like you and me."

"Someone dreamed up 'Forty-Nine Bottles,' " Earl recalled. "Are you sure you're not the culprit?"

"Quite sure. I didn't do it," Harry summed up, "but I almost wish I had. I've an excellent memory, considerable industry, and as much taste as the next fellow. But I lack inspiration."

All too soon, the Crawfords' visit was over. Jean's school term began right after Labor Day. "I can watch the Little Woman off to her job, and then settle myself with the morning paper and an extra cup of coffee. There's a lot to be said for a working wife," Earl proclaimed.

"One thing I hope can be said for her," his mother-in-law retorted. "I hope she leaves the breakfast dishes for you."

Jean Crawford laughed. "Sometimes the stacked dinner dishes, too, that first hectic week. The more domestic type of wife would be better in the kitchen, but—"

"But not so interesting to talk to at the table," Earl finished for her. "Board and bed is the standard phrase, isn't it? Nothing said about the kitchen sink."

The Labor Day weekend was not just another business weekend for Waverley Book Shop; it had a character of its own. There was the usual holiday stampede of New Yorkers to get out of town, with the resultant traffic jams and traffic accidents. Right here, on a leading thoroughfare which led to tunnels and to ferries, the Martins got their share of the din and the reek. Conversely, there was the holiday influx of tourists who came to the Village in search of thrills, preferably illicit thrills. The usual oddities, such as the self-conscious Bohemians who patronized the grubby Superb Cafeteria on the corner north of the shop, were right there and very much in evidence.

Alice was sometimes driven to tell the more persistent of the curiosity-seekers, "I wouldn't know about that. I just work here. I live in Brooklyn." Brooklyn had a reputation not only for respectability but for dullness. Actually the Martins had come back to their second home with its late quietness and rooftop view of the city scene.

But Harry enjoyed the game of giving the answers which might reasonably be asked in a book shop. "If you mean Mark Twain's house," he would say innocently, "that's quite a way from here. Washington Irving the Second's house is right across the Avenue here. It's marked, and you can't miss it; but the tablet is misleading. It calls him 'Junior,' and of course he wasn't. Washington Irving, who wrote 'Rip Van Winkle,' lived and died a bachelor." For good measure he would sometimes even point out the house where Tom Paine wrote "The Crisis." If they had never heard of Tom Paine, so much the worse for them. They could use a stalwart work on United States history. Waverley did not stock textbooks; but there were interesting volumes for the lay reader.

It all kept the Martins from missing Jean and Earl too much. Missing was the price you paid for having; the more precious the possession, the greater the gap it left. Loneliness was not too high a price, even in those first acute moments. Some in-laws were missed just the way that you would miss an aching tooth. Some children were loved because they belonged, and their presence tolerated because that was the custom. But in this respect the Martins had been singularly blessed—in this respect as in so many others. They had a great deal to be thankful for. Thankful even over Labor Day; there was no sense in putting off gratitude to the Last Thursday in November, when Harry carved the turkey.

Monday evening they put the shop to bed rather earlier than usual. "I do not know where 'the Bohemians' live," Alice said as they were locking up, "if you mean by 'Bohemians' people who ought to be in jail or in a madhouse. We do not keep any dirty books under the counter. If any of our competitors do, they're welcome. I feel contaminated somehow. Shall we wash up here and go somewhere for dinner? Or shall we call it a day and go home?"

"I vote for home and a shower. But how about stopping in at the corner delicatessen and getting some vittles? You could stand having things a little easy tonight, can't you?"

"I could stand eating out of the paper containers and not having any dishes for either of us," Alice decided. "You can let me have first whack at the shower, too, if you'll be so good. I can get pure while you're mixing the drinks."

"But can you wait while I shower?" he demanded. They were both laughing when they locked the shop door.

The telephone was ringing when they let themselves in at the door of the Commerce Street apartment. "Now who on earth can that be at this hour?" Harry wondered as he laid the packages on the table.

"I suppose a good way to find out would be to answer," Alice retorted. But just at that instant the phone ceased ringing. When Harry picked up the receiver, there was nobody on the line.

"Probably a wrong number anyhow," he concluded. "Still, it might be Jean or Earl long-distancing for a report. Go ahead and take your shower. I'll go after the ice cubes. Bathing suits and the roof tonight. No dinner preparations, you know."

"Not unless a call comes through," she decreed. "It may not amount to much; but if we neglect it we'll be afraid we're missing something."

She had finished her shower and was on her way to the bedroom for a negligee when the phone did ring again and Harry answered. With nothing more than normal curiosity he said, "Yes?" Then, with pleased surprise, it was, "No?" Listening then for a minute, he ejaculated in succession, "Really? You don't say! You wouldn't kid me, would you? Don't stop now! Tell me some more."

He was not only pleased; he was overjoyed; but then along toward the end, he was also holding out on her. Alice, who had stopped in her tracks, waited for a clue. Then, tired of being teased, she shrugged and turned on her heel.

That did it. "I know you want to tell your own good news," Harry said. "Your mother is right here." Extending the instrument to her, he revealed, "It's Jim."

It was indeed Jim, talking from the West Coast and as plainly audible as if he were right here in New York with them. "This is official," he said. "I'm writing you tomorrow; but I wanted you to have the good news by word of mouth. I've been promoted and transferred to the Chicago office. I'll be second in command there, with a nice increase in salary."

Prestige, recognition, salary; they were all fine. Jim was getting what he had earned, and he made no attempt to conceal his gratification. His parents were as pleased as he was that things were coming his way. But for them the crowning touch was his accessibility. Chicago was only an overnight ride from New York: closer by a good deal than Minneapolis, for which a person not only had to change trains but often change stations.

Jim went ahead and put Kathleen on the wire. She must talk not only to Alice but also to Harry. Kathleen was the most reserved of the four; but even Kathleen was a little drunk with happiness, which is a very heady brew.

She wound up, "If the baby is still awake, I'll put him on the wire. Talk to Jim again while I find out."

Jim explained that due to Daylight Saving, there was a four-hour difference in time. "I would have let you listen to him before this; but Kathleen said there was no sense in calling you all across the country just so that you could listen to a baby crying. He can talk now, after a fashion. At least, *we* call it talking."

The baby presently da-da'd at them. He was Harry's godson as well as their grandson: more important in some ways than President Hoover himself, though Mr. Hoover was blissfully unaware that he had been superseded.

The telephone conversation was over presently; but the glow remained to transfigure succeeding hours. Harry sang in the shower; not satisfied even with "Forty-Nine Bottles," he essayed, "Hail, Columbia!" Their drinks were nectar, their potato salad and deviled eggs ambrosia. Harry even went so far as to suggest that they long-distance Jean and Earl in Minneapolis. But he accepted Alice's veto meekly. Jim must be allowed to tell his own good news, and in his own time.

"They won't feel quite the way we do about it," Harry agreed. "The Minneapolis people are fine; we all get along beautifully together. But Earl and Jean are not, after all, Jim's father and mother."

"They are not," agreed Alice. "You have such a telling way of putting things."

He was still putting those same things even when at a decidedly late hour the Martins cleared up the remains of their meal and went to bed. Alice put out the light and stifled a yawn. Harry finally went to sleep in the middle of a sentence. He was the talkingest man that Alice had ever been married to. But for once he had a subject to which not even Harry Martin could do justice.

5

MARRIED COUPLES HAD THEIR OWN WAY OF DATING THINGS.
"That was the year we set up Waverley Book Shop," the
Martins might say. "That was the year Jim finished high
school." "That was the year Jean got her degree." Their calendar read like a record of achievement. No reason why it
shouldn't; on the whole they hadn't done so badly. Anyhow
officially people dated from memorable events: Harry's beloved Romans from the founding of the city, modern occi-
dentals from the beginning of the Christian era. So 1929
would go down in the Martin annals as "the year Jim moved
to Chicago." Earlier it might have been labeled as "the year
we moved to the Village."

Eventually indeed it might revert to that. Chicago wasn't
actually in the senior Martins' back yard. But Jim was going
up in the world as well as coming east in the country. Good
luck seemed to have settled down in the Martin family.

When Alice remarked that to Harry, he admonished, "Rap
on wood when you say so. You're not superstitious, of course;
but it can't do any harm."

Alice carried out his suggestion, remarking as she did so, "How the children used to love it when they were small and I said, 'Where's some wood to rap on?' and then tapped my own head!"

"Just as funny to them the two hundredth time as it was the first, too. I wonder where that superstition orginated? Everything has to start somewhere."

"Rapping three times might be for the Trinity, and wood might be because the Cross was made of wood. Or the practice may be much older than that. There's no telling."

"It isn't like Tom Paine or Washington Irving; that you can look up," Harry agreed. "Look'ee, Alice, that's one story I'm going to have in my anthology, 'Rip Van Winkle.' It's not only a superb story; it hasn't appeared in too many other collections."

"Sometimes I think anthologists copy other anthologists instead of going to the sources."

"They save work, and cheat themselves out of fun. On the other hand, though, an anthology can't be written on the margins of other anthologies. A certain amount of overlapping must be allowed for."

"That is definite, then?"

He nodded, and made a memorandum. So far he had done a lot of reading and made numerous memoranda. He had also arrived at several important decisions. "The Bible is out, and Shakespeare is out. Those two absolutely and automatically. Just as certainly, Aesop is in. All those wise wonderful old stories! Some of them have passed into the language so completely that everybody recognizes the reference. 'Sour grapes,' for instance, and 'dog in the manger.' But if we set down the complete fable, the reader will have the pleasure of greeting an old friend."

"You're going to include the one about the man, the boy, and the donkey, I hope. You know, the man has his son riding the donkey, and a passerby says it's awful to make the old man walk. When the father takes the turn at being the rider, the next passerby says it's awful to make the poor child walk. When they're both loaded on the animal's back, the poor beast gets the sympathy; they are told they might better carry him. They do, tying him to a pole. No fun for any one of the three. Then, when they're crossing a narrow bridge, the poor struggling animal works loose and falls in. We don't have to have it drown, do we, to prove that you can't satisfy everybody?"

"In the shop, we have to try to do just about that. But in this book, Harry Martin, Editor, will be the one who must be pleased. I declare, Alice, that's one reason I'm not saying anything to anybody about it. I don't want any advice." He ended that sentence sharply, then added with ludicrous haste, "Except, of course, from you."

"From me least of all," said Alice sweetly. "You can use me as a sounding board."

Harry grinned. "One poem I'm certainly going to have: the one about the man who didn't take his wife's advice. And about the many men who don't.

> 'Ah, gentle dames, it gars me greet,
> To think how many counsels sweet,
> How many lengthened sage advices,
> The husband frae the wife despises!' "

"Oh, 'Tam o'Shanter'! Harry, that is absolutely the most unmoral thing I ever read—and about the funniest. The habitual drunkard gets to attend a witches' Sabbath, sees grossly improper sights there, and gets off scot-free, though his poor mare loses her tail. I hope your anthology isn't going to run up against too many instances of cruelty to animals."

"I'll have to include one or two of Burns in a serious mood. He could be absolutely heart-rending."

[54]

"There's a Caxton Burns in the Brooklyn apartment," Alice recalled. "But maybe I can dig a cheaper one out of the warehouse for you. Want me to try?"

"So far I'm just taking notes. I won't wear out any copy." Harry penciled one more memorandum. He kept some of these in the Commerce Street apartment, some in the Brooklyn flat. While he was working on them, indeed, some of them were thrust between the pages of volumes in the shop; but such a volume was always stuck out of sight when he wasn't using it.

It was a mammoth undertaking. So far Harry Martin didn't even know how large he was going to make his book. Prose and poetry together. Selections of what had especially appealed to him: things he liked to reread, to think about between readings, to return to over the course of the years. That was the idea, and he had it clearly in mind. But countless details would have to be settled as he went along. Settled, and perhaps resettled, and then again re-resettled. Infinite labor lay ahead, and infinite pleasure.

Even when he had the selections pretty well sifted out, there would be the question of format. There would be finding a publisher and clearing copyright. But such details were very far in the future.

Alice always assumed most of the burden of reading the new books which Waverley laid in regularly. But Harry read, or glanced at, enough so that he could do an intelligent selling job. He had to keep a firm hold of the mail order end of the business, too. That was profitable, it was fun, and it was tricky. Though Bill Thayer had proved an invaluable assistant, he couldn't do Harry's thinking for him. Alice sometimes did; but the sly puss had had long practice and knew how the old man should be handled.

Planning his anthology offered Harry Martin a chance to ransack the ages. (That was Browning, wasn't it? He would be a difficult author to select from; but Browning was certainly coming in. His case presented an embarrassment of riches; this one would need a lot of narrowing down.) The anthologist drew from the richness of the past; he made no promises for the future. He would complete his work one of these days; and he didn't care how long it took.

Harry was simply digging in that year: the year of grace 1929. Autumn was upon them now; and autumn in New York was always a lovely season. The very air smelled crisp and clean, even on Seventh Avenue. "Everybody" was back in town. Waverley Book Shop did a fabulous business with the new fall volumes; "used books" were brought in for a time faster than they went out. The new clothes were catching on well, after the first silly styles had had their day in the newspapers and the fashion shows. The Broadway openings were crowded as usual; Ben Johnson, the Martins' drama-critic friend, had his hands full with openings. October got off to a flying start.

It came to a crashing finish. The deluge burst. The bottom dropped out. The "new economic era" fell over its own feet, and lay prone. The year 1929 became publicly known as the year of "The Depression." The stock market crashed.

Not only that; it went on crashing. The first profound shock was succeeded by incredulity, then by panic. No one needed to turn to the financial sections of the newspapers for the dire particulars; they blazed forth from the front pages.

Buyers on margin were wiped out overnight. It couldn't happen! But it *had* happened. What had gone up must come down; the only question was how far down. Each time that it seemed the bottom had been reached, the stock market found new low levels. "Coolidge prosperity" had gone the way of Nineveh and Tyre.

Business at Waverley Book Shop fell to a minimum. The gossips still gathered there to talk over each fresh disaster. Everybody wanted to tell about his own hard luck; nobody wanted to listen. As an excuse for hanging about, many of

[56]

them bought "used books." Some benighted souls brought in secondhand items for sale; the price on those fell as sharply as had the stock market. Alice was eventually driven to mark down prices even on the new fall issues.

Curious phenomena came to pass. Men thrown suddenly out of work took to selling apples on street corners. Where all those apples came from was a mystery; and here in a thickly settled part of New York there were barely street corners enough to go around.

"It reminds me of Mark Twain's old joke," Harry Martin remarked, "that the Chinese must earn their living taking in one another's laundry." Being a soft touch, he sometimes took fewer apples than he had paid for. Alice, on the other hand, tried to get her money's worth. She ate apples herself. She fed them to Harry, with cheese for dessert, or cut up in salad. She made applesauce. She even ventured on apple pie, but only the once. That took too long to make, and she could buy better at an excellent French bakery just around the corner from the Commerce Street place.

The large hospital a few blocks to the north of Waverley Book Shop opened a soup kitchen. Alice stared with amazement at the characters who lined up for their dole; you could tell just to look at them that most of those men hadn't worked in years. How did they subsist in times of "prosperity"?

The hospital soon came to the same conclusion that Mrs. Martin had; their bread line closed after a few weeks, and the patrons thereof crawled back into the holes they had come out of. Apple-selling ceased almost as abruptly as it had begun.

Business at Waverley picked up slightly. After all, reading was a cheap pleasure. William Thayer ventured to say, "I've been waiting for the ax to fall." Harry Martin told him, "Not yet a while." Harry's gilt-edged stocks had fallen, fallen in

[57]

some cases below what he paid for them. But they still paid dividends. He saw no reason to despair.

He was different in that respect from many of his fellow Americans. The stock-market crash had brought on a perfect epidemic of jumping out of windows. A spectacular way to commit suicide, and very inconsiderate of other people. The jumper never could tell what or whom he would hit.

Alice blamed the newspapers for giving such prominent space to these suicides. "I'm glad Ben made the grade to drama critic," she remarked to Ben Johnson's wife Bess, who had come into the book shop to invite Alice to attend a matinee with her. "Not only on account of the passes, though I always do love to see a show for free; I'd hate it if he were still a reporter and had to go around and write up all these messy suicides."

"Passes are easy to come by nowadays." Bess smiled faintly. "The established plays are having fair runs, though. Money to put on new plays has become as scarce as hens' teeth. Ben has few openings to cover."

Ben himself had had a play produced in the not-too-distant past. He had from time to time sold options on others. If that source of income should dry up, he still had his salary to depend on. It would not only pay the rent and buy the Johnsons food; it would also cover Bess's bills for postage. She was a poet largely unpublished; indeed many of her poems remained unfinished. With Ben having so much more time on his hands, she would get less writing done than ever. The worst part of being congenially married was the way a loving couple chatter-chatter-chattered to each other.

"Let me return your favor by giving you two or three books," Alice said. "Or would you rather I lunched you before the matinee or took you Broadwaying after it?"

"Either way will cost you money," Bess demurred. "Passes don't cost me a cent."

"But you've always seen the show with Ben on the opening

[58]

night. When you take me to it, you practically recommend it."

Bess smiled. "If I can sit through a show a second time, I've earned a restorative afterward. Broadway it is, and thank you."

"We'll both have that to look forward to. There's always something to look forward to, isn't there, even if it's only a cola drink and a third-hand book? That's why I can't see why people ever commit suicide, though I've heard that there for a short time before the end they experience a wonderful sense of satisfaction. They feel that they have finally found the answer."

"Maybe they have," said Bess, "I can see what makes some people take an overdose of sleeping pills, though even that is a silly thing to do. But when a man jumps out of a high window, he must know one awful moment."

"You mean that when it's too late he must realize—?"

Bess nodded sadly. "He must reach for something to hold onto, and find there's nothing to grasp."

Alice suppressed a little shudder. "Nothing to grasp," she said slowly. "Nothing—to—grasp. You ought to write a poem about that, Bess."

Harry Martin caught those last words and turned away from the shoppers who had not yet gotten around to buy anything. "Is the Little Woman bossing you too, Bess?" he asked.

Bess Johnson turned up her nose and retorted, "She thinks too highly of my ability, that's all."

"What else are friends for?" demanded Harry.

Alice's tension vanished, she smiled broadly. "Harry Martin talks a lot, Bess; but every once in a while he says something. I think he might help us pick out two books, one for you and one for Ben. Something that will be nice to read in bed, now that nights are getting chilly and openings are few."

[59]

Alice regularly read the new books in bed at the beginning of publishing seasons. It was by no means the most distasteful part of her job. The living room davenport in the Commerce Street apartment was good for an extra-late session: just as good as the second bedroom in the Brooklyn flat had long been. She was getting to feel very much at home here. If The Depression continued, it would be prudent to give up this second establishment and go back to Brooklyn for keeps. But that seemed like acknowledging defeat. Defeat in only a minor matter, perhaps; but Alice didn't like the feeling of it.

She would cross that bridge when she came to it, anyhow. The Depression couldn't last forever. Actually in lapsed time there hadn't been so much of it. Not yet, that is. It only seemed a long time because people got attached to the subject and made the most of it.

This apartment could be given up at a month's notice anyhow; and the davenport would look fine in the Brooklyn living room. Not nearly so much to unload as if the Martins had taken the Burgesses' advice and saddled themselves with an estate on Long Island.

What the Burgesses themselves thought of their encumbrance was another matter. There were some questions that simply were not asked even among friends—or perhaps it would be more accurate to say: especially among friends. But a person could always listen.

Harry did so one afternoon when Don Burgess came into Waverley Book Shop. Alice happened to be out on an exploring expedition. It had struck her that some of Waverley's competitors must have been forced out of business; if she attended their closing sales she might pick up a few bargains. Just as well, she might be accused of gloating over a defeated rival—that is, if she were recognized. In that case, she could always pretend that she was "searching."

Don was waiting when Harry had satisfied a solitary customer and seen her on her way. When the two men were alone, Mr. Burgess began, "I've never descended that low professionally: never tried to get suspense by saying, 'Had he but known—!' Personally, however, that is my theme song nowadays: 'Had I but known!' "

"You sinned in good company. It isn't as if you had nothing left, either."

"I have a country place which would sell for good money, if anybody had the money to buy it. I have a car which will last me for some time, and which I can't afford to turn in on a new one even if I wanted to. I have a very fine servant couple whose salaries I've had to reduce."

"But they're staying?"

"They are staying. There's not much market for their services. Besides, they happen to like Virginia and me."

"Bill Thayer is staying, too. This is his day off. I suppose it does pay to treat one's help decently."

"That isn't why we do it; but yes, it does pay."

"You have a lovely wife, scarcely more than a bride," Harry urged.

"A working wife, too. The best investment I ever made." Don's face softened suddenly. "I never dreamed two people could be so happy together. What she sees in me—!"

A customer came in just then. Shortly afterward Alice returned and dumped two packages of books. She was the victim of a new idea; but it waited until after Don Burgess had had a visit with her, and had picked up a few cheap items and departed with them to catch a certain train on the Long Island. "The victim of a timetable!" Alice jeered at parting.

"The suburbanite's plaint," he agreed. "But the theme song of the dear old Village is:

> If time was money, I'd be a millionaire.
> I ain't got no money, but I got time to spare."

"Spare us some, any time you feel like it," said Alice. "Wait just a minute, though, and take along a book with my love to Virginia. I have something I'm sure she'll like."

"Giving away the profits!" Harry teased as soon as Don was out of earshot.

"He's sort of a sweet thing, and he's playing in hard luck. Look, Harry. I've picked up some books which would do well for children. I can buy some additional comic books later on, and sort out the cheaper items from our stock, here and in Brooklyn. I'm going to start a new 'Used Book' table. A low one, especially for children. Some of the books won't actually be 'used' to begin with; but they'll get that way soon enough." Running out of breath, she caught his eye and faced his grin. "That is, if you think it would be a good idea," she added hastily.

The Martin's stock of comic books had always been kept on two or three low shelves, were small-fry might spot them while their elders were busy with something on a different level. But this was a bid for the children's own coins. "I suppose you have the tables all picked out," Harry jeered.

"Oh, sure! There's a 'stock and fixtures for sale' in a secondhand clothing store right near here. The stock looks to me pretty mangy and moth-eaten. But there are a couple of tables that only need the legs sawed off to be quite usable."

"It's going to make extra work, with very little profit," Harry objected.

"I'll do the work, and we can pool the profit."

"The profit, if any."

"The profit, if and when." Alice opened the cash drawer. "I think I'll go back and arrange about those tables now. Oh, look who's headed this way! He has been passing by on the other side lately."

It was Thomas Carroll who entered the shop now. Alice smiled and waved and went on her way. She didn't even pause to ask, "How's business?" Business was bad all over;

[62]

but in an uptown art gallery it must be much worse than in a Greenwich Village book store. There was no chance of inexpensive sales and resales there, or of new ideas which might bring in a penny profit.

This new idea of hers was entrancing. There was a real zip in the air today, too. There well might be; Thanksgiving was less than a week away. Then would come Christmas, with Jean and Earl here to share it, and the junior Martins settling into their new surroundings. Alice's step grew even lighter. She began to hum a carol.

At the door of his shop she almost collided with a man who did electric repairs and installation. Like so many people in this neighborhood, he was an Italian; like so many others, he was a character. They both laughed at the near mishap. Then Alice said, "Cheerful as ever, aren't you, Mr. Angelotti! Don't you know we're having a Depression?"

He was carrying an order to be delivered; from its shape and size, very likely a toaster. He thrust it under his arm to free both hands, and began to gesture as he replied, "So there is, so what? If I'm sick and I worry, does it make me well? If I'm broke and I worry, does it make me rich? If the country is going to the dogs and I worry, does that set the country back on its feet?"

"People must enjoy worrying, or they wouldn't spend so much time at it," Alice argued.

"The time they spend that way—!" His shrug was so eloquent that he nearly dropped his bundle.

"They really enjoy other people's bad luck," Alice concluded.

She hadn't meant that the way it sounded. But Angelotti was now in full spate, and took her remark in his stride. "This they enjoy: 'What, Mr. Angelotti, three dollars for a little repair it couldn't have taken you ten minutes to do? The man in the next block never would have charged me that much.'"

[63]

Over her laughter Alice managed to say, "It can't be as bad as all that!"

"Bad? It's worse." This time the package really started to skid; he retrieved it only just in time. Resuming her way on her errand, Alice reflected that this would give her something to tell Harry when she got back to the shop.

She'd better hurry, too. He might need help with the customers. Business might be picking up a little. Just a little, it might.

6

THERE WAS A RENAISSANCE POPE, A MEMBER OF THE MEDICI family, as Alice recalled it, who is supposed to have said, "God gave us the papacy, therefore let us enjoy it." That might not be a deeply religious remark; but it certainly made sense. Not so much could be said for the feeling which seemed to prevail over much of America during the year 1930. It was that the Devil, or the Republican Administration or wicked, wicked Wall Street, "gave us the Depression, therefore let us wallow in it."

The suicide epidemic was over. Nobody starved to death in the street. Some of the wiseacres knew when the bottom had been reached. It was still possible to obtain funds for speculation; it was also easy to send good money after bad. Harry Martin was tempted, especially after he had been listening to Don Burgess.

"Why follow Don's advice now?" Alice demanded. "You were smart enough not to take it before; and look what happened. We're not sitting pretty on Easy Street, exactly; but we still have a foothold on Commerce Street. Food prices are lower, too. Let's outlast the Depression. The Depression with a capital 'D' has ceased to depress me; in fact I'm getting most confoundedly sick of if. I have to listen to customers, of course. But when you and I are alone together, can't we please talk about something else?"

"We could even refrain from talking," Harry suggested. "Silence is an art in which I've never had much practice. For the next hour by the clock, I'm going to make believe that I'm a Trappist monk."

"That is the order which enjoins silence on its followers, isn't it? I wonder how it got its name." Alice reached for a dictionary, and read aloud, " 'From La Trappe, abbey in Normandy where the order was established in 1664.' Oh, so that's it! I knew it couldn't possibly be because they were in the habit of keeping their traps shut."

Harry guffawed. "I'm afraid your dictionary would classify that as slang. I don't promise to make it a habit; but right now I'm going to keep my trap shut for a full hour; and you can time me if you like."

That enjoined silence on Alice, too. It was an amusing game. She must remember to mention it to Bess Johnson, who had reported on how she and Ben chatter-chatter-chattered. Virginia Daly and Don Burgess might be different. There would be no harm in reporting to them, though.

On fine spring days the outdoor tables at Waverley Book Shop always did a flourishing business. That was where "Used Books" had been displayed ever since the Martins opened the establishment; now the two new tables were crowded with children after school and on weekends. Alice didn't mind a particle if the children read more than they bought; and after enough exposures to street dust and juvenile readers, the books often had to be marked very low indeed. Alice's forays with a damp washcloth helped a little. Washing the dirty hands of the neighborhood children was a good deed in itself, even if it couldn't be rung up on the cash register.

[66]

In May Earl and Jean Crawford sent word that they would be in New York for some time this year. They were both enrolling in summer session at Columbia. Earl wanted a refresher course, for spiritual as well as intellectual reasons; he had sat in the seat of judgment for some time now, and wanted to take his turn at looking up to the rostrum. Jean would do some work toward an advanced degree.

They would like to stay in one of the Martins' apartments, and pay rent for it, of course. If that arrangement didn't suit Harry and Alice, they must feel prefectly free to say so.

The Martins' first impulse was to say that the young people were welcome to stay as long as they liked, but it must be as the parents' guests. That of course would have been all wrong. Guests had certain obligations, fully as binding as the hosts'. Also there was a large claim on their time. The young people were coming here to work; they must be free to work.

They could take one apartment, leaving the other to their elders. There was very little question which one; even the Commerce Street apartment was a long subway ride from Columbia. There Earl and Jean would set up their own housekeeping arrangements, while Harry and Alice retreated to Brooklyn for the duration. What a blessing that they had put in an electric refrigerator there! Harry was going to get his money's worth out of it now. He wouldn't tote any new wine in old bottles for a while, either. Earl and Jean were welcome to whatever was in the place already, of course. The Martins' Carrie, who had been with them for years and years, would look after the Crawfords' cleaning and help with the cooking. She adored "Miss Jean," and sympathized with Mrs. Martin because her daughter lived so many miles away. Her own daughter had married right in Carrie's neighborhood.

Harry and Alice left Bill Thayer in charge of the shop the evening of the Crawfords' arrival. They gave the young people a warm welcome and a bang-up dinner, and accepted

[67]

a check in advance for the rent during the young people's entire stay. Earl had added an extra thirty dollars, partly for the provisions with which Alice had stocked up the place, partly to cover the gas and electricity bill. "That should be higher than usual," Earl explained. "We'll burn the midnight current a good many nights, I suspect."

"We live largely by artificial light ourselves," Harry protested. "That 'early to bed, early to rise' pap was written in the days of farm labor and homemade candles, anyhow."

"By Benjamin Franklin as the wisdom of a fictitious character," Alice supplemented. "Poor Richard was supposed to have said that. Old Ben himself liked the light of the chandeliers at court, if my memory serves me."

"Early to bed and early to rise
Is what I don't practice, I simply advise,"

Harry parodied.

"Bright boy, Harry Martin," Alice said sweetly. "Somebody once laughed at something he said; and he's kept it up ever since."

"I've heard worse," said Jean. "If one of my students handed that in, I think I'd give it an 'A' grade."

"This time I inform, I do not advise:
It certainly pays to advertise,"

Harry capped himself.

"That *is* worse," said Jean. "You can take a 'B minus' on that one."

"Mr. Martin's dry wit calls for a drink," Earl decided. So the evening was off to a flying start.

It ended much too soon. There was never another one quite like it. Harry and Alice saw something of the young

[68]

couple on subsequent weekends; one or the other of them would drop into the shop on the way home and pause for a chat and to exchange their small news. But the Crawfords needed some of their scanty leisure to see New York for themselves. It might have been different if the Martins had lived in Oskaloosa, say, or in Kalamazoo. Then again it might not. There was no point to being dogmatic about a thing like that.

The Martins got back easily into the routine of the long subway ride. On their way to the shop in the morning, Harry read his newspaper; returning to Brooklyn of an evening, he alternately read and dozed. He could count on Alice to rouse him when they reached their station. She was a sound sleeper; but she had never been able to see the fun of catnapping. Just as well she hadn't, too. It would have been very sad if they both slept past their own station, and had to pay another fare back at a late hour, and by so doing miss an hour or two of proper rest in bed.

At the end of the summer session the Crawfords treated themselves to a week's real vacation, in which the Martins were deeply enough involved to make their loneliness all the more acute when the young people finally went westward.

There toward the end, however, Harry managed to throw a rainbow bridge in the direction of the future. "Another year you must come to New York again, Earl, and really get away from the academic life for a time. Maybe from married life, too. Alice can join her daughter in Columbia. While the girls are in school, you can either help me out in the Book Shop or loaf around New York and get acquainted."

"I'm scheduled to go back to school with Mamma for chaperone, while you two bat around the Village and see strange sights not fit for our innocent eyes?" Jean protested.

"Suppose you put that up to Earl and let him do his own

[69]

refusing?" Harry insisted. "Or simply bear the thought in mind, and let your parents hear from you later on?"

"I'd be willing to bet that you haven't even put it up to Mamma. But it is a nice idea," Jean acknowledged.

Next summer was a long way ahead. By that time Jean might well have other concerns to attend to besides graduate work at Columbia. She and Earl had planned to produce a family one of these days; so far that plan, too, seemed to have remained "a nice idea." On this particular subject, not even Harry Martin could go asking a whole lot of intimate questions.

The future was vast, anyhow. Even summer of next year lay a considerable distance ahead. By that time, there was no telling what might have happened.

One thing happened this very year of 1930; that too just before Labor Day, when "everybody" would be back in New York, and the Depression would be looking forward to its first birthday anniversary. Their landlord, whom the Martins knew principally as a name on the rent check, came looking for them. He wanted to make them an offer.

"The apartment in the ell is twice the size of this one," he explained. "The bird who lives there is the last of three bachelors who used to share the place. One of the others left for the Coast while the going was still good. The second married a widow and moved in with her. The third owes me money which I'm never likely to get."

"I've noticed him going in and out," said Alice. She had also noticed him bringing a dame in at the cocktail hour: a woman who always avoided Alice's eye, and who more than once had actually tiptoed from the head of the stairway. As if "going to a man's rooms" was a proof of iniquity, the way it had been in a *fin-de-siècle* drama. As if it were any of Alice's business anyhow!

"I want somebody I can count on to pay the rent," the

landlord went on. "You can have it for what you've been paying here. Care to take a look at it some time soon?"

The Martins took a look. This apartment was at the back of the building. Being in the "L," it had light and air on three sides; it gave almost as stunning a view up and down Seventh Avenue as the Martins had been enjoying from the roof. It had a kitchenette twice the size of their present one— which wasn't saying much; if the Martins wanted a decent kitchen, they had to go back to Brooklyn. It had a foyer which would accommodate several tiers of bookshelves. It had two bedrooms, both with cross ventilation.

Harry's eyes began to gleam. "We don't need two bedrooms," he whispered to Alice. "But I could use one of these for my anthology."

Alice nodded, and brought up the question of refrigeration. But the bargain was too good to be resisted. This was crowning proof that the country was indeed experiencing what the jargon termed "a buyer's market."

That was a pleasanter expression than "Depression," with a capital "D." As for depression with a small "d," that occurred largely in one's own mind. Alice and Harry weren't constitutionally subject to it; Harry was even less so than Alice. Loneliness was different. Lonely in a general sense the Martins were not; but lonely for a special person or persons they sometimes were. The feeling was always at its worst when the people had only just left; almost as bad when their departure was imminent. That was actually what had made Harry dream up that notion about the Crawfords' visit to New York next year.

But now this year was filling up very neatly. The very next day after they had agreed to take the new apartment Alice was in the neighborhood bank. At a moment when business was slack, the guard came up to her. He was a handsome Irishman in his fifties, very likely a former policeman, though he was too spare and otherworldly to suit the common idea of a "cop." He looked, instead, as if he ought to be a prelate in the Catholic Church: a bishop at least, if not in fact a cardinal.

"You've heard the news?" he asked sadly. "The bank has reduced the interest on savings accounts again."

"It has?" The Martins carried a small reserve fund there; she hadn't given the matter much attention lately.

"Yes, ma'am. They pay only one per cent now."

"One per—? That is awful. Of course it's only temporary. But it shakes a person's confidence, doesn't it?"

He nodded sadly. "It scares a person. Some of the customers are even cashing in their securities and putting the money into their deposit boxes."

Alice stared; then she smiled. "The only reason I know you're not making that up is you couldn't possibly make up anything so silly. It simply has to be true."

He smiled back at her. "It always makes me feel better to talk to you, Mrs. Martin," he said gratefully.

"It makes me feel better to be told that," Alice assured him. She was on the point of reminding him of what a wise man had advised years ago, what the newspapers ought even now to be reminding people, instead of lining up with the prophets of doom and the reporters of disaster. "Never sell America short," he had said: old J. Pierpont Morgan, who had made a great deal of money and amassed a priceless collection of beautiful art objects.

Alice did not get a chance to remind the bank guard, "Never sell America short," for there behind him materialized somebody whom she saw all too seldom, and was always delighted to see: Emil Koenig, the sculptor friend with whom she had once visited all those secondhand furniture stores. Emil, whose hard-earned apartment she had helped him settle. Emil, whom she had introduced to the charming girl he had married. Now he filled the doorway as he entered: a huge

[72]

hulk of a man, with that special gentleness which seems to be the birthright of so many large people.

"Emil Koenig, as I live!" cried Alice, and put out both hands to him.

He grasped them and drew her toward him; for an instant Alice thought he was going to embrace her right there in front of the bank guard and the few stray customers. But he held himself in check. With Alice, he had always held himself in check. He had had to; even back when he wasn't married, she was.

"The weather is up and down," he contented himself by saying. "Business is mostly down. How's yours?"

Emil had risen to the place where he did architectural sculpture. It gave his talents the largest possible scope. It was also his first chance to make big money. He had arrived just in time to depart, Alice feared. Now he contented himself with a hazy generality.

"Let's get our business done and then swap the news," she suggested. "Your business won't take too long, will it?"

He grinned. "My business in here never does. I'm not in a class with the Morgans and the Rockefellers."

Alice told him then of the wise man's counsel, "Never sell America short." Told it to the bank guard, and added, "Never sell anything short would be my advice. That's just hoping the other fellow will have bad luck so that you can take advantage of it." Then, their small errands transacted, she went on, "Come into the shop and see Harry, won't you? We haven't laid eyes on you in ever so long."

Her good news wouldn't keep until they got to the shop, however; Alice had to tell him that she and Harry had taken another and larger apartment in the Commerce Street building, "so we're doing what we can for America while benefiting the Martins too."

Back in the shop they listened to Harry, who rolled his eyes expressively at the "browsers," greeted a new customer, found

[73]

time to tell the classic joke: "The question is, 'What's worse scared than a banker?' The answer is, 'Two bankers.' " Emil asked Alice to look up a few used books for him. "I haven't bought much lately. Kitty had a lot of things given her by a friend."

But all this time Emil was looking and looking at Alice. It was a special sort of look. It made her faintly uneasy, though after he had presently taken his leave she forgot all about it in her pleasure at having seen him again, at finding him so solidly and enduringly himself.

Less than a week later she discovered the reason for that scrutiny. He returned to the shop with a package wrapped in tissue paper, and presented it to Alice with a grin and the words, "Housewarming present. I wanted to surprise you."

It was a portrait bust of Alice Martin in painted terra cotta, about fourteen inches high. It represented her as a slightly younger woman, and even more piquant than Alice had ever looked. Whether you knew the subject or not, the statuette could stand on its own merits; it was a delightful piece. Anybody who did know her, or who saw her and this treatment of her together, experienced an additional thrill.

"But Emil, it's too lovely! It's too much!" she cried.

"It's too much!" Harry repeated after her, a little grimly. For a moment a flicker of jealousy appeared in his manner.

"She really should be done in porcelain," said Emil. "Complications there, though. That will have to wait."

"A Dresden china figurine. Complications, indeed!" Under Emil's noncomprehending stare, Harry had the grace to look sheepish. He hastened to make amends. "It's hard for me to realize that a big man who does big things can also make anything small and—you might almost say dainty."

Emil grinned. "Why not go ahead and say it? Is 'dainty' a fighting word?"

Alice had got her breath back. "A housewarming present demands a housewarming. I hadn't thought that far ahead.

[74]

The place is going to have a hard job living up to this beautiful gift, Emil. I'll put it in the middle of the living room mantel, and start from there. As to living up to the statuette myself, I shan't even try. Beauty is in the hand of the artist; but he has to start from somewhere. It's just my luck that this time he started with me."

"You have a conversation piece for the party. You also have the conversation pretty well thought out," teased Harry.

"Well, I'm not a Trappist monk, and so far as I know they never had Trappist convents." Alice was delighted that harmony had been restored. It would never do for Harry to go getting silly notions.

When Alice began to settle in her newly decorated apartment, she placed the figurine in the middle of the living room mantel, as she had said she would. It was flanked by her silver candlesticks and two framed photographs, and by nothing else. That was the keynote of her new apartment: lack of clutter. The Brooklyn flat was crowded, the shop was crowded, the warehouse was crowded; in the new place she actually had some empty space.

The bedroom was much as it had been in the smaller place. In the room which he would use for a study, Harry had the freedom of the house; he could even sing "Forty-nine Bottles" while he was shut up there. In the study closet Alice hung their out-of-season clothing. At the end of the living room she set up the folding table and chairs. The place was half empty. That was part of its newness, part of its charm.

A very great part, but only part. From one of the bedroom windows you could glimpse the Woolworth Building, which was for so long the architectural treat of downtown New York. From a window of the study you could see the new Empire State Building, much larger, much haughtier, and erected just in time to stand half empty. From the second windows in both those rooms, and from all three windows of the living room you could look down into gardens: those lovely little backyard gardens with which city dwellers did so much. In several gardens both here and on the other side of Seventh Avenue could be seen the graceful ailanthus trees: something which the Martins had never glimpsed in Indiana or in upstate New York, but a characteristic and very welcome piece of urban scenery.

The Martins set a Saturday for their housewarming. They had a buffet supper, with both Carrie and Phyllis in attendance. The guests were the same faithful souls who had been friends and customers before—oh, go ahead and say it!—before the Depression. (You might almost as well have said, "Before the Flood." Noah's gang certainly must have dated from that occurrence. Did they have reunions in later years, and did they enjoy talking over those past hardships though they had never enjoyed the hardships themselves?) The food was magnificent, and cost only about half of what it would have cost before—well, *before*. The drinks were potent and palatable. The guests were free to come and go pretty much as they liked. Actually they came and stayed.

They had brought along various gifts, some potable, some staple, including a new radio which several of them had clubbed together to buy. It was Ben Johnson, however, who made the finest gift of all, and that an immaterial one. Settling himself in the living room after a tour of inspection, he announced, "You two will never need to leave this place, no matter how rich you get."

Rich, when everybody must make a fetish of being poor? Rich, when Alice had had qualms about taking this place? Rich when—and when—and when—

Maybe it was just that the party spirit had got into him. If so, that alone was reason enough for giving the party. It had been wished on her by another friend. She had the nicest friends. They were worth a party any time.

Right now they were here, and this was a party, and that figurine was impossibly lovely. Alice Martin had never

[76]

looked quite like that. But the statuette had a beauty all its own. That beauty was a fact. Not only did it exist in the same world with less pleasing facts; at moments it could make a person forget them. One per cent on savings; yet in that same bank Emil Koenig could size up his old friend Alice and decide to put her into terra cotta.

He had his wife here with him tonight, of course. They had been married only a few years; but they had developed a certain pattern in their marriage. Kitty was small, though not so small as Alice; she was very good looking without being exactly beautiful. She was years younger than Alice, and for that matter, than Emil. Perhaps that was one reason why he sometimes looked at her in company the way a good old Saint Bernard dog might look at a frolicsome kitten.

Or perhaps he looked at her quite differently in moments when he had her to himself. Or perhaps he planned to do a terra cotta of her some time. Or perhaps—or perhaps—or perhaps—

It was a going party, anyhow. Now that she had this proper setting for her entertaining, Alice might well keep it up. This year of grace was rounding into its final quarter. The home stretch might well be the very best part of the race.

7

"You want me to take the blame," said Alice Martin "while you go ahead and share in the fun."

"I sure do," Harry agreed unblushingly. "Adam ate the apple, didn't he, and then said the fault was all Eve's? She gave it to him. You don't hear anything about his exerting his superior masculine intelligence, though, and saying before-hand, 'I don't think I'd touch that forbidden fruit, darling. There are plenty of other things growing in the garden.'"

Alice fell back on the defensive. "I know this may be a poor time to pick, when we're already supporting two establishments, and the dear delightful bank has reduced interest payments, and Recovery is like Repeal: something to look forward to, but don't count on it. Yet Waverley Book Shop is still making money. We have a grandson we've never yet laid eyes on. We're neither of us getting any younger."

"Times may get worse before they get better, too. All right, Mrs. Martin, we'll invite ourselves out to Chicago for the Christmas holidays. Bill Thayer can be left in charge of the shop. Another year we may not be able to afford even Bill

Thayer. All right, Mrs. Martin, go ahead and make the arrangements. We'll need something pleasant to talk about when we get to the poorhouse."

Their daugher-in-law had long since informed them that she didn't approve of house guests, and never stayed with them when she was in New York. But when Alice wrote asking Jim to make reservations for them at a moderate-priced hotel not too far from the apartment where the junior Martins were now living, Kathleen amazingly came across with an invitation to "camp out with us and make the best of it."

"That will save us a hotel bill, but it will put us under an obligation," Alice objected.

"Which we can discharge any time Jim and Kathleen and little Jimmie come to New York. Don't forget, we can put them up in the Commerce Street apartment just the way we did Jean and Earl this past summer. The retreat to Brooklyn is always open."

To Chicago the Martins went, arriving the afternoon of December 24. Kathleen's widowed mother had preceded them. She shared the connubial chamber with her daughter, while Jim bunked in the living room; the guest room was allotted to the senior Martins.

"They are making a point of putting themselves out for us," Alice muttered to Harry. Then she bit her tongue and added hastily, "They do have a guest room. Kathleen has changed her tune." Not that that made it much better. The senior Martins had not learned of the existence of the guest room until they invited themselves to Chicago.

Jean and Earl were the ones who put up at a hotel. That gave the New Yorkers a chance to see something of Chicago. Alice would have liked to see more. It was a city with a glorious view over Lake Michigan. But very few of the natives even knew there was a view; to look at it was to acknowledge oneself a stranger. The steam-shovel watchers who abounded in New York had no counterparts here.

[79]

The little boy was a darling in anybody's eyes, in the grandparents' a paragon. They not only enjoyed his Christmas rapture; it took them back to the days when their own children had been little, sometimes even to those faraway days when they themselves had been very young, and had been first devout believers, then in a small way participants at making Christmas for other people.

How much time had flown since then! It had left them with this rich store of memories. Christmas was the official season for remembering. It added a great deal to the richness.

This visit in its turn went by all too fast. Here 1931 was upon them. How would this decade go down in history? As "The Terrible Thirties?" History was, to be sure, something that a person studied in school, then later read about in memoirs and standard or "period" novels. At the time it happened, however, it wasn't history at all. History was the common, or sometimes personally important, things that happened to ordinary people like Harry and Alice Martin— who thought very little about today as history because they were too busy living it.

Parting was tough. Partings generally were. But this one was different. This time the senior Martins were the first to leave. There was novelty in that. So often at the end of a holiday they had been the ones who were left.

Then, too, they had a lot to go back to. It wasn't as if Harry had had a routine job and Alice had been condemned to associate with a lot of other married women who had time on their hands. Waverley Book Shop was waiting for them, with its myriad delightful tasks and its hosts of customers and friends. There were two dwelling places of their own; and much as a person might enjoy a delightful visit, home was home. Also, when Harry had caught up on his sleep, there was the anthology opening infinite vistas. According to the old adage, well begun was half done. That would do to tell timid youth. It would also be a wholesome doctrine to spread in the Village, where all too many of the denizens talked about the work they were going to do, but didn't get around to a good beginning. But actually well begun was well begun, period. There were not only months but in all probability years ahead of the ambitious anthologist. He wasn't sure yet of how he would arrange the text or even how he would handle the material; and most of the delightful work of selection still lay ahead of him.

The Burgesses came in for professional as well as personal reasons. Virginia was again in quest of source material. "Biography will remain my standby, I suppose," she informed them. "But right now I plan to do something different. I want to write a history of the Underground Railroad. You know, the organization that helped fugitive slaves escape to Canada. I've been curious about it for years."

"There's a novel in it, too," said Don. "A novel which I may do one of these days; or Virginia and I may do it together."

"Don't hold your breath until we collaborate," Virginia warned. "It may come to that one of these days. So far, however, our separate careers have been a great bond between us. We may not do much to further each other's work; but we can grouse to each other and be certain of perfect understanding."

"What are your publishers going to say to this new undertaking?" asked Alice.

"They're going to say 'Hell!' " Don answered for her. "They're going to say, 'Your speciality is biography. Why don't you stick to biography?' "

Harry supplied, "Aren't they also going to say, 'Don't you know there's a Depression on?' "

Virginia beamed. "It will be just too bad if they do. A novelty would attract new readers, methinks. My faithful public may be just a little bit tired of reading about the Civil

War. Anyhow I can get back to it one of these days and tell them all about Admiral Farragut."

"Novelty is what I sigh for." They were taking advantage of the dinner-hour lull in business; so far no customer had interrupted them. Don sighed gustily. "I've tried some new plot twists, and given one more yank to the old ones. But my future would be assured if I could dream up a great new detective character."

"Sherlock Holmes was the archetype, of course," said Harry. "There have been a lot of other good ones, too, most of them English. The highly paid consultant is one variety, the noble amateur another."

A customer came in just then; Alice waited on him. Then a middle-aged couple; Harry kept them in play. New business these; it did happen. The tinkle of the cash register was sweet music to the Martins' ears, all the sweeter because the slack season was upon them and they hadn't yet made up for the extravagance of their Chicago trip.

When the next pause came, Don was ready for it. "How about having a neighborhood bookseller as the noble amateur?"

"Too far fetched even for a detective story," Alice said quickly.

"Then how about having him for the Dr. Watson? The detective character could try out his theories on such a guy, and perhaps really beat something out on the anvil of his stupidity."

" 'The anvil of his stupidity' is good," said Virginia. "Better write that one down before you forget it."

"You'll remember it for me. You know you will. But here is a real idea: use the bookstore as a vantage point for observation."

Harry Martin laughed. "A lot of queer characters do pass here. If I had much time to stare out into the street, I could tell you even more about them. I never tire of the passing show. But alas! I'm an industrious man."

"That's another good speech. Lend me pencil and paper, will you, Harry? I want to write it down."

"Mean to say you don't carry a notebook? Mean to say I have to supply you with stationery as well as with ideas?"

"All right, then, sell it to me. If you make me a present of the idea, I won't object to paying for the paper and pencil."

Harry provided them, and Don tendered him a dime. Harry accepted it, then handed him a nickel in change. It was a cash-register transaction. The only trouble was that when their bit of clowning was over, both of them had forgotten the speech in question.

Virginia remembered it, however, as well as "the anvil of his stupidity." Don wrote them both down, then went on, "You can't sue me for slander even if you think you detect a resemblance, Harry. The publishers run the usual disclaimer in the front of every volume. Besides, it's a form of flattery. A popular and talkative bookseller, then, who sometimes takes time from his tasks to look out at the passing show, though he is 'an industrious man,' according to his own say-so—"

"And who would call in the police if books kept disappearing from his ten-cent table," Alice Martin interrupted.

"There's an idea!" shouted Don. "A capital start for a story. The police set him down at first as a crank, though of course a likable crank. They deal with such all along; some of them can be real pests. Then a plainclothesman falls into the habit of talking things over with him; and presently the bookseller either supplies him with the answer, or gives him the necessary lead for discovering it himself."

"It's an idea, at least," said Harry Martin. "Don't write it down, though. If it's good enough to use, it will be good enough to remember."

"That's all you know!" Don began to scribble.

[83]

"Oh, all right, all right, all right! Have it your own way. Better make it the twenty-five cent table, though. By the time a book hits the dime class, it's pretty shabby: hardly worth a police complaint." Harry made this last statement in front of an entering customer, a stranger who looked slightly astonished. To her he said, "You mustn't mind us, madame. Say, 'It's just the Village.' "

Don Burgess drew Alice aside. "I think there's a possible second idea here. You couldn't say from memory what's on one of your bargain tables, could you?"

"Good heavens, no! I remember the regular stock, and can answer questions about it. But the bargain tables offer customer's choice. I don't even glance at the used books if I notice from which table they've been taken."

"But you do glance at them when brought in for resale?"

"Have to, or I wouldn't know how much to offer. It's a matter of making the nickels count."

"The secondhand books have often been scribbled in?"

"They sure have, especially inside the back cover. That is a great place for memoranda and phone numbers."

"Why wouldn't it be a great way for one crook to get a message to another?"

"It would. The message would mean nothing if it fell into the wrong hands. But if it miscarried, communication would be broken."

"That's the start, dear lady, the start of the whole thing! The objection you mention is very important. If enough messages miscarried, that could be crucial. And if the police got wind of the system, and inserted a message or two of their own—!"

"Pleased with yourself, aren't you?" asked Virginia Daly.

"Pleased with this lovely lady and the information she has just handed me. Give the gent another nickel and get me another sheet of paper, will you?" Don began to scribble furiously.

[84]

Virginia shook her head in disclaimer, but her smile was understanding. Right now Don was in Seventh Heaven. Descent would come later. Let him have his fun while it lasted.

This man write a historical novel? He'd better stick to his last. His wife had the more solid talent, if you could rank such things. But why should you? Leave that to the reviewers, who made their living trying to sound wise about such matters.

Oh, let Don write a historical novel if he chose to do so! The Civil War, so many of whose great men Virginia had written books about, would furnish him with an excellent background for one. A fascinating period, and the best documented in American history. If the love interest was commonly a little obvious—Southern belle balancing to Northern beau, or the reverse of it—that was natural enough. A Capulet falling in love with a Montague. The old people's feud was a prime advertisement.

But the Underground Railroad was no subject for a novel, Alice felt from the beginning. She felt it increasingly as the days went on and she looked up books for Virginia Daly.

Not only looked up; she read them all. Finding them in a corner of the warehouse where she had stowed them from time to time, she took them first to the Brooklyn flat. Then, one at a time, she honored them with a careful reading; her conclusions she noted on slips of paper which she laid in the text.

The first two were published in the same year, 1859. Contemporary stuff; history written down while it was still going on. One of them, indeed, was issued at Syracuse, a fact which gave Alice a strange sense of kinship, since she herself was a native of upstate New York.

It was entitled *The Rev. J. W. Loguen as a Slave and as a Freeman*. It was dedicated *To the Friends of the Under Ground Rail Road—in America and Europe*. That alone was tremendously suggestive. It had a preface, a very adequate preface, but unsigned. The book was anonymous, indeed, though it dealt with its hero very circumstantially.

The very beginning got Alice Martin going:

We must devote a brief chapter to the parents of Mr. Loguen.

The genealogy of an American Slave may be traced with certainty to the mother, rarely to the father, never beyond them on the male line. It is the condition of the mother *de facto* that makes the slave. She is mother *de lege* only to the intent that her offspring may be an outlaw. As to the progenitor on the male side, he is rarely known as the father in fact, never in law. The slave has no father. Slave legislation makes no use of the paternal line, and refuses to acknowledge one. It acknowledges a mother, not in respect to any natural relation, but for accommodation, as the medium of titles, not of affections and obligations. Legally speaking, the slave has neither father nor mother.

Slavery, of course, has no records of conjugal relations. Should the Clairvoyant translate and publish the secrets of its history, the domestic relations of the South would be broken up, and society sink in the abyss of vulgar passions. It owes its existence to the fact that its sexual history is faintly shadowed in the varied colors of the abused race.

Hold hard! thought Alice. *There is a novel right here. But I don't see Don Burgess writing it. It would be much too deep, dark, and deadly.*

Unfortunately not all of the book lived up to its opening. It was fictionized, which was allowable, and overwritten, which was forgivable. But also it betrayed the amateur's hand, which was just too bad. Alice said as much in the note which she wrote for Virginia Daly.

The second source book was entitled *Fifty Years in Chains;*

or, The Life of an American Slave. Alice drew a long breath, and remembered that Booker Washington had called his memoirs *Up From Slavery*. Booker Washington had experienced emancipation, and could set down his story in freedom. The preface to this other book recalled how different things were in 1858. It read simply:

The story which follows is true in every particular. Responsible citizens of a neighboring State can vouch for the reality of the narrative. The language of the slave has not at all times been strictly adhered to, as a half century of bondage unfitted him for literary work. The subject of the story is *still a slave* by the laws of this country, and it would not be wise to reveal his name.

Very different indeed from Booker Washington, who had been given his chance at "literary work," and had succeeded in it. He was a great educator, too. His name was not only revealed but recognized at the top. He had been invited to lunch at the White House, and had been addressed by the President of the United States as "Mr. Washington."

This narrative was absorbing, especially during those passages which recorded the observations of an eyewitness; then the ghost-writer sometimes forgot to be polysyllabic. Sandwiched in among all the cruelties and horrors, too, were scattered memories of early happiness. One that Alice found especially touching was the hero's very early memories of his father. For this man did know who his father was: a slave on a neighboring plantation in Maryland. Sometimes of a Saturday night he was permitted to come over for a visit with his wife and children.

He always brought us some little present, such as the means of a poor slave would allow—apples, melons, sweet potatoes, or, if he could procure nothing else, a little parched corn, which tasted better in our cabin, because he had brought it.

When there was a question of his being sold down river, the father, who "had been formerly of a gay social temper," ran away and was never heard of afterward. It was after being sold down river, and witnessing tortures and indignities worse even than what he himself was exposed to, that our hero himself ran away. Legally he remained a fugitive; but at least he had lived to tell his story.

Alice Martin would read for a time in utter absorption. When the going got too tough for her, she would lay down the book for a time. Then every so often she would place a known figure from her own life in the situation of which she had just been reading. Imagine her Carrie, who had been friend as well as employee all these years, and whose grown daughter Phyllis was an occasional and very welcome substitute at "Miss Alice's"—imagine her Carrie as a young woman with her baby girl torn from her arms and sold into alien bondage. Imagine Carrie being cruelly beaten if she ran alongside her baby's new owner and implored him to buy her too. Imagine—

Well, no, you couldn't imagine it. But to have such happenings dug up and reexamined might give present-day readers something to get their teeth into. This needed telling as a fact book, however. Let Don Burgess go ahead with his new yarn about a bookseller whose bargain tables had become a private and illicit post office for a gang of crooks. It was an original idea, as far as Alice knew, and not much more implausible than whodunit readers were accustomed to.

Alice endorsed this book, "Excellent. Ghost-written, but seems authentic and contains a lot of straight stuff." Some people had cared, even in those days. Some people had done something about it. It did not solve the main problem; but to certain individuals it made all the difference.

There was the novelist's business, in the realm of the individual. Or rather, in the relations between the individual and the group. Some people simply took what was handed them. That was the slave mentality, in any age or any system of social organization. Some people took part of what was handed them and rejected the rest. What they did with what they took made all the difference.

Careful, Alice! You're getting sententious. Better get back to your proper job. Leave drawing conclusions to those who are paid for doing so.

Mrs. Martin began now on source books which had been published after the Civil War, and which told the story of the Underground Railroad in various localities. Published locally, too, those were. Interesting in their various ways, but chiefly to the student or the researcher for an end, like Virginia Daly.

While checking out three of them, Alice began to note down items which she had heard or read over the years. For instance, in *Uncle Tom's Cabin,* that greatest of propaganda novels, one very exciting scene was not only true to life but typical, that was the fight in the glen. The "fighting Quakers" ran a whole series of stations on the Underground Railroad; and in defense of their fugitives, when they shot, they shot to kill.

Then there was Thoreau, whose *Walden* was one of the less popular New England classics. The neighbors wrote him off as a crank; so did the authorities. Both the neighbors and the authorities were right to a great degree. But his isolated cabin at Walden Pond was an established station on the Underground.

Alice mentioned these facts to Virginia Daly when she delivered the first five books and mentioned that those ought to last her for a while. They would, Virginia assured her. Right now she was doing some preliminary research at the New York Public Library.

There she had unearthed one circumstance which startled her: the great Allan Pinkerton, Lincoln's bodyguard and the originator of the famed Pinkerton Service, had been up to his neck in Underground Railroad affairs before the critical election of 1860. That was how he happened to get the job.

"All of which will be great stuff in your book," Alice pointed out.

"It's going to be an awfully big job." Virginia smiled. "Great good luck for me that the expenses of the Long Island place are mostly up to Don. He's living a bachelor existence there these days except at weekends. I live in my old apartment, eat my own cooking, and work in the American History Room hour after hour. It keeps us from quarreling, anyhow. I come with fresh zest to the weekends. I think Don looks forward to them, too."

"Is he really writing a whodunit with a bookseller in it?" asked Alice.

"I suspect that he is. In fact, he has pretty well completed a synopsis of the plot and is talking contract with the publishers. But about his work I know only what he chooses to tell me."

Virginia meant of course that about her husband's work she told only what she chose to tell; that was, in a phrase beginning to come into common use, "No comment." Don himself had told something about his next book; Burgess was a great fellow to groan in public.

But so far the generally garrulous Harry Martin was keeping his literary undertaking private. For a very good reason, indeed: he didn't want the whole thing to evaporate in talk. He was getting on with it; but the mass of the work still lay ahead. His anthology was such an ambitious project; if it remained unfulfilled, it would provide a whole block of paving on the road to the nether regions. A road on which he had no intention of helping. Competition there was already too severe.

8

ALL THROUGH THE SPRING HARRY MARTIN WORKED DILI-
gently at his precious anthology. The title still baffled him;
but there was plenty of time for that. Selection and arrangement were what he had to deal with now. He hadn't even
settled the important question of how he was to handle the
text.

He was in the habit of marking a possible choice, making a
note of it, and laying the book in a special place with other
volumes similarly delegated. Sometimes for sheer love of it he
copied an extract longhand. Some of the poems he wrote
down from memory and then looked up. It was astonishing
how even a good memory could trick a person on details. In
actual reproduction, too, even the punctuation should be followed. Not that his readers (his readers!) would ever notice
the difference. But it was all a part of the job; and in such a
job as this, no detail was unimportant.

He considered the scissors-and-paste method of dealing
with his copy. But that would involve mutilating one book, if
not two, for every selection he cut out and pasted up. It

seemed a wicked waste of lovely volumes; and what was he going to do with all those mutilated books? They could scarcely be offered on the ten-cent table, even; and at the very idea of selling them as waste paper, Harry felt a distinct qualm.

Everything would have to be copied, then. That was not a job for H. Martin, Esquire, who could perhaps have typed a label on the hunt-and-peck system if he had been simply forced into it, but preferred to leave all such typewriting chores to Mrs. M., who did them habitually for Waverley Book Shop, and who had worked in an office while she was still Alice Frederickson.

There was not a chance of asking her to undertake this tremendous new job. She had enough on her hands anyhow; she always had had, and the more time Harry devoted to his anthology, the more responsibility was Alice's to keep the shop running and to direct Bill Thayer's activities.

Harry would have to hire the typing done. It would be a nice bit of business for some keyboard artist. Or perhaps for several of them; he could parcel the work out and compare results and prices. These days there were more people than ever who needed the money. That wasn't to say that the level of competence had risen. Decidedly, he would do well to parcel the work out, especially just here at first.

Having decided that much, Harry went back to his selecting. He could just as well consider and in many cases reconsider before he sank any solid cash into his undertaking. Already it was proving expensive in time.

He would include, then, besides "Rip Van Winkle," that lovely story of Mary E. Wilkins about the little lost ghost: the one who came wailing, "I can't find my mother," and who was finally carried off to peace and presumable bliss by a heart-hungry woman who had never borne any children. "The Devil and Daniel Webster" would come naturally in here: another story of the supernatural which was so vivid

[92]

and convincing that it made the whole thing seem natural. That was a modern, Stephen Benet. To get back to the classics, there was Henry James's "The Turn of the Screw." Harry marked that down as a possibility. These were early days yet; and he mustn't go overboard on ghosts.

Along quite different lines, another short story was a natural for his collection: Anatole France's "The Procurator of Judaea." That told how an aged and ailing Pontius Pilate met another veteran of the Roman Foreign Service at a health resort. They grumbled about their past hardships and lack of recognition; and at the end Pilate could not even remember that certain man whom he had once tried to save from the Jewish rabble.

Harry recalled the thrill with which he had first read that story. It was the perfect, yet the infinitely tragic, apologue. If his anthology could bring anything like that thrill to a handful of readers—! The first freshness was now gone for him. Yet rereading too was great fun. That was the pleasure Editor Martin was having now. "Would-be Editor" was perhaps closer to the mark.

In poetry it was easier to make a definitive choice. From Tennyson, "Crossing the Bar," "Ulysses," and "The Last Fight of the Revenge at Sea." From Browning, "A Toccata of Galuppi's," "A Grammarian's Funeral," "The Bishop Orders His Tomb at Saint Praxed's Church," "Childe Roland to the Dark Tower Came." With Browning it was hard to know just where to stop. This would do for the present, however.

With two American poets he was on safer ground. From James Whitcomb Riley he selected, "When the Frost Is on the Punkin," that superb dialect variation on the "Ode to Autumn" theme, and an infinitely pathetic piece which came off oddly enough here in the depth of the Depression. It was all about the isolation and shock of sudden riches.

[93]

Pap's got his patent right, and rich as all creation,
But where's the peace an' comfort that we used
to know afore?
I'd like to go a-vistin' back to Griggsby's Station,
Back where we used to be so happy—and so poor.

With Eugene Field he would start out by recalling the
bibliomaniac's dream of bliss, chancing upon the catalogued
item: "a First Edition, boards, uncut." There would be two
lullabys, "Sleep, Little Pigeon, and Fold Your Wings," and
the one with the story about "Wynken, Blynken, and Nod."
Of course Harry's anthology would include that lovely lyric
about "The Dream Ship." It went back to the dear dead days
when a dream was a dream, and brought "revenge or recom-
pense." That anticipated Freud's dogma, "Every dream is a
wish-fulfillment"; but it did not tag along with Freud's thesis
that the human mind is a sewer, and sleep stirs up its deepest
depths.

Perhaps, too, Harry Martin would make room for "Apple
Pie and Cheese." But "Little Boy Blue" must perforce give
way to two infinitely sad poems by Coventry Patmore. A dead
child was pathetic enough, in all conscience. But a child who
might die, a living child whom the father had wronged—:
Harry copied those poems out longhand, and took pains to
make his penmanship legible, for once. The first one was
"The Toys." It began:

My little Son, who looked from thoughtful eyes
And moved and spoke in quiet grown-up wise,
Having my law the seventh time disobey'd,
I struck him, and dismiss'd,
With harsh words, and unkiss'd,—
His Mother, who was patient, being dead.
Then, fearing lest his grief should hinder sleep,
I visited his bed,

But found him slumbering deep,
With darken'd eyelids, and their lashes yet
From his late sobbing wet.
And I, with moan,
Kissing away his tears, left others of my own;
For, on a table drawn beside his head,
He had put, within his reach,
A box of counters and a red-vein'd stone,
A piece of glass abraded by the beach,
And six or seven shells,
A bottle with bluebells,
And two French copper coins, ranged there with careful art,
To comfort his sad heart.
So when that night I pray'd
To God, I wept, and said:
Ah, when at last we lie with trancéd breath,
Not vexing Thee in death,
And Thou rememberest of what toys
We made our joys,
How weakly understood
Thy great commanded good,
Then, fatherly not less
Than I whom Thou hast moulded from the clay,
Thou'lt leave Thy Wrath, and say
"I will be sorry for their childishness."

The other one struck Harry as even tenser. It was, "If I Were Dead."

"If I were dead," you'd sometimes say, Poor Child.
The dear lips quivered as they spoke,
And the tears broke
From eyes which, not to grieve me, brightly smiled.
Poor Child, poor Child!
I seem to hear your laugh, your talk, your song.

It is not true that love can do no wrong.
Poor Child!
And did you think, when you so cried and smiled,
How I, in lonely nights, should lie awake,
And of those words your full avengers make?
Poor Child, poor Child!
And now unless it be
That sweet amends thrice told are come to thee,
O God, have Thou no mercy upon me!
Poor Child!

Some slight expiation, those two poems. Little Boy Blue
had died in his sleep, but he had died happy, having given his
little toy dog and little tin soldier his last happy good night.
Oh, damn it all, put that one in too! There was a consolation
in remembering a happy child, even if you had lost him.

The first person to whom Harry confided the secret of his
new enterprise was Bess Johnson. She brought the subject up
when she came into the shop looking for something to read.
"Both of us have a lot of time on our hands these days," she
remarked. "No chance of my selling any of my poems; the
magazine editors are all scraping the bottom of the barrel.
The managers haven't renewed the options on the two plays
Ben has out; they've joined their elder brothers in a bottom
drawer. It's a good thing he has a steady job as dramatic critic.
His salary goes on, even if there isn't much to be reviewed
any more."

"So you stay home and read," Harry concluded. "Go ahead
and browse as long as you like. I can make you a good price
on almost anything you find."

She obediently poked around until she was the only customer in the shop. It was Bill Thayer's day off, and Alice had
gone out on one of her exploring trips. Then Bess said,

"What ever became of those Latin translations of yours? Have you done anything about getting them published?"

"I hope to include them in a larger book," said Harry, and went on to tell her about his anthology. Manners, and a hint of genuine doubt, led him to say, "That is, if I decide to include them. Translations may be something of a weight on the undertaking as a whole."

"They shouldn't be!" Bess decided. "Indeed they shouldn't be. A translation opens gates to people who would otherwise be barred from a rich field."

"A nice figure of speech," said Harry. "I might use it as an introduction. I haven't yet decided how much in the way of notes or explanation I'm going to use. The whole thing is still very much in the tentative stage. And—but surely I don't need to tell this to *you*—'mum's the word.' "

"Oh, absolutely!" Bess assured him. "I won't tell even Ben." She went back to looking over books. Alice presently returned; then Bess took herself off with enough reading matter to last her for some time.

But the matter did not end there. She came in a week later with a typewritten sheet which she handed Harry. It was headed, "Translated By—" and under that line she went on to poetize.

> Writings which lose in translation
> May still translated be,
> To give us some faint notion
> Of lands beyond the sea.
>
> Of other minds than our own mind.
> The savor of other climes
> May come to us through our English words,
> And hints of olden times
> Chime in with alien rhymes.

"But Bess!" Harry cried. "This is just what I needed."

"You're welcome to it for what it's worth," she assured him.

"I don't know what it would be worth in any other market. But I can pay you for it. Would twenty-five dollars be enough?"

"Twenty-five—? You're out of your mind. Take it if you want it; but I would like to see my name in print. That has happened to me all too few times."

"Your full name, Bess, is—?"

"Elizabeth Davis Johnson. Harry, you don't really mean it?"

He did, however. He wrote her out a check on the spot. "Really, do you mind if I tell Ben this much?" she asked.

Harry didn't. At this moment he wouldn't have changed places with—Was there a jingle to the effect, "I would not change places, With kings, queens, or aces"? If there wasn't there ought to be. Certainly Harry Martin wouldn't change places with poor President Hoover, who here in the advancing spring of 1931 was being held responsible for a Depression which was, after all, worldwide. Public opinion demanded a scapegoat. Public opinion derided Mr. Hoover's advice to go ahead and buy. Every nickel spent would be a nickel put into circulation; these days it would buy a cup of coffee, and a second nickel would buy a doughnut—out of which the lunchroom proprietor could pay the baker and the coffee vendor their cut. But two nickels were still two nickels. Self-pity was much cheaper. Anybody could wallow in that for free.

One member of the inner circle at Waverley Book Shop was missing that spring. The Donald Burgesses were expecting an heir; and things were going very badly with Virginia. She had always enjoyed remarkable health, and had taken for granted that she always would enjoy it. Now she found herself the victim of morning sickness, which she had supposed went out of existence about the time Queen Victoria died. She was puzzled and dismayed, though she did her best to put a brave front on it. "I don't like this," she would whisper to Don after one of her paroxysms. "I don't like it at all."

Don came into New York, hauled Harry Martin off to the apartment where Virginia Daly had been so happy and so single, and mixed stiff drinks for the two of them. Over them he told Harry about Virginia's troubles, and wound up, "It makes me feel so damn guilty."

"Nature is hard on women. You didn't arrange it that way," Harry consoled.

"I'm not talking about 'women.' I'm talking about Virginia," Don groaned. "God! We were getting along so well before *this* happened."

"It has happened. You're looking forward to the baby, aren't you?"

Don brightened a little. "It's a long look. But I can at least pay Virginia's maternity expenses. These independent career women! Oh, I'm sorry! I never think of Alice that way, perhaps because you and she are in business together."

"Virginia's career must be halting a little these days. Plenty of time for her to get on with that, though. She can still be writing books when she's seventy."

"But the time for her to have her children is now? Her child, rather. I can foresee a very small family for the Donald Burgesses." There for a minute Don looked to Harry rather pitifully young. The wisdom of the ages might be distilled into books—yes, and then redistilled into anthologies; but there were some things a person had to experience for himself.

Harry refused a second drink and suggested, "Let's go back to the shop and pick out a few books which might amuse Virginia. Something cheerful, for a change. She's in no state now to deal with the Underground Railroad."

Don rinsed the glasses and took a final look around the little apartment. "She never thought, when she lived and

[99]

worked here, that some day it would serve as a spot for her husband to do his grumbling." That was what he called it when he worried over her, "grumbling." Fellows like Don Burgess always tried to act tough; that was their form of defense.

Two days later the Martins had a letter from their son Jim. "Prepare to be grandparents again in November," he wrote. "Kathleen says the second baby will be just as much fun as the first, and not nearly such a source of anxiety. . . . Your grandson is so cunning—and so naughty! . . . Business is not good; but I notice we continue to eat every day."

So very cheerful about everything! By way of thank offering, Alice decided to spend a few hours with Virginia on Long Island. Or at least she would phone and propose the visit; Virginia could always use her health as an excuse.

Far from making an excuse, Virginia jumped at the offer. "I hesitated to ask you. I know you're busy. It seems ages since I've seen you. It's lovely out here; but it's awfully far from—well, from people like the Martins."

The country was indeed lovely in late April. George, the Burgesses' man of all work, met Alice's train. Don joined the ladies for luncheon; he was now in full tide of his new book. But he left them alone afterward.

Virginia showed Alice around the place. The house afforded both Virginia and Don privacy for work; the rest of the rooms were delightfully companionable. George's wife Daisy kept everything beautifully. They were a handsome Negro couple in their forties. Did Virginia see them when she read about the Underground, Alice wondered, but she forbore to ask. Better not remind Virginia of her neglected research.

She allowed herself to be persuaded to stay for dinner. Actually she had warned Harry not to expect her until he saw her. "I never do," was his unabashed retort.

Don himself drove her to the station. "I can't tell you how

much good you've done Virginia," he said. "She's been more like herself today than she has since the heir announced himself. Sometimes another woman needs a woman to talk to. Not just any old woman: a woman like Alice Martin."

Alice pressed his hand, but she said flippantly, "There are no other women like Alice Martin. I suppose Harry Martin sometimes thinks it's just as well there aren't."

Don offered to see her home. Alice refused. That would make him too late in returning. She could take a taxi from the station. She would be perfectely safe, and she would enjoy the trip.

Alice had had very little experience with New York taxis; the subway was quicker as well as much cheaper. But tonight she climbed into one and gave the address crisply. The driver looked at her blankly for an instant. When she repeated, "Commerce Street," he asked, "Where's that? Brooklyn?" He made "Brooklyn" sound like a fighting word.

"It's in downtown New York. Get over to Seventh Avenue, and drive south," she directed carefully. "It's below Fourteenth Street. I'll tell you when to turn." Then she sat back and enjoyed herself. She felt as if she had been away for a week. She had been out of the shop all day; and she had sampled a sort of life which was quite foreign to hers.

She was just paying off the taxi when her fellow tenant Thomas Carroll came along from the dead end of the street. He was alone. It occurred to Alice that several times lately she had seen him alone.

He held the door of the building open for her. Alice paused an instant to ring her own doorbell, and Harry clicked the release. Then she thanked Carroll, entered the hall and preceded him up the stairs.

On his own floor he paused and looked as if he wanted to say something. Alice waited; but he thought better of it. Or perhaps it was just her imagination or a moment of awkwardness on his part.

9

Harry Martin had not actually expected his program for this summer to go into effect. When he suggested that his daughter and his wife both do graduate work at Columbia while he and his son-in-law alternately worked together at Waverley Book Shop and poked into the depths of Greenwich Village, he had merely been dangling a bright idea for the spectators to stare at. Of course it might have caught them; or at least some part of it might. Worse suggestions than that sometimes found acceptance in certain quarters.

What happened in that summer of 1931 was that the young Crawfords stayed at home in Minneapolis. Earl taught the summer session at his university, Jean studied there during her high-school vacation. Not only that, however, which wouldn't have been too hard to take, but they decided against any visit at all to New York that year.

"We're going to loaf right here at home," Jean wrote. "Sleep late in the morning, go out for meals whenever we happen to feel so disposed. I would like some of those New York clothes that I'm accustomed to flashing around in, however. Mother, won't you go ahead and buy them for me? I can trust your taste in selecting things; and I'm a standard size. If the enclosed check won't cover, let me know and I'll make up the difference."

"A polite word of regret at missing her visit here; but she doesn't sound heartbroken at the prospect of not seeing us," Harry grumbled.

"They're happy with each other. Would you like it better if Jean were the kind who came running home to Mother every time they had an argument?" Alice retorted.

"There is a happy medium."

"There is, theoretically. But when it comes to knowing where to find that—how do your classics put it—that 'golden mean,' it's another story."

"You have reason to be self-satisfied, Mrs. M. Your daughter wants you to select her new wardrobe for her."

"Flattering, isn't it? I'm properly flattered. It shows too that Jean still feels free to ask the old folks for a favor."

"She also wants marked-down summer clothes which she can wear next year. That doesn't sound as if she's planning to extend her family very soon."

"Good gracious, what a hurry you're in! Do you think all the young people care about is providing you with grandchildren?"

"I don't think that that is their first consideration, or even their second. I suppose it will happen when and if it happens." Harry remembered that he had seen even Bess Johnson grow a little misty-eyed and wistful at the holiday season; she and Ben were among the chronically childless and ordinarily didn't appear to give the matter a second thought.

Alice too was thinking, *An ordinary domestic woman might feel the lack of grandchildren just as keenly as a business or professional woman; she would have a harder time filling in the gap.* Alice too wondered how long her daughter would be satisfied to go on as she was now. Though who on earth was ever completely satisfied? Heaven was the place for that, and Mrs. Martin was in no particular hurry to get on toward the celestial regions.

"Something amuses you?" said Harry.

Alice pressed his hand. "I'm disappointed, too, not to see the young people again this year. When all the nestlings have taken to their wings and flown—and flown so far—! But there are children enough around this neighborhood, goodness knows. What was that phrase I read somewhere lately? "Metropolitan sterility!' It hasn't hit the dear old Village. We won't need as much money this summer as we should if we were entertaining the young people. I think we can afford to reduce the prices on our children's books a little more."

"Enjoy somebody else's pleasure instead of wallowing in your own disappointment? It's a nice idea."

"It's a nice idea; and if it helps even a little, it's that much to the good." Alice had succeeded in cheering Harry up—and herself into the bargain. It so often worked that way. Nevertheless, Alice hoped that Jean would start her family before too long now. Those things went much harder with a woman if she put them off too long.

In the full tide of summer, Virginia was sitting things out on Long Island. She felt considerably better, and was getting some of the preliminary work done on her book. Alice went out to see her almost every week. Don was working away now on his new detective story. The eccentric bookseller was all very well so far as he went; he might indeed be used again later, though even his creator did not expect him to turn into a second Sherlock Holmes. All the better if he didn't, maybe. How earnestly Conan Doyle had striven to get away from that too-successful character! Even to killing him off and then having to resurrect him. Not that that was such hard luck as the author made himself believe that it was. Authors were kittle cattle anyhow.

The summer went by fast enough; it always did when anybody kept as busy as the Waverley Martins managed to. Late in August Alice did Jean's shopping for her, and managed to keep it within the limits of the check—almost. She forbore to bill Jean for the difference; whereupon Jean, in a letter expressing delight at her mother's selections, enclosed an extra fifty dollars anyhow. That was a nice way to handle financial transactions in a family. There was always a chance of awkwardness when the "undue love of money" threatened to rear its ugly head.

Alice was hard at her fall purchases of new books, too. The publishers' lists announced that they were bringing out "fewer and better books." That might be a good line so far as the trade went; to Mrs. Martin it seemed to reflect on their previous practices.

Then one afternoon when there was a deceptive hint of crispness in the air, a huge hulk made its deliberate way into Waverley Book Shop. The Martins had seen very little of Emil Koenig for some time; he was still busy with that project on which he had embarked before the historic crash now two years agone. Kitty came in sometimes and picked up a few volumes. As soon as the honeymoon glint was out of her eyes, she had gone back into her office on a part-time basis. What little housework she did wouldn't keep her busy; more important still, she had missed the office atmosphere to which she was accustomed.

Emil threw a gigantic arm around Alice and clapped Harry on the back with a heartiness which did not realize its strength. "Behold a galley slave released from his oar!" he boomed. "Now I'm free to get reacquainted. Kitty West can lay the can opener back in the drawer, too. I'm going to cook the dinner any time the Martins are free to come and eat with us."

The Martins had known Emil when he was very poor indeed, had watched him get a start as a sculptor who did garden pieces for wealthy people's country estates, had rejoiced

[105]

with him when he began to do architectural sculpture for a large and well-established firm. Such people would fulfill existing contracts wherever it was humanly possible; but they would beware of entering into fresh commitments. Anyhow business on that level was mostly at a standstill; it wasn't a case for going out and buying a doughnut and a cup of coffee.

Alice's color rose faintly. She released herself from Emil's encircling arm and said, "Not quite so loud, please. We'll love to come. Bill Thayer can take over for us at a day's notice; but I always like to have a little time to look forward to a particular pleasure."

She sounded almost prim. Harry stared at her for an instant; then he said, "All right, Emil. Give her time to make up her mind which dress she's going to wear. Any evening she selects will be all right with me. My other suit is always hanging there in the closet."

After they had set the date for two evenings later and Emil had taken himself off, Harry found a moment in which to say to Alice, "I wonder whether Emil wants a chance to talk things over with us. Still, he wouldn't do that in front of his wife, would he? She's an interested party."

"How do I know what Emil wants? Wait and see."

"There's no harm in guessing."

"Go ahead and guess, then. It will add to the interest of the game for you. You do that while I make up my mind which dress to wear." Alice turned away to join the bargain hunters at the sidewalk tables.

Actually Alice was reliving a moment which she seldom allowed herself to think about, though it was always there for her to turn to. It had occurred shortly before Emil and Kitty were married. Alice Martin and Emil were alone in Emil's working studio. He had taken both her hands and told her that he had been in love with her for years. There was no future in their love. It had the briefest possible present, when they kissed each other and she lay for an instant in his arms. But their avowal was as real as their renunciation. It meant that they would see even less of each other in the future; but they could both of them cherish the memory of their acknowledgment. That was in fact the way their relationship had worked out.

On the appointed date Alice wore a blue outfit which Harry did not remember seeing before; Harry's "other suit" was fresh from the cleaner's. They walked to the one-room apartment which had been Emil's bachelor quarters for a time before he was married: a place which realized the aspirations of his early poverty-stricken days because it had a fair kitchen and a really well-appointed bathroom.

Kitty too was wearing a becoming dress; obviously she had returned from her office with plenty of time to freshen herself. Emil was in his shirt sleeves, with his hair still wet from a recent shower. He served them cocktails; but the real appetizer was the odor which had greeted them on their entrance.

Emil had combined chicken with a dozen different vegetables in a stew which would have made the reputation of any restaurant that could have boasted it as the "chef's special." For salad he served simply very crisp lettuce with a tart dressing; there were browned rolls and unsalted butter. For dessert he had made an old-fashioned peach shortcake. His coffee was the crowning treat.

In response to the Martins' compliments Emil grinned and said, "Sure! The only reason Kitty married me is because I'm such a good cook."

"The only reason you married Kitty was because you couldn't get Alice," Harry retorted. Then he was horrified at his own rudeness.

There was an instant's awful pause. Kitty came to the rescue. "Quite true, Harry. When a woman like Alice is taken out of circulation, it gives the rest of us a chance. Is there any coffee left in the percolator, Emil? I could stand half a cup more. Anybody else?"

Emil brewed fresh coffee. Then he began, "I've saved some money these past few years. But how would it pan out if we lived on my savings while my wife works? She can quit her job if she wants to. There, Mrs. Koenig, I've made the offer in the presence of witnesses. What have you to say to it?"

Kitty smiled demurely. "I say it isn't the only offer I've had. My boss says that in spite of the Depression it's just as hard to get a *good* secretary as it ever was. The same thing goes for a *good* cook, his wife tells him. The good ones may be working for less; but they are still working."

"I suppose a bad worker can get just as hungry as a good one," Alice said slowly. "After the astonishing dinner that I've just put away, the very idea of hunger seems farfetched."

"Kitty has given me an idea," said Emil. "If worse comes to worst, I can go to work in a restaurant. I think I might honestly enjoy that, at least for a while."

"If worse comes to worst, will there be any restaurants?" asked Harry.

"I'm not looking that far ahead." Emil paused for an instant, then went on, "When I was young enough so that I could really make such a decision, I decided that as between an easy life and an interesting one, I would choose the interesting."

"I don't remember thinking it out in so many words," Alice said quickly, "but that is what I have done."

"Does that mean me or Waverly Book Shop?" Harry demanded.

Everybody laughed and relaxed. Harry set to work to efface the bad impression he had made earlier. What had ever made him say a fool thing like that? The jealous husband was always a figure of derision. How would Harry Martin like to be married to a woman nobody else wanted?

[108]

All the same, when they were back in the Commerce Street apartment, Harry stood for a moment looking at the portrait bust of Alice on the living-room mantel. Then he burst out, "I'm sorry I said what I did tonight, Alice. All the same, I could sometimes feel it in my heart to be jealous of that big clown. But I suppose it's really your beauty he admires. Artists are different."

"That bust is beautiful," Alice said slowly. "Emil's skill is what made it so. That's what he is interested in."

But she felt an instant's trepidation after they had retreated to the bedroom. Harry always went to sleep very promptly after he went to bed, or else made love to her. Somehow tonight she did not want him making love to her.

He didn't do so. Lying there beside him, Alice thought, *It isn't poverty that Emil is facing. Poverty alone would not frighten him; he has known what it was to be very poor. What he faces is complications.*

Didn't we all? It must have been so much simpler back there in the amoeba stage. The amoeba had no brain and presumably no sensations to speak of. No sex certainly; it reproduced by fission. It missed a great deal of trouble; but it also missed all the fun.

Alice smiled in the darkness. She must remember to tell this to Virginia Daly Burgess next time she saw her. Virginia's baby would be born in January. Next January would see them all once more in a Presidential year.

Mr. Hoover would have his own troubles and the country's too to answer for. But Alice Martin couldn't do anything about that tonight. Tonight? It was already morning by the clock. Alice turned farther toward her own side of the bed, readjusted the sheet, and finally sank off to sleep. Tomorrow would be another day. Not so good as this one, probably; this had really been a banner day. But at least tomorrow would be different.

When Alice Frederickson was a little girl in upstate New

[109]

York, Labor Day had always cast a certain gloom over her spirit. It meant the end of the long vacation and the beginning of the school year. Not that Alice disliked school at all; and the first day of the new term was a sort of holiday, when a little girl was dressed up, had a reunion with her fellow pupils, and tried to see which one could outbrag the others about the delights of the past two months. But it marked the end of picnics and boat rides and tea parties with other little girls in their back yards or in hers: the end of those days when a single afternoon was longer than a whole week seemed in later life.

That was all changed now. For the long weekend, a great many of the natives went on auto trips, with every prospect of spending many wasted hours in traffic jams and an excellent chance of figuring in a traffic accident. The banks closed, the department stores offered special sales. Out-of-towners came to New York, tried to pack three weeks' sight-seeing and merrymaking into three days, and wondered how the residents stood it. Waverly Book Shop was overwhelmed with persons asking questions. Some of them were pertinent enough. It was a confusing neighborhood; Alice herself could remember once in her early days when she had struck the celebrated spot where West Fourth Street crossed West Tenth, and had wished for an instant that she was back in the old Main Street town where she grew up: where blocks were square, and streets were laid out by a surveyor instead of following the trail of old cowpaths. Other questions verged on the insulting, such as, "Is this Greenwich Village? And what's so remarkable about it?" Still others did not stop at verging; they sought information as to pornographic and other infamous joints. Alice never got over a feeling of outrage at such applications; but Harry, who was appealed to oftener than she was, found a certain pleasure in answers along the lines of, "You'll have to tell me about that. I just live here."

There were always genuine customers mixed up with the unduly inquisitive. Old customers, known by sight if not by name, made up the backbone of the business. (They and the mail-order people, of whom a faithful nucleus remained after the past two years.) The customer who came in off the street (that was the way Harry labeled chance purchasers) might add slightly to the profits, but could not be counted on to help defray running expenses. But people moved to New York as well as came visiting. There lay the Martins' great hope for the future.

On the afternoon of the Tuesday which followed this particular weekend, things were decidedly sluggish. Bill Thayer was having the day off, and Alice suggested to Harry, "You might as well go back to the apartment and put in a couple of hours on the anthology. Or take a nap if you feel like it. I can phone you if trade gets brisk."

"What's the fun in catching a nap if I'm put to bed like a child?" Harry demanded.

"All right, then, if you want to tend shop, I'll sit down with my back to the public and get on with one of the fall books." Alice picked up a brand-new volume, shucked off its jacket, and encased it in one of the brown paper covers which she kept for the purpose; that prevented new merchandise from getting shopworn. She had just completed the task when the door opened and a stranger entered.

It was a girl in her early twenties. Her face was piquant rather than pretty; the nose and chin were both too sharp. But she had intelligence and dash. Surveying the store and smiling at both the Martins, she looked a little like an actress "taking" the stage.

"Good afternoon," she said. "This is a very attractive shop you have here."

"Thank you, we try to make it so," said Alice. "My husband and I are in business together. He's Harry Martin; I'm Alice."

The girl smiled her acknowledgment. "I'm Peggy Pratt. I come from Portland, Oregon. I graduated from the State University last June. I've come to New York to seek my fortune."

They came in by every train at this season. Not nearly so many as had come in other years, but enough. In Alice's view, more than enough; they risked deadly disappointment. She felt a pang of pity for the poor young thing—a pity for which Miss Pratt obviously would not have thanked her; the young lady was one who considered the world her oyster.

"Are you living in the neighborhood?" Alice asked politely.

"I've taken a furnished apartment on West Tenth Street for a year. My Dad is backing me, just the way he would for a year of graduate study. I've come here to write a novel."

Alice's sympathy evaporated. Here was just another would-be to hang around Village resorts and talk about the wonderful things she was going to do.

"This looks like a place where a lot of writers might come," young Peggy swept on.

"I do searching for some of them," said Alice noncommittally. "That is, I look up rare or out-of-print books which they need in their work."

"Then you know a lot about such things. You must know a lot of the right people, too. You have a very good idea of how they go about being successful authors. Not that I expect to become a best seller overnight," Miss Pratt disclaimed modestly. "But I would like to learn enough about the market to get my book accepted."

"The first step toward getting a book accepted is to write it," Harry informed her.

"That's exactly my point; only I would consider it the second step. In writing my book I'd like to give the publishers what they want. If I were writing advertising copy, I would do just that. Why not take that into consideration when writing a book?"

"That's an idea," said Alice. Harry, who had opened his mouth to say something else, contented himself with, "It's quite an idea."

"Could you recommend anything that might help me?" demanded Peggy Pratt.

Alice's sympathy came back in full flood. Here was an appeal from youth. Youth: so courageous, so often mistaken, so pitifully *young!*

"I have one of this fall's books which I've enjoyed very much," she said. "Here it is. You might like it. Some of last spring's better numbers have returned and are on the 'used books' tables. Do you want to come with me while I pick them out? You may see something else that you'll like."

Peggy Pratt bought five books altogether. Before she finished doing so, she was calling the Martins by their first names. A nice girl; a likable girl. She made a good impression on the cash register, too.

After she had left, Harry said consolingly, "That's as good a way as any for her father to spend his money, I suppose."

Alice nodded. "She is bound to enjoy her year in New York, anyhow. Westerners have a way with them, haven't they? I hope she comes in again soon. I'd like to take her somewhere for a cup of coffee."

10

Emil Koenig had had his architectural sculpture photographed from various angles. He brought around a set of prints, and presented them to the Martins with the offhand remark, "I believe there's an incinerator in your apartment building." It had taken some time for this gate to shut; there was no indication as to when it would reopen.

"It's a magnificent accomplishment," Alice consoled. "Nobody can take that away from you. Your work will be standing, and people will be admiring it, long after Waverley Book Shop puts up its shutters for the last time."

"No one will remember my name," Emil answered bitterly. Making another grasp for lightness, he said, "Not that very many people know it now. It's a hell of a name anyhow. 'King' of what am I?"

Harry looked up from the photographs. "I know it's easy to be optimistic about other people's troubles. But when I first knew you, if you could have looked forward and seen yourself sitting where you are today, wouldn't you have thought that it was a startling success?"

Emil flushed. "Thank you for reminding me of that. A good friend you were in those days. Many was the bowl of beans or dish of chili you helped me to, under the pretext of keeping you company, when often I actually needed the feed."

"You've repaid any kindness I ever did you," Harry insisted. "But actually it's fun now to talk about the old days of your poverty, isn't it? Now that you have money in the bank and time on your hands. Think of this as a breathing space."

Alice turned to wait on a customer. She was grateful for the reprieve. If Harry could talk cheer into Emil, so much the better. To Alice the sculptor's plight appeared bitter indeed. He had arrived, just as in his lean years he had dreamed of doing; but he had arrived only to depart again.

She was grateful for a flurry of business which kept her occupied for some time. When she was free to rejoin the two men, their colloquy was winding up. "I suppose that's the right way to look at the whole thing," Emil was saying. "You've cleared the air for me, Harry."

Harry had indeed atoned for his rudeness at the Koenigs' dinner party. Maybe Alice hadn't been quite so chagrined at that *gaffe* as she had supposed she was. At her time of life, she might even have been secretly flattered.

Back at their apartment for dinner, she told Harry how well he had acquitted himself. "Words are my trade," he explained. "Other peoples' words are in the way of earning a living, perhaps; but I do have a certain feeling for speech. Give Emil something he can see and touch and he's a marvel. He must have an artist's imagination, too, a great deal of it. But thinking his way through a situation is different. I'm glad if I could help him a little."

After dinner they studied the photographs together, arranged and rearranged them, and finally laid them aside. But just before she followed Harry into their bedroom, Alice suddenly turned back to the packet. "Don't wait for me," she said. "I'll be with you in another minute or two."

Actually it was half an hour before she rejoined him. Harry, more than ready for the night, pointed an accusing finger at the bedside clock.

"I succumbed to an idea," explained Alice, kicking off her shoes and unfastening her dress. "Those photographs of Emil's sculpture should be mounted together, I think in a straight row. I've been trying various arrangements, and have hit what I think is the right one. It will look stunning hung above our living-room mantel."

Harry snorted. "Behind the bust of sweet young Alice, who really should be done in porcelain too?"

"Balancing it," said Alice sweetly. "Original, striking, and very easy for Carrie to dust."

She went ahead with her scheme. Harry decided that it looked very nice, "for a change." The arrangement wasn't irrevocable. It pleased Emil very much when the Martins told him about it. Soon after that the Koenigs came up for dinner. Kitty too approved the framed strip, and asked permission to duplicate it.

Emil's working studio had been his dwelling place too in the days of his early struggles. Now he decided to let go and indulge himself there. He stocked it up with all sorts of sculptors' materials, and threw in a few painters' supplies as well, just in case he should get another urge. He bought them all at record low prices. He had had a reasonably good store of them already, and an outfit of wonderfully fine tools.

"If I had had any idea, in the days when I used to figure whether I hadn't better walk a long distance in order to save a nickel subway fare or save my shoe leather and ride—if I'd had any idea then that I'd ever reach the stage where I could buy artists' materials that I may never be able to use up—!" Emil gestured his bewilderment.

"I hope you never will," said Alice pertly. "I hope the next thing you know there'll be such a demand for your services that you'll be swamped with offers."

Really, Emil was off her mind. That is, she worried about him no more, and she was trying once more to thrust him into the background of her thoughts. She had a lot of other things to think about: business, and the prospect of her second grandchild, and the troubles and blisses of some of her other friends. On the whole, the happiness outweighed the distress. Thanksgiving was looming closer and closer; Alice Martin had a great deal to be thankful for.

That grandchild, first and foremost. Very obligingly, he put in his appearance just after the middle of November. That would not only give his parents a great reason to be thankful, Kathleen would be home from the hospital with the new arrival and would have begun to get her strength back by that time.

It was another boy. "Two boys, double joys," Harry sing-songed. Nobody wanted a long string of one thing or the other; but two boys made a fine start on a family. The newest Martin was named John Carter, the Carter because it was his mother's maiden name, the John at his father's instigation, because the usual strong plain names were always best in the long run. If Harry Martin was slightly disappointed because the new baby was not his namesake, he ought to be ashamed of himself. James Earl Martin was not only his first grandson but his godson as well.

"Think we can afford a Christmas visit to Chicago again this year?" Harry asked Alice.

"I don't know whether we can afford it; but I think we can manage it. We can live on bread and water and owe the landlord until we get square with the world again," Alice decreed.

"Owe which landlord?" asked Harry. The Chicago trip wouldn't be their first major extravagance, though it might very well be their last—at least for some time.

It wasn't as if they had had Peggy Pratt's father to back them. That enterprising young lady had been in the shop from time to time, to buy books and report progress. "I have a title for my novel," she announced on one visit. "I'm calling it, 'You Don't Say So!'"

"Well, you're the author," said Harry reasonably. *You will be when you are* was his mental annotation. But the title would be something to write Papa in Portland. Four words to the good, at least.

Another time she told the Martins, "After Thanksgiving I'm going to make a regular business of calling on editors. I've tried a few so far; but they send their secretaries out to see me, or else some dame in the waiting room asks, 'Have you an appointment, Miss—er—Miss Spratt?' I have learned this much: from now on I'm going to make appointments."

Alice was enough interested to tell the Burgesses on one of her visits how a newcomer was tackling the problem. Don Burgess said flatly, "How can a writer give the publishers what they want when they don't know themselves what they want?" Virginia supplied, "They want a very original work which has the added advantage of being exactly like the last best seller put out by a competitor."

"It's a silly way to make a living, being a writer," Don went on. "Oh, I don't mean the kind of books Virginia writes! A person can learn something from them; they're quite worth rereading. But a detective story, even at its best, is nothing but an elaborate puzzle. Once it's finished, it's not of the slightest further interest."

"I wouldn't say that," Virginia demurred. "A good one, like yours, is worth rereading just to see how the author turned the trick. A puzzle is fine entertainment anyhow. These past months, when I've been so much less active than usual, I've done a lot of crosswords. I've even learned new words from them. Not that anybody I know wants to talk about the fourth caliph and an Arabian garment and a room

[118]

in a harem; but as entertainment it's more to my taste than all that fine needlework on which women used to ruin their eyesight."

"You're buying your layette?" asked Alice.

"Every last bootee and pinning blanket. I bought them only lately. Queer, when it lies ahead of you, nine months seems like such a long time. But when I feel that life stirring within me, and know that only next January the baby will be *here*—This is all an old story to you, Alice."

"It's never an old story to the mother. You've been wonderful not to complain. But of course the first month or two is generally the hardest. They do say a first baby is often the hardest, too. All those old wives' tales!"

"What's an old wives' tale and what's the wisdom of the ages?" demanded Don.

They were all so happy that evening, they might have been tempting Providence. Three days later Virginia was rushed to the hospital. Her baby was born two months prematurely and placed in an incubator.

Everything was going to be all right, the Burgesses were reassured. Mrs. Burgess was in splendid condition. The baby was a doll. What were they naming her? The nurses exuded cheer. Don adjusted himself to the changed situation, and made friends with other fathers who saw their poor little premature babies under such strange circumstances. But Virginia was inclined to be bitter. She had to go home from the hospital alone. The lovely new nursery was still awaiting its tenant. This was going to make a strange Thanksgiving.

Alice went out to Long Island, visited the hospital, got Virginia aside in her own house and gave her a good talking-to. "Premature babies used to die oftener than they lived. Even nowadays some babies do die. You still have your baby to look ahead to, but now your plans are being fulfilled. You know the baby is all right. You've seen her and started to get acquainted. What did you say you're naming her? Joan?

[119]

That's a pretty name. You wouldn't want to name her after yourself. That would be too confusing."

Virginia actually smiled. "We could be Virginia and Jinny, maybe. But a nickname acquired in childhood may be awfully hard to shake. Big Virginia and Little Virginia wouldn't do at all. Old Virginia and Young Virginia would be even worse."

"There isn't any satisfactory feminine form of Donald, is there?" Alice went on. "You picked a good name anyhow. That's very important."

"There is a good feminine form of Harry. But I noticed you didn't name your daughter Harriet."

"That can happen to one of my grandchildren, I suppose. Virginia, don't cheat yourself out of anything right now."

"Don't cheat Don, you mean, don't you? Alice, you've done me a world of good. Now tell me about your Thanksgiving party. Don and I will be able to imagine ourselves there."

The Martins were giving their Thanksgiving dinner party at the old railroad flat in Brooklyn. This was the season for tradition. It was also the season for "the stranger within thy gates." Alice invited Peggy Pratt to dine with them "unless you've decided on some more exciting way of celebrating. You've been in New York now long enough to get acquainted. The Village is a friendly place, too. Haven't you found it so?"

"I'm finding it so right this minute. It's lovely of you to invite me. I've become well acquainted in New York anyhow. It's been easy."

"Another thing," Alice went on, "we won't want you to get lost, so Bill Thayer will call for you and guide you into the wilds of Brooklyn. You've seen him around the shop sometimes. He's a nice fellow."

"But isn't he married?" asked Peggy in some surprise. "That is, he seems like the marrying type, and—and—"

"He's past the first flower of his youth, too," Alice supplied. "He's in his thirties, which is a very good age to be, and he did have a heart interest a year or so ago. I don't know what ever happened to it. I'm awfully glad you're coming. You'll meet some of my other friends; for many of them it will be a reunion."

Alice had already invited Emil and Kitty, and Ben and Bess Johnson. Now she searched out an elderly man who had been a neighbor of theirs a long time, and whom they used to see on an average of four or five times a year. The Martins had neglected him lately. Alice's conscience pricked her on that score. It must be hell to be old and alone in the world: a world otherwise so full of married couples and new babies and young authors with the world ahead of them and a title to a future opus already nailed down.

It occurred to her that she had promised Bill Thayer's services without consulting him. So when Alice invited him for Thanksgiving dinner, she suggested, "Isn't there somebody else you'd like to bring with you? Or, if you've made different arrangements, just say so and I'll excuse you."

"I had invited somebody for a restaurant dinner," Bill acknowledged. "That may sound to you a little bit forlorn; but we odd numbers do well enough at keeping one another company."

"Would you rather stick to that, or do you want to switch around and ask your guest to be mine instead? Is it anybody I know?"

"You don't really know her; but you were responsible for my meeting her in the first place."

Alice's nostrils twitched; here, if she mistook not, was the scent of romance. "A bookshop pickup?" she hinted.

Bill shook his head. "Not exactly. When you decided that you wanted an assistant in Waverley, you had plenty of applicants for the job. You weeded them out; I was one of the lucky three you passed on to Harry for him to make the final selection."

"I remember. The other two were women. One of them had had librarian's training, the other had worked in a chain book store."

"She still works there. She goes around with me, but she keeps me at arm's length. I thought I'd met wonderful women before, but she is—" Bill broke off in embarrassment. "Hell! This isn't an 'Advice to the Lovelorn' column. You said something about a young girl, didn't you? Back there two minutes ago, when you were inviting me?"

"Yes, I said I'd like to have you escort young Peggy Pratt into the wilds of Brooklyn. Think your friend would come along? She would round out my party for me. If you'll give me her phone number, I can call her and extend the invitation firsthand."

"It seems a splendid idea. She holds me at arm's length. But that Martin hospitality will do something for me, if only for the one day. And Alice, you'll—you'll put the whole thing on the ground of a favor to yourself, won't you?"

For once, Alice did not object to having words put into her mouth. Bill Thayer was actually appealing for help. Also, he was giving his would-be hostess a chance to meet the lady and size up the situation.

The lady's name was Marion Murdock. Her voice over the telephone was lovely: low-pitched, full, warm. She was just sufficiently responsive, too. "Oregon is a long way from New York," she said, and, "You're sure you want me? I can let Bill out of his date if that's going to help anyone," and, "That's very kind of you. I shall look forward to it."

Not half as much as I shall, thought Alice. She laid the whole matter before Harry that evening when they were relaxing in the Commerce Street apartment. She was going back to Brooklyn Wednesday to make final arrangements. Her turkey was all picked out at Staymann's, a meat market which was as much of a neighborhood institution as Waverley Book Shop itself, and considerably older. This was an occasion for tradition; the cranberry sauce and the pumpkin pies and all the rest of it must be seen to. Between the upcoming holiday and the return to Brooklyn, Alice had a sense of homecoming herself. If she and Harry ever had to choose between the old place and the new, they would feel that the old railroad flat was practically the Martin homestead.

Marion Murdock turned out to be a woman of substantial dimensions. She had lovely dark-brown eyes, and hands which looked accustomed to the feel of beautiful things. She wasn't extremely young, and she didn't try to look it; as a background to Peggy Pratt's youth, her maturity took on an additional charm.

She talked to Harry, talked to the old man who had been coming here so many Thanksgivings, looked around at the Martins' many books. But she scarcely talked at all to Bill Thayer. He was not part of the getting-acquainted process. "Arm's length" went just as well on this side of the river as it had in Manhattan.

Peggy Pratt, during her preliminary inspection of the flat, contrived to draw her hostess aside. She displayed a diamond solitaire on the ring finger of her right hand.

"I declare, if that were on the other hand, I'd feel that it was an announcement," said Alice. "Is it somebody you've met since you came here, Peggy?"

"It's a boy at home, and the engagement is only provisional," Miss Pratt confided. "We graduated together last June, and he wanted us to be married in the fall, but I thought after I got my book written I'd be better satisfied to settle down."

"That's right, do your deciding beforehand," Alice approved. "You never wear this ring around New York?"

"I keep it in my deposit box at the bank most of the time," Peggy answered. "But today I guess I was just a little lonesome, it being Thanksgiving and all."

At dinner she sat between the old neighbor and Ben Johnson, who was extremely gallant to her. At the head of the table Emil Koenig did the carving; then he slipped into a seat next to Alice's and let Harry go ahead with the serving.

Alice and Emil talked quietly. She gave him the news of the Burgess baby, told him of the Martins' plan to visit the new grandson over the Christmas holidays, held up crossed fingers when she told him how well everything was going with the Martins. Betweentimes she kept a hostess' eye on the table. This alone was enough to make the holiday for her: this sitting beside Emil in quiet conversation, with both of them realizing that although this interval couldn't last, right now it was here, and it was theirs, and when time took it from them, time took it into its own keeping and made the moment immortal.

Once Emil said, "That Miss Murdock! I would like to do a portrait bust of her some day. She has strength, great strength; but she has no peace. Something is troubling her."

"You see right through people," Alice answered quietly.

"See through people, and see the statue beyond. That Miss Pratt, she is trivial. But I should like to sketch her some time."

"You can sketch her from memory, can't you? You have a good memory, Emil."

"Yes, a good memory," he agreed. From then on they were silent with each other. They were both afraid of saying too much.

Ben Johnson, finishing his second helping and refusing a third, proclaimed, "Of course Bacon wrote Shakespeare. He couldn't get my namesake, Ben Jonson without the h, to do it for him. Some of those boys spent too much time at the Mermaid Tavern. Willis the Shakes was the worst offender."

Carrie came in to change the plates. The dinner proceeded to its close. The guests examined the choice books in the long hall, listened to the radio in the living room, regrouped themselves. Emil found pencil and paper and sketched the party. The guests all signed the sketch, and Alice dated it and put it into the *Nurenberg Chronicle.* Carrie's daughter Phyllis came to replace her mother. There was a pickup supper with cider cup. It was very late indeed when the guests departed; there was no sign of life anywhere else on the street.

"Don't think of opening until late afternoon," Harry said to Bill Thayer at parting. Alice said to Marion Murdock, "I'm going to call you again and have you come to see us in New York. It's been lovely meeting you."

Then they were all gone. Alice turned out lights and yawned her way to the familiar bedroom. There she remembered to tell Harry about Peggy Pratt and her "provisional" engagement ring.

"Peggy Pratt prattles," Harry jibed. "But I can see now why her father staked her to a year in New York. He wanted to give her engagement time to wear off."

"You don't think she'll ever get her book written?"

Harry chuckled. "Not in time to make the 1932 fall catalogues, anyhow. I told Bill about opening up tomorrow, didn't I? I guess that's all for now."

It was the shortest "after party" on record. But it had been a long party, if a good one. Perhaps, too, even the voluble Harry was beginning to run down. When two people had been married as long as the Martins had, there really wasn't much more to be said.

11

ALICE COULD NOT LET THAT WEEK COME TO AN END WITHOUT corralling Bill Thayer and telling him how much she liked Marion Murdock. "You two have so much in common," she wound up. "So very much in common!"

Bill was obviously pleased by those kind words; but his smile was a little bit wry. "I'm not the one who needs convincing."

"But why on earth should she stand you off, Bill? Obviously she thinks a great deal of you. A woman doesn't alter all her plans and journey into the wilds of Brooklyn just to get a slice of turkey."

"She's standing me off for my own good. At least, that's her story."

"A hard sort of story to shake, you've found? But Bill, how does she figure that one out? If she places your welfare ahead of her own, that's the perfect foundation for marriage."

"You're telling me? That's what I've been telling her."

"Not that it's any of my business, really," Alice hastened to back-pedal.

"That was what the scribe and the Pharasee said when they passed by on the other side. Well, you see, Marion is older than I am."

"Not conspicuously. She uses that as an argument against marrying you? It doesn't carry much weight. How much older, if you don't mind telling?"

"Between six and seven years. I say just over six; she says just under seven. Anyhow, she has been married before and is divorced."

"A burned child dreads the fire? But that's putting herself ahead of you. It doesn't agree with the rest of your story."

"All right, then, if you must have it. She has outgrown a lot of the old unhappiness. Lived it down. She realizes that all men are not like her ex-husband."

"Her *first* husband," Alice corrected.

"Thank you. What bothers her worse than the difference in our ages is this: she knows she never can have any children. She says that under those circumstances marriage to a man like me is quite out of the question."

Alice couldn't think of any glib answer to that one. Her children had been such an important part of her own marriage that she tried in vain to imagine what a childless marriage must be like. It turned out that way sometimes without much apparent reason; Ben and Bess Johnson were a case in point. But that was altogether different from steering into the situation deliberately.

"Marion Murdock is a very wonderful, a very generous person," Alice said slowly. "Bill, you can trust me not to mention this to anybody."

"Not even to Harry?" asked Bill with a faint smile.

Alice shook her head. There were some things that people just didn't discuss. It would seem too much like enjoying other people's bad luck. This world held too much unhappiness anyhow; it didn't pay to dwell on that. You did what you could for family and friends. You ran your business and ran your household, Mrs. Martin. And you really had to sleep sometimes.

This was always a busy season of the year in Waverley Book Shop. Alice and Harry had to get ready for their trip to Chicago, too. On top of all the other expense, she suggested to Bill Thayer, "Can't you get Marion into the shop for a little while during the holidays? Have her get leave of absence from her regular job and help you out?"

He couldn't, of course. Like him, Marion would have some straightening up to do; but she would do a little celebrating with him. She came across with Christmas handkerchiefs for both the Martins: a nice return for their Thanksgiving party, and one more proof of what a fine person she was.

Behold Mr. and Mrs. Martin, then, actually taking their crowded train for Chicago: an overnight train that would land them at their destination just in time to unpack and get over to the junior Martins for the Christmas Eve festivities. Jean and Earl Crawford had preceded them; Grandma Carter was the relative in residence. There was the newcomer, already beginning to know people, if you listened to some of his elders. There was little James Earl, a host in himself. Those same elders believed, or tried to make themselves believe, that he remembered them.

The stockings were hung, and little Jimmie was old enough to enjoy being read to about "The Night Before Christmas." The Martins had brought along an elaborately illustrated edition of that classic. It must have been put out in hundreds of different editions. It had been read to millions of children. How difficult to realize that anybody had ever written it! Surely it had always been there, like the snow and the stars.

Alice had wondered whether Peggy Pratt wouldn't go home for the holidays. But Peggy had planned to spend Christmas in New York; Portland was too far to go for such a short time. Most of the gifts which she sent to the Coast she had the Martins gift-wrap and mail for her. Alice told her not to miss the carol singing at Wanamaker's. (She wouldn't go there unescorted, if Mrs. Martin was any judge.) She must take in the Times Square New Year's Eve celebration, too. How far away all that seemed now! What was real and immediate was the family circle, the recurring joy of the holidays, the dear, dear children. One's own, grownup and out in the world now, but blessedly here for this season of reunion; more than the children, even, the doubly miraculous grandchildren. Poor Marion Murdock!

The holidays ended all too soon. The Martin clan dispersed. There was always a letdown after the holidays; but in some ways the letdown was welcome. It meant that Harry Martin could get on with his anthology, and Alice could straighten up the clutter in the book shop and get ready for the spring catalogues.

One great event happened the middle of January: the Burgesses were allowed to take their baby home with them. Virginia, who had been looking forward to this great event for two months, suddenly found herself panic-stricken. To have the care of a new baby was an overwhelming responsibility. Other mothers had made out under the same circumstances; but other mothers were different. This wasn't any other mother; this was a profoundly loving, and a highly inexperienced, Mrs. Burgess.

Don had suggested that she take a nurse home with her from the hospital and keep her for at least two weeks. Virginia knew that recent heavy expenses were weighing him down. She agreed, however, provided she was allowed to pay for the nurse out of her own money.

Don lost his temper. She was casting slights upon his position as head of the household. They actually quarreled about it: they, who were surely the happiest couple in the country, and should have been the most united. Then they both gave in at the same minute. Later there were moments when they both regretted that yielding. Being a parent turned out to be very intricate.

The first night that they had their baby at home, neither Don nor Virginia got much sleep. They were both alert for the cries that might come from the nursery. But after her ten-o'clock bottle Baby Joan wakened only for the two-o'clock. Virginia, feeding and changing her, allowed Don to do most of the running. They were sharing one more incredible bliss, one more of those "firsts" which never quite fade from memory even when the experience itself has become routine.

At six in the morning Don was again allowed to help. When that was over, they did get some sleep. Then, preparatory to the ten-o'clock feeding, Virginia gave the baby her bath. It was an ordeal for both of them. The new mother handled the child awkwardly. The child yelled. The father added to his wife's embarrassment by making suggestions, "Do you want me to take her for an instant while you get your breath back?" and "Shan't I call Daisy in? I'm sure she must have bathed babies before." He heartily wished that they had brought a nurse home with them. A nurse knew how.

Great beads of perspiration stood out on Virginia's forehead; but she shook her head mutely in answer to his suggestions. This was her baby, and she was going to give that baby her first bath here in her home.

When small Joan was finally bathed and swabbed and dressed, in only about the time that it should have taken to bathe an elephant, Virginia let Don see about the bottle. With her child in the crook of her arm, she relaxed suddenly. "I've had two months to get my strength back, and look at me!" she said with a derisive smile. "Yet this very minute some mother of only a few days' standing is undoubtedly giving her baby its first bath and doing an expert job."

In an access of tenderness Don leaned over, kissed the top

of the baby's head, kissed Virginia's forehead. "Now she belongs to us," he pronounced. "Before this, she belonged to the hospital. No fooling, darling, she is the prettiest small baby I ever saw."

"Is your judgment entirely unprejudiced?"

"Good heavens, no! What kind of monster do you take me for? My own child; my first child." *Very likely my only child,* Don added in his own mind. But he was careful not to breathe this sentiment aloud. There were some things which simply were not said.

Physical parenthood did not convey supernatural wisdom, Virginia knew. But it affected a person's judgment in many ways. Now when she went back to her poor slave mothers in the Underground Railroad days, it was with even added sympathy. Was her motherhood making her a better writer, or did it simply add a deeper color to her private emotions? Probably every personal experience affected a writer's writing. That would be one additional reason—and a very highly specialized one!—for having children.

The baby's regular schedule now formed the pattern for Virginia's research schedule. She phoned Waverley Book Shop that she needed new material: everything that Alice Martin could lay her hands on. It was splendid to be back at work again, and on such an absorbing project. If for an hour or two she forgot all about her lovely baby, that made coming back to her all the more wonderful.

Alice not only delivered an armful of research books in person; she brought along a package of gifts. There was a series of three "Baby's First Books," all printed on linen and boxed together: the alphabet, toys, animals. There was also a first edition of *Baby's Own Alphabet,* illustrated by Walter Crane, and a modern reprint of the same text.

"Am I giving little Joan her first books?" Alice demanded. "The collector's Walter Crane, of course, is either for her mother or to start the young lady on her own collecting."

"A little early, aren't you?" asked Don.

"I don't think so. Literary taste is formed in the cradle; but not the baby's own. In the grandfather's cradle, at least."

Virginia caught fire. "Nursery rhymes must in many cases have been passed down orally, and often by the grandparents. Alice, how simply lovely of you! You must autograph this book for Joan. Not 'autograph,' that is, but inscribe."

"And date," Alice acquiesced. "She may turn out to be a poet herself."

"Just let me catch her at it!" Don made gestures of choking.

"I don't want too much to be expected of her," Virginia said hastily. "This setting up a pattern is too hard on anybody. She has her own life to live."

"The gifted child of gifted parents," Alice reminded her.

But now it was Don's turn. "I don't want to imagine her growing up, like other people's children. In fact I can't imagine it. To me she's just a baby, a doll herself, a toy. I want to enjoy her as she is."

"Do that," agreed Alice. But she felt a twinge of sadness. It was wonderful to watch them grow and develop. No two children were exactly alike, though along general lines there was a wonderful similarity. Even if you didn't love them half to death, they were the most marvelous thing in the world to observe. But as they grew, they grew away from you. Oh, you were resigned to it! They had their own lives to live; they were only repeating the pattern which you in your day had followed.

Virginia began to look over the books which she would use professionally. Don bethought himself of his duties as a host, and invited, "Now tell me all about your trip to Chicago."

She told him the high points, at least. She was careful also to pass on her daughter-in-law's comment that "The second child is almost as much fun as the first, and not nearly so much trouble." What she did not dwell on was the great glory of being a grandmother. To the young parents, that was just too far in the future.

Later on, however, when she told Harry Martin about her visit, she allowed herself to comment, "Joan must inherit brains, and she is an awfully pretty child. Some day she will make some nice boy a charming bride."

Harry guffawed. "Don't tell me you're matchmaking again! Which of the small Martin boys have you selected as the bridegroom?"

Alice smiled sheepishly. "The boy was never born that Don Burgess will think good enough for his one ewe lamb. All the same, she will naturally know our grandsons."

"By the time that another generation has arrived at the marrying age, we'll be too old to care," Harry said gloomily. He had had another birthday just after Thanksgiving. He was beginning to show his years, and to feel them. Still, that was better than if he had indulged in that "I'm-just-as-young-as-I-used-to-be" nonsense. Men felt their age more in a certain way, Alice supposed. But there was no point in going too deeply into that. Rival book stores might have certain works which they kept in a back room and trotted out only for customers who were in search of illicit thrills. The Martins were not in that line of business.

There was an idea for Don Burgess: a bookseller who was on the shady side of the law. He would have to be the victim, of course; there were a good many possible false leads here. She'd better not say anything about this, however, until Don's new book came out and she learned whether he actually had made use of a noble amateur something like Harry Martin.

What a little princess Baby Joan was! This was an instance where everything had come out most beautifully. Some stories led naturally to a happy ending. What an awful lot luck had to do with it! Alice's own luck had been good all her life: so good that it sometimes frightened her. But very few people ever died of an excess of good fortune. Or of too much happiness. There was a lot of happiness in this world, but just not enough to go around.

Alice, taking a look out of the window one winter afternoon, caught the glance of a little girl who was a stranger to her. A child of about eight, with a certain wistfulness about her; pretty enough, but perhaps slightly forlorn. Mrs. Martin had smiled at her instantly; when her smile was returned, she somehow felt an urge to go further. She stepped to the door and said, "Don't you want to come in and get warm? We have other books here inside, too."

"I'm afraid I—I haven't much money," faltered the child. Hers was the instinctive timidity of a young person who has all her life found herself more or less unwelcome.

"We don't charge for our heat," said Alice. It was a joke on the eight-year-old level. The little girl loved it.

Indoors Alice pointed to a low shelf and said, "I haven't seen you before, have I? I'm Mrs. Martin. That man who is waiting on a customer is Mr. Martin. We used to have a little girl of our own; but she's grown up now."

"You kept her at home and took care of her there?" asked the little girl eagerly.

"Yes, we did. Don't you live at home?"

"I've been living with Aunt Edie. She isn't really my aunt; but I called her that because I lived with her. Now she's sick, she had to send me to my mother."

No mention of a father; another case of a broken home. A child farmed out was a child who had found herself to be in the way. This one was old enough to recognize the difference.

"I hope Aunt Edie gets better very soon," said Alice. "Here are some books you can look at. My daughter is named Jean."

"My name is Nina. Nina Babcock. My mother is Mrs. Babcock, really; but she calls herself 'Anita De Byles,' She sings and dances."

"That's very, very nice," said Alice. "I can sing a little bit myself; but I leave dancing to the young people."

I'd like to take you home and fill you up with lamb chops and creamed potatoes, she was thinking to herself. This was that kind of child. She was a little too thin, a little too hesitant about her welcome; her clothes were showy but shoddy; her coat had seen better days. Alice meditated about inviting her to go out for a cup of cocoa, and decided not to rush things.

An immediate measure lay in her grasp. A child who apologized for not having too much money was old beyond her years; she probably hadn't any. "I'm going to give you a book, just to show that we're friends," she announced. "Pick out anything here on the lowest shelf. I'll write your name in it."

Small Nina was in an agony of indecision. After a quick glance to make sure that her hostess really meant the offer, she turned to the indicated shelf, and began to handle its contents with little paws which, on a happier child, would have called for prompt work with Alice's washcloth.

Harry finished with his customer; and Alice explained in a voice loud enough to be overheard, "This is Nina Babcock. She's come to spend a few days with her mother while her Aunt Edie is sick. I hope she likes us."

Harry caught the child's forlornness. So likewise did Bill Thayer, just back from his coffee break. He had brought in coffee and doughnuts for the Martins. Alice shared her doughnut with small Nina. Thereupon Harry shared his, and Bill his. Alice had an excuse to use her washcloth after that.

Warmed and fed and welcomed, Nina Babcock went back to the picture books. She took so long at the task that Alice was finally driven into saying, "If you can't make up your mind now, come back tomorrow. It's getting late."

Nina looked startled, and made a hasty choice. Perhaps she had too often been put off with a flimsy excuse. But when

Alice had inscribed and signed the book for her, she put up her face to be kissed.

Alice, kissing her, said, "Come again soon." Then she stood at the open door watching the child scurry down a side street toward the east.

"I'm afraid you've wished a constant visitor on yourself," said Harry.

Alice picked up Nina's second choice and stood turning the leaves for a moment. Then she laid the book carefully behind a row of adult books on a fairly high shelf.

"Giving away all the profits!" teased Harry.

"Anything to keep the stock moving," said Alice. "Profits on the children's table don't amount to much anyhow. But I love the idea that one of these days, when you and I have joined the Great Majority, some gray-haired old lady may look back and think, 'That was a nice book Mrs. Martin gave me just after Aunt Edie was taken sick,' and then maybe go out and buy a picture book for some child who isn't in the least expecting it."

"You're entitling yourself to the gratitude of generations yet unborn. While you're about it, have the book mean everything to the little girl. Have her decide on the strength of it that she's going to be a writer herself. Have her go on from there to fame and fortune. Oh, here comes another customer and Bill's busy! To be continued in our next."

The child had been hungry for affection. Shunted to "Aunt Edie" because her mother couldn't, or wouldn't, take personal care of her, Nina had now been failed by Aunt Edie. Alice Martin couldn't solve the big problem; but she had done a little something to help.

Besides, if Harry Martin thought he was all that smart, he just wasn't. The book which Alice had so carefully laid aside would be right there for him when it was his turn to give. "Anita De Byles" was a silly name. But perhaps in Anita's walk of life, the sillier a thing was the more romantic it seemed. It wasn't everybody who had the good luck to be born Frederickson and to marry Martin.

A given name like "Alice" reflected good taste on the part of one's parents. Unlike "Elizabeth" and "Katherine," it didn't lend itself too readily to nicknaming. Kitty West signed things Katherine; but around the apartment or in the Martins' society, "Kitty" seemed to suit her.

"Peggy Pratt" suited that lady, too, when it was just a question of casual conversation. To Alice's ear it didn't sound like a writer's name. Was Peggy really trying to interview editors these days ?If so, how was she succeeding? Nothing had been heard lately from her or from her proposal to give editors what they wanted. Alice would have to wait for further confidences on that score. She didn't plan to hold her breath while she was waiting.

12

PEGGY PRATT HAD BEEN IN THE SHOP TO SHOW THE MARTINS the fur stole which her father sent her for Christmas. "It will serve to impress editors," she announced. She had had a wonderful holiday season; now she was really starting on her quest of inside knowledge.

"She now has a fur stole and a title," Harry summed up after their visitor left—with another selection of used books; she was reading her share, even if she didn't seem to be writing much. She was their final customer that evening; they closed the shop on her.

"That's more than either of us has," Alice agreed. "I should think, however, that an editor would be more impressed by a good manuscript than by a Persian lamb stole."

"She has a new approach. I don't know how good it is, though." Harry began to chuckle. Heading for home, he went on, "I remember one artistic soul I saw in the movies when I was in college. Movies were a nickel a throw in those days, and sometimes worth the money."

"Was it as bad as all that?"

"It was bad enough for me to remember. This bird had

fallen for the heroine's wiles. He was a sculptor; he wore a smock and beret. Full in the eye of the camera he made gestures which looked to me like setting-up exercises; then the words flashed on the screen: 'My soul is seething with passion. I will now create a masterpiece.' "

"Did you ever get a chance to see the masterpiece?"

"It looked to me like a piece of cast-iron garden statuary. I suppose somebody made those, too, in the days when public parks were decorated that way; but weren't they mass-produced?"

"Harry, how on earth can you remember a caption like that?"

"How could I forget it? It deserves a prize for silliness. But that was a world apart. We didn't go to the movies for what we could see in the street or at home."

"Or learn in the classroom. Harry, one thing I remember is the behavior of a doctor in the films. He wore a Vandyke beard, a thing which doctors hadn't done for years. He seated himself on the side of the patient's bed; I don't think they ever did that. He took the patient's pulse with his thumb. I know no doctor would ever do that, because what he felt would be the pulse in his own thumb. Then he would shake his head mournfully, to indicate that the sufferer was in a bad way."

"As well he might be, with such a doctor. Then again, Mrs. Martin—?"

"A family breakfast always began with grapefruit; and that was as far as it ever got. I know nobody would want to stick around just to watch actors eat breakfast. But just once in a while we could have seen the grapefruit shells being removed and the bacon and eggs served. Or they could have begun with orange juice."

Harry took his turn. "The cowboys always had plenty of time to ride to the rescue of virtue; they never had any cattle to mind. They rode beautifully, though; and the spread of scenery was a lovely background. It made a wonderful change after a hard week's hash-slinging, with Monday classes still two days ahead and the chance of an extra hour's sleep Sunday morning."

"Did you always do your movie-going Saturday nights? And with whom did you go?"

"As if you hadn't heard me say! Or haven't you? Or have you forgotten my cherished confidences?"

She had heard a lot of it over the years. But if he wanted to put it together and perhaps draw a conclusion from it, Alice was willing to listen.

For an instant Harry appeared on the point of making a confidence. Then he shook his head and said ruefully, "It happened a long time ago."

Alice patted his hand. "There's something else I remember about movies. When they wanted to pass over a lot of time quickly, they used to show a succession of very short, not very distinct scenes. They would even flutter the leaves of a calendar."

"Oh, that was later! It was a good device, too. A person doesn't always have to remember the worst of everything."

"A person named Martin is trying to put together the best of everything."

"Or thereabouts. Thank you for reminding me." Half to himself, Harry went on, "Sometimes of a Sunday evening I used to go calling on a girl, and then after an hour or so walk her downtown for ice cream. I was in no position to give a girl a serious rush; but it was nice while it lasted. A young man can dream dreams."

"All this because a young woman has had a strip of pelt presented to her!" gibed Alice.

Harry nodded. "The young lady is having an extremely good time for herself. I don't think she really knows much even about writing copy for an advertising agency—which can't be as simple as it looks. But while Papa comes across

[140]

and her fiancé sits the thing out, she can parade around and tell everybody that same thin story."

"It will wear out in time." Alice yawned. "Dinner is ready, if you are. After we've finished, you might do a little work on your anthology. I brought up the first of the new books to have a go at tonight. Spring is in the book catalogues, if not in the air."

"And the politicians are getting set. Election years do come closer together than they used to, don't they? I remember one October day when two dames behind me in the streetcar were talking away. One of them predicted bad weather right in the face of the autumn sunshine. When her friend demurred, she said, 'Oh, but you're forgetting! Election is next week, and we always have bad weather after election.' "

Alice had heard that one before. Heard it more than once, in fact. But in a long married life a person got used to a considerable amount of repetition. What was remarkable was that now and then Harry came across with something she hadn't heard before.

Small Nina Babcock had become a frequenter of the shop, though she was far from being a customer. Alice gave her a share of attention every time that she came in, generally managed to smuggle her something to eat, bestowed an occasional book on her. Mrs. Martin was going to miss the little girl if "Aunt Edie" recovered and reclaimed her.

For the child's own sake, however, Alice wished that it might happen. Once when Nina came in she had obviously been crying; she leaned against Alice to whisper, "My mommy was mean to me." Another time she confided, "I woke and had to go to the bathroom. I didn't know there was anybody there with her. It was a man; and they were mad at me when I interrupted." She was seeing and hearing things which were not suitable for a child to witness. Nina might not understand them now; but she sensed that there was something not right, something secretive and shameful.

[141]

It was not a case for the authorities, even if Alice had been justified in interfering. The child was not physically abused; she had a home of sorts, and was kept in school. Anita De Byles might not be a model mother; but she did provide for Nina. Alice could scarcely have obtained redress anyhow. The authorities nowadays held that even a relatively poor home was better than an institution. Perhaps a baby placed in an orphan asylum was not too much to be pitied, even aside from the chance of its being adopted, which in normal times in New York was very good. But a child old enough to remember would be fearfully unhappy even in surroundings of good physical care and merely routine kindness.

Things like this were not precisely Alice's responsibility. Still, she did take an interest. For one thing she was extremely thankful: all her life long, when there was a genuine appeal to her for help, she had always been in a position to do something about it.

"Aunt Edie" did not get better. Or at least, the arrangement for her to keep Nina was never renewed. Instead, Nina came in to report, "I'm going to stay with Aunt Agnes this time. It's right here in the neighborhood, so I won't have to change schools. I'll maybe be able to come see you again sometimes."

Alice and Harry both gave her books this time. Bill Thayer, coming in on the end of the transaction, said, "Wait a minute," dashed out, and came back with a bag of candy bars. It was a real bon-voyage party.

After Nina had had her cocoa and doughnuts, brought in by Harry Martin, he walked her to her own corner so that he could carry her packages. "If she goes ahead and eats candy bars until she makes herself sick, all the better," he told Alice on his return to the shop. "That poor kid has had very few chances at a legitimate stomachache."

"I wish I could buy her a new wardrobe for Easter," said Alice. "I'm not going to need much myself this year."

"You'd like to buy little Nina Babcock some spring clothes just for the pleasure that you get out of it?"

"I sure would. Of course I know what that shows about me in the eyes of every amateur psychoanalyst in Greenwich Village. Not that I like children and enjoy making them happy because that's the natural thing to do. Oh, no! Nothing so simple and sane as all that. The reason I try to be kind to her is that I have a Christ complex."

"If that's what you have, for heaven's sake keep it!" interjected Bill Thayer.

"Here comes a customer," Harry informed Alice. "You even like customers, don't you? Suppose you take this one?"

It was a new customer, a woman. Alice showed her around the shop and bade her take her time. "If there's anything you're especially interested in, maybe I have it or can get it for you. This is a small shop; but we have a fairly large warehouse."

The outside tables began to do business. People were coming home from work; some of them did not care to spend the evening yawning over the newspaper or twiddling with the radio dial. Movies cost money, too, and didn't leave you with anything which you could resell at the box office. Gone were the happy days of the jitney movie; not even the Depression had brought that back.

"Do you want tomorrow off, Bill?" Mrs. Martin asked presently. Tomorrow would be Thursday, a slack day in the book business; Bill Thayer generally had it off, as well as Sunday.

Bill did. Couldn't he put the shop to bed for them? No, but he could help Alice handle the post-dinner business; let Harry go up to the Commerce Street apartment and have an hour or two to himself.

Harry gestured his thanks. Now that he had a study of his own, and the business in the shop was almost too easily taken care of, he was getting deeper and deeper into his great undertaking. The mail-order business, however, he kept firmly in his own hands. He was not going to be one of those men who were spoiled by too capable wives.

He was just turning toward the washroom when Ben Johnson came in. Harry turned back. "I want something to take home to Bess," Ben announced. "There are so few openings any more, she and I have a lot of time to read. Of course I do theatrical notes from time to time; but between the press releases and the phone, they are easy enough to take care of."

"I tell you what, Ben," said Harry, "You should put in some of your spare time writing lectures. Or a lecture. Something on the Drah-ah-ahma with a broad 'a.' You could get a lecture bureau to book you to women's clubs around the country. The overweight, overdressed dames would hang on your words. You're not only a New York critic; you're a produced playwright."

"I was, once. Now the last of my options has expired; and I'm not writing anything more to join my unproduced plays in the old trunk. It did me good in one way, being a produced playwright. I'm a little bit easier now on the poor birds whose plays I review."

"That just shows what a nice guy you are," Harry assured him. "Some people in your position would be jealous, and would take it out on the other fellow."

"He has a Christ complex," said Alice, and proceeded to enlighten Ben on the Nina Babcock episode.

Ben received the news with unexpected seriousness. "That may make a difference in her whole future life. You showed the poor kid that somebody thinks all that much of her."

"It made me happy, too, in a different way. But I never thought of it as important." Alice was delighted at his approbation; but it made her slightly uneasy. She didn't deserve all that. With the means at her command, perhaps she should do more for other people than she did.

Ben sensed her embarrassment, and was quick to change the subject. "Talking about the Drah-ah-ahma might be all right for a season, though I'd never be asked to play a return engagement. At least, my remarks would be deliberately addressed to a public. I remember how disappointed I was once when I was still a boy in my teens. I had a job down in Birmingham ushering in the theater. There was a 'road' in those days, and we got some really good attractions. Well, I spotted two actors loafing between the matinee and the evening performance. I eavesdropped to find out what those creatures from another world would say. One of them said, 'Rotten town, isn't it?' The other agreed, 'Yeah, rotten.' "

The Martins laughed. Alice said, "You poor kid! You expected them to be talking about Shakespeare, maybe."

It made a good story afterward; but those things weren't funny at the time they happen. Alice sometimes felt awfully sorry for young people. Their natural cockiness was only their protection against experience; it was an armor full of chinks.

Ben finally selected his books and left. Alice had given him a nice discount on his purchases. Waverley might not show much profit on today's business; but it was one of the most rewarding days that Mrs. Martin had ever spent in the shop.

"Do you think he'll really be easier on the playwrights?" she asked Harry a few minutes after Ben had left.

"He was never much toward the 'sour grapes' side. I wonder how many other drama critics have unfulfilled aspirations and a trunkful of unproduced plays. I wonder, too, if Ben will stick to his new path when times pick up and managers are again taking options."

Alice turned to wait on a customer, but presently wandered back to Harry and to the topic. "I wonder, too, whether Ben will take your suggestion of making a lecture tour?"

"He should. I can just imagine Madame Chairman introducing him. That story about the actors in Birmingham might come into his lecture too, mightn't it? But I've an idea Rare Ben has something else up his sleeve. It isn't like him just to settle back and let well enough alone."

"Who does? Only shiftless people. More power to Ben in his new enterprise, whatever it is."

There was no secret about another friend's new enterprise. Don Burgess appeared in the shop carrying a bulky envelope. It contained a thick wad of sheets covered with close-packed and considerably scribbled-over longhand; but there were a few typed pages at the beginning. It was Don's new opus, complete with title and dedication, "To my daughter, Joan Burgess."

"The most important page in the book," announced the author. "Possibly the only one to which there will be no editorial objection. I can get a better idea when it's back from the typist's and I undertake to copyread it."

"Has Virginia read it?" asked Alice.

"Yes, and as in duty bound has objected to some details and called my attention to some minor discrepancies. Her verdict is on the whole most kind."

"She couldn't write this sort of book if her life depended on doing so," said Harry. Obviously there were times when men must stand together and try to keep women in their place.

"She wouldn't if she could," retorted Alice. "There, that was what you wanted me to say, wasn't it?"

Both men laughed; but Don sobered suddenly. "I think she sometimes wishes she could. She's getting in pretty deep with her escaping slaves."

"It isn't a cheerful subject," said Harry. "All that misery, and in the background a deep fundamental wrong. She isn't thinking of dropping the work, is she?"

"Good heavens, no! She finds it fascinating, that whole

[146]

business of the Underground Railroad. She is beginning now to wonder what the escaped slaves did when they got to Canada, and who helped them there. The source material so far hasn't helped her much with that."

"There's an idea in that for a novel," said Alice. "But which one of you is going to write it?"

Don shrugged. "It's way beyond me; and so far Virginia has confined herself to writing about facts."

"You'd prefer to choose your own subjects, too, wouldn't you? Don, have you really written a whodunit with a talkative bookseller as one of the leading characters?"

Don's good spirits came back in a rush. He grinned teasingly. "I could hardly write about a deaf-mute bookseller."

"Get along with you and dump your script at the typist's," Alice ordered. "Stop in on your way back, though, and let's have a visit."

"It must be a relief to get your book finished," Harry supplemented. "You beat Virginia to that dedication, too, didn't you?"

Don's face lighted with sudden tenderness. "Sometimes I can't believe it myself. Joan is there, and she's mine, and she's reached the age where she is beginning to recognize people and learn things. As soon as I've slept off this book I'm going to take over the two-o'clock-in-the-morning feeding. That will give Virginia a little more rest."

"Speaking one word for Virginia and two for yourself," said Alice saucily. But just for an instant there was a suspicious moisture in her eyes. Fathers were somehow very touching. Why did silly people try to make a joke of them?

When he had left she ordered Harry, "Take Don up to our apartment for a drink if you want to. I think he must get a little homesick sometimes for masculine society, though he's too polite to acknowledge it."

"Alice, you're a wonderful wife—and a wonderful partner —and the prettiest mature woman in Greenwhich Village. But there are times when I'd like to wring that smooth little neck of yours. You send me out to roll my hoop as if it were an assignment. Takes all the fun out of it."

"All right, then, you stay here and tend shop. I'll take Don up to Commerce Street, fourth floor, and give him some more feminine society, in the hope that he will realize he's getting too much of it."

"Were you ever caught without an answer?"

"Seldom. If I'm in any danger of that, a customer always comes in."

Sure enough, one came in that instant. A new customer, too. Harry turned away hastily; but Alice advanced with her usual greeting, "Would you like to look around, or are you in search of something special? If you are, perhaps I can help you find it."

If Mother Eve had had the first chance there when explanations were called for in the Garden of Eden "in the cool of the evening," she would have brazened out that little affair about the serpent and the forbidden fruit. It was that poor zany Adam who gave the whole show away.

13

Don Burgess came into Waverley Book Shop bearing the typed copy of his new opus. He deposited the bulky envelope on Harry Martin's desk, opened it, and said, "Looks encouraging, doesn't it, all those pages of neat typing? Quite a change from my hen scratchings and rescratchings. The original manuscripts of the Burgess books ought to be in some museum, maybe; but they look to me as if their natural destination is the ash can."

Don's longhand manuscript was indeed deplorable. Harry managed to decipher the first page, then compared it to the typed version. "This does look quite different. Does your typist charge you more because your copy is pretty messy?"

"Are you asking that out of idle curiosity, or with some worthy end in view?"

"I may need some typing done some day myself. Is this dame good at the job?"

"Alice types your labels and such odd jobs. You're speaking about quantity production, I gather?"

"I thought I might ask a simple question," Mr. Martin parried feebly.

"In what shape would your copy be?" Don drove on.

"Well, printed."

"Printed?" Don drew his conclusion, and grinned. "Not by any chance working on the Waverley Book Shop Anthology, are you?"

"I have no title." Harry's thoughts wandered for a second to Peggy Pratt, who had one, and who had reported that she was really going around to see editors now, and about time too, wasn't it?

"You see I have." Don flashed the title page, where Harry read *Murders on the Sidewalk*. "That sounds as if our pavements were 'with bloody corpses strewn.' Next title to be announced much later. Probably 'Death something-or-other.' 'Death' used to be a dignified word. Now it merely means 'spilled red ink.' "

"You groan an awful lot," said Alice, excusing herself to a customer and coming over to the desk. "But you really like what you're doing. Nice typing this. Do you want to leave it here with me, or do you prefer to take it with you when you and Harry go up to the apartment for an interval of—well, for an interval?"

"There she is, trying to send us away for a bull session again," said Don, "and too polite to use those words."

Just for that, Alice brought over the customer and introduced Don. She found two of his published books, too, and trotted them out for inspection. The customer, a middle-aged woman, enjoyed the act if she didn't buy the books. She was still in the shop when Harry and Don went across Seventh Avenue for their promised recess. Don carried his burden with him, of course. There would be no further pauses by the way once he got started for home.

Relaxing in the Martin living room, Don proclaimed, "I'm famous for getting my copy in on time. The best part of being a writer is that you can do your punctuality all in one burst and get it over with. Not like the Army, where I was bugled into bed and out of bed, to meals and to drill. You know what Sherman said war was."

"That's all over now," Harry consoled him.

"Sure is. We made the world safe for the Democratic Party. I can't be too hard even on the Army, though. I was a schoolteacher befoah de Wah. I told you about that, didn't I?"

"Once," said Harry with a grin.

"And once is enough? I don't blame you. But have patience with me for just a moment. 'Look here upon this picture, and on this.'" Don indicated the bundle of manuscript with one hand. Then with a leer of false kindness he mimicked, "'Willis Smith, will you go to the blackboard and make a diagram of today's first proposition?'"

"Geometry. A nice subject," commented Harry.

"Nice if you're doing it by yourself. Nice the first few times over, maybe. But year after year, with the stupid, the lazy, the unwilling—! Just think, Harry, if I'd stayed with the noble profession, or if I'd gone back to it after I was dempbbed— pardon my French, Mr. Martin. After I was demobilized, mustered out, sent back into civilian life with the blessing of a grateful country—"

"I understand," Harry assured him. "I speak very fair colloquial English. I've lived in this country a long time."

"All right, then, if I'd gone back to the ghastly grind, I might have been a high school principal by this time. I might have been spending my days trying to convince a lot of luckless brats that tardiness is the sin against the Holy Ghost."

"A tougher life than teaching? My daughter likes teaching."

"Some people do. Some people like carrots. Some people like string beans. Some people like oatmeal." Don grinned and watched Harry pour a refill. "It would serve me right to have Joan turn into a schoolmarm."

"More power to her if she likes it."

"That's a long look ahead, anyhow. I'm looking into a vastly different world, the world of might-have-been."

"A very sad world, if you can take Maud Muller's poet's word for it."

"I'm not thinking about Maud Muller in the hayfield, I who have Virginia Daly waiting for me at home. I'm speaking of the wife Principal Don Burgess might have married: so all-fired prim and proper."

"But with a secret vice," Harry put in. "Reading detective stories."

"Which he reads even more secretly." Don tried to keep his face straight, but failed. "It's a nice picture, though; makes me feel better. I do give innocent pleasure to some people. Besides, it isn't as if I were serving a life sentence. Some day I may even get over into that next field, where it always looks just a little greener."

"It sometimes is, too," Harry assured him.

Don stared for a moment, took another pull at his drink, then said, "You really are working on an anthology, aren't you?"

Harry nodded. "I figure that I'm about halfway through the preliminary work." He went on to tell how he proposed to include his translations from Latin, and how he had bought a poem from Bess Johnson. It was high time he got some typing done and began to consider arrangement. So far he hadn't even thought about a publisher.

"I've been reluctant to talk about it," Harry summed up. "Afraid of breaking the charm, I guess."

"Afraid that you'd be like too many other Villagers: take it out in talk instead of getting down to work."

"Not that so much, but I'm superstitious. If you talk about your good luck, you may drive it away."

"What's lucky about choosing a job and buckling down to work on it?"

"It's good luck to pick a job as compiler. An editor lives off somebody else's work. I'm planning to live off both the writers' work and the editors.' I feel a good deal like a new father, in a way. I take all the credit when somebody else has really done the spadework."

"So you think there must be a catch somewhere? Keep your fingers crossed, then, if you think that will do any good."

"It can't do any harm," said Harry, and rose to replenish their glasses.

But Don declined a third round. He had a train to catch. Lugging his precious manuscript, he accompanied Harry to the door of the book shop and waved farewell to Alice. Then he took his departure for the wilds. This was the man who had once enjoyed being a bachelor!

Harry smiled derisively; yet just for an instant he was envious. Don had completed a big job, and it was a job which only Don Burgess himself could do. Editors and compilers were all right in their way; the editors, at least, were a necessary evil. Yet they were actually nothing but middlemen, living off the fruits of other people's productive labor. More than that, Don was going home to a young wife and a miraculous firstborn from whom the newness had not yet worn off.

Nonsense to envy Don, of course. Harry might better reflect on how much happiness there was in this world, in spite of the crape-hangers and in the face of some very deplorable facts. Anyhow it did no good to rebel against the passage of time. Which version was Harry going to use of that much translated, and often well translated, classic, "Where are the snows of yesteryear?"

There was another poem somewhat along that line, but with homesickness added to wistfulness over the flight of time —those dedicatory lines which Robert Louis Stevenson had addressed to a cousin from his exile in the South Seas:

[153]

It's ill to loose the bonds that God decreed to bind;
Still will we be the children of the heather and the wind;
Though far frae hame and friends, yet it's aye for you and me
The broom is blowing bonnie in the North Countree!

There would be none of *The Child's Garden* in Harry's collection; "little me" might climb up into the cherry tree as much as he cared to, and the "Land of Counterpane" might lie spread before him; but it must be between other covers. Harry would include one short story by Stevenson, that lovely parable "Will o' the Mill," all about a man who let life pass him by. But there would be a nice fat selection from the published Letters. In the days when people still wrote letters, some of them did so with an eye on publication, Mr. Martin feared. Still, all that effort deserved some encouragement, even if it was only from hope.

Walt Whitman, too, would be represented by a selection from those letters which he wrote his mother when he was tramping the wards in Civil War hospitals. *The Wound Dresser* that book was called. Whitman had had the misfortune to be made the object of a cult. That was one form of bad luck which might happen to any writer; but in this case it was especially ironic because Whitman had always defended the common man and tried to interpret him to his fellows. A few years ago an admirer had made a valiant attempt to rescue Walt from alien altars by writing a biography of him told entirely in his own words. Harry wondered how well that book had done; his shop hadn't sold many copies. All of which wouldn't bother the Good Gray Poet very much in whatever Happy Hunting Ground his spirit was now holding forth.

Harry decided to commit himself. He looked up Don Burgess' typist, a damsel of some fifty frosty winters, who held forth as public stenographer in a small hotel a few blocks east of Waverley Book Shop. He told her he had a large job for her if they could come to terms. The work would be easy and she could fit it in to suit her own time; but he wanted a substantial discount from her usual rates.

Avarice and curiosity struggled in her breast. She informed him that she had a regular schedule of prices, and maintained it for her steadiest customers.

"Who all, including Mr. Burgess, need their work done promptly," said Harry. He had come empty-handed on purpose; he knew too well the temptation, when you have lugged in a package, to deposit it.

"If you could give me some idea—" she temporized.

"Most of the time you would be transcribing from the printed page. You could go at least twice as fast as you do when you have to type from Mr. Burgess's longhand, and with far less strain on your eyesight and nerves."

She hesitated for an instant, then went on, "You said, 'most of the time.' The rest of the time—?"

"You would be struggling with my longhand, which is only a shade better than Mr. Burgess's. But there wouldn't be too much of that."

"You're planning some sort of collection?"

"I am. I'll make you a sporting offer: half your regular price for everything you transcribe from print, twice your regular price for everything you have to puzzle out from my penmanship."

She gave up and began to laugh. "Bring in your material and let me get started. Do you expect me to wait for my money until it's all over?"

"Bill me for the first batch of copy when you finish it. I'll bring it in tomorrow."

He was committed now. A vinegary sort of person, this Sylvia Norton. It still remained to be seen whether Harry Martin had got the better of her on their business deal. The important thing was that he was now committed in more eyes than his own. In Alice's he had been right from the beginning, in Bess Johnson's for some time, in Don Burgess' rather lately. But irrevocably committed in his own; that was the important thing.

It would be some time yet before he had to talk to a publisher. Harry must be prepared to say in what respect his anthology differed from other anthologies, and presumably surpassed them. He had an idea that he might make a running commentary: not much of it, but a thread on which to string together all the various gems which he had selected, and would select. For the present he would call it "Another Treasury." A working title. Not bad, though it did not quite satisfy him.

If it took all this work, and involved all this uncertainty merely to find an acceptable title, what must the actual writing of a book involve? Yet here was he, as a compiler, sitting in judgment on books which he must assume to be of permanent worth. Even that was a long and difficult task, much as he enjoyed it. But in the ordinary way of business, he made his living selling books over the counter, just as he might have sold any other article of merchandise.

Or no, it was not just the same. He thoroughly enjoyed selling books; he wouldn't have got anything like the same satisfaction from selling groceries, say, or men's clothing, or shoes. Why were shoe clerks regularly such discouraged-looking men? Presumably because not one of them had ever started out with that as his life's ambition; he had come to this because it was one way to earn a living.

To earn a living doing what a man loved to do was surely to succeed in life. Here too Harry Martin had much of the rough work done for him. Alice read the current books first. What was served to H. Martin, Esquire, was simply the cream of the crop.

Harry was in a mood of exultation. He had learned from experience that the only thing to do with such a mood was go ahead and indulge it. It was by nature ephemeral. A person had to come back down to earth; in fact he was lucky if nothing very disappointing happened afterward.

What happened ought to have been highly pleasing to Harry Martin. It was highly pleasing, of course; but he had to nudge himself into acknowledging that fact. Emil Koenig was a friend of both the Martins. He was perhaps the finest person in their little circle: certainly the most talented. Alice had made the match between him and his pretty wife. It was an all-around satisfactory marriage; if he had never been madly in love with Kitty West, at least he made her a kindly, considerate husband; she for her part filled a gap in what had been his lonely life. The whole thing was so sensible; it was such a livable arrangement. Harry was a fool for wishing that the sculptor would give him a pretext to blow up and break off the friendship between the two couples. But to that extent Harry Martin *was* a fool. Everybody had a blind spot; and this was his.

Now here came Emil Koenig bracing into Waverley Book Shop and half filling the narrow space left by shelves and counters. He was a big man physically, as well as in talent and emotion. Under one arm he carried a sheaf of drawings. He bided his time about showing them; he waited first until Harry was at liberty, then he drew Alice away from customers who were taking their time about making up their minds. Harry expressed perfunctory admiration; Alice displayed real interest.

Well she might. The drawings were partly in crayon, black and colored, partly in India ink; the subject of them all was the same. Three or four of them showed Alice Martin in all sorts of costumes and poses; the other two sheets were filled with tantalizing fragments: a head half turned away, a hand holding a flower, a foot dangling a slipper.

"All done from memory!" Harry exclaimed. It was rather feeble enthusiasm, but it was the best he could summon up at the moment.

"From memory, with a touch of genius added," Alice amended.

A customer pricked up her ears and turned toward them. Alice went to wait on her. This time Harry did better. "I always knew that you were good, Emil. I didn't know that you were all this good."

"Good up to a certain point," Emil agreed. "That point has now been reached. I've come in to see about the next step." Again he bided his time. Harry paged over the sketches once more, and reminded himself that the husband of a beautiful woman mustn't expect other men to be blind. If the other men happened to be artists, that simply made their admiration more valuable.

When Alice rejoined them, Emil opened up. "What I want now is a study in the round. A study from life. I'm not one bit satisfied with that fanciful bust I made a while back. Alice, if you could come up to my studio some afternoon before too long, I could do a fairish clay model of you in a single sitting."

"I'd be flattered," Alice said promptly. "That can easily be arranged, can't it, Harry? Just so it doesn't come on Bill Thayer's afternoon off."

"Bill is working for us, not we for Bill," Harry snapped. He could always vent his vexation on a trifle.

"Then, after that," Emil went on, "Kitty and I would like it if you joined us for dinner at the apartment. She will get home from the office in time to set the table and make the salad. I'll prepare the main dish that morning: something that only needs heating up."

At last Harry could manage to sound cordial. "That is an offer which would tempt an anchorite. Your cooking is as good as your sculpture, Emil. That's saying a lot."

"If the Depression lasts long enough, I can always take a job as chef." Emil grinned. "I wouldn't mind taking a job as janitor, for that matter. But such a way of earning a living

[158]

would be beneath the dignity of Katherine West's husband."

The Depression would end some day. In the face of such widespread misery and suffering, Harry Martin was almost ashamed of the fact that he was able to sit back and not only enjoy a comfortable living from the book shop but also get ahead with an enterprise of his own. Emil Koenig was in much the same position. He and Kitty hadn't handicapped themselves with any children, either. Harry conjectured it was from choice. Anyhow it was their own business. Some things still were a person's private business, even in the small circle which centered at Waverley Book Shop, right here in the heart of Greenwich Village.

"All right, then, Alice, you name the day," said Harry. "In all such matters you're a free agent. The marriage service doesn't say a thing about having your picture taken or your likeness sculptured."

They set the date, subject only to confirmation from Kitty, who telephoned it as soon as she got home from the office. The following Thursday afternoon Harry spent in the shop, mostly busying himself with his anthology and keeping his mind off the fact that to an artist like Emil even a decorously clad woman might just as well not have been dressed at all; he could see her body right through her clothes. Harry sent Bill out for an early dinner, then went himself over to the Commerce Street apartment to freshen and change.

Shaving for the second time that day, he realized how he was beginning to show his age—realized it not for the first time. That lusty giant of a man, Emil Koenig, couldn't be much younger than Harry himself. If he was, he was a little younger than Alice, too. Suddenly cheerful again, Harry whistled a tune while he shaved and dressed. His whistling wasn't quite as bad as his singing. Nothing could be. But at that it did fair justice to that unique ditty about those bottles which might fall to the floor in succession.

It was a very successful evening. Alice was quieter than usual. She admitted that she was a little tired, "though goodness knows why. All I had to do was sit or stand or lie down as I was told to. I didn't have to be polite to a single customer all afternoon." Emil too was silent; but that was nothing new for him. Harry talked a lot; Kitty sometimes batted the ball back to him, sometimes contented herself with laughing at his sallies. At a suitable hour the guests took their leave.

Harry Martin escorted Alice back to the building where they now occupied a large top-floor apartment. Where they shared a bedroom, just as they always had in Brooklyn. Shared a bed, even if it was a comparatively new bed. She was *his* wife. She belonged to him; she would continue to live with him and to like it. He would see to that.

Only, that evening she seemed a little cold and distant. When he attempted to make love to her, she drew slightly away and whispered, "Not just now. Later, darling. Later."

But later she pretended that she was asleep. When Harry himself awakened from his first sound sleep and tried to draw her close to him, she turned away from him and cuddled deep into her own pillow.

If that was the way she felt about it, very well. But two could play at some games. Harry Martin would show her how he felt about all this business. He didn't yet quite know how; but he would show her. Those two and the high plane on which they insisted in their relationship! A high plane probably offered them some sort of rarefied delight; they breathed thin air, and their pulses beat faster.

Which did not alter the fact that God the Father had created them male and female, and their entire relationship was founded on that fact. Harry's jealousy tormented him to his own disgust. He really ought to be above such nonsense. He, too, might learn to like thin air, once he got used to it.

14

THE ACADEMIC YEAR WAS NEARING THE CLOSE OF ITS FIRST semester. Like the publishing world, it had seasons of its own. The Martins' academic relatives out in Minnesota were giving examinations and grading papers. Peggy Pratt faced the fact that her year sponsored for a New York safari in place of work for a master's degree was now half over. It had not shown any great positive accomplishment.

"I'm getting so I can find my way past the secretaries," she reported in Waverley Book Shop. "What few editors I've seen listen and are polite, but they don't tell me much."

"Did you expect a magic formula like 'Open, Sesame'?" demanded Harry Martin. "That's only a story in *The Arabian Nights*, you know. It's not a guide to practical conduct."

Peggy shrugged an indignant shoulder. "All right, then, if you don't care to listen, go outside and mind the bargain book tables. I'll talk to Alice."

"Editors," grumbled Harry, "are on salary. I wish that I could be paid for sitting in a comfortable office and listening to a pretty girl and saying, 'Yes. That is, No. What I mean is, Well, maybe.'"

"You couldn't confine yourself to so few words for the fattest salary in the country," snapped Peggy. Then she gave in and laughed. "Oh, have it your own way! One of them said, 'Are you going to write your book anyhow, Miss Pratt? We'll be glad to look at the manuscript when you have finished it.'"

"That told you something," was Harry's comment. "It will be your book. Write it your own way."

"Another one said, 'Everything that comes into this office is read. We have no rigid specifications.'"

That really told her everything, in Harry's opinion. The publishers themselves didn't know what they wanted. If they had done so, what would it have availed them? They had to make a selection from what was offered. But this time Mr. Martin held his tongue. If Peggy Pratt didn't understand anything as plain as that, there was no sense in trying to interpret it for her.

"A third said, 'We are accepting very little these days. Times are not good.'"

"The dear Depression! Times aren't as bad as all that, or I wouldn't be still in business," Harry said. "Has there been a fourth editor yet?"

"The fourth one said, 'We have our regular authors. It is difficult for a newcomer to break in.'"

"That man was really talking sense. But weren't all the regular authors beginners at one time?" Harry moved toward the door. "I will go out and mind the sidewalk tables now, and let you two good ladies wait on the customers."

The only bad feature of being in the book shop business was that customers sometimes interrupted gossips with friends. But customers in Waverley Book Shop were seldom in much of a hurry.

Harry hadn't been at the outside tables three minutes, however, when a customer in search of a cheap book wherewith to while away the evening stopped to ask, "Have you heard the latest Depression story?"

"If you asked me had I heard the *last* one, I could have said, 'I hope so.' But I didn't realize there were Depression stories still going the rounds. I thought we were so used to our Depression that we no longer noticed."

The customer proceeded, "It seems the bookkeeper in this business said to the boss, 'Hurrah, we're out of the red at last. Look here at the figures.' The boss looked and said, 'But the figures are in red ink.' The bookkeeper said, 'Oh, I can't help that! If we spend ten cents for a bottle of black ink, back we go in the red.' "

"That joke," said Harry, "is so bad it's good. In exchange I'll give you two ten-cent books for the price of one. And I'll use your dime to buy me a bag of chestnuts."

Peggy sauntered out of the shop presently, drawing her Christmas stole tighter around her shoulders. She had bought a book, which was clutched against her handbag. Harry suspected that not all her evenings were passed reading in the furnished apartment which she had rented for her New York year.

Later on, in an interval between customers, he said to Alice, "I'll miss Peggy when she goes back to Portland and her fiancé. I only hope New York hasn't spoiled her for living in Oregon."

Alice raised her eyebrows. "What makes you think she's going back there?"

"She came to New York to get established as a writer. So far she hasn't put her foot on the lowest rung of the ladder, and her time is half up."

"There are other ways to make a living besides writing.

Peggy could get a job in an office or a department store, if she decided she wanted to stay here."

"You don't think she's dead in love with the Oregon chap?"

"I think she's in love with love. Like all normal people, she wanted to get married. She had a chance, and took the first step. Those are only my ideas, mind you. She hasn't confided in me a thing that she hasn't told you."

"Like all normal people, she wanted to get married." Those words echoed in Harry's head after Alice had turned to wait on customers and he had gone out to straighten up the sidewalk tables. What a singularly flat way of putting the thing! It had its prosaic side, to be sure: years enough of diapers and dishes for a young wife, of monotony and weariness for the erstwhile Romeo. Poetry was truer in its way. It lasted longer. Harry remembered that beautiful quatrain by Austin Dobson:

> All passes. Art alone
> Enduring stays to us.
> The Bust outlasts the throne,—
> The Coin, Tiberius.

Harry wondered what made him so damn discontented lately. He had not only his marriage and his book shop to depend on, he had the ever-widening world of his anthology. The mail order business gave him an opportunity to get out and stretch his legs. Surely he had a nice life if ever a man did.

Already the publishers' spring catalogues were arriving; Alice was selecting and screening new books. Sure enough, Donald Burgess' firm was bringing out his latest opus. Don came in with an advance copy. The Martins always rated presentation copies of Don's whodunits; but this one had a special, and a very saucy, inscription, "For Harry Martin. If he thinks any character in this book bears resemblance to any person in real life, let him rest assured that the resemblance is intentional. And let him make the most of it!"

"Does that mean I can sue for libel?" asked Harry. "Or does it mean that I'm entitled to a small percentage of your royalties?"

"It means that you can read some of your nifties in print. Recognize them if you can. Reclaim them at your peril. Now that Ben Johnson has retired from writing plays, you can't have your bright remarks come flashing back at you over the footlights any more; be satisfied with second-rate enjoyment. Has Ben really retired, by the way?"

"Sort of the way a drunkard reforms, I guess. Not a single one more—until the next time. But I really can't read inside men's minds, Don. That is left for you writers with imagination."

"We read only inside the minds of our own puppets," Don assured him. All the same, he had that certain smile popularly described as "like the cat that has just swallowed the canary." Harry suspected why, and that night, when he read right straight through the opus dedicated to Don's infant daughter, he discovered that his suspicions were correct. The garrulous bookseller was the man who, thinking along lines peculiarly his own and in some ways downright peculiar, still managed to give the police just the assistance they needed.

As for Ben Johnson, he came in not long afterward with an offering which he too had inscribed for his dear friends the Martins. It was a very expensively manufactured magazine entitled *The Dramatic Arts Quarterly*. Very heavily subsidized too, Harry suspected. Yet those well-upholstered and well-corseted dames who attended lectures on "The Drahma" might well subscribe to a periodical such as this. It would look very impressive on the living-room table.

Ben's article led off the issue. A note on the "Table of

Contents" page set forth his standing and achievements in a way that must have impressed even Ben himself, let alone the readers of the publication. The article was "Ten Minutes' Grace." It went on to explain that for the first ten minutes after the first curtain, the audience didn't care a continental what happened. They were there to settle into the play as well as into their seats; they were simply waiting for the thing to get going.

Ben went on to give instances of how this must be done. The dramatist now had his chance to get in his exposition. An old-fashioned way had been to have two servants gossip about their masters' affairs. Nowadays a telephone conversation might serve the same purpose. He went back to the classics; he used instances drawn from published or other standard plays. He put the thing into words of one syllable. They were vastly entertaining words, however; and they certainly drove home his point.

Harry glanced over the article, approved it warmly, asked, "Do you intend to keep on with this line of work?"

"I certainly do!" said Ben happily. "As long as they like me, I'll keep it up."

"But Ben, the author of a magazine article is so far behind the scenes! It's bad enough to write books, I should think, though a book writer may get fan letters and certainly gets reviews. But to anybody who has ever heard those first-night cries, 'Author! Author!'—"

"When and if they come," Ben said sharply. "By the time they do, he is too tired anyhow to care; and they die away in a very few minutes. But this sort of writing is fun to do. I can do it at my leisure; so different from my reviews of plays, which have to be hurried. The form is semipermanent, too. Of course my name appears at the head of all my reviews; but I'm only too well aware that today's newspaper lines tomorrow's garbage can. Even a review sometimes has to be cut for space. This sacred text appears exactly as I wrote it."

Ben's burst of enthusiasm left Harry breathless. Rather weakly he asked, "You already have an idea for your next article?"

Indeed Ben had. It was an argument in favor of reading printed plays. (Ah there, ladies in the hinterland!) When Hamlet said, "The play's the thing," he did not mean that the play was all-important, though he was often quoted as if he had meant just that. He had predicted that the play was the thing in which he would catch the conscience of the King. But in a very real sense, Ben Johnson would go on to inform his magazine audience: the play was what mattered; and in an actual stage presentation all that the audience saw was the actors.

Harry had often seen Ben enthusiastic, almost as often depressed; but he had never before seen him so happy and contented. Queer, the way things worked out. Very queer indeed, the new quirks that old friends developed.

Of course Ben Johnson, having a good job and a settled income, could have sat back and let nature take its course. That argument would apply with equal force to Harry Martin; he too had a certain standing in his own profession and earned an adequate living even in these times. But both men had that push to go ahead and do something additional on their own hooks. Ambition, egotism, inner drive: call it what you would, it certainly started fresh undertakings off and kept them going. It gave a person a feeling of accomplishment, too, of effort well spent.

One question was forever forbidden to poor weak mortals: Is all of this really worthwhile? Harry Martin was afraid to face such an issue, and the question would simply never have occurred to Ben Johnson.

"Peggy Pratt has a sweet little racket," Harry Martin remarked to Alice one evening when they sat down to their late dinner. "She kicks up her heels around New York for a year at Papa's expense. Then she goes back to a sure thing and marries her intended. In the years ahead, whenever she gets mad at her husband, she can tell him that she gave up her career to marry him, and just look at her now."

"If she really wanted to write a book, she'd sit down and write it," Alice agreed. "Still, who am I to judge? New York may have gone to her head; it does to lots of young people's. Once she's back on the Coast and married and out of the hubbub, she may yet settle down and write her book."

"She may, at that. Girls nowadays are amazing. Her father will be glad to have her back in Oregon." Harry sounded a little wistful. His own girl was a long way off. She might be back for a visit this summer. But only for a visit. She was as much married to Minnesota as she was to Earl Crawford.

So the Martins settled Peggy Pratt's future for her. As a good classicist, Harry should have reflected that although most everyday events are fairly predictable, important happenings still remain on the knees of the Gods, when they are handed down to mortals, if not perhaps quite haphazardly, still with amazing results.

Only two days later Peggy Pratt came into the shop wide-eyed with excitement. Something had happened. Yes, something important. She needed Alice's help. But she couldn't explain about it here. Wouldn't Alice come out with her for coffee?

There was only one sort of thing that could make a girl look like that: only one sort which could make her come to Alice for help. Alice was as good a matchmaker as she was bookwoman; she hadn't had much practice lately either, what with most of their intimates safely married off and Bill Thayer in a hopeless stalemate. Alice responded with alacrity. The two of them bustled off to a nearby lunchroom.

Over their coffee Peggy made her disclosure. "I was beginning to get a little bit discouraged about talking to editors. But I do make a memorandum of what they tell me. It gives me something to write home to Daddy, too. He never asks for an accounting. But after all, it's his money that is keeping me here. So yesterday afternoon I had another appointment."

"This man really told you something?" Alice encouraged.

Peggy shook her head. "I make it a practice to get there a little early for my appointments. I was sitting in the waiting room when an office door opened and a man started to show someone out. He caught sight of me and lost track for a moment of what he was saying. Then he completed his errand, walking with this man as far as the outer door of the office. On his way back he stopped and spoke to me. He asked, 'Were you waiting to see me?' "

"Well, were you? Did things get off to such a fine start?"

"No. I was waiting for the book editor. When this man introduced himself, he turned out to be the editor of the magazine which the same firm publishes." Peggy went on to give the firm's name and that of the magazine. They were both well known to Alice.

The girl went on, "Then he asked me, 'He has a manuscript of yours?' I said no, I had just come to ask him some questions about writing. He said, 'Ask me instead. I'm fine at answering questions.' He took me into the book editor's office and introduced me. The next thing I knew I was in the magazine office with Mr. Ferrar."

"Ferrar? Oh, yes!" said Alice vaguely. Editors' names were a little out of her line.

"Walter Ferrar. He gave me a copy of the current magazine before I left. I looked to make sure."

"So then you asked him your question? Asked him what the office was looking for in a book?"

"Just that. He said, 'The same thing I look for in a short story. Something which will catch and hold the reader's attention.' "

"Another package answer," commented Alice. "True enough, to be sure; but I don't see how it helps you much."

"He went on, 'If you'll come out for coffee with me, I can tell you more.' So we went out for coffee, and he told me more. I can repeat it almost verbatim. I hope I'm not boring you."

"It's very interesting, I'd say. Books are my business," Alice reminded her gently.

"Mr. Ferrar took me to a very nice restaurant right in the neighborhood. He seemed to be known there. He suggested that I have French pastries with my coffee. I accepted with pleasure. I always love to have them bring that beautiful tray around and give me my choice."

"A wonderful moment of suspense," Alice agreed. "I like it even better than I like the pastries."

"Afterward I generally wish I'd chosen another one," said Peggy. "I had two and refused a third. There was the usual small talk until we had finished eating; then Mr. Ferrar drew a long breath and said, 'Writing is largely a losing game. You'll soon find that out. In an average year, ten thousand short stories reach our office. We publish thirty-six. Figure the odds out for yourself.' I said, 'Ah, but you *do* accept thirty-six.'"

"Nice going, Peggy. What did he say to that?"

"He looked a little sheepish for a minute; then he said, 'True, a magazine is due to get all the worst of it. Robert Louis Stevenson remarked something to the effect that "Anybody can write a short story—a bad one. But not everybody can write even a bad book. It is the length that kills." ' And then he really let me have it."

Peggy sat silent for a minute; she must get this next part exactly right. Then, almost as if she were listening and then repeating after the absent Mr. Ferrar, she began, "He came bang out and advised me, 'Write your own book! Write it just as it comes to you. Take yourself for your central character if you like; most beginning authors do. Write about a woman who is young, sensitive, eager, more than half con-

[170]

vinced that the world is her oyster.' I said, 'You make her sound a little bit brash.' I was trying not to admit even to myself how thrilled I was; I added, 'Is that the right word?' He answered, 'Brash is the word, perhaps. But behind the impudence of youth lies a terrible uncertainty.'" Peggy drew a long breath and came out of her trance.

"That was wonderful!" cried Alice. "I think he really gave you an idea. Mull it over, and perhaps you'll find that you can actually get a start on your book." Incongruously that title of Peggy's recurred to her: *You Don't Say So.* Alice hadn't heard her repeat it in some time. Perhaps young Miss Pratt had reached the place where she was the one who didn't say so.

"I thought you'd like it. I think you'll like him." Peggy spoke slowly, and the color rose in her cheeks.

"I—will like Mr. Walter Ferrar? When and where—?" stammered Alice.

"He told me there was a lot more to talk over, but he had to get back to the office. Then he went on, 'Won't you come out with me for dinner some time soon? Then we'll really have a chance to take our hair down. I'm unmarried, a middlewesterner, seldom go beyond my second cocktail, and have no police record. Please say "Yes."'"

"He sounds amusing." Alice's tone was flat.

"He sounds glib—and practiced. I think he has used that speech before."

"So you went ahead and turned him down?"

"Turn him down? After coming all this distance and spending all this time here in New York? He really may have something to say to me! Besides, I—I sort of like him."

"You accepted, then? Did you set the date?"

"We set the date, and the place. I suggested that he call for me at Waverley Book Shop."

Alice laughed aloud. Peggy had undoubtedly had other experiences with men in the Big City; and she had not come here out of a nunnery. By this maneuver she not only protected herself but afforded her friend Mrs. Martin a chance to give him the old family look-over.

All of this was duly reported to Mr. Martin, who rolled the morsel under his tongue. "A young woman who wears her engagement ring on her right hand, if at all, and a man who brings up the subject of love an hour after he meets a new girl! I would say young Peggy could write a book about that—if she can write a book at all, which still remains to be seen."

Walter Ferrar duly appeared to keep his date. He paid his respects to the book shop, too. He was fortyish, nice looking without being precisely handsome, never at a loss for something to say. He made a very good impression on the Martins. Just before the two of them went off to keep their date, Peggy whispered to Alice, "Mind if he returns me here just this once? It won't be later than ten o'clock."

Walter Ferrar duly returned her, and Harry Martin walked her back to her own apartment. On the way Peggy confided to him that she had given Ferrar her phone number, which was listed in the name of the man from whom she sublet the apartment.

On a second date, then, she let him pick her up at home and return her there. A third date followed in due course. Then Peggy decided that she wished to have him in for dinner. He couldn't misunderstand that, could he? And what should she give him to eat?

He didn't strike Alice as the sort of man who would turn a home dinner for two into a wrestling match. The fact that he was still a bachelor at his age might not mean a thing. It might mean that he fell in love with every pretty face he saw. In that case, they would soon find out. Give him steak and one cocktail before dinner.

"I wonder how much writing Peggy is doing these days," Harry Martin speculated to Alice.

[172]

"I have no means of guessing accurately, and I don't like to ask," Alice said demurely. "There was an old story handed down in my mother's family about a farm boy who was given the job of hoeing corn. Some time later he was asked for a report on what he had done. He answered, 'Soon's I finish this one an' that one an' them two an' two more, I'll have six.'"

In Alice's mother's family! Young Miss Frederickson from upstate New York. Young Harry Martin had picked her up in a bookish way, too; had indeed spoken to her for the first time in the New York Public Library of a dull Sunday afternoon. *He* had taken *her* out for coffee, and thereby started something. Eh, but that was a long time ago!

"She has from now till the end of June to make up her mind about him," Alice went on. "That is, if it comes to a question of making up her mind. The affair is yet young."

"And so is she," Harry said with lingering relish. "But look here, June won't make it a year for her. She came to New York last fall just after Labor Day."

"It's the academic year. By that time she will know where she stands, too."

"She will stand at a crossroads. There's an old story by O. Henry, I remember, 'Roads of Destiny.' It takes a man down all three of those possible roads. It will be a very good story to include in my anthology."

Oh, but he was very happy with his anthology! He was getting around to Kipling now. Harry would certainly omit all the old grinds. Legend had it that the author had thrown "Recessional" into the wastebasket, whence Mrs. Kipling's pious hands rescued it. If the author had really wanted to get rid of that screed, he could have destroyed it properly instead of publishing it.

"The Ballad of East and West" was out, too. A little too English and old school tie and Don'-che-know. So was "Mandalay," that victim of all bad baritones. And "If," that cheering erection of false standards which doctors read to their "nervous" patients. But most decidedly in was that lovely short lyric about how the Queen of Sheba and King Solomon "talked to butterflies when they took their walks abroad." In was the one about the Builder who built in vain, but did manage to leave a message for others vainly striving. In was Diego Valdez, High Admiral of Spain, discounting his fabulous career and yearning for the hardships of his youth. In was aging Queen Elizabeth, who refused to look at herself in a mirror, dance though she might.

I'm getting so I envy youth, Harry thought grimly. *Envy youth, and almost hate the young.* And he must remember to include those infinitely sad lines of Charles Lamb about "the old familiar faces."

Though the biggest credit of all must go to "that great author Anonymous." Harry made a note to that effect, and at once felt better.

Aloud he said, "A neat little drama is working itself out on our doorstep. We are lucky to have box seats. All I hope is that young Peggy Pratt doesn't fall between two stools."

"It just might happen," Alice agreed. Then she smiled suddenly. "If she should, by any chance—though I don't see her doing it—that young person would get quite a jar. But she would presently pick herself up and reach for a third stool."

" 'You don't say so!' " chimed Harry. Once more they laughed together. The Martins had laughed together for so many years. Surely too they had years enough ahead in which to keep on doing so.

15

Children were great collectors. make one of them a promise, and the child would take care that you kept it.

Little Nina Babcock showed up at Waverley Book Shop every Saturday afternoon. Alice always gave her a book of some kind. She took Nina out with her, sometimes to the soda fountain in a neighborhood drugstore, sometimes to the lunchroom where Alice often had coffee with a grown-up friend. The men behind the counter knew her now and called her by name. That too was important. Young or old, we all crave recognition.

Mrs. Martin loved doing this much for the little girl. In her way she enjoyed it just as much as Nina herself did. But she had the feeling that it just wasn't enough. A regular treat like this meant a good deal to a child; she not only enjoyed it while it lasted, she also had it to look forward to all week, and she had something to take home with her afterward to brighten her evening and perhaps her Sunday too: something to add to a growing collection. How important that was Alice remembered vividly from the days when she used to give parties for her own children, and always saw to it that each small guest had something to take home from the party. A trophy prolonged the festivity; it helped a short memory, too.

Ah, but the "home" to which Nina Babcock took those weekly books of hers wasn't like the home Jim and Jean Martin had known in their childhood! It wasn't like the homes to which their little friends had returned in good old Brooklyn. It was where Nina boarded with "Aunt Agnes." It might be as satisfactory as the place where she had boarded with "Aunt Edie." It was surely better than a public institution. Presumably it afforded a decent measure of comfort. But how about that emotional security which was so important to a child? If Nina were allowed to grow up without that, she would be very badly equipped to face the complexities of adult life.

Strictly speaking, this was none of Alice Martin's business. But she had grown very fond of the little girl. Kindhearted bystanders could always associate themselves with treats for children, and enjoy sharing in the fun; enjoy making themselves liked, too, of course. But since the responsibility was not theirs, they could step aside afterward. It was the customary, and the common-sense, way to act.

But Alice was deterred not only by her affection for Nina. She remembered so vividly the time when with quivering lip the little girl had reported, "My mommy was mean to me." Mrs. Martin could not very well go poking into the affair herself. But if she could manage to find out a little more, find out possibly through somebody else . . . A second point of view was highly desirable, and would keep Alice from implicating herself too deeply.

The following Saturday she not only gave Nina a book to take home with her and read; at the last minute Alice added a small dictionary. "You're getting to be such a big girl now, you must often want to look things up. Not in the new book, maybe; that might spoil the fun. But when you read the old ones over, there may be things you find you haven't quite understood. Mr. Thayer will carry your package home for you. Here, Bill, tie this up and deliver it, will you please?"

Nina protested, but not too hard. Being escorted home would prolong the party. She might even ask him to come in when they reached Aunt Agnes': to come in for a minute and get warm. Aunt Agnes had made one or two slighting remarks about "those Saturday friends of yours," though she wasn't all that fond of having Nina underfoot the whole live-long Saturday.

Mr. Thayer picked up the parcel and the two of them set forth. Nina was proud to show him the way; she chattered along as they proceeded. Bill loved being sent on this errand; he only hoped that Mrs. Martin was setting a precedent.

He owed her a report, however. Back at the book shop he gave it rather dryly. "It isn't a place where I'd like a daughter of mine to live. There are four little girls packed into two bedrooms; Nina has to sleep with one of them in a bed only about big enough for herself alone. She has her books all lined up, though. She introduced me very proudly and properly."

"You're glad you went?" asked Alice.

"I'd like to do more than that for the little girl. But Lord, a bachelor and a bookman—!" Bill shrugged despondently.

He was a bookman from choice. There were other ways to make a living, some of them more remunerative. Many of them, in fact, though this one had its special joys and satisfactions. But he was a bachelor simply because Marion Murdock insisted on refusing himself for his own good.

An idea was shaping itself inside Alice's head. An idea so gorgeous and glittering that she scarcely dared acknowledge it even to herself. "A daughter of mine," Bill Thayer had said. There you were: the American male with his cherished ideal

[177]

of the perfect child. In making his factual report, he had no idea how completely he'd given himself away.

The next step was going to take time. Meanwhile, however, Alice would suggest that Bill walk Nina home on other occasions. He needn't always have something to carry for her. Nina would love his escort any day; and if the Martins chose to pay Bill Thayer a salary for doing things which were not, strictly speaking, book shop business, that was between him and them.

Marion Murdock refused to enter with Bill Thayer into a marriage which must be childless. Alice Martin loved her children, missed them now that they were so far away, kept in touch with them the best she could. But she honestly felt that producing children wasn't the be-all and the end-all of marriage. The Johnsons had no children, and appeared not to feel the lack. In fact, Ben opened up that very spring with a fresh opportunity for Bess.

She came into Waverley Book Shop to report it. "Ben just thought up an opening for me. I've been writing verses for our greeting cards for years. It makes the whole thing seem so much more personal than if a person just buys a handful of cards and directs them. Well, Ben typed off a couple of my past efforts. They were still lying around the house. Oh, I'm sure I have a copy here!" She rummaged in the depths of her handbag and drew forth two slightly crumpled sheets. "Here we are."

Alice read off the shorter:

> I'm thinking of you,
> As I so often do,
> And I'm telling you so!
> Else how would you know?

"That's to be printed on the inside, I find now," Bess explained. "When I wrote it I gave it a title: a different title for each recipient. But now it will just say on the outside, in large decorative letters, 'Thinking Of You.' Then here's another one. This I wrote for last Christmas, and called it, 'It's Coming!' "

Alice had received one of those cards; but she read now with closer attention:

> The twenty-fifth is almost here—
> The day which all of us hold dear.
> Christmas greetings and Christmas cheer.
> All my best in the Brave New Year.
> Pluck up hope and cast out fear.
> Sail ahead! The coast is clear.

"I never realized that anybody wrote these," said Alice. "I won't say I thought they 'jest growed,' like Topsy. I never thought about the matter at all."

"Neither did I. But Ben wrote a letter on his office stationery, and sent these two to a big greeting-card firm. He said they were his wife's work. They sent me a small check and said they'd be glad to see more of my work."

"But Bess, how lovely!" Alice waited until Harry was free to give him their attention, then she laid the case before him.

"A versicle like these will never snatch the laurels from the brow of Keats or Shelley, or even Ben's namesake 'rare,' Ben Jonson," Bess explained. "I won't even have the fun of seeing my name appear in print. But an acceptance is an acceptance; and Ben is altogether responsible. Isn't that darling of him?"

"Are you going to have the check framed?" asked Harry facetiously.

Bess laughed. "I spoke about that. But Ben had the check photostated, so that I could keep it and spend it too. Only I'm not spending it. I've opened a savings account with it—after all these years."

Alice began to count on her fingers. "There are other holidays in the year. There are birthdays and anniversaries. There are 'get-well' cards."

Bess nodded. "The best part of it all is that Ben thought of me. Since he no longer writes plays, we have lovely quiet evenings together whenever he doesn't have to catch an opening. He works at his articles, or just sits back and reads, or even listens to the radio like any other husband. I've had him to myself more even than I used to have him when he was a run-of-the-mill reporter and we were newlyweds."

"Wait until the Depression ends and the theater picks up again and producers begin once more to buy options on plays," said Harry in a voice of doom.

"Killjoy!" Bess lunged for him with her handbag. It was not firmly clasped, and the contents proceeded to spill out all over the shop. The Martins helped her gather up the miscellany. At the last minute Harry redeemed himself by saying, "Somebody even makes up the crossword puzzles, I suppose. There are lots of different ways to earn a living. Most of them are safer than sticking up a bank, too. The police often catch their man, even when it isn't in a whodunit by Donald Burgess and they haven't any assistance from a garrulous bookseller who is smarter than people give him credit for being. Which is not saying much!"

He had some further light on another way to make a living only a day or so later. A new customer came into the shop. She was a shapely piece somewhere in her thirties or early forties; she was wearing no make-up except a very vivid lipstick, but she sported a rather noticeable perfume. Alice Martin, who never used anything stronger than lavender toilet water, wrinkled her nose slightly; but she smiled her greeting. "Good afternoon. Come in and look around. If you're in search of something special, perhaps I can help you."

"Just looking for something to read," said the lady lightly. "Something as far as possible from what I write."

"Tell me what you've written," Alice encouraged. "Perhaps we have some of your books in stock."

"I don't sign my stuff." The lady answered Alice; but she was looking at Harry. "My name is Gloria Gregory. I may make it famous some day; but meanwhile I have to keep the pot boiling. I write for the 'confessions' magazines."

Alice had more than once picked up a selection of such magazines in a drugstore; odd numbers she had seen at her hairdresser's before she switched to the present Village establishment. The stories were all presented as fact; they were all written in the first person; they were all of a deliberate sexiness which stopped short of absolute pornography, yet constantly skirted the subject. The utter stupidity of the performances amazed Alice. Doubtless there was a public for this sort of diluted slime, or the magazines couldn't have remained in business. But that there was a living in writing it—!

"A lot of your readers must believe that all those things actually happen," she said noncommitally.

"That's one of the tricks of the trade. It's not nearly so easy as it looks."

Gloria Gregory eventually made her selection entirely from the bargain tables; but it was a fairly large selection. "You deliver?" she asked. This time she not only looked at Harry; she spoke to him.

Alice answered for him. "Mr. Martin will carry your package home for you. Is it right in the neighborhood?"

It was. Gloria Gregory gave an address on the other side of Seventh Avenue, west and south of Commerce Street. Alice had sometimes explored around that neighborhood; it was where Greenwich Village got very Villagy indeed. Now it was Harry Martin's turn to poke around there; but he could do it in the sacred name of business.

He took his time about it. But he was back in Waverley

Book Shop for a chance encounter. A strange man stopped in to verify the time. Harry would know him again. While he was about it, the stranger seemed to size up the shop and its proprietor. Doubtless he in his turn could have described Harry Martin.

Something in the encounter struck Harry as just a little suspicious. He must remember to describe it to Don Burgess the next time he saw him. Since Don had been gracious enough to put Harry into a book, the least return Harry could make was to offer Don a little material.

The next time Don came into the shop, Harry remembered to tell him about the episode. "Something fishy there somewhere," he wound up. "Looked as if he was establishing a false alibi."

"The oldest trick in the business," Don agreed. "Between the covers of one of my books, it would be such an old trick that the only way I could intelligently use it would be to have the transgressor do it deliberately. Or have him a plainclothesman who wishes for some reason to be mistaken for a crook. But right here on Seventh Avenue, in what we laughingly call 'real life,' I suspect that he was just a bird who was late for an appointment with his wife."

"Why with his wife necessarily?"

"With his sweetie he would be on time. Elementary, Watson, elementary. Still, it sounds like an interesting episode. Describe him to me."

That just wasn't so easy to do. "He was fiftyish, average height, medium coloring, sturdily built, well dressed—"

"What impressed you most about him?" Don asked when Harry hesitated.

"His lips were pressed together in a straight line."

"That's better. He talked—?"

"Very little. Something like, 'Can you tell me the exact time?' and, 'My watch is right, then, after all.' "

"And his voice?"

"Just a good average voice. No foreign accent."

"It sounds like the perfect description of an equivocal character." Don couldn't quite keep the amusement out of his tone.

Harry's suspicions came alive. He repeated. " 'An equivocal character.' You think you know who it was?"

"I couldn't take my oath on it; but your description sounds like my publisher."

"In here by coincidence?"

"Most unlikely. The man has been interested by that character who so libelously resembles you. Wants me to put the noble amateur, the bookseller, into another production. When I had received his suggestion I went on to mention your anthology project. Not unkindly, you may be sure. He may have dropped by to have a look at you in both capacities."

"Does that sound likely?"

"Unlikely enough so that I'd never get it past him in one of my scripts. The subordinates in such a firm as Knowles & Wingate are kept busy enough; but the higher-ups have a hard time keeping themselves in work."

This had been Peggy Pratt's experience. Long as Harry Martin had been in the book business, he was lately getting new sights on it.

"This might be Mr. Knowles, or Mr. Wingate?" he asked.

"Sounds to me like Old Pop Knowles himself. Mr. Herbert Knowles, at your service—more or less."

Sure enough, the stranger reappeared a fortnight later, looked over the used-book tables with an especial eye to publisher's names, and came inside to compliment the shop.

"Thank you for those kind words," said Harry. "You're in the business yourself, Mr.—?"

"Knowles," supplied the stranger.

"Any relation to Herbert Knowles the publisher?"

"I'm not all that famous. My given name would scarcely

have penetrated far in the trade. Somebody has been talking."

"Somebody did make a guess at your identity. He's a good friend, Don Burgess."

"And a good author." They shook hands on it, and Knowles added, "Don't quote me as saying that." As if Harry wouldn't! As if Knowles had really expected him not to!

"I've looked your place over. Suppose you come up and do the same for mine one of these days. Just give your secretary my name and she'll be glad to make an appointment," Mr. Knowles invited.

Harry said he would, and felt a warm glow at his heart. His anthology was by no means as good as accepted. But it always pays to know a man. When the man in question makes himself known, the indications are very hopeful indeed.

Harry took another batch of work to his typist. He went over his lists of selections, and was pleased and a little startled not only at the variety but at the amount of matter they showed. Already he had enough for a thick volume. An anthology must have size; he had handled enough of them at Waverley Book Shop to know that. Much of the arranging was as good as done, too, and many of the short forewords were written.

There still remained to be entered that greatest of all stories, "The Man Without a Country." There was that wonderful screed of Elbert Hubbard's, "A Message to Garcia," all about how hard it was for an employer to get even the simplest task performed promptly and properly. Copies of both those works, Harry thought, they had in their Brooklyn flat.

He consulted Alice, who agreed with him. Did he want her to go over and fetch them? Harry did not. He wanted to go over and read them there.

Alice smiled. "The Brooklyn place is still home to you? I've thought sometimes perhaps we were a little extravagant to keep that and the Greenwich Village apartment too. But the old railroad flat is where we lived when the children were small; we spent some very happy years there. It gives us a chance to house Jean and her husband when they come for a visit; we see more of them that way than if they put up at a hotel. It gives us a chance to get a little change while we're still running the shop for all it's worth."

"Are you arguing down your own feeling that it's an extravagance?" Harry patted her shoulder. "Wait until my anthology comes out, and we'll be wealthy beyond the dreams of avarice."

"Scarcely that; but it should have a steady sale," said Alice judicially. "We'll make a double profit on all the copies we sell in the shop."

The Brooklyn flat was always stocked with staples; the Martins' Carrie saw to it that the place was kept clean and two beds always freshly made up: that in the front bedroom, where the couple slept, and that in the one which had been Jean's, where it had been Alice's habit to do her late reading. It made a delightful change for the Martins. Even the subway ride was fun when you didn't have to keep taking it as a matter of course.

Behold the Martins, then, entering their Brooklyn first floor armed with a steak and suitable accompaniments for their late dinner. "It's a real change," remarked Alice. "I shall not say, like the Vicar of Wakefield's migration from the blue bed to the brown."

"Those literary allusions are fun: saying that you won't say what you are saying," remarked Harry.

"Only just don't make a habit of them, you mean? Cocktail, Harry? I think we still have the makings of one hereabouts."

Over their dinner Harry remarked, "This is still our voting residence, isn't it? Of course in New York, where we have to register afresh every year, we can easily change that. But

[185]

when we register in October, are we going to do it here in Brooklyn?"

"Here in Brooklyn is my guess. We've registered before—I don't like to think how many times. There was no woman suffrage, was there, when this building was erected?"

"No, and the living room was called the parlor. Some things change—" Harry slipped back into one of his Latin quotations. Were they actually going to see the light at last? If so, he could claim credit as translator. As editor, he was running some of his own work in his compendium. That was one way to get your writings published. If published! Bright as his prospects seemed, this was still the time for Harry Martin to keep his fingers crossed.

Alice had not brought along any of her taskwork. This once she was free to read purely for pleasure. But when they established themselves in the living room with Harry's two selections, she said, "You take the one you're going to read first and give me the other."

Harry obediently handed over "A Message to Garcia."

"Music?" asked Alice, gesturing toward the radio.

"Not for me, thanks. I want to take this full in the face."

Harry read; and it was as if he were reading "The Man Without a Country" for the first time. A good writer had got hold of a great subject; he wrote as if inspired, and for this work alone he was remembered. Harry recollected, indeed, that when it was published the work had made such a sensation that Edward Everett Hale had to come out publicly and admit that it was fiction.

It carries such conviction, Harry thought. *But so far as I'm concerned, "Rip Van Winkle" is the same. While I'm reading it I believe it.*

Alice had already finished her first assignment. Exchanging volumes with her, Harry said, "To write or edit or publish or sell anything like this is a treat. But it does bring with it its own problems."

"There are some kinds of problems it's fun to solve. You're up against one right now, I take it."

"I sure am. I've tried ever so many titles; and I haven't yet hit on one that is really satisfactory."

"You can submit them all. Or better, perhaps, submit the one which is best, and hope that they will like it better than you do."

"No title is final until a book actually goes into print; and 'Another Treasury' is still far from reaching that stage." Suddenly Harry began to laugh. "I'm different from Peggy Pratt. She started off with a title and nothing else. Alice, what's the name of her Oregon suitor? The one she's engaged to on the wrong hand. Did you ever hear it?"

"His given name is Frank. If I ever heard his surname I've forgotten it."

"I don't think it's really worth your memorizing. If she ever goes back to the Coast and takes it for hers, I suppose they'll send us a wedding announcement."

"It's none of my business," said Alice, "but I can't help wondering what she is up to these days."

"Must you always be so suspicious?"

Alice shrugged and picked up the book with which Harry had finished. He tackled the one about hired help. It had been published back at the turn of the century; but it held true all these years later, held true even during these days of the continuing Depression. Only too many hirelings were interested, not in the job, but in collecting their pay and in doing as little as they possibly could to earn it.

Harry read over once more, "It is not book learning that young men need, nor instruction about this and that, but a stiffening of the vertebrae which will cause them to be loyal to a trust, to act promptly, concentrate their energies, do a thing—'carry a message to Garcia.'" He went back and read the opening paragraph about how during the Spanish-American War President McKinley needed to communicate with

[187]

the Cuban guerrila General Garcia, whose whereabouts in the jungle was unknown, was told that "a man named Rowan" would carry the message for him, and sent for Rowan. Rowan did just that.

Harry scribbled, "This is so sadly true! That there aren't many such people around. It will require a footnote on Rowan, perhaps." He had not yet considered the question of footnotes.

Aloud he said, "We were mighty lucky when we hired Bill Thayer." Alice waved for silence. Harry sat back, and a bit of doggerel began to run through his head.

> Hip, hip!
> I had a good job and I quit!
> Then why don't you work like other men do?
> Why, how can I work when there's nothing to do?

It put the depressionist's philosophy very well indeed. He forbore to mention it to Alice, however. When she finally closed her book and winked away a few tears, he said quietly, "I hope Bill Thayer never quits."

Alice was startled. "Bill? Has he said anything about—?" Then she caught herself and smiled. "He would be hard to replace. Harry, when you've seen your anthology through the press, I'll be glad for more reasons than one."

"You hear a lot too much about it?"

"Not a lot, but perhaps just a little. I was thinking more, though, about what Bess Johnson said when Ben gave up playwrighting: she's happy now to have her husband to herself."

That was very good hearing for Harry Martin. Perhaps it was the influence of the return to their old home. Perhaps the fault was in him rather than in her, for lately Harry had been sensing, or imagining, a coldness on her part. But that night they had a loving time together, and once more it meant everything to him.

Later in their different ways they both recalled it with a certain bitterness. 1932 was not only the year of a Presidential election, and the triennium of the Depression; it marked a turning point for the Martins.

16

ALICE KEPT CALENDARS AT THE SHOP AND AT BOTH RESI-
dences as a matter of course, though she seldom consulted one.
She had heard of solitary people who blocked out each passing
day; it seemed to her a forlorn thing to do, though perhaps it
gave them some queer kind of satisfaction. A glance at the
newspaper was enough for her if she needed help; but in her
busy life she seldom did. She could tell the days of the week
by the customers. The weeks themselves moved in seasons, as
publication and personal dates indicated.

Easter was a lovely season. The great annual rebirth stirred
everything to fresh life. Its celebration might take any one of
many forms; but celebrated it had to be in one way or another. The great force must find vent.

It had no particular impact on the book business. Perhaps
Alice Martin enjoyed it all the more for that reason. Not that
Waverley wouldn't have done the work and pocketed the
profits if books had become as popular for Easter gifts as they
were for Christmas. The way things stood, however, the flo-
rists and the greeting card people now had their harvest sea-

son. With the Martins, about now outgo always exceeded income. But then, Alice Martin reasoned, what was the good of having charge accounts if a person never used them?

She intended this year to use one of hers harder than ever, and try to make up the difference later. Or if she didn't manage to do so, that would be right in keeping with the spirit of the age. Poor old President Hoover had kept bumbling about how "The budget must be balanced." The country had gone sailing along with an unbalanced budget. But if you stopped to think about such discrepancies, you never would get anything done.

What Mrs. Martin proposed to do was buy Nina Babcock a complete Easter outfit, which would include not only stylish togs for the great day itself, but enough stockings, underwear, and plain frocks to take her through the spring season and the summer as well. This was not the first time she had made purchases for Nina; nor was an enlargement of the scale any feature to be remarked on. What was different this time was that Alice proposed to have a collaborator. She asked Bill Thayer what would be a good time for her to get in touch with Marion Murdock.

Telephoning Marion, Alice announced that she had a favor to ask. "You must feel quite free to say 'No' if you feel that I am asking too much." After that opening, of course, there was no denying such a simple request as to meet Alice and a good friend of hers at Wanamaker's the following Saturday afternoon. "It won't take more than an hour or so of your time. What I want is the advantage of a younger woman's judgment . . . You will? Oh, that's lovely of you! I do appreciate your taking the time."

Marion caught step with them promptly. She gave Alice the benefit of her advice only to a very limited extent; but she added a few items of her own choosing. An overwhelmed Nina was presently escorted back to Aunt Agnes' by two ladies carrying so many packages that they looked like the enthusiastic shoppers in the cartoons.

Nina took them in with only a casual introduction to Aunt Agnes, who might be a kind woman in her way, but was desperately common and to Alice's eye not quite clean. The little girl who happened to be at home in their overcrowded bedroom Nina didn't even introduce; she simply said, "Hello, there." But she displayed with infinite pride the carefully stacked books with which Alice had regularly presented her.

"I let Gracie and the others look at these on Sundays if their hands are clean," she said. Then, as an afterthought, she pulled Alice's head down and whispered, "I can let them have my old clothes now, can't I? And maybe just a few of the new ones. Their mommies are poor like mine."

"Share your gifts by all means," Alice said, and kissed her. She forbore to look at Marion Murdock; but she knew that the byplay hadn't gone unnoticed.

Alice paused to give the landlady a five-dollar bill and to wish her a Happy Easter. But she realized to the full what Bill Thayer had meant when he said he wouldn't want any daughter of his to live like that.

At the corner the two ladies parted, Marion to return to her own concerns and Alice on her way back to the book shop. Marion shook hands almost too hard; and there was a suspicion of a choke in her voice when she said, "Those things go on around us all the time? Thank you for giving me a chance to help."

"Lonesome children stuck away in a corner somewhere," Alice emphasized. "Still, it's better than herding them into an institution."

Back in Waverley Book Shop she reported to Bill Thayer, "Marion Murdock was awfully sweet this afternoon." He waited for her to go on, but Alice didn't. Let Marion tell her own story, if she had really been as impressed as she seemed.

Mrs. Martin had fish of her own to fry, anyhow. Her spouse

hated to shop, and ducked the task shamelessly. It was a part of her wifely duty to see that he had adequate shirts and underwear and socks. Why didn't they tell brides those things, instead of all that nonsense about the birds and the flowers? As long as a suit was clean and whole, he saw no reason for replacing it. Men's hats, he insisted, looked all alike to him. People came into the book shop to look at the books, not at the proprietor. When he went anywhere with her, people looked at Alice, not at him. The same old threadbare excuses, and no action.

More than once she had bulldozed him into going with her to the large and elaborate Men's Store of her favorite emporium. Harry had on the whole enjoyed the experience; but he had learned no lesson from it. The struggle would be just as bad the next time.

The following afternoon Harry went off on one of his mail-order errands. During a lull in business at the book shop, Alice laid the case before Bill Thayer, and wound up, "Couldn't you offer to go with him when he does his Easter shopping? He might not feel so silly if he were led around by a man instead of by a woman who is so obviously his wife."

"Offer to go? How could he help knowing that the offer was prompted?"

"You could tell him that you want to buy Marion Murdock an Easter present, and suggest that he do the same for me. Then once you got him in the store, you could steer him."

Bill was doubtful, but said he would try. The transparent trick failed. Harry Martin grinned and answered, "It's a splendid idea. You go ahead and buy two scarfs or blouses or something. Charge them both to me. You can settle with me when the bill comes."

"I want to buy myself a new hat, too," Bill persisted. "I'd like the benefit of your judgment."

"My judgment isn't worth a red cent," Harry answered

cheerfully. "Why don't you take the woman Alice with you? She has excellent taste."

"All right, then. You guessed it. Mrs. Martin thinks you need some new clothes, and she suggested that I accompany you when you buy them."

"Why didn't you say so in the first place?" asked Harry. "You don't give the poor old bookman credit for very much brains. Sure I'll go. Just settle with Mrs. M. on a date when she can spare both of us."

This unusual docility made Alice a little suspicious, though of what she could not say. Her suspicion vanished quickly. It was just too bad if she found herself disappointed when she looked for trouble and didn't get it.

Alice actually spent most of that designated afternoon listening to Peggy Pratt. Peggy as usual wanted to take Alice somewhere where she could confide in her. Finding that Alice was tending shop alone, she made her confession in spurts. But make it she really must; she was full of emotion which demanded an outlet.

Peggy was doing a great deal of writing these days. She had not formally started a book; or if she had, it was not a novel. She wrote down things as they came to her. She had told that to Walter Ferrar, but hadn't yet shown him anything she wrote. He highly approved of what she was doing. "Get it out of your system," he had counseled. "Get into the habit of writing, too. It isn't a thing which a person can pick up at intervals, like a piece of needlework." Or again, "You're very new at the job. But you *are* beginning."

All of that meant little or nothing in Alice's opinion. Still, it helped to keep the couple out of mischief. Walter Ferrar wasn't the first person who ever acted as if he knew what he was talking about, nor Peggy Pratt the first who ever dirtied up a lot of fine fair paper. Mrs. Martin gave them her approval; or at least she listened and forbore to discourage.

"He wants me to spend Easter Day with him," Peggy

wound up. "Attend the Easter Parade uptown, and then go somewhere and eat, and then maybe take a bus ride or hire a taxi or something."

"Take a horse-drawn cab around Central Park. That's one of the features of New York. You mean you haven't had that experience before?"

"No, though I've seen the old buggies drive off with couples in them. It always looked to me like a—a quaint thing for them to do. Do you think it would be all right for me to suggest that?"

"Quite all right. It will give you something to write home about." Alice couldn't help it if she sounded a little dry.

Peggy had the grace to blush. She rose rather hastily. "I've written to Daddy that I'm doing a lot of writing now. He's very much pleased with that. He says he's always been sure that I could do whatever I set out to do."

"I know. When you're young it's hard to make up your mind." Alice waited for further remarks along that line; but they were not forthcoming. She was driven to tell her reasons for being alone so long in the shop. She still hadn't learned fiancé Frank's surname. Or was he only half fiancé? Or by this time former fiancé? There were some questions a person simply couldn't ask. But Alice had done her bit for today, not only by listening, but by putting in that suggestion about the horse-drawn cab. She hoped, however, that Walter Ferrar would have sense enough to broach the idea himself.

It gave Alice a pretext for intervening once more in a case which was after all closer to her heart. When Harry Martin and Bill Thayer tumbled in with part of their purchases and their tale of the rest, she listened and approved. Then she presently found a chance to put in a real two cents' worth. She hesitated an instant before she did so; it is possible that a well-wisher may sometimes be downright meddlesome. But finally she blurted out, "Bill, if you're taking Marion Murdock out on Easter Day, why don't you arrange to pick up little Nine Babcock sometime during the afternoon? You two could take her for a ride around Central Park in a horse-drawn cab. Do it, and watch the little girl open her eyes. She has never had an experience anything like that."

She was going pretty far. Bill actually stammered when he said, "I—I'll speak to Marion about it. I don't know what she'll think of the idea."

"Tell her I'm to blame for it," said Alice saucily. She opened the cash register, extracted a five-dollar bill, and held it out to him. "Here, let me pay for it. Then I can feel that I'm sharing in the fun."

Bill suddenly realized the full beauty of the scheme. He not only accepted the money; he shook Alice's hand heartily. Then they were both a little embarrassed. Harry helped them out by launching into a highly colored account of their afternoon's expedition. Alice was up to her old interfering tricks. But poor little Nina Babcock could do with all the happiness that kindhearted adults managed to bestow on her.

So Easter was all set. Alice looked forward to it, and refused to look beyond it. She was doing very well thus far. There were times when it paid to take the short view; this was definitely one of them.

Alice had bought a new hat; with a new blouse and accessories, last year's suit would do very nicely indeed. Harry was the member of the household who was getting the new clothes this time. So Alice held until Holy Week itself. Then, when the stocks had been pretty well picked over, the saleswomen were tired, and there was the usual rush of last-minute shoppers, she bought herself a new suit anyhow. She was, after all, just as good as the masculine member of the firm. She was the one, too, who loved and appreciated good clothes.

Jean and Jim both telegraphed flowers. Alice kept the tributes in the shop until they closed on Easter Eve; then she had Harry and Bill lug them up to the apartment. She herself lingered for a moment to unearth and display their "Closed Today" sign. It was almost never used. Even apart from the absence of the sidewalk tables, a shop with no sales-people on duty could clearly expect to do no business.

Alice hummed a little tune as she ran up the stairs of the apartment building. The Martins were going out for dinner tomorrow. A greater luxury still, they had a long evening to spend at home.

She found Harry already enjoying it. Divested of his coat and collar, he was deep in his newspaper. She disposed of the Easter flowers to the best advantage, reread all the Easter cards, and put them back on the mantel. She visited the kitchen briefly, made sandwiches and salad and put them in the refrigerator. Then she put on her best negligee and re-entered the living room. Without even glancing up from his newspaper, Harry handed her the second section.

Alice let it lie in her lap. Clasping her hands behind her head, she leaned back in her armchair and stared up at the ceiling. Harry, coming to retrieve the second section of the newspaper, saw that she had not touched it and demanded, "What on earth are you doing?"

"As nearly as possible, nothing," said Alice sweetly. But the charm was broken. She began to think. Presently she went for paper and fountain pen. Using a magazine laid on her knee for a desk, she began to write a letter to her daughter:

"Jean darling, It's Easter Eve. I'm writing to thank you for your lovely flowers, which I'm at full liberty to enjoy. Your father and I closed the shop early and came up here for an hour's relaxation. That is, I relaxed for an hour. He read his newspaper, which is simply a routine daily duty, like brushing one's teeth.

"How did primitive man put in his time, do you suppose, before civilization imposed its round of tasks upon him? In animal satisfactions alternating with physical distress? Per-haps there were spells of fantasy even very early."

Alice rested a minute, and read over what she had written. She would have hated to live before there was writing and reading. But the spoken word must go even farther back. Tradition was a powerful force among unlettered peoples.

Was she getting in a little deep? At least she was writing a letter, and that was better than scanning the ceiling for possible cobwebs. The hardest thing for Alice to do was to do nothing. That was an awful sentence; she would never dare to put it into a letter. But she did know what she meant.

"We have some lovely plans for tomorrow," she scribbled on. "A good plan is fun in itself, isn't it? The eve of a holiday may be given up to plans, which impart to it a charm all its own. Christmas Eve has been immortalized in a classic. How all children love that one! Easter Eve hasn't yet been done, so far as I know. Perhaps the material isn't really there. Perhaps a thing like that ought to be seen through the eyes of children."

Glancing up, Alice caught Harry's eye fixed upon her. "I'm writing the things out the way they come to me, just as Peggy's Walter advised her to," she explained. "Only I'm putting them in the form of a letter to Jean. I started out to thank her for her flowers; but I'm afraid I wandered pretty far from the subject."

"You could have said, 'Dear Jean, thank you for the flowers. It was sweet of you to send them. Your father joins me in all good wishes.' You could even have bought a card which has 'Thank you' printed on it. That would be better than no acknowledgment at all. They do say letter writing is a lost art nowadays. You and Jean don't seem to have found it so."

"All right, then. You may add your two cents' worth. Then I'll lay it aside until Monday. Or no, maybe I'd better not. I'll finish it off and let it go for what it is. Another day a person can always write another letter."

While Harry was writing his message, Alice began to track another line of thought. We habitually said "primitive man" as if primitive men were all alike. Of course along certain broad lines the generalizaton held true: "primitive man" differed from "modern man," for instance, when it came to believing in magic. But one modern man differed so intensely from other modern men! Yes, and plenty of men alive nowadays, and civilized enough in lots of ways, still threw spilled salt over their shoulders and rapped three times on wood after they found that they had bragged. Humorously, perhaps; but even their humor helped to keep the superstition alive.

Alice fetched a notebook and pencil and wrote all this down. Later she copied part of the letter to Jean, and added her reflections about the force of tradition among unlettered peoples. This might be fun to read over some day. She had scribbled down a good deal of nonsense here and there, and had mislaid most of it. But at least she got it out of her system.

The Martins slept very late on Easter Sunday. On rising they had coffee and toast. Then they groomed themselves at length and dressed in all their Easter finery. They had a marvelous dinner at a midtown restaurant. Everybody was friendly with everybody else. For this one day the entire population, residents and visitors alike, was unified, smiling, in harmony.

A pity it couldn't be like this every day, Alice reflected. But that was a silly thought. How was one to tell the heights if there were no depressions between them?

When they finally finished dinner, including a second order of coffee over which they unmistakably dawdled, Harry asked, "What would you like to do now?"

It was on the tip of Alice's tongue to suggest that they seek a horse-drawn cab and make the circuit of Central Park. They could pretend they were out-of-towners; pretend they were honeymooners; or acknowledge the truth that they had done their sight-seeing in New York when they were newcomers. Or they could just go for the ride and listen to their driver and watch the other passengers. This would be a second or even a third trip for most of these vehicles; the afternoon was drawing on. But she checked herself. She didn't want to run the slightest risk of spying on the people whom she had sent to take the tour.

A different idea occurred to her. "Let's go and sit in the shop, just as spectators, and watch the rest of the world roll by."

They did just that: sat in their shop, waved to passing acquaintances, pointed to the "Closed Today" sign when a few would-be purchasers showed indications of stopping. "Box seats at the crossroads of the Village, and they're not costing us a cent," Harry remarked.

When Emil and Kitty Koenig appeared, however, Emil paused to pantomine a drink and pointed in the direction of his apartment. Alice half rose from her chair; then she thought better of it, sank back, shook her head and pointed at the sign. Emil and Kitty went on their way.

Ten minutes later the telephone rang. "Better not answer that," said Harry sharply. But when Alice did answer and it proved to be Ben Johnson, he was glad to accept an invitation to join the Johnsons for drinks. They had already tried to reach the Martins at their apartment, and had rung the shop as a last resort.

By next year Bess would have an Easter card of her composition in the shops, she explained over the drinks in a neighboring speakeasy. It was like being in the fashion business; you always had to be a season ahead of the retail trade. By next year Harry Martin would have an anthology in the shops, the way things looked now. But why bring his heavy artillery to bear against her little popgun? Especially since her popgun was, after all, inside the citadel, and nothing had actually been decided in Harry's case.

There was no need for Harry to catch her up, however; she caught herself. "Now look who's talking! Talking my miserable little shop talk, too, in front of a man who really has a great undertaking on hand. What luck are you having, Harry?"

"All that I can use and more than I deserve. The Johnsons' calling us at the shop was the perfect way to round out the holiday for me." Harry lifted his glass toward his friends. Where they would all of them be next year was much less to the point than where the Martins and some others would be tomorrow.

On Monday Waverley Book Shop was open for business. If there wasn't much business, at least there would be some reports.

Bill Thayer turned his in early. "That little Nina is the sweetest thing I ever saw in all my born days, Harry. During our expedition she was happy enough for two little girls. The driver in Central Park thought we were a family party, of course; that flattered Marion. Nina was so busy turning to smile up first at one of us, then the other, she scarcely had time to look at the sights in the Park. It was quite a while before she remembered to tell us, 'My mommy came to see me. Wasn't that nice? She doesn't do it often.' "

"That tells a lot," said Harry rather grimly. But Alice looked pleased. She was certain that the remark hadn't been lost on Marion Murdock.

About the middle of the afternoon Peggy Pratt dashed in. "I can't stay a minute. I've got to get back and write it all down. Those horse drivers are really characters, aren't they? I want Walter to take me there some other Sundays, so that we can watch some other ones putting on their act."

So now the reports were in; they were highly satisfactory. Alice wrote a second installment of her letter to Jean; then she began a letter to Jim. She was just well into it when a voice at her elbow interrupted, "Mrs. Martin, isn't it? I wonder whether I might speak to you for a minute."

Alice looked up. A rather small young woman stood beside her: a pretty brunette, just a little too much made up, a little too flashily dressed. Alice had never seen her before, certainly; but there was something about her that was vaguely familiar. "At your service, of course," Alice said. She laid aside her unfinished letter and rose.

"I'm Anita De Byles," the stranger announced, as if that ought to mean something. Then after an instant she added in explanation, "Nina Babcock's mother, you know."

After all this time, the lady had materialized. "Do sit down," Alice invited, and motioned toward a chair in the far corner of the shop.

Mrs. De Byles—no, they were always "Miss" when they used their stage names—Miss De Byles perched rather uneasily on the edge of the chair and announced, "I won't take up a minute of your time. I know you're busy."

"Not just now," Alice reassured her. "Not to you, anyhow. I'm delighted to meet you. You have a very lovely little girl."

"Thank you. I'm glad you like her." Miss De Byles hesitated for an instant. The resemblance to Nina, which was what had bothered Alice there for a moment just at first, was gone now. This woman was hard. Hard as nails. Harder than one so young had any right to be. But right here and now, she was uncertain of her ground.

"Very lovely," Alice repeated encouragingly.

"You've been extremely kind to her," the newcomer went on. "I don't see as much of her as I'd like to. I'm a night-club entertainer. I have to get my sleep at odd hours."

"Yes indeed. It must be an exhausting life," Alice murmured sympathetically. Not too sympathetically, she hoped. The creature might be leading up to something.

"I went over Friday to see my little girl," Miss De Byles continued. "I planned to take her to the Thrift Shop to buy her some clothes. Children that age outgrow things so fast."

"Indeed they do," Alice agreed.

"I found that you had outfitted her beautifully. Mrs. Smith —'Auntie Agnes' Nina calls her—says you've given her a lot of books, too. It must be nice to be in a position to do that for a little girl. I came in to say 'Thank you.'"

"It is indeed nice. It's a pleasure to do for a little girl like Nina. You and she are more than welcome."

Without another word Miss De Byles jumped to her feet. With a wave of her hand toward Harry, she was gone.

Alice's first slight resentment was swallowed in pure pity. Later, when her uneasiness returned, it returned as pure wonder. Beyond identifying their caller, however, she said nothing to Harry about her. A woman left with a child to take care of; a woman presumably without much natural ability, certainly without any such practical training as Alice Frederickson had had; a woman driven to earn a living—or mooch it—as "a night-club entertainer": secure, respectable, prosperous Alice Martin was not going to cast a stone at her.

There the woman was. On the other hand, there was childless, child-hungry Marion Murdock. It sometimes seemed to Alice that most children got into the wrong families. Still, there was a chance of straightening out this tangle. Or perhaps of watching it straighten itself out. People did Alice Martin the honor of confiding in her. Alice was really a very lucky woman. So lucky, indeed, that her luck sometimes frightened her. It was just too good to last.

17

"Miss De Byles" had come into Waverley Book Shop to thank Alice for her kindness to Nina, to make a poor mouth, possibly to size Alice up. All of which might mean much, or it might mean nothing at all. In her youth, Alice Frederickson had often thought that it would be fun if people's heads were made with removable tops, so that a superior being, by which of course she meant somebody like herself, could lift off the lid and see what was brewing within. Now she was not so sure. That would have entailed a godlike responsibility about desires and motives. Poor weak mortals had to be satisfied with trying to figure the whole thing out. It constituted one of the principal interests of the game. It provided a blanket excuse, too, for wholesale failures on the part of poor fallible humanity.

Nothing excused not trying to help the other fellow out. There were questions of when and how; but before that were questions of *if*. Alice did go out of her way to borrow trouble. But she was not only concerned about Bill Thayer and his

Marion (at least, Alice hoped that Marion would soon be his); Alice had also grown very fond of dear little Nina.

There now! When you came right down to it, the reason why you did things for other people was in order to gratify yourself. Or at least that was one of the reasons. A thoroughly enlightened selfishness amounted in the end to the same thing as intelligent unselfishness.

Alice would better write that observation down, too. It sounded as if it might mean something. One of these days, if she ever got time enough, she might try to cast her observations into some sort of form. Or maybe she'd better not. Maybe they were not so gemlike that they deserved a proper setting. It must have been nice in the medieval monasteries in one way; the inhabitants had leisure to debate questions like, "How many angels can stand on the point of a needle?" Not so nice in other ways, to be sure; those places must have smelled like the very devil. How many germs can the unwashed harbor? Alice remembered a professor of hers in college who came out flat against a cult popular at the time, "If you do not like the Middle Ages, it is because you do not understand them." He defined them morosely as "a thousand years without soap."

That next Saturday when Nina came in for her regular visit she was still prattling of the joys of Easter. But the following week she had a news item: "My mommy came to see me yesterday. She kissed me good-bye. Then she talked for a long, long time to Auntie Agnes. Twice she handed her something in an envelope. Then she came back and kissed me again."

It was a pretty enough little scene. Nina's recital of it was touching; she was proud of these marks of her mother's affection, certain that they would be of interest to Mrs. Martin. But it sent a quick stab to Alice's heart. Coming on top of Nina's mother's visit to Waverley Book Shop, this might well mean that the lady was not just saying good-bye for a week or a few weeks: that instead she was bidding a long farewell.

At the next lull in business, Alice consulted the telephone book. Sure enough, Anita De Byles was listed at an address on a neighboring street. Alice must have been through that block on her rambles. If she walked past it again, she could spot it; and that would tell her precisely nothing. Some lovely homes lay behind some unpromising façades. That was the way of the Village. There were beautiful old houses, too, many of them now divided up into apartments. A "floor through" would not only afford light and air, which were at a premium in the Big City; it might give a chance for a tiny back-yard garden.

That was one feature the Martins didn't have in their fourth-floor apartment. But oh, the lovely summer evenings they might look forward to spending on the roof! The privacy, and the strange sense of power it gave them to look down on that city scene of which Waverley Book Shop was a feature!

Back to Brooklyn they would go this coming summer, however, if daughter Jean and her husband came on for their expected visit. That was something else to look forward to. Later on, perhaps, the senior Martins could again make a trip inland. Once Harry got that compendium of his off to the publisher—and the publisher took it, of course.

Virginia Daly Burgess telephoned from her Long Island home and came in for that very purpose. She delivered the manuscript of her work on the Underground Railroad to the publishers and came down afterward to visit the Martins. They took her out for dinner at an hour when a suburbanite might reasonably be accustomed to dining; they had both gone without their midday snacks in order to have something of an appetite.

"It's the most fascinating book I ever wrote," she told them over the table. "Fascinating to me, that is. But it has had me in emotional turmoil a great deal of the time. Can you imagine getting so stirred up over events that happened all those years ago? Bygones are bygones, and the people are dead. But the great issues never die, do they? That's what I tell myself."

"You'll find your next book a little easier on you, I hope," Harry Martin consoled.

"My next?" Virginia shuddered. "Give me time to recover from this one, please. But I am going back to Civil War biographies. The terrain is familiar to me. In a sense too it was one of the greatest wars ever fought. It began as a war to save the Union; more and more it turned into a war to free the slaves. The Underground Railroad played its part, not only by the slaves it freed but by keeping the idea to the fore." She broke off and began to laugh. "Quite a little lecture I'm treating you to. I'm afraid I'm quoting from my own work, too. You'll have to excuse me if I sound a little silly."

Alice attempted a diversion by asking about the baby. Virginia smiled faintly. "Joan will go from me or her father to George or Daisy any time. There are times when I think Don is just a little jealous."

"People have a talent for making themselves unhappy," Alice sympathized. "Just wait until she reaches the marrying age, though. The boy was never born who was good enough to grow up and marry your Joan."

This time Virginia was actually diverted. "That's a long look ahead," she parried, and promptly began to relate the exploits of her little daughter.

Presently she began to ask for news of their family, then of the old friends who used to gather around when she was still Miss Daly and lived in the Village. "What ever became of—?" drew blank so many times that Alice was finally driven to apologize, "If people no longer come into the shop, I can't very well call up and ask them why not. I might mean it as neighborly interest; but they would certainly think I was trying to drum up trade."

"I'll have a little trade for you again one of these days." Virginia glanced at her wrist watch. "I must be getting along in a few minutes. The suburbanite is the slave of the time-table. We sold ourselves into bondage, though, so we shouldn't complain. Worth it, too, when Missie has all outdoors to play around in."

Both the Martins escorted Virginia to her train. It was only at the last minute that Harry remembered to ask her, "What are you calling the book?"

"Quite baldly, *The Underground Railroad*. I've thought once or twice that there might be a novel in the story of how the escaped slaves lived in Canada. It was an alien civilization, after all; they were still a people set apart. But I'm not a novelist to begin with. There probably isn't a novel there anyhow. Facts are hard enough to deal with. There! I've about talked my head off. But it was so nice to be with you dear people."

She kissed them both good-bye; she took their messages for Don; she waved to them from the train window. "I suspect she's really done a definitive book this time," Harry said when they turned away. "Yet she looks just like any pretty young housewife on her way back to home and husband."

"To be met at the station in the family car, and to report on her visit with us," retorted Alice, "while we wend our way back to the shop to put it to bed, and meanwhile bury Virginia under a shower of platitudes." Harry stared at her for an instant, and she added, "That sounded horrid. I didn't mean it that way."

"What's a platitude between friends?" he asked. "I'll take you home, if you like, and then go rejoin Bill Thayer for an hour."

"We'll both go in there, and listen to Bill report business, if any. There's my platitude for you. 'It takes a good old platitude to give a person latitude. You understand my attitude?' I won't need to write that one down, will I? It's so bad I couldn't forget it."

"Write it down and give it to Bess Johnson. There's nothing like making somebody else a present of something you have no possible use for yourself."

By the time they reached Waverley Book Shop, Alice had forgotten about her burst of annoyance. What remained with her was the recollection of people she used to know and had lost track of. There had been a goodly company of them over the past few years. Having them called to mind was something of a treat.

They told Bill something about their pleasant evening. Alice repeated her rhyme; now she added a fourth line, " 'Oh, thank you for your gratitude!' " "I had accused Harry, not of using platitudes, but of being about to use them," she explained. "How far can a woman go out of her way when she wants to be annoying?"

Bill shook his head slowly, then turned to wait on a late customer. The three of them together locked up. Virginia would be well toward home by this time. You might think Don would have come into town with her on such an important occasion. But the writing Burgesses not only respected each other's working hours; apparently they also gave each other occasional solo dinner dates in the Big City.

Virginia Daly had an inevitable title. Harry Martin had titles enough, but none which quite suited him. Peggy Pratt had had a title; but that had somehow got lost in the shuffle when she met Walter Ferrar and began to write down those impressions. The opening of an office door at a special moment might make all the difference in a woman's life. The accident of a mislaid page of manuscript had led to the meeting of Virginia Daly and Don Burgess in Waverley Book Shop. To such a triviality small Joan Burgess owed her very existence.

All that was ancient history. But sometimes a person got to remembering; sometimes, again, to speculating. Virginia had spoken of a possible novel on the Underground Railroad, and had regretted that she was not a novelist. Don Burgess wrote detective romances; he was almost at the other end of the writing business from his wife. Yet perhaps some day the two of them might collaborate on the very novel that Virginia had just mentioned and then pushed aside. One of the couple could supply what the other writer lacked. But that was all on the knees of the gods.

Harry Martin, putting the finishing touches on his anthology, was impressed by its very bulk, and by the professional look of all those neatly typed pages and their snappy little italicized comments. The dedication page, however, was in longhand, and there was no carbon copy. The dedicatee was inevitable; but he wished, if possible, to keep the fact from the lady until she actually saw it in print.

The exact wording, too, eluded him. "To My Wife" said it all in the fewest possible words. On the other hand, that would deprive the lady of the satisfaction of seeing her name in print. "To Alice Frederickson Martin" avoided that difficulty, but did not specify whether the lady was wife, daughter, or even mother. To run both the name and the relationship sounded as if he were particularizing which wife this one was. Eventually he suppressed the longhand page altogether. It would be presumptuous to include a dedication in a book which was only now being submitted for publication.

At long last, it was finished. Harry made an appointment to see Howard Knowles, of Knowles and Wingate. He hired a taxi to help him get the bulky thing to the publisher's office. He had an amicable, if short, interview with Mr. Knowles, whose lips made a very compressed line indeed when he glanced over the first few pages of the opus. He promised to read it himself, and as soon as possible.

Then it was all over. Harry found himself out of the building, in the public street again. He felt triumphant in a way, yet curiously at a loss: something the way he used to feel as a small boy when the long-looked-for last day of school set him free for the leisure of the vacation, yet also left him aimless. He walked all the way back to the shop; along the way he devoted a good deal of attention to store windows.

Alice excused herself to a customer long enough to ask, "How did it go?" Harry shrugged and said, "All right, I guess." And there you were. And just exactly where were you?

The title under which he submitted the work had come to him as an inspiration while he was wrestling with the matter of the dedication. He had scribbled it down, looked at it, consulted Alice, picked out the letters on her typewriter, finally decided that he liked it. He called it *Reader's Choice*.

The world did not hold its breath while Harry Martin was waiting to hear from the august firm of Knowles and Wingate. That very next Saturday something distracting happened in the little circle which centered in Waverley Book Shop. In the afternoon, when William Thayer walked Nina back to Auntie Agnes', that lady fixed him with a grin which was almost a leer, and announced, "She paid me an extra week, all right. Handed the money to me this time; gener'ly it came in the mail. But she told me that after this you'll be paying Nina Babcock's board."

"*She* told you?" gasped William. "You mean Nina's mother?"

"Yup, Nina's mother. Mean to say she forgot to tell you?"

Miss De Byles hadn't forgotten it. She had neglected it deliberately. Now William saw light on the little scene which Nina had so innocently related: the two payments to Mrs. Smith, the two farewell kisses. This meant that Nina's mother had finally deserted the child: had left her for alien hands to tend, for strangers' love to shelter.

He got his breath back and announced, "Nina's mother settled all that with another friend, Mrs. Martin, the lady who always gives Nina books and who bought her her Easter outfit. One woman can talk more freely to another about things like that, don't you think?" But all the way back to the book shop his head was whirling. Nina was as good as his now: his and Marion's. If Nina was his and theirs, Marion Murdock must be his, too. But it was Alice Martin he must speak to first. The whole thing pivoted on Alice.

He beckoned her into the street outside the shop and poured forth his story. Alice looked concerned; but all she said at first was, "Tell me that again, and slower."

Bill did so, and Alice nodded. "She has left us a good deal in the dark. We'll have to find out for ourselves. It looks to me as if she had flown the coop."

Alice had recourse to the telephone book then. Her call elicited the information, "That number has been disconnected."

"I'll go with you to see what we can find out," Alice said. "The sooner the better, too. Harry can tend shop in our absence."

They found the address easily enough; it was in a shabby building, but a respectable neighborhood. There was an "Apartment for Rent" sign on display. They were lucky enough to find the landlord. He assumed that they were house hunting; when he learned that they were looking for a former tenant, he at once became cagy.

Alice smiled, and took charge of the interview. "This is not Miss De Byles' husband," she explained. "Nor is he a boy friend of hers, or an ex-boy friend. I am interested in her little girl, who lived here with her for a short time. Mr. Thayer was good enough to walk over here with me."

The landlord shook his head. "She was a—a night-club type, you might say. She knew her way around; but the other tenants didn't complain. In the Village, you can't be too nosy. She was fairly prompt with the rent until just lately."

"She left owing you money?" asked Bill Thayer.

"Sold her furniture for what it would bring and lit out. You say you're interested in the little girl, ma'am? I can't tell you anything about her."

They didn't get much more out of him; but Alice gave him the shop's business card and told him to be sure and let her know if he had any word of Miss De Byles. "Though it's really the little girl I'm interested in," she repeated.

Alice led Bill into a lunchroom on their way home to the shop. She ordered coffee and announced, "I want to get my breath back before I face Harry. I suspected something was due to happen. Just the same, this is a facer."

"I got the impression that the lady did not leave alone," said Bill dryly.

"Either she left with a man, or she has simply deserted her child and covered her tracks. You're willing to go on paying for Nina's keep until we decide what's best to be done?"

"I want to assume Nina's keep for good and all. You know that as well as I do. But I'd like to get her out of Mrs. Smith's place as soon as I can."

"Where would you take her from there?"

Bill grinned sheepishly. "One step ahead of me, as usual, aren't you?"

"One step behind the plot, I'm afraid. In many ways I prefer books, where a person can safely leave things in the hands of the author. I don't know what to make of all this. Stand me the coffee, will you, Bill? We'd better be getting back to the shop."

When they stopped for traffic, she enjoined him, "For the present, the less said the better." She was deeply uneasy at the turn events had taken. That Bill and his Marion and their to-be-darling Nina should have plain sailing from now on was just too good to be true.

[213]

That was not Harry Martin's view of the case. When he was favored with an outline of what had happened, he rolled Miss De Byles' possible elopement under his tongue. Alice's sharp rebuke, "This isn't funny," drew only the comment, "It certainly isn't tragic. A good riddance to bad rubbish. What more do you want?"

"Some sort of assurance."

Harry shook his head. "You read too many books. You expect everything to be neatly rounded off in real life, the way it always is in novels. Ragged ends lie around us all the time in everyday life. Why not let them lie there?"

He was of course reminding her that this was none of her business—further, that is, than to help Bill and Marion out a little. Alice thought it over for a minute; then she said slowly, "There are more fools than knaves in the world, I suppose. I don't know which kind does the greater harm."

"I don't know how to tell them apart." Harry stifled a yawn. He had just said about her what Alice had said to Bill about herself, in pretty close to the same words. There were times when Alice preferred the symmetry of the finished product to life in the raw. So did a great many other people, luckily, or how could Waverley Book Shop earn a living?

Alice started to share the reflection with Harry; remembering his yawn, she checked herself. Harry had been a little strange lately. Was it mere fatigue and reaction after completing his anthology? Was it the suspense of waiting for a verdict on that opus? Was it creeping ennui?

Now Alice was really looking for trouble. First she worried because the Nina affair had gone too smoothly. Now she was fretting because Harry Martin seemed a little different lately. Why shouldn't he seem different? He really was different. He not only looked older; he was occasionally moody and absent-minded. Suppose she let him alone for a change? She might go off for an afternoon by herself sometimes. Generally her daytime expeditions were limited to infrequent matinees with Bess Johnson and excursions with a visiting daughter, and of course those neighborhood explorations which she had undertaken since the Martins had a Village apartment. On the other hand, she could tend shop and give him an afternoon's freedom. Those mail-order rambles of his took him time enough, heaven knew. But why shouldn't he for a change join the other sitters on park benches, and exchange idle gossip and share opinions, and do a little all-around loafing?

There she went again, the managing wife! The next thing she knew, she'd be writing to one of those Helpful Advice columns in the newspapers.

Oh, but wait a minute! She could write such a letter, not with the idea of posting it, but purely to get the thing down on paper. If it proved amusing enough, she might show it to the gentleman himself. If it sounded as dull as she feared it might, there was always the wastebasket.

Dear, soothing thought, the wastebasket! Alice finished her letter and read it over. She decided not to show it to Harry; it might simply put ideas into his head. But she felt much better for having written it.

Now if she really wanted something to worry about, she could turn her attention to the state of the country, which was really enough to worry any responsible citizen. After that she could worry about the Republican Party. Was there a wastebasket large enough to contain the Republican Party? She feared that there was, and that the Party was headed for it.

Glancing up, she caught Harry's eye. He inquired, "What are you smiling to yourself about?"

That was marriage for you. Try to talk to your husband and he yawned in your face. Keep your thoughts to yourself and he wanted to find out what they were.

"Don't you wish you knew?" teased Alice. She began to tear up her letter. No sense in provoking him by letting him see that arraignment. If put to it, perhaps he could have written a tidy letter about her. She got busy on her proper concerns.

Late that night, when she was just about to take her place beside a husband already comfortably installed, Alice felt a sharp stab of pity which amounted almost to physical pain.

She had just thought of Anita De Byles, getting into bed here or there, but almost certainly not alone. Whatever else happened to her, Anita had to sleep sometimes. When she slept, did she dream, sadly, strangely, perhaps in queer disguised forms—dream of her little Nina?

18

BILL THAYER, ESCORTING NINA BACK TO AUNTIE AGNES' THE following Saturday, was ready to pay her board bill; on his way over he realized that he didn't know how much he was expected to pay. He hated to ask Nina; he was not even sure that she knew. The whole transaction had been unbusiness-like; yet throughout it money had been very much to the fore.

"I didn't know as you'd show up today," was the lady's greeting. She was a tough nut; but the people with whom she dealt were not calculated to make a woman tender.

"I'm paying," said Bill curtly. "I'd like a written receipt, please."

Mrs. Smith glowered at him and muttered, "The kid's mother gener'ly just mailed me the money. When she come here and paid me, she didn't ask for no fancy frills. What's the sense in makin' such a fuss over ten bucks?"

"I want the receipts to show Nina's mother in case the question ever comes up," said Bill steadily. He produced his pocket notebook and fountain pen. "I'll write the receipt out for you if you have no stationery handy; all you'll have to do is sign it."

A very disagreeable woman; but better than a public institution, Bill reminded himself. Poor Anita De Byles had never completely given up her child until now. Bill was extremely thankful that she hadn't. It had taken an actual Nina to break down Marion's long resistance. If indeed it was broken down. Bill would talk more to Alice Martin on that score. She shared his doubts and hesitations.

Harry insisted on the jocular side of things. "This is the farthest possible from a shotgun wedding."

"The very farthest," said Alice sharply. "The whole point to a shotgun wedding is haste. This one bids fair to drag along until hot weather, at least."

Bill put his receipt back in his pocket. "I think I'll keep this and its successors for Marion's benefit. They will show her how much money we'll save by taking Nina into our own household."

He waited until Harry was out of earshot; then he tackled Alice again. "I have a queer feeling that this marriage arrangement of mine isn't going to turn out. My heart is so set on it; I suspect maybe that is one thing which makes me fearful. But it is going through, isn't it? Alice dear, it is, surely?"

This was an appeal for sympathy, which Alice gave promptly and profusely. But she sounded more confident than she felt. Her own uneasiness returned in full measure; there were just too many unknown factors here.

Then all at once something clicked. In her recent talk with Virginia, they had mentioned former friends who had now dropped out of sight. Alice had deplored the fact that she couldn't very well look them up; her friendly interest might be mistaken for an activity on behalf of Waverley Book Shop. But now she could scout out one of them, and for a much deeper motive than that. She had her qualms about doing so;

but after all, the worst the gentleman could do was say "No."

Back in the days when Virginia Daly had still been Virginia Daly, she had had a persistent suitor by the name of George Scudder. He was considerably older than she, but distinctly an eligible: a lawyer with a very well-established downtown firm, a widower of many years' standing, a member of the Harvard Club, tenant of an apartment very handy to that club. Virginia had certainly accepted his attentions, had even encouraged them. But after her marriage to Don Burgess, George had ceased to frequent Waverley Book Shop. It was too far uptown from his office, too far downtown from his club and his residence, perhaps. Perhaps, also, it would bring back too many memories.

Alice recollected the name of the firm. She telephoned there one afternoon and asked to speak to Mr. Scudder "if he is in the office and not too busy. I'm not sure that he would remember me. Please tell him I'm Mrs. Martin of Waverley Book Shop."

George Scudder came on the wire in a surprisingly short time. He remembered her perfectly. He asked about Harry. Then, after a barely perceptible hesitation, he asked what he could do for Mrs. Martin.

"I'd like to consult you about a small legal tangle. It concerns a good friend of mine. Not," Alice took pains to assure him, "not Virginia Daly. She was asking about you the last time I saw her; but I had to tell her you never come into the shop any more."

In this connection, of course, that wasn't a bad thing to say. "That has been my loss," George Scudder said quickly. "If I can be of some service to you now, just call on me. Would you like to come down and see me here at my office? My secretary will give you an early appointment."

His secretary did: an appointment the following week.

Alice left the shop in plenty of time to visit her apartment and make a special toilet in George's honor. She was glad she had done so when she entered the imposing offices of the firm. It was one of those old houses where the original name was kept, though the original partners had gone to meet their Maker; but Alice was gratified to note that George Scudder's name appeared only two lines below it in the sign on the office door.

George himself was impressive against the background of his private domain: much more so than he had ever appeared in a book shop on Seventh Avenue. His greeting was very cordial, however. He complimented her on her appearance, asked after Harry, drank in her news about Virginia and ordered a copy of Virginia's new book. These polite preliminaries over, he leaned a little back in his chair and asked, "Now what can I do for you?"

"I know your firm specializes in corporation law," Alice began.

"That and estate work, yes. Business law, you might say."

"My problem is vastly different. It isn't even my problem, really. It belongs to some friends of mine; and I'm here without their knowledge."

Alice went ahead to give the particulars of the De Byles–Babcock imbroglio. George Scudder soon began to ask questions; then he began to make notes of her answers. "I don't know whether my friends have run afoul of the law," Alice wound up. "But I do think the whole business should be clarified before they go much farther."

"Your friends might have adopted a child through the usual channels," he suggested. "It isn't too late for them to do that, of course. But I suppose it would do no good to suggest that they change their minds?"

Alice shook her head. "The whole thing is desperately personal."

"You take a deep interest in it, too?"

"It I hadn't, should I have come here? I'm afraid it's not

worth your time; but you're the only lawyer I really know, and I thought perhaps I—perhaps you—Oh, is it quite beneath the dignity of your firm? I'll pay you as much as I can afford." She suddenly blushed scarlet. What a time to mention money! Her kind of money, too, in these august surroundings!

George suddenly smiled. There for an instant corporation law and the Harvard Club and all the rest of his background faded into insignificance; he looked like a much younger man, and singularly attractive.

"Don't mention money in this connection," he said heartily. "I'll be glad to do what I can for people who are so much interested in doing for others. It will give my underlings something to do, too. Let them run around and get a few depositions and maybe take things to the proper court. Mind if I ring for my secretary now? I'll need some names and addresses, and I want to go over certain particulars again."

He summed up for her twenty minutes later. "It could be done on an informal basis, which I suppose was what your friends had in mind. But the actual mother might turn up again some day. She sounds unscrupulous; she might be desperate."

"You mean—blackmail?" stammered Alice.

"Exactly. A mother feels so strongly drawn back to her child sometimes, especially when there is money involved. We'll have to go ahead and have the little girl made a ward of the court and all the rest of it. Your friends will have to know."

Alice threw up her hands. "Then they will find out how I've interfered?"

Again George Scudder smiled. "You're the only long headed person in the whole transaction, really. I'll be seeing you from time to time about this business. Speaking selfishly, I'm glad it happened."

One last anxiety of Alice had to be appeased. "But can I

tell them to go ahead with their arrangements? They have been planning so much, and of course they do want to get Nina out of that dingy environment as soon as they can give her a real home."

"Tell them to go ahead by all means." George Scudder rose to walk her to the door. "Virginia is happy with her whodunit husband? Is he still in excellent health?"

"I don't see half enough of them any more. Long Island sometimes seems dismally far away." Turning toward him at the door of his private office, Alice impulsively gave him both her hands. "Oh, if you knew what a load you've taken off my mind—!"

"It's been a pleasure. I'll keep in touch with you." George pressed her hands, and held them just an instant longer than was necessary. For all his success and his fine connections and whatever interest he might take in women who would be delighted with his attentions—for all of this, George Scudder was essentially a very lonely man.

Oh, stop feeling sorry for everybody, Alice, you goose! Her sense of warm gratitude was something to pause and savor. In return for the tremendous favor that he was doing her, she had brought into his life the knowledge that he was somebody people could turn to. You didn't ask favors of people unless you liked them. It had been an experience for George Scudder, too. There for the long minute when he and Alice Martin stood hand in hand, he had not been a lonely man.

The worst of her worries was over; something was being done about it. But that in turn brought up another matter for her to settle; just how much should she tell? It was a delicate job. There is a point at which explanation may slop over into apology. On the other hand, there is the danger that it will seem like bragging.

She dealt with Harry easily enough. She told him, "I've been seeking out an old customer who has fallen by the wayside. I have hopes of bringing him back into the True Faith."

"I'm not good at guessing riddles," Harry countered. "As for the men you date, it's a good thing for me that dueling has gone out of style."

Alice made him a bow. "I wonder how popular it ever was. It must have been very flattering to know that rivals for your hand had ordered coffee and pistols for two; but that certainly didn't give the lady much choice in the matter."

"If given her choice, the lady might have decided to flip a coin for the result. That would be very deflating to the male ego. All right, Mrs. Martin, whose leg have you been pulling this afternoon?"

"I was down at George Scudder's office talking law business with him. But the book business may profit in the end."

Harry stared at her. For once, Alice had taken the wind out of his sails. When he got his breath back, he demanded, "No fooling, you went to George Scudder for legal advice? Could it have been about this mix-up with the little Babcock girl?"

"Could have been. Was. He proved most sympathetic and helpful."

"Couldn't Bill Thayer have attended to his own business? You're not the one who is planning to adopt the little girl."

"Bill doesn't know anything about my visit. I'm wondering just how much to tell him. I can't let him be drawn in without warning. He may not thank me for my interference."

"Probably not. That is, in case you thought of something which he should have foreseen."

"I did his thinking for him, yes. But I couldn't very well consult him beforehand. In the first place I might just have been dreaming up bogies to frighten myself with. In the second place, how did I know George Scudder would even look at such a case? His Wall Street firm does corporation law and suchlike stuff. It is distinctly Big League."

"Yet you sound as if you had succeeded."

"George is going to help us out, yes. Help our friends out,

rather. But I think it was the idea of making a child happy that appealed to him."

"If you can't get something out of a person, nobody can. I'll bet you put up a good story; I wish I could have heard it. All right, you'd better think things over a little more and then take Bill out for coffee while Papa minds the shop. I'm looking forward to the sight of Bill's face when you offer him the date."

Bill's face actually looked apprehensive. He feared that something more had been heard from the missing Anita, or at any rate from her landlord. But when Alice had set forth the state of the case, he was divided between chagrin and relief.

"I wish to goodness I'd held a pistol to Marion's head when I first fell in love with her," he announced. "I should have bullied her into marrying me, and promised her that if she would do so, we'd take a baby out of an institution. That's getting to be a popular sport hereabouts, isn't it?"

"So I've heard. In New York the supply of babies offered for adoption isn't equal to the demand. But if you had put a pistol to Marion Murdock's head, she would simply have told you to take it away again. It isn't *a* child she wants. It's Nina."

Bill again looked disconsolate. "I can't bear to load all this worry on her. It's going to come out all right in the end, isn't it? It *has* to."

"That's just what we're planning to make it do. If I were in your place, I shouldn't say too much to Marion about this. After all, you two have a lot to do before you can even offer Nina a proper home."

"Such as get married and set up housekeeping?"

"Getting your joint establishment ready is an undertaking in itself, especially since you're both of you working people." Alice switched her mind from the fact that Marion had been through that experience once before. What difference did that make? Old unhappiness, instead of poisoning present bliss, might well be the dark background which would throw it into relief.

"There are lots of vacant apartments these days," Alice went on. "You might do a little scouting when you have an hour free."

"House hunting on your time, dear Mrs. Martin?"

"Go out when one or both of the Martins is certain to be there. That way you'll get a place within easy walking distance. Or if word gets around of what you want, somebody may come up with a good lead. It's amazing how much business is done that way in this neighborhood."

It was the middle of May before they found what they wanted. Bill signed a lease beginning in June and gave word for the house painters to move in. Actually they would pay less than their separate rents had amounted to. They could sell some of their superfluous furniture. Marion would have the say about most of that; American women did. When the weeding out was pretty well finished, she would go looking for a double bed.

Bill had asked her whether she would prefer twin beds. After all, he had been sleeping alone for a great many years, and Marion ever since the collapse of her first marriage.

"Certainly not!" she said, and blushed like a sixteen-year-old. "I think it's horrid for a married couple just to get into bed together on certain occasions."

She made one stipulation, however, which rather took him aback. "Bill, I expect to be happy with you. I intend to be happy with you. But there's one thing I want understood right from the beginning: if we ever do separate, I'm to have the custody of Nina."

"Let's not even think about that," he answered hotly. He was prepared to take on this ready-made family; he even welcomed it. But it seemed to him sometimes that Marion wasn't marrying him for his own sake; she simply wanted to give the little stranger child a permanent home.

Bill too loved Nina. He was gratified that, according to what he learned both directly from George Scudder's henchman and through the agency of Alice Martin, legal difficulties were cleared out of the way. But if at the last moment they should be disappointed, he would have settled for another child, and this time have had something of a say-so in picking her out.

He would never have mentioned this to a living soul. He felt disloyal even when he had stray thoughts that a little boy would be a saner choice when you had your pick this way; boys were safer among the temptations and traps of a big city. But most steps in his domestic undertaking he talked over with Alice Martin.

Not so much with Harry. Harry was sometimes facetious at the wrong moments. Anyhow he was much wrapped up these days with his own concerns.

Herbert Knowles had in his own good time come across with a verdict on Harry Martin's anthology. He wrote saying that Knowles and Wingate had read Mr. Martin's anthology and decided that it would be an acceptable publishing venture. Would Mr. Martin like to come in some afternoon soon to discuss terms?

Mr. Martin would, and did. He found the discussion somewhat one-sided. First there was the stipulation that times were bad in the publishing business; the best contract the firm could offer was—the days of a fifteen-per-cent royalty were gone forever—in a work of this character there were always copyrights to be cleared—

Was this publishing or was it horse trading, Harry Martin wondered. But he had sense enough to listen instead of talking. He agreed in lukewarm fashion, "I can see your point, of course." "True enough, to be sure." "I'm in the business myself, you must remember." He left the office an accepted author, though still months away from being a published one.

This was something which Harry could tell Alice about,

[226]

and strut when he told it. There were other things these days which he was doing his best to keep from Alice's knowledge. These mail order errands of his to the post office were genuine enough, as they always had been; but now his return was by a certain route, and a route with a stopover. Lately his relaxing walks had all been in the same direction. He was giving the author of those "confessions" magazine stories something to confess.

The day in the book shop when Gloria Gregory had insisted that the proprietor deliver her purchases, Harry Martin was indulging one of those moods which had been frequent with him lately. He was beginning to show his age, and to feel his age. To feel it in one respect particularly, though Alice did not seem to notice any deficiency. Perhaps she cared less about him in that way; perhaps it was all a part of her damned high-mindedness. But Harry realized that his specific male powers were diminishing. One day they would fade out altogether; but until they did, he was put on the defensive.

Gloria Gregory was a transparent enough little baggage. In other years Harry would have considered her merely a part of the passing spectacle. As it was, she presented a challenge. Harry Martin had to show her that there was life in the old dog yet.

He had showed her on that very first occasion. She invited him to sit down and get his breath back. He complimented her on her apartment, a one-room, kitchenette-and-bath affair; it was indeed comfortable enough, though a little flashy. Gloria asked him whether he would like a drink. Harry said, "Does anyone ever refuse?"

That very afternoon their intrigue had begun. They had arranged their system of phone calls and window-shade signals. Harry, just before he took his leave, handed her a folded bill and said, "Buy yourself a bottle of gin." Gloria demurred, but she took the money. If she glanced at the denomination of the bill, he didn't catch her at it.

When Harry was with Gloria, he felt like a young man again. In betweentimes, he realized that he would do well to break with her before she broke with him. She might have commitments with other men anyhow; might be simply amusing herself with this fish who had swum so readily into her net. Harry Martin saw her only at certain afternoon hours, saw only one side of her at that. Actually he knew very little about her.

Getting back to the book shop after his interview with the publisher ("my publisher," Harry could now say), Harry found George Scudder there. He greeted Harry like a long-lost brother. Over his shoulder, as the two men shook hands, Alice caught Harry's eye for an instant. She lifted her eyebrows. Harry nodded to her.

Brief as the interchange had been, George caught it. "Perhaps you two would like a minute to yourselves," he said quietly, and turned toward a neighboring shelf.

"We don't need it," Harry assured him. "Good news can always be shared with a good friend. I have a small business undertaking which has been in the works for some time. It has finally gone through."

"Words of mystery!" cried Alice. "Let me tell him, and spare your blushes."

She took George Scudder aside to talk to him. Once Harry caught the words, "terrific amount of work." Later she said, "Don Burgess claims he used Harry as a model for a character in this book." She swooped on it, then presented the volume and a fountain pen to Harry. "Give George this with your compliments. Let him see whether his lawyer's mind can trace any likeness."

George Scudder insisted on paying for the book. "It cost you money, didn't it?"

"But you're giving me legal advice and not charging," Alice pointed out.

"It is not advice in your own case." George grinned. "The

only legal advice you two will ever need is on how to make out your wills. But I suppose that matter is already taken care of."

Alice stared as if she saw a ghost. "Years ago we both made out wills in each other's favor. That was when the children were young and we had nothing much to leave. Wouldn't those wills still hold good?"

"Only one of them would, in the very nature of the case," George answered.

Alice winced. Harry knew what had gone to her heart: the idea of herself as a widow. Generous, loyal Alice, who was always doing so much for other people. Alice, his helpmeet and his business partner. Harry Martin didn't half deserve Alice. He never had deserved her, and lately he had been more unworthy of her than ever.

"I'll have to do something about rights in my anthology, won't I?" he said, and closed the subject.

The only flaw in the senior Martins' marriage was certainly Harry's fault. Yet when he finally turned in the dedication to his anthology, it was with the savage reflection, *Here I am doing something for Alice that Emil Koenig could never do.*

19

"If you could find it in your heart to come out with me for coffee once more—!" pleaded Peggy Pratt. "I realize that I take up an awful lot of your time. But you can't realize what it means to me to have somebody to talk things over with."

"I'm an older woman, if I'm nothing else," Alice murmured sympathetically. "Around the Village, anyhow, we always have plenty of time to talk, and to listen."

The two ladies proceeded to a nearby lunchroom. It was a little early for the afternoon crowd. That suited their purpose; at their corner table, they had the advantage of privacy.

Peggy Pratt stirred, sipped, then sought Alice's eye and smiled radiantly. Her face told the story before she confided in so many words, "Walter Ferrar has asked me to marry him."

"That is big news, but no surprise. You've told him Yes?"

"I've told him Yes." Tears sprang to Peggy's eyes. "Alice, this time it's the real thing."

This time! Peggy needed somebody to talk things over with. She needed a shoulder to weep on, indeed. How much had she told Walter beyond the word of assent? What, if anything, had she done toward getting off with the old love before she was on with the new?

"I suppose it's too early for you to have made any plans?" asked Alice.

Peggy's smile was proud; but her voice was just a shade forlorn when she answered, "He says he hopes I won't keep him waiting."

"That is easy enough to understand. But for my part I hope you will." Alice paused, sipped her coffee, paused again. "These things cannot be settled on the basis of emotion alone. Too many people's happiness is at stake."

Peggy nodded sadly. "Things which were so important at the time—it wasn't so long ago, either—but now they seem so far away! Almost as if they had happened to someone else."

It's the real thing this time. Yes, but once that same feeling for another man had been the real thing. That earlier ardor had had a chance to cool. The long miles between Peggy and her Oregon suitor, the days passing into weeks and the weeks into months, had done their work. But who was to say that with conditions reversed the experience would not be repeated?

"Walter Ferrar said he hoped you wouldn't keep him waiting." It was Alice's turn to say something, and this was the best that she could do.

Again Peggy's troubles were swept aside by the incredible fact that Walter Ferrar loved her, that he was claiming her for his. "He said he was older than I, and by all that much had spent more time waiting for our meeting. But now that we had met, he said, the rest of it couldn't come too soon."

"People meet in such a variety of ways," Alice mused aloud. "Harry Martin picked me up on a dreary Sunday at

the New York Public Library. He asked me out for coffee."
Alice took another sip at her half-finished cup. "What would a woman say if she didn't drink coffee, I wonder?"

"She could always take tea."

"Virginia Daly and Don Burgess met in Waverley Book Shop just by a small quirk of fate. If Walter Ferrar hadn't happened to open his office door just when he did, your whole life might have been different."

"Ah, but he did open that door just then! Ready for more coffee? No? Then you really think I should take my time about marrying Walter?"

"There isn't all that much hurry about getting married," Alice pronounced. "Goodness knows the honorable estate lasts long enough after you're in it."

Peggy gulped, but she said gamely, "I'll tell Walter that. Thank you for listening." They discussed impersonal topics after that, and the interview soon ended.

Peggy had revealed more than she told in words; still more she had kept to herself. Her Oregon swain might have been told little or nothing about the great and only Walter Ferrar. But how much had she told her father? Her mother, too, of course; but her father was the one Peggy always talked about. He was the one anyhow who had financed this trip in search of a career. A crack-brained idea, and perhaps he knew it: that anybody could go sailing off in search of a market to satisfy. Perhaps, like many American fathers, he could deny his daughter nothing. Perhaps, like Alice, he couldn't see the hurry about getting married. Middle-aged people seldom can when the fate of younger people is at stake. In their own youth, they surely hadn't felt that way about it.

Peggy had been using Alice as a sounding board. That was all to the good, of course; it had helped the young lady to sort out her own impressions. So many people asked advice when what they really wanted was approbation; but that at least Alice had not vouchsafed. Very likely Peggy Pratt would go ahead and marry her Walter; but actually Alice had called her attention to her complicated responsibility.

There were plenty of other things to think about right now. The Republican National Convention for one thing. As if the continuing Depression hadn't been enough! But now the Convention put through a straddle plank on Prohibition. That wasn't bad luck; it was sheer bad judgment. The Democrats could plume themselves on the coming glory of Repeal.

Then Bill Thayer and Marion Murdock were married: a very quiet ceremony at City Hall, with only the Martins for witnesses. Afterward the four of them "breakfasted" at an East Side hotel; then the newlyweds went off for a three-day honeymoon. By the first of July they were in a position to get acquainted with their new status and to get used to living in their new home. Enough of the formalities had been complied with so that Nina could be packed off to camp for the summer.

Nina Thayer she was now. So registered at camp; so she would enter another school year. Nina would have a lot of new things to get used to. With the easy adaptability of youth, she could do so. Doubtless she would be spoiled; that was a thousand times better than being neglected. Could anything ever erase certain unhappy memories of her childhood?

Peggy Pratt made her decision along about this same time. Walter Ferrar had now come across with a specific plan: she was to marry him as soon as possible. Preferably right here in New York, say, at the Little Church Around the Corner. Then the two of them would go west and confront her parents with the established fact.

Peggy wavered for a minute. She came to a decision which she hesitated to explain to him. If absence had cooled her ardor for Frank out on the Coast, it must have its chance to do the same for Walter in New York City. She must go back home to Oregon and break her engagement there in so many words. It was lapsing, possibly; but a lapse was not enough. Everything must be set straight now if it were to remain straight in the future.

"In the fall," she said firmly, "if you haven't changed your mind before then."

"Then let me go out to Oregon some time during the summer. I can meet your parents and talk to them. I can make the trip again in October, if that's the way you want it. Meanwhile, how about an engagement ring?"

"Later on," said Peggy, and found herself blushing. A girl shouldn't have two engagement rings at the same time, even if one of them was in the course of being returned.

So Peggy went on back home. Alice Martin missed her. She had grown very fond of the girl. What she hadn't figured on was inheriting Walter Ferrar. He found it convenient to come around to Waverley Book Shop every twice in a while. He would ask with false casualness, "What do you hear from Peggy Pratt?" As if he didn't hear from her ten times oftener than the Martins did! Those letters of Peggy Pratt would be carefully saved, would go to join that account of herself and her days' doings which she had been writing to please Walter Ferrar. If she ever wrote a book, Alice would miss her guess. There were enough books written anyhow. Many more written than published, Alice suspected. But an awesome number were being published even in a Depression and Presidential year. The fall catalogues were already beginning to come in.

Then one afternoon into the book shop came Bess Johnson with two more specimens of her handiwork. "For Easter and Valentine's Day, 1933," she announced. "Easter will have to be renewed another year, I suspect. The valentine verse is different. There is always a fresh crop of children coming along. They don't read their valentines anyhow. They count 'em."

Her valentine verse was entitled "The Fourteenth of February," and ran:

> Dear Valentine,
> This heart of mine
> Is twin to thine.
> For thee I pine.
> Sure, "That's my line."
> I hope you're fine.

"Doggerel, to be sure," Harry Martin pronounced. "But it's amusing doggerel."

"Fun to write, anyhow. This one took some thought." Bess handed over a sheet headed "Easter Meditation." The Martins read:

> I hate to think some day I'll have to go,
>   To leave behind me all this brave bright earth,
> The scene of my small triumphs and defeats
>   And the country of my birth.
> Eternity on high may do for some;
>   Impatient I would find it last too long.
> I'll linger here and love it while I can.
>   Faint heart, be strong!

"That's too good to waste on a greeting card," said Harry. Alice agreed with his verdict.

"But it's not good enough for a magazine, I'm afraid." Bess was easily discouraged. "That 'impatient I' isn't right somehow. Oh, well, let it go for the present! Perhaps something about an Easter hat would do better for the grown people. For the children, I can do something about Easter eggs and the Easter rabbit. That's the best part of this greeting-card racket, really; I can add to the children's fun."

"Easter is a long way ahead," Alice consoled. "Meanwhile,

can't you and Ben arrange to come down soon and eat with Harry and me? We'll all talk fondly of the good old days when we were younger. We'll give Carrie sway in the apartment during the afternoon, and have her get something which can be served whenever we get around to it."

To tell Bess that her poetry was good was a sure way to discourage her, apparently. Alice would offend in that way again, probably, if she were given the chance. One subject she must remember to keep off during their planned evening was politics.

Thomas Carroll came into the shop soon after Bess Johnson left. He was a good customer as well as a fellow tenant in the Commerce Street building; he seemed to have money left even after what must have been pretty lean years for art dealers and their functionaries. Once or twice Carroll had made friendly overtures to her. That tickled Harry's sense of humor; he knew he need fear no rivalry from that quarter.

One particular evening shortly after the Johnsons and the Martins had had their evening of reunion, Alice went home a little early. Harry had indulged in one of his afternoon prowls, from which he returned looking only half-wilted. She didn't see how he managed it; even with the fans going, the shop hadn't been really cool, and even cursory attendance on the sidewalk tables was a chore. She excused herself therefore and went home for a shower and a change. Then she set up their folding chairs to be ready when Harry joined her for a drink.

She was only halfway through the brief task when Thomas Carroll joined her and offered to help. He lingered then as if he would like to talk to her. Impulsively she decided to give in and get it over with. "Won't you sit down and keep me company while I cool off?" she asked.

Sitting down, he leaned toward her and asked suddenly, "Do you believe in thought transference, Mrs. Martin?"

[236]

"I have no fixed opinions on the subject," Alice said cautiously. "I believe there is some evidence in its favor."

"Between two people who are emotionally very close? Between mother and son, for instance?"

"I have a son of my own. I used to guess ahead what he was going to do. But no, I never did any better than guess, as I remember it now."

The story came rushing out then. Carroll had been the only son of a mother widowed early. There was money in the family, too, and she had been able to keep him always at her side. All this the son revealed, though not baldly. It led up to the fact that as an elderly woman his mother had had to go to the hospital for an operation. It had been completely successful, the authorities assured him. Back home three days later, he had suddenly heard her voice, "as distinctly as if she were right there in the room with me,"—her voice saying, "Good-bye, Tom. I'm dying. Good-bye, my son." When the telephone rang five minutes later, he knew what the message would be. He was right; indeed he had told the hospital, as soon as he answered and before the doctor identified himself, "I know what it is you want to say."

"After she died, I never cared about another woman," he summed up, "and so I've never married, or had many friends."

Alice had listened in silence. But what on earth was she to say in answer?

"That isn't like anything I've ever heard before," she managed to say. "Thank you so much for telling me." Then her quick ear caught a sound on the staircase. She added, "Here comes my husband to make sure that I haven't jumped off the roof."

Harry grinned. He had caught the words, "Thank you so much for telling me." People told Alice everything. That is, most people did. Harry himself was the one who kept some-

[237]

thing from her. He had been over at Gloria Gregory's again this afternoon.

Alice picked up the ball. "I've heard stories of second sight. Of prophetic dreams, too, now that I come to think of it. But isn't it always for disaster?" With her question hanging unanswered, she shifted in her chair. "Come and sit down with me, Harry. Tom Carroll and I were talking about telepathy."

Carroll scrambled to his feet. "I must be going. Take this chair, Mr. Martin. Mrs. Martin has been kind enough to listen to something that once happened to me."

"No hurry," urged Alice. She put detaining arms around Harry and buried her face on his shoulder. She wanted the good hearty male smell of him, even if the heat had made him perspire. Just for an instant she fancied that she caught another odor, too; but before she could place it, she forgot about it.

Tom Carroll resumed his seat, but tentatively. Perhaps he dreaded the thought of a lonely evening ahead. Perhaps he was really interested in the subject he had started. He talked for half an hour or so about extrasensory perception, and talked well. He accepted the drink which Harry offered, too, but refused a second. Throughout the interview he called them "Mister" and "Missus"; Alice called him "Tom Carroll." In these first-name days, that probably indicated something.

Seldom had Alice felt so sorry for anybody. This was something, too, that she didn't feel she could tell even to Harry. A confidence must never be betrayed, and Harry was inclined to take too facetious a view of some things anyhow. To love too passionately and exclusively, as Tom's mother had, and thus to ruin the object of one's adoration, was indeed a dire fate.

Settling down with Harry in their apartment, Alice not only accepted that second drink, she reached for a cigarette. She was a very moderate smoker. Like many women of her generation, she had started the habit as a protest against out-worn conventions: what was sauce for the gander was most decidedly sauce for the goose in these enlightened days when "woman's sphere" so largely overlapped man's that for a good deal of the time they appeared to coincide. But from observation as well as mother wit she had deduced that like alcohol, nicotine was a good servant but a bad master. When a person ceased to enjoy a drink or a smoke, habit was passing over into addiction.

Harry lighted cigarettes for the two of them. Alice took a long pull and a short sip, and stared at the ceiling. Mr. Martin held up a warning hand to an imaginary audience. "Don't disturb the lady. She's thinking."

"With what?" retorted Alice.

The Martins hadn't thought of that quip in years; it brought back a host of memories. There had been a season when it was a standard household joke. Jean, just entering her teens, talked slower than her brother did. (Just as his father, on the whole, talked more than his mother did. Who ever said that garrulity was sex-linked?) There for a season, every time the poor girl began a sentence, "I thought—" Her big brother would chip in, "With what?"

Alice and Harry smiled in reminiscence. "You tried once or twice to stand up for your daughter," Harry recalled. "But a reproof is no good when you have already laughed."

"They were fun at that age," Alice agreed. "But that was when they began to grow away from us. You want them to mature and get out in the world; yet you can't help resenting it."

"Just the age-old dilemma. Parents want to eat their cake and have it, too."

Tom Carroll's mother had solved the problem in one fashion: she had kept her son exclusively hers, while devouring him as thoroughly as that particular spider which banqueted on its offspring.

Alice sheered off that subject. "I look forward to seeing Jean this summer. It won't be long now to wait. But she's been holding back on the details."

"Creating a little suspense, maybe. You don't suppose she's really decided to start in having a family?"

"I suppose just as much as you do. I know just as little. I should get a letter any day now."

As a matter of fact, that letter came the very next day. Jean would arrive the second week in August. She would stay about a month, "if you find you can stand me that long." She was coming alone.

"Oh, my divining soul! You don't suppose they've had a quarrel and are separating?" Harry groaned.

"No, I don't suppose so. Even if they were, we'd have to keep quiet and let them tell their own news."

So here was one treat more in immediate prospect. Peggy Pratt continued to keep them supplied with tidings from the Coast. Bill Thayer showed proudly the letters Nina wrote them from camp. Marion once took Alice aside and confided, "To think I ever hesitated about marrying Bill! Every day now I'm finding some fresh reason to love him." A remark which Alice found touching and just a shade ridiculous, since their marriage was not yet dry behind the ears.

Alice sometimes thought that in this world there was never quite enough happiness to go around. Right now it seemed that there was.

She was thinking of saying as much to Harry one afternoon when he came in from another of his neighborhood prowls. She had him to herself for a minute; Bill was waiting on a customer at the other end of the shop.

"You look remarkably pleased with life," she announced. "Almost as if you had partaken of a little stimulation. Let me smell your breath."

"I may have had a drink," he acknowledged. "But what's a little stimulation between friends?"

He leaned toward her. But instead of smelling his breath, Alice put up one hand and closed his lips with her fingers. Then she kissed him in the middle of his cheek, right where the prick of the beard behind the skin would have its full effect on her.

It did for an instant. Then Alice started as if she had had an electric shock. She had detected an odor which was not native to that spot. This was not the first time she had smelled that special smell. It had assailed her nostrils the night Harry sat down on the chair with her while she was talking to Tom Carroll on the roof of the apartment building. That time, however, she had ignored the sensation. Now it suddenly connected itself with something else. Something significant. Something dire.

The scent was that of a woman's perfume. One of those strong perfumes which are supposed to be extremely alluring to the male of the species. A perfume which she had smelled once before right here in this very shop. Alice, who never wore anything stronger than lavender cologne, suddenly remembered noticing such a whiff. She drew back. Her voice was low and quiet and seemed to come from a distance when she said, "So you've been kissing her!"

"I haven't!" snapped Harry. Then, after that too-hasty denial, he must go blundering on, "I don't know what you're talking about. I did stop in at what looked like a promising joint. I had it pretty much to myself; there was nobody there I knew. I was going to tell you about it, if you hadn't been so hasty."

Alice turned on her heel and walked away. She joined Bill Thayer and the customer; she was just enough mistress of herself so that she took care not to kill his sale.

That kiss, and the one which had preceded the moment on the roof. These two—and how many scores, perhaps hundreds, which Alice had never suspected. It didn't stop at kissing, either. Not these days. Not with a susceptible male who was challenged to show what he could do. Not with a baggage like the one who had come in here all those weeks (or was it months?) ago and insisted that the proprietor must deliver her purchases.

She had stayed away consistently since then, at least so far as Alice knew. It didn't take much angling to get a bite out of that poor fish. Doubtless the lady was an experienced angler. What was her implausible name? Oh, yes, "Gloria Gregory!" A writer for "True Confessions" magazines; a dame who made a living by feeding garbage to the gullible. By supplementing her income in other ways, too, perhaps. A man had to compensate in some way for the favors he received; Harry Martin had free access to the cash register at Waverley Book Shop, and if he chose to take additional money out of it from time to time, there was no way of catching him in the act.

After all these years, to have this happen! In a stable, well-rounded marriage, a marriage which like an enduring house was built on a firm foundation, to which every year of mutual affection and shared interests and the incidents of daily living had added another course—to have this wretched thing happen!

The first shock of realization was followed by a strange numbness. It carried Alice through the next hour or so. She did not speak to Harry; she scarcely looked at him. She hadn't the vaguest idea what her next step would be.

Yet a next step of some kind was inevitable. She couldn't just casually wait here with him, placidly close the shop, go home to their charming apartment across Seventh Avenue, dine *à deux* and go to bed together. As they had done so many times in the long, loving years they had spent together. As they had continued to do these latter days when Harry had been carrying on with this creature.

The next move was up to her. That was plain enough in any man's language. Alice took advantage of a lull in business to say, "Bill can help you out for the rest of the evening, can't he? I'll go back to Commerce Street and wait for you."

"I'll go with you if you like," said Harry. He forced himself to meet her eye. But under Alice's cool gaze his face reddened. It was a slow reluctant flush: an old man's flush. Instead of arousing Alice's sympathy, it simply added to her anger and humiliation. Silently she shook her head at him.

She went across Seventh Avenue and up those three flights of stairs to what had only lately been a charming refuge for the two of them: an indulgence which was almost like a honeymoon nest in some ways. But not tonight. Not any night henceforward. It would be to Alice now, not the place where the senior Martins had been so happy together, but the hearth that Harry had betrayed. The worst of a transgression like his was that it not only darkened the future, it cast a strange and dreadful light upon the past.

20

Her sense of incredulity persisted. The walls of the apartment stared down at her like some strange stage setting, or like a background dimly perceived in a dream. This was home: the home which she and Harry had permitted themselves to indulge in, the second home so well suited to their years of maturity. This was home—once.

It couldn't happen. Yet it had happened. It happened all around and all the time; yet unless there was something very spectacular about it, it wasn't even news. It was simply the kind of thing that went on constantly. But not where the senior Martins were concerned. After all those long fruitful years together, the eternal triangle was certainly ruled out. Only it wasn't. Not even in the case of that ardent advocate of matrimony, Alice Martin.

She had given him a little time to himself. That avoided an open quarrel; it also gave him a chance to collect himself. It must have been a shock to him that she had finally made the discovery. For her part, she felt like a fool not to have found it out long since.

There were always certain motions to be gone through; it did no good to neglect them even in times of emotional crisis. Alice showered, put on fresh clothing, brushed her hair into sleek, shining waves. Forlornly she remembered having read somewhere that a frog with its forebrain cut out could still eat, drink, and scratch itself. That was just the sort of small joke she had liked to share with Harry back in the days when the sharing was good.

He kept her waiting long enough so that Alice began to get a little uneasy. A glance at the clock, however, showed that it was not as long as it had seemed. She would still have time to listen to him, to see that he was made physically comfortable, then to leave him here and take the subway ride back to Brooklyn. It was a long ride; it would be a lonely ride if she took it all by herself.

When he finally came in, he brought the evening newspaper, which he tendered her with only a nod of greeting. Then he spent a long time cleaning up. He should have removed the traces of Miss Gregory's perfume earlier. Or he might have set up his intrigue with a woman who used a delicate odor. In that case Alice would have gone right on being hoodwinked.

Until the affair wore off? Until the lady sickened of the situation and demanded a showdown? Alice almost wished that something like that had happened. It hadn't, however. She must deal with the disastrous—and ridiculous—facts.

"Drink, Harry?" she asked when he finally presented himself in the living room.

"You must need it by this time," he said. "Business was good tonight. Wine or a gin concoction?"

"Wine for me, please. There is some ready chilled." Alice glanced at the newspaper while he tended bar. It wasn't until they were seated together at what should have been the finest hour of their day that she said coldly, "Well, I'm waiting."

"I suppose you feel that you have some kind of explanation

[245]

due you," he began. He got on with his story: how he sometimes met acquaintances while he was on his rounds, how one
particular girl had asked him up to her apartment for a
drink, how he had kissed her good-bye. "Not that it meant
anything much to me, but she seemed to expect it."

Alice allowed a significant pause. She knew now the meaning of the good Edwardian expression, "He lied like a gentleman." She said coolly, glancing up from her drink only
for an instant, "The woman gave you the apple."

He began to flounder. He was pitiful, and he was disgust-
ing. Alice listened, shrugged, once or twice agreed faintly.
But at least the facts of the case were growing clear. It had
happened, and she must take some sort of step toward making
an adjustment.

She prepared a small cold supper, for which neither of
them had any appetite. Then she said quietly, "I had thought
of going over to Brooklyn to spend the night; but I don't see
why I should penalize myself. I'd have to meet you in the
shop tomorrow anyhow. There is always business to be attended to."

"You mustn't dream of that!" he protested. "Going poking
off by yourself like that."

"I'll need time to think things over," Alice went on. "Jean
is due here very soon now. In front of her we'll have to put
up a pretense of being still married."

"A—a pretense?" stammered Harry.

"If I can trust you to stay over on your own side of the bed,
I'm sleeping here tonight," Alice announced.

Harry was so relieved that he forgot for an instant his pose
of injured innocence. "I knew you'd understand when you
stopped to think it over," he said. Then he bit his tongue and
looked embarrassed. He had conceded that there was something which she would have to "understand."

Apart from being such a sleepyhead, Harry Martin had a
sensuous love of bed anyhow. His bed companion was an

[246]

essential part of his comfort, a sort of charm or fetish, like the things children take to bed with them, dolls and teddy bears, or a tattered picture book or even a fragment of an old blanket. Both Jim and Jean had derived that childish comfort from bedtime toys.

Actually that had helped greatly in the early days of their marriage. Alice, though mature enough in most ways, was pretty much unawakened on one side of her nature. All the better if she was, of course; it had been her bridegroom's delightful task to arouse her latent passion. The idea that they should now sleep like a couple in legend, as if a drawn sword lay between them in the middle of the bed, was a regression to very early days indeed.

Still, it was better than if she had insisted on leaving him. Much better, indeed. Time and propinquity would do their work for him. He could bide his time, and humor her.

Harry slept badly that night, Alice scarcely at all. She lay there in a carefully relaxed pose; she breathed evenly and quietly, so that he would be deceived if he woke and listened. But she was thinking both backward and ahead. There was a lot to be cleared up in the Martin ménage and the Martin business. She must begin now to train herself so that she wouldn't give in accidentally. This wasn't anything that called for a public breakup: not a sudden dramatic breakup anyhow. The Martins had their business and their family to consider. But the private estrangement was deep and serious. The very fact that theirs had been a many-sided marriage made the present situation much harder to deal with.

Were other marriages as happy as they seemed? Here daughter Jean was coming on to New York without Earl Crawford. What, if anything, did that augur? How much would she tell her mother anyhow? Could the unhappy situation here be kept from Jean's sharp eyes?

Harry discontinued his explorations west of Seventh Avenue. He still attended to the mail order business; but he came back promptly from those excursions to the post office. Had he broken with Gloria Gregory? If so, how and when? It looked as if he had. There were a few unexplained phone calls to the shop. When Alice answered, there was "nobody on the line"; when Harry did, he informed the caller, "I think you have the wrong number." It might be simply that there were that many mistakes. It might be that Gloria Gregory was biding her time and feeling her way along.

Daughter Jean arrived as promised. She was lovelier than ever, and more affectionate. "I'm going to have one more fling at New York and being a girl again," she announced gayly. "Earl deserves a matrimonial vacation anyhow. He can electioneer for the New Deal if he likes. He can eat at restaurants or take his chances at home and let the dishes pile up in the sink the way they do in the cartoons. He deserves a break, and he's getting it."

She insisted on sleeping in the living room of the Commerce Street apartment most of the time; but twice she asked her mother to go back with her and spend the night in the old Brooklyn flat. Jean slept alone in her old bedroom, Alice alone where she had for so many years shared accommodations with Harry Martin. Here too Alice slept badly, though there was no mythical sword lying down the middle of the bed. These surroundings, in these changed circumstances, brought back too many memories.

Jean was all joy. "I'm bidding farewell to my girlhood once and for all. Oh, I know I've been a married woman for quite some years now! But Earl and I have just jogged along with our eyes on the present. I've finally decided that it's time we started our family."

"You don't mean that you——?" Alice was startled.

"No indeed! Your eagle eye would have detected it if the miracle had really come to pass. I'm waiting—and I'm hoping."

Alice was touched. Jean had confided her secret dreams and

aspirations: proof of how she loved and trusted her mother. It was also proof that she trusted fate. In a matter so close to her own heart, Alice would never have dared speak aloud; it was too much like inviting trouble.

Or was it simply that she had had nobody to speak to? Even if Mrs. Frederickson had been still alive when Alice was married, she would have been no candidate for such confidences. Alice's mother and her contemporaries discussed among themselves certain of the more intimate aspects of femininity with a gusto and detail which Alice found faintly revolting; yet they kept a taboo on others. You might sometimes have thought they still believed that the stork brought the babies. The tradition which had prevailed in the days of the Dear Queen was still strong enough to carry on the assumption that men were "like that," and it was a wife's duty to submit. An assumption which reduced one of the loveliest things in life to slavery, and a very degrading form of slavery at that.

Jean and Earl Crawford took for granted that they had full control over the practical side of the situation; their very confidence must help them there. Emotionally they were at full flood: a higher tide possibly than they would have enjoyed if they had set about the undertaking earlier. They were spending these few weeks apart in order to get full perspective on their happiness.

"Waiting and hoping is a part of life," Alice assured her daughter. "One of the loveliest parts." She leaned over to kiss Jean. At that moment they were both close to tears. But an instant later the younger woman became offhand again; there was nothing left for her mother to do except to follow suit.

There were no sentimental episodes with her father; Jean commandeered Harry for repeated dates, but between the two of them it was always some sort of game. She had him take her to movies, a form of entertainment which did not ordinarily fit into Harry's scheme of things; she told him this was doing a lot to broaden his horizon. She suggested walks about the Village and rides on the open-deck Fifth Avenue bus; during these she pretended that this was her first visit to New York, and she was not an overintelligent tourist. Stupid or not, she came up with some questions which displayed Harry's ignorance. She insisted on an afternoon trip to a speakeasy for a drink. Once she pretended she was a foreigner; talking in bad vaudeville dialect, she inquired what would happen if "ze police found out about zis place." Once she was a disdainful dame from the old home town, and demanded, "Isn't there somewhere else to go for a drink in the Village? Somewhere where you meet interesting people?"

To that last question Harry replied in tones of mock offense, "So you don't think *I'm* interesting?"

"After two drinks, maybe you will be," retorted Jean.

Another time his response was, "I hope you carry mad money. Another crack like that, and I'll stalk out of this place and leave you to settle the bill."

" 'Mad money'? I hadn't heard that expression in ages." Jean began to laugh. "I always did carry along a little money. Not only is it a handy thing to have; it's awkward to do without."

"A sage saying," commented her father. "You get your talent for epigram from me."

"Mother can always hold up her end," Jean reminded him.

"Oh, we get lots of practice! The place in the Village where you meet interesting people isn't a speakeasy, I find; it's Waverley Book Shop."

"Credit that one to 'Advertisement,' " Jean suggested. "But come to think of it, there have been times when I slipped my escort a bill. Under the table, of course, so as not to humiliate the poor chap. Can you imagine the embarrassment, Dad, of being young and taking a girl out for a good time and then running short of money?"

"Imagine it? It has happened to me. Happened more than

once in my impecunious college days. But I was never forced to stoop so low as to get money from the girl. Both times I raised a loan from a fellow in the crowd."

" 'Both' times? You remember it as well as all that?"

Harry nodded and suddenly went back to their impersonation. Memory was a tricky thing. Generally a man's distant youth took on rainbow hues when it was recalled in middle age; nostalgia was one of the privileges of maturity. But every once in a while some tricky incident, forgotten for years, would again pop up its ugly head. Almost always an ugly head. One didn't forget the joys of youth; one simply exaggerated them.

It was during one of these forays that Alice, tending shop with Bill Thayer, spotted a woman gazing attentively into the windows of the book shop. Seeing herself observed, the newcomer feigned interest in the outside tables. That gave Alice a good chance to size her up. Kindling suspicion drove Mrs. Martin out to the sidewalk, where she said, "We have a lot of other used books inside, if you'd care to look them over. I was just about to add some volumes to these tables."

"It will be cooler inside." The newcomer followed Alice indoors. Sure enough, she was wearing a heavy perfume. Not the same one which Alice remembered only too well, but a more recent variation, or possibly something recommended especially for summer use.

"Just take your time, in case you like to browse around," Alice invited. "Or if there is something in which you are especially interested, I'll be right here to help you."

"Perhaps a detective story or two," murmured the woman. "They make good summer reading."

It was Gloria Gregory all right. Harry must simply have dropped her; he had refused to talk to her on the phone, he had not gone off on long absences lately. Had he broken with her in so many words? How did anybody break with a woman like that? It was a challenge to her to whistle him back. But perhaps one reason for her coming here was to find out if the wife knew.

Alice was tempted. She could say, "Aren't you Gloria Gregory? We haven't seen you around here much lately." No, that was all wrong. In this neighborhood customers came and went; only steady patrons rated the honor of special mention. She could say, "If it's my husband you're looking for, he's out for the afternoon with his grown daughter." That would be even worse: sheer cattiness from a respectable married woman, and a nasty slap at Harry.

Alice thought of a better one, "I'm not sure I have a used copy of that particular book. But Don Burgess, the detective-story writer—Are you familiar with his work?"

"I'm not sure I remember him by name," murmured Gloria Gregory.

"He's well known, as such things go," Alice assured her. "He's a good friend of ours, too. We have a full line of auto-graphed Burgesses at home. But what I started to say was, he vows that the noble amateur detective in his last book is a character founded on my husband."

"Your husband?" Gloria tossed the ball right back at her. Miss Gregory might never have suspected that Alice had a husband, let alone that anybody had put him into a book. She had a momentary advantage; but she pushed it too far. Instead of waiting for Alice's reply, the newcomer gestured in the direction of Bill Thayer, who was waiting on a new customer at the other end of the shop.

"Oh, no!" said Alice sweetly. "I supposed you knew. That is Bill Thayer, our very able assistant. I'm Mrs. Harry Martin. Bill and I are married, but not to each other."

Gloria Gregory managed to smile. "You say Mr.—was the name Sturgess?—put your husband into a mystery story? That might make it more interesting to you personally. But as far as the reading public goes, that is hardly a consideration."

"True!" Alice agreed. "The name is Burgess. But since

[252]

that means nothing to you, let me pick you out one used Burgess for a sample. The fellow really knows his business, I think, even if he is a friend of ours."

Gloria did better this time with her smile. She wasn't finding out much; but at least she could put it down to her score that she hadn't given herself away. "Do pick out some Burgesses, and one or two other whodunits," she ordered. "You have the cheaper books on the tables outside, don't you?"

She presently took herself off. A good-looking gal, if you liked them a little on the overblown side. More to an iceman's taste, Alice would have said, than to a bookseller's. Still, very much the sort that might encourage some men to show that their prowess had not vanished with increasing years.

Alice couldn't very well mention this to Harry. Couldn't mention it in Jean's hearing, of course; when Alice and he were alone together, they now had very little personal conversation. Shop talk, yes; matters relative to their keeping board and bed together even on opposite sides of the bed, yes, that too; concerns of their visiting child, certainly. But one of the worst features of their estrangement was that the senior Martins no longer chattered away when they were in private. In company too they now gave the other fellow more chance; but perhaps that was something of an improvement. The silences between just the two of them were bitter. Even Jean's proximity helped them very little.

So another small stone was added to the wall that had grown up between them. When Harry and Jean presently returned, Alice asked for an account of their outing; on her side she merely reported a fair afternoon's business, and added no particulars.

She had her turn again at Jean's society, though they never again got in as deep as they had right there at the time of the daughter's supreme disclosure. Alice accompanied Jean to matinees of the few plays which had held over, and to one of an early opening which was not selling out. Ben Johnson got them passes; Ben himself had retired from the playwrighting game, but his drag as a drama critic was as good as ever. The two of them went shopping together, too. Jean could buy almost the same clothes in Minneapolis for about the same price; but they would lack the New York cachet. It was more fun to go shopping with Mother anyhow, and Alice on her part allowed herself to be talked into buying more things than she really needed, though doubtless they would all be put to good use.

Jean modeled some of her new clothes for her father. When Harry suggested that Alice do the like, she shook her head and assured him, "You'll see them soon enough."

Harry looked rebuffed. Jean, puzzled, assured him, "Mother is afraid she'll steal my thunder."

"Mother wants to keep her nice comfortable seat as part of the audience," Alice amended. "You must realize that we spent three afternoons as well as a young fortune buying these things. We're through now, I hope, I hope, I hope! Mamma is bushed."

That was the way she used to sound, the way Harry liked her to sound. Alice was keeping up appearances, of course. But even that was something gained. He moved his chair closer to hers and reached out to take her hand. Alice moved it at that instant. By chance, possibly. Just possibly.

"I'm sure I'm through," said Jean graciously. "I think I'll let the other things stay in their boxes until it's time to pack for the trip home. I brought my suitcases half empty, just looking forward to this."

Unwelcome reminder of how soon she would be leaving! Harry cleared his throat. "Do you think, for a change, you and I might go somewhere in serious earnest? Go to one of those places where New York residents visit with their out-of-town relatives in tow?"

" 'In serious earnest,' you say. You sound as if you were tired of my clowning."

"Never! But if you could find it in your heart to journey up to the Metropolitan Museum of Art and trundle through some of the exhibits with me, I'd enjoy it very much."

"I might look at the exhibits so hard I'd forget about my escort." But Jean smiled radiantly. "Name the day, Dad."

Harry consulted Alice, of course; but he did name the day. Then it was Mrs. Martin's turn to do some inviting. "Wouldn't it be nice if we had a few people here for dinner, Jean? We're both obligated to Ben Johnson for those theater passes. Harry and I owe Emil and Kitty Koenig; have owed it ever since the Flood. I'm sure the Burgesses would come in town for the occasion, too. Perhaps you have some friends you'd like to invite?"

Jean shook her head. "You haven't noticed me bothering much with my contemporaries, have you? I've lost track of early New York acquaintances; your friends here are now my friends. But could you arrange such a large party here, Mother? We might have to go back to Brooklyn for it."

Between the apartment and the roof, Alice thought she could. Besides, all the people invited might not come.

Virginia Daly Burgess refused for the two of them; but she wanted Jean to come out for luncheon and to see the baby. "Jean and you, Alice, if you can possibly make it," she urged.

They could, and did. It was right along the line that Jean's emotions were pursuing anyhow, to view darling little Joan. Alice remembered that Virginia too had been a woman who thought she had full control over the family situation. Events had finally justified her, too.

Jean had by this time made her reservation on the *Commodore Vanderbilt*. That was the New York Central's second luxury train. The dear old *Twentieth Century* was still the train which had prestige, and charged accordingly. School-teachers and their mates paid for luxury when they could afford it; but they were in the habit of getting their money's worth.

She intended to stop over in Chicago and see Jim and his family. Her idea was to make arrangements in advance and then forget about them. Earl might meet her in Chicago and then again he might not. She had an idea that he would; he had been writing her what amounted to love letters. Separation was on the whole a fine idea; but it would be a long time before Jean again tried to put it into practice.

Her cultural expedition with her father was a decided success. Harry proved the perfect companion; he listened more than he talked, and his occasional comments were interesting and to the point. *It's too bad he feels that he has to clown so much of the time*, Jean thought. His own fault, of course, for encouraging the idea. But he did seem different lately. Or perhaps it was merely that she was seeing him in a different light. She saw everything in a different light these days; she felt kindly toward everybody.

The dinner party went off swimmingly, too. Emil Koenig carried a plateful of fried chicken and other delicacies across Seventh Avenue to Bill Thayer in the book shop. From the roof Jean watched in company with Ben Johnson and a man named George Scudder, whom Alice had invited in to balance up the party. Harry Martin had gone down to the apartment to put together another round of drinks. Bess Johnson and Kitty Koenig had preferred electric fans in the living room to what passed for fresh air on the roof.

The senior Martins were like that, always looking out for everybody. Jean would remember to tell Earl about this when she wrote him tomorrow. The last letter she would write him from New York. She almost hoped they would open it together in Minneapolis. But if he didn't meet her in Chicago, she must remember not to be disappointed. It wouldn't be long to wait, anyhow.

Smiling, Jean turned away from the parapet and began to do her duty as guest of honor. Some duties were more like privileges. Right now, Jean Martin Crawford was enjoying her full share of them.

21

Fall was a splendid season in New York, a city which luckily had other attractions besides its climate. Summers here were long and hot, winters slushy, springs alluring only in spots. But with autumn a lovely crispness came into the air. Life leaped into high gear. Everybody came back. The few millions who hadn't been away had taken advantage of the relaxed atmosphere which the heat engendered; as keenly as the returning absentees they enjoyed the new tautness. The theaters reopened. The shops displayed their magic. Telephones rang and night spots were crowded. Even returning school children had an extra week's vacation; public schools opened that much later here than they did in most other places.

Among those who entered New York this September was little Nina Thayer, fresh from her summer at camp and beginning to be accustomed to her new surname. She was now a child with a latch key of her own: an apartment-house dweller, free to come home by herself and make the best of what she found there.

She was terrifically proud of her new responsibility. For the first few weeks she paused every afternoon at Waverley Book Shop to show her key and demonstrate how promptly she was going to use it. To her, the new Thayer ménage was an Aladdin's cave. She had a room of her own, with her play clothes hung on a special hook in the closet and her fruit and milk waiting for her in the refrigerator. On fine days she could disport herself in the small back-yard garden until it was time for Mamma Marion to arrive home. If it rained, she could fall back on her cherished books. Then, when Mamma Marion came home, Nina would set about her homework, which at her age was not heavy. Sundays and generally Thursdays Daddy Bill ate with them. Saturdays Nina saw him at work when she paid her customary visit to Waverley Book Shop. Mamma Marion had told her she must no longer expect regular gifts from Mrs. Martin. All the same, Nina often left the shop richer than she entered it.

Another romance was coming to fruition these days. Peggy Pratt had set the day when she would marry Walter Ferrar. She had set the place, too; that was another of the bride's prerogatives. The Little Church Around the Corner it would be, the last week in October. Meanwhile she and her parents were coming from Oregon to New York in plenty of time to get through the necessary preliminaries. Or at least that part of them for which the bride's presence was necessary. Walter must do all his part and get hers laid out for her. When she and her parents appeared, it would be simply to complete arrangements, do a little last-minute shopping, and give their final sanction.

"And pay the bills," Harry Martin remarked in private to Alice. "Peggy is certainly making it easy for Walter."

Was Peggy running away from memories? Alice wondered. Thanks to her own entanglement she was always looking these days for the flaw in the gem, the rift in the lute. Things just weren't all that lovely. The Prince and the Princess didn't live happily ever afterward. The dream was lovely enough while it lasted; but it wouldn't last. That was simply one of the pretty stories people told to children.

Aloud she remarked reasonably, "The Pratts seem to have money enough for a good many cross-country trips. The way Peggy sends Walter in here to report to us, she must feel that we figure in the proceedings some way."

Peggy did. She not only wrote regularly to Alice; twice she long-distanced the Martins at their apartment. It was only the shank of the evening on the Coast; but it was late enough in New York so that she was reasonably certain to find them at home.

At home, and delighted to have their privacy interrupted. Alice and Harry were still on those same width-of-a-sword terms. In addition they were still acutely lonesome for Jean, now back home and with an eager eye turned toward her own future.

"I want the two of you to come to my wedding as my witnesses," Peggy said during her first call. During the second she made detailed arrangements for the Martins to meet the Pratts as soon as they were established at their New York hotel.

"Now I'm glad I have all those new clothes," said Alice complacently. "You're the one who had better do a little modeling now, Mr. Martin. You'll have to look your best to live up to Peggy's description of you."

"She may have described me as a Village oddity," said Harry rather bitterly. "Good old Harry Martin, who is such a character that an author put him into a book. He's all right in his way, to be sure; but everybody knows that he doesn't weigh much."

"Is there a pun involved there?" asked Alice. "Let's look in your closet, though, while we're on the subject." His newer clothes were hanging in the closet of the room he used as a study; but he still kept a few things in the closet of the bedroom. He dressed and undressed there, too. If Alice had now taken most of those incidental intimacies to the bathroom, well, so much the worse for her.

They looked in his closet. She had him try on one coat, helped him settle the shoulders, gave him a short nod of approval. "It will do very nicely for chasing around this fall. But for the wedding itself, I think you'd better get a new suit. I can tend shop some afternoon while Bill Thayer goes with you to pick it out."

"Got it all fixed up in your own mind, haven't you?" he retorted.

"I really should have let Jean lead you into the men's department. I—I'm afraid I was a little selfish with Jean. But her visit was so short."

"Too short," Harry agreed. "Did Peggy tell you where they plan to be married?"

"At the Little Church Around the Corner. Bless her innocent little heart, how romantic she must think that will be!"

"But—but that's where you and I were married!" stammered Harry.

"It is. But we didn't take out a patent on the idea, did we?" Alice's voice was crisp, but she avoided his eye. "We thought at the time that we had. Probably they think so too."

If he pressed her now, he might break down her resistance. Just as well, he might strengthen it. Better wait for some suitable occasion, such as the approaching wedding, which might well put Alice into a sentimental mood.

Then all of a sudden he wondered what he was worrying about. She had caught him in a flagrant affair; she was punishing him for his offense. Yet she continued to keep up appearances; she worked as industriously as ever at their joint business; right this minute she was urging him to spend money which he would just as soon have saved.

"Is Peggy an only child?" he asked. "I never heard her talk about any sisters or brothers."

"She has a married sister some years older than she. I gather that the two of them have never been very close. Anyhow she didn't say anything about the sister's coming with her to New York."

The sister didn't. It was a very quiet little wedding. Walter Ferrar's brother came from Ohio to act as his best man; three men from the publishers and their wives were also present at the ceremony. Afterward the bridal party breakfasted at the Waldorf. Then the young couple left for their honeymoon. They were going to Asheville, North Carolina, Peggy had confided to Alice. After a month there they would return to Walter's bachelor apartment for the winter.

Meanwhile Mr. and Mrs. Pratt were staying on at their hotel. "We thought after we came so far we might as well spend a little time here," Peggy's mother explained. Her father caught Harry's eye and nodded rather sadly. They had come so far. Presently they would return so far. There they would face that awful emptiness.

In a sense they were prepared for it. They had even asked for it when they staked their daughter to that crucial year in New York. Only they had expected her to come back and marry her Oregon Frank, or write that promised book and come home after she was an established author.

"You must come down and see our shop," Alice invited. "Dinner afterward in the attic where we live. Right at the crossroads of the Village. Can't we set the date now?"

"It's just too good of you to ask us!" protested Mrs. Pratt. "But Peggy has told us so much about that fascinating shop of yours—!"

"Peggy is just too kind," said Alice. "I hope you won't be disappointed!"

Now it was Mr. Pratt's turn. "We will love to see your shop, of course. But why not let us be the hosts for dinner, in a place of your choosing?"

Something about that speech was wrong. 'You choose the

place and we pick up the check.' The Martins just weren't all that poor. Alice said sweetly, "We eat at home most of the time now. The good places we used to know have been ruined by uptowners."

Mr. Pratt had the grace to blush. "Dinner in your home, then. We shall look forward to it, shan't we, Margot? I'm sure we can suit your convenience."

That was the important part: something to look forward to. All four of them were suffering now from a letdown feeling. The distant future, though promising enough, sometimes looked too distant. Let them set a date for the party; setting it would do them all good.

They did exactly that. A date for dinner, though Harry felt as if he couldn't eat again for a week. Their farewells over, the Martins had to wait an instant while a taxi was summoned for them. This was indeed a rarefied atmosphere, where a man couldn't even flag down his own hack.

"You want to go into the shop for a minute and let Bill Thayer look at you in the splendor he helped you pick out," Alice said. It was a statement, not a question.

"I do, darling. But first I'm going to land you safe back where you put your corsage in the refrigerator and have a long drink of ice water." Harry helped Alice into the cab which drew up at that minute. Scrambling in after her, he asked in the weary tone of one who expects a stupid answer, "Do you know where Commerce Street is, down in the Village?"

The driver was a tall, handsome man about thirty. In a brogue which sounded fairly like stage Irish, he answered, "Yis, sorr-rr-rr, I know ivery strate on Manhattan Island."

Harry instantly went on his dignity. He drew himself up with an expression which said as clearly as words, 'You needn't think you can get the slightest hint out of me, you sassy Irishman.' Alice caught onto the little byplay; instead of watching the street in his rear-view mirror, the driver was

[263]

watching his fare. He took the shortest way downtown, turned west at the proper corner, and inquired, "Phwat numberr-rr-rr did you say, sorr-rr-rr?"

Harry Martin hadn't said any number. He did so now, and chuckled when he said it.

When the cab had been paid off and dismissed, Alice said to Harry, "I'll see you at the shop in an hour or so. You can yarn to Bill between customers. When I spell you, you can come back here and change."

"Make it as snappy as you can," begged Harry. "I don't want to get book shop dust on these wedding clothes of mine."

Entering her top-floor apartment, Alice tried to view it as a stranger might. It was undoubtedly clean and comfortable; also, it was not the sort of place where out-of-towners would expect Village characters to live. It might almost have been a cottage in Alice's native upstate New York. It might have been a bungalow in the Pratts' Oregon. Or did they have bungalows in Oregon? Alice supposed so; they built those affairs pretty well all over America.

Why try to do the other fellow's thinking for him? Alice wrote down the agreed date (not that there was much chance of her forgetting it). The menu would center around Carrie's fried chicken. Drinks as usual. Alice scribbled another memorandum. Then, with a welcome feeling of getting back down to earth, she disposed of her wedding finery, put on fresh and somewhat lighter make-up, and followed Harry's suggestion about drinking ice water. She had thoroughly enjoyed today's festivities. But it was great to have home to get back to. Home, and that other spot where she functioned so naturally, Waverley Book Shop. In some ways Alice preferred the shop to the apartment, now that—Oh, damn it, she wasn't going to let that woman intrude into her thoughts now! Not now, when it had been such a thoroughly satisfactory day.

She rejoined Harry in the shop and informed him he was

now free to go home and change. While he was doing so, she favored Bill with her account of the wedding festivities. Her mind veered off to the bridal pair, then to her own wedding night. Luckily a customer came in just then; Alice signed to Bill that she would take him.

When Harry returned to the shop, she sent Bill home. Home to his wife and ready-made family. One good thing about children was that they kept the parents from seeing too much of each other. Bill was in no danger on that score, perhaps. Tonight he could eat with both Marion and Nina. That would round things off nicely.

Alice's mind was still on the wedding festivities next afternoon when she sat down in the shop to write all about it to daughter Jean. She was halfway through the letter when in came somebody who must be told by word of mouth: that old married man and seasoned campaigner, Don Burgess.

He listened to her news and wished her well of her dinner guests. Then, as usual, he proceeded to groan upon her shoulder. He was in the process of writing a new book, and found himself up against a new set of obstacles.

"This time I am trying a real variation," he announced. "Instead of producing a corpse right at the beginning and then going on to deal with various suspects, I am now building up an atmosphere of suspense and suspicion. Next I intend to plant the weapon. From there on I can more or less trust the old formula. Because the good detective stories have all been written. I myself had a share in a few of them. Alas, how good I used to be! So good I acknowledge it myself."

"You're not exactly a galley slave chained to your oar," Alice reminded him. "There are other ways of making a living besides writing books. You could get a job as floorwalker in a department store, I should think."

"I was once a moderately successful schoolteacher," Don recalled. "I hated the routine; but at least when the bell rang for dismissal, all I had to do was correct papers. Still, I could get through it by using about half my mind. Now I beat my brains out week after week, month after month, and what does it all amount to?"

"You help to keep honest booksellers in business," Alice answered promptly. "You make tired businessmen forget their cares. You distract housewives from their darning and dishwashing. You can point with pride to a small shelf of volumes with your name on them. Need I go on?"

"You needn't. There is something in what you say. But I have thought sometimes of going up another alley. I'd like to deal with the great historical mysteries, such as the Lost Colony of Roanoke Island."

"Why not do just that, as soon as you can find the time and energy? You could even start a second career under another name."

"A great idea!" This time Don allowed his amusement to show. "Call myself Burgess Donaldson instead of Donald Burgess. Or—here's the dodge that all mystery writers fall back on sooner or later: people who change their names often do not change their initials."

"In an escaping criminal, he might be taking his luggage with him, and it might be marked with his initials."

"Right! My luggage doesn't make so much difference; it's gathering dust in an attic on Long Island, and is likely to remain there. But my initials, D. B.! D. M. B., now that I come to think of it. I used the middle initial, as an initial, in the days when I used to explain to unlucky kids that the square erected on the hypotenuse— It's a queer American custom, that of middle names which are never used in full."

"They go on wedding invitations and announcements," Alice insisted.

"Woman, were you ever caught without an answer? Now wait a minute! Here's one for you, and maybe one for me. You remember that the old nursery rhyme asks, 'Who killed

Cock Robin?' There is prompt confession. The sparrow says he did it with his bow and arrow. We get a lot about the funeral and the mourners. But we never see justice done, and we never learn what was behind it all."

"This time you score," said Alice. "You can tell us all that about Cock Robin."

Don smote his brow. "Damned if you haven't given me an idea! I come in here with a grievance, and you hand me a new scene already made—maybe a whole series of scenes. 'A good riddance to bad rubbish.' Is that the idea? Just for that, sweet-Alice-Ben-Bolt, put me together all of last spring's books that nobody else has taken off your hands and I'll give you my check for them."

"And may the check be better than the books?" Alice chimed in. "As a matter of fact, our spring books moved very well. I'll give you a nice selection from used copies, and let you have a discount at that. Now talk sense for a change, if you can. Tell me all about Virginia and Joan."

Don turned to Harry and an amused customer. "I had already told the woman Alice she's given me an idea; she had perhaps inspired another of my works of genius. Now she invites me to talk sense. Just for that I'm going to ignore her while she looks up a few likely books for me. But I don't mind telling you, Harry old top, that my wife is fine and flourishing, and a better writer than I am any day in the week. As for my daughter, I carry snapshots of her around with me all the time, and inflict them on people at the slightest excuse."

Alice sold several second hand Burgesses right in front of him, just to show Don. He bought most of the books she had given him to select from. Then he possessed himself of some paper and jotted down notes about Cock Robin and luggage and middle names. Pocketing them, he glanced at his watch and announced, "I hate to leave this pleasant place; but like all good suburbanites I have a train to catch."

Alice turned back to the letter she was writing Jean. "Don Burgess has just been in," she scribbled. "I don't know anybody else who groans as much as he does. He turned author anyhow only because he hated teaching; that is, if you listen to him. He's a customer, though, as well as a friend. Sweet music to my ears, the tinkle of the cash register! To get back to yesterday—"

Mr. and Mrs. Pratt had been invited to appear at the shop about nine o'clock. The early evening trade would be over by that time; but there might be stray customers for another hour. This was on an ordinary weekday evening; Fridays there was generally a rush of business, because so many people were paid on Friday; Sunday evening there was a second, smaller rush, often to the used-book tables. Not that you could count on anything in this business. Guests would simply have to take their chances.

The Pratts were very much interested in Waverley Book Shop. Roger wondered at the large stock they had packed into a small space, and was informed about their Brooklyn resources too, in the old flat and the warehouse. Margot loved the way that, thanks largely to its outside table, the life of the shop blended into the life of the street. "No wonder you say this is the crossroads of the Village!" she exclaimed. "If I didn't know better, I'd say that a parade must have passed somewhere nearby, and the crowd had only just broken up."

Tom Carroll was one of the customers that evening. Alice introduced him as "my neighbor in the building." William Thayer had been introduced earlier and then sent home. The Martins would put the shop to bed tonight; that was a part of their act.

Inside the Commerce Street apartment, Alice showed the visitors around the place, after having them deposit their wraps in the bedroom. "This is Harry's study," she announced proudly. "He has to have some place to go when he feels that he simply must get away from me."

That gave Harry a chance to explain about his anthology. "In the course of my reading, I've so often come across something which made me think afterwards, 'That is exactly what I should have said myself, if I had only had the brains to say it.' So I thought I'd bring together a lot of those choice items; maybe some publisher would be interested."

"One was." Alice took up the tale. "Harry, don't you want to bring the drinks in here? While you're mixing, I'll tell the Pratts how a publisher came looking for you."

They had much more good talk of books. Then, over their excellent dinner, the Pratts thanked Alice "for all you have done for our daughter. If Peggy hadn't found a confidante in you, we doubt whether she would ever have reached her present happiness." Ah, that habit of speaking in their joint names! It told so much of conferences behind the scenes, of a joint verdict arrived at and proclaimed.

Yes, and of the habit of putting up a front. Sometimes Alice wondered whether chronic married couples were ever as happy as they seemed. Contented, maybe, or simply accustomed to it. Anyhow, it was the common lot of mankind. As for her own lesser half, he was doing very well by them tonight.

The four of them moved back to the study for their after-dinner coffee. By that time the Martins had learned that the Pratt money came from real-estate development. No wonder they had expected Peggy to come back home eventually: Peggy, who was planning to spend this coming winter crowded into Walter Ferrar's bachelor apartment.

But now they were back on the subject of Harry's anthology. "Surely you had to do some writing on it yourself," Roger Pratt suggested.

"I had to write a preface, of course," Harry acknowledged.

[269]

"That bothered me at first. I once heard of a man who proposed to write a general history. He opened up with a detailed explanation of what he expected to do. It ran to three hundred pages headed 'Preface.' Then all he had left to say for the body of the book was, 'Well, that's it.' "

"Harry, I never heard that one before!" cried Alice. Then, at his smug smile, she added, "Did you make it up?"

"Somebody has to make things up," said Harry. "That's 'invent,' isn't it? In my extreme youth, I thought that Benjamin Franklin invented electricity. Just the way I thought that Paul Revere galloped through the country shouting at the top of his lungs, 'The British are coming!' "

"All American children think that," Margot Pratt assured him.

"I supposed that Queen Isabella *did* pawn her jewels to finance Columbus," Alice contributed.

So the desultory talk went on. It was very late when the Pratts took their leave. Harry Martin accompanied them down to Seventh Avenue and waited with them for a cruising taxi. On his return he found Alice still a little keyed up from the party, though at this hour and after such a day she must be tired enough to make the idea of bed very welcome.

Harry reached around to help her unhook her dress. "Alice, sweetheart, tonight surely we can—" he whispered close to her ear.

She hesitated for just an instant; then she slipped out of the arms which had come up to encircle her. "Not tonight," she said between set teeth.

"Then some time soon? Tomorrow, perhaps?"

This time her resistance was curt and very, very definite. Into her mind had flashed the recollection of his fancy woman in her new perfume coming to seek him. That memory again came between them. Tonight they lay farther apart than ever.

Like the figures on an Etruscan tombstone, Alice thought drearily. Presenting a united front to the world; intending to keep right on doing so. But oh, the frozen misery she took to bed with her that night! It was enough to last her all the rest of her life. But at least, she was no longer afraid that she might give in accidentally. She had sealed her own fate. She was justified in her decision. Make no mistake about it, she was justified. But that did not sweeten the bitterness which lay at the bottom of Alice's cup.

22

ALICE MARTIN WAS RIGHT IN STICKING TO HER DECISION THAT
Harry must keep his distance from her. Of course she was
right. Only at intervals did lurking doubts rear their ugly
heads and an inner voice hint that perhaps she had got very
far indeed up on her high horse: so far that if occasion arose,
she would find some difficulty in getting down again. Why
should any such occasion arise? The present difficulty was
not of her making. She was simply the person who shared the
consequences.

She herself missed those intimacies which were such an in-
tegral part of the married relation. Of late years they had
been a far cry from bridal bliss; yet since she had passed the
age where there was a question of having children, Alice had
found a new significance in their close endearments. There
had been moments, indeed, when Alice thought that an experienced husband sometimes made the offer rather because he
thought it was expected of him than because it was what he
himself desired. His pride, too, would keep him from letting
her think that he was beginning to fade out a little.

There was one factor in the situation which Alice never suspected. Harry himself had not put a finger on it. He had read a lot, seen a lot, listened a lot to other men in stag sessions. But fundamentally he was a comparative innocent about the whole matter. In his young manhood he had had a few surreptitious and highly unsatisfactory experiences, though in company with his male cronies he had talked big. It was in its different way as much of a revelation to him as it was to her: that lovely flowering of passion, that halcyon season when dreams came true and the world began all over in the coming together of this man and this woman; when young Harry Martin would half wake in the summer dawn and lie there contemplating the miracle of his lovely bride sleeping beside him, most incredibly there, most incredibly his.

A more experienced man would have behaved more shrewdly. A shrewder man, even when caught red-handed, would have managed somehow to engineer himself a better deal.

But the way things had happened, appearances were saved, the business of the book shop went on, friends continued to circle. The heavens had failed to fall, even if the private estrangement continued. The world wagged on.

It wagged a little faster, if anything—or at least, a little too fast for Alice's tastes. The Republicans had been blamed not only for a worldwide and continuing Depression, but for practically everything else that the citizenry disliked or found unprofitable. In November Hoover was stunningly defeated at the polls.

The November election owed its placing to the fact that in the days when it was initiated the country was primarily agricultural; politics had to wait until after the crops were in. That was as good a time as any for voting. But other antiquated customs held on when they had outlived their usefulness. The Electoral College, for instance, had long since outlived its usefulness. The wise men of the country did not get together and select a President, the way the Founding Fathers had expected them to. The form had in some instances actually defeated the will of the people. At best, its function was to delay.

Another outmoded usage was due for reform, though only a measure of reform. That was the long delay between election and inauguration. After the impending inauguration, the date would be shifted from the Fourth of March (or actually the Fifth, publicly, if the Fourth happened to fall on a Sunday. So much religious observance was still practiced even by an ungodly generation). It would be the Twentieth of January. At least the lame-duck session of Congress would be shortened.

A "lame duck," Harry Martin remembered, was a congressman who hadn't been reelected, but who had still to serve out his old term. Probably with this session shortened, important business could now be deferred; Congress was always good anyhow at deferring important business.

So let the Democrats bring in their New Deal come spring; let their opponents call it "the Raw Deal." This was still November, with Thanksgiving in the offing. There was plenty to be thankful for, too. *Reader's Choice* was now definitely in the offing. Yet another grandchild was on the way, too.

Jim had written them the news from Chicago. "If it's a boy, he will not be called Franklin D. Roosevelt Martin. A girl would be a nice change. You know; you had one. Twin girls would even the score nicely; but I'm afraid the chances are all against that."

Now that the weather was getting so chilly, Alice decided to shift dwellings for a time. "Let's go back to Brooklyn for most of the week, and save the Commerce Street place for Saturdays and Sundays," she suggested. "That will give us both a nice change. That is, of course, unless you'd prefer to spend some time alone in New York and let me voyage to Brooklyn by myself."

"We work together, thank you; and I'm a decent enough escort if I'm nothing else," Harry said stiffly. The imaginary sword was bad enough; she needn't go trying to put the breadth of the city between them.

The newlywed Ferrars were back in New York and Peggy was again a steady visitor at the shop. Her first purchase was a cookbook. "Steaks and chops are all right; but I may as well begin learning something different now that I have the time. Alice, dear, what cookbook do you recommend? My mother told me to ask you. She took a great liking to you."

Alice returned the complimentary speech. She also sold young Mrs. Ferrar not one cookbook but two. Her personal advice on the subject, however, was, "Use your own ingenuity. So long as you take a real interest, you can't go far wrong. New York is the greatest food market in the world. Go out and stroll around. It will give you ideas. But you and Walter must come to us for Thanksgiving."

This was hospitality. It was also a strong hint to Peggy to get her marriage off on the right foot. The young husband had lived here much longer; but matters like the celebration of holidays should still be Ladies' Choice.

The Ferrars were asked around a lot, to be sure. They ate at restaurants both as guests and on their own. But Peggy's decision to do some cooking at home was soundly based for more reasons than one. Housekeeping was a trade, and like any other trade took both learning and practice. Also, she must now learn to live on an editor's salary budgeted for the two of them. That was quite different from being backed by a wealthy father.

Marriage had its financial side, even when the participants were not in business together. Perhaps in cases where they were not (and those cases were numerically in the vast majority) it was even more important. If a man supported the household, he was entitled in his turn to a well-run household.

As well as to so many other things! Alice Martin had always been something of a matchmaker. Sometimes she had simply given the advice which she knew the recipient was dying to hear. Sometimes she had acutally given a shove in the right— or at least positive—direction. Marriages might be made in heaven; but the details had to be settled right here on earth. You couldn't expect Almighty God to do too much for you; He had a great many other things on his hands.

But since she had been having all this trouble with Harry, Alice had begun to look on marriages with some doubt. Perhaps no marriage was completely happy, or happy for very long. Perhaps even when everything seemed to be going very well, the load was gradually building up until the marriage could no longer bear the strain.

Perhaps even her own children—But that was carrying the thing too far. Jim was doing so well he could even afford to make fun of his own dreams and hopes. All that blather about twin girls! Jean had added refinements of bliss: she with her vacation from a husband, and her aspirations so charmingly confided, and even the added seriousness of her special expedition with her father.

As for Bill Thayer and Marion and little Nina, the Martin invitation to them for Thanksgiving was practically a royal command. Alice felt a warm glow at her heart when she remembered the little girl whom she had first known as Nina Babcock. There was a small person who really had something to be thankful for.

Emil Koenig and his Kitty were due for an invitation, of course. So was the old Brooklyn neighbor whom the Martins now saw only on occasions like this; he was the only one remaining who had shared their Thanksgivings when they first moved in here. But high up in the ranks of seniority were the Johnsons. When Alice invited them, she also made a request. "Bess, won't you bring along one of your poems and read it to us? It doesn't necessarily have to be about Thanksgiving; doesn't have to be timely at all, in fact. But it will keep us from being too dreadfully dull. Something perhaps a little reminiscent?"

Bess began to laugh. "Oh, the dear old days in the Village, when we were all young and interested in any sort of naughtiness! We thought we were being so terribly sophisticated; really it was just like little boys using four-letter words that they have learned from bigger boys."

"That was a little before my time," Alice encouraged. "But I've heard you and Ben talk about it."

"The palmy days when the Village really was the Village! A popular resort was Three Steps Down, where the customers were allowed to write their own tabs for the food they ate. All the girls wore smocks in summer; looking back at it, I'd say we had long summers then. Everybody carried a copy of Krafft-Ebing. The simplest remark was evidence of the direst passions. For instance, if you said, 'I'm planning to go up to Forty-second Street this afternoon and look for a pair of new shoes,' it meant that you were in love with your grandmother."

"*Little Red Riding Hood* must have been a saga of sin. All that about her grandmother and getting into bed with animals. But I suppose," Alice philosophized, "all folk tales go pretty well down to the roots of things."

There you had it: at bottom we were all animals. Still, the animals were a great advance on lower forms of life. The glory and the grime were all mixed up together. It would have been much simpler if we had all stayed back in that primeval goo—what was the name of it? Protoplasm! But no, the amoeba came along and proceeded to reproduce by splitting. From then on, it was only a question of a few million steps and a few billion years to Krafft-Ebing and Greenwich Village in the palmy days—and to Thanksgiving dinner in

[277]

Brooklyn with the hostess arranging for a little special entertainment after dinner.

"You can get Ben to cue you in after I've given the signal,"
Alice urged. "Bess, do you think Ben misses his playwrighting and the hope of being produced?"

Bess laid her finger lightly on her lips. Then she went on to
assure Alice, "He'll cue me if there is anything to cue. The
only trouble with Ben is, if I do write a poem, he'll think I
ought to submit it to a magazine."

"Maybe he's right. He often is."

"Oh, but the awful shame of getting a rejection slip! Alice,
you lucky woman, you sell the stuff. Harry sits back and harvests from previous harvests. I sound ungrateful, don't I?
Harry actually did buy one poem from me. When is his anthology coming out?"

It would appear some time next year; the *annus mirabilis*
of the New Deal. There were some subjects best not mentioned between friends, however; politics headed the list.
The Johnsons were Southerners and hereditary Democrats.

"Before too long," Alice replied to Bess's question. "I'm
looking forward to it just as much as he is." *Stress the things
which you two still have in common, Mrs. Martin; present a
united front to the world.*

That blessed last Thursday in November meant to some
unenlightened souls the big football game of the season. To
schoolchildren it meant a holiday with another free day to
follow; after that, all small-fry would have Christmas to look
forward to. The Martins would look forward to it in quite a
different way; to them it meant a rush of business which left
in its wake tidy profits and physical exhaustion.

When Alice reported the Johnson plan to Harry, he inquired, "Why make Bess Johnson sing for her supper? You're
not going to charge any of your other guests, are you?"

"The others may bring bottles; our guests often do. Harry,
won't it be fantastic if we do get Repeal? I can remember way

[278]

back when people often brought flowers to the hostess. That was in the Dark Ages, when a great many women didn't drink."

"Many men stopped at one or two," Harry recollected. "I used to think I was celebrating if I had a few beers with the other fellows on Saturday night."

Sure enough, on the festival Thursday several of the guests brought bottles; Walter Ferrar's was excellent Scotch, one each from himself and Peggy. The Thayers had remembered flowers; little Nina had drawn, and colored with her crayons, a picture of a Pilgrim Father, a turkey, and an Indian rather incongruously wearing his war paint. The old man from the neighborhood contributed a gallon of that "dago red" which had made former icemen such popular and successful figures. Emil brought gin; his Kitty who knitted beautifully, had made scarfs for both host and hostess.

"The loot alone is cause enough for Thanksgiving," Harry proclaimed. "Thanksgiving and Christmas rolled into one!"

The Johnsons were the last to arrive. They were regularly the last ones to arrive anywhere. Ben's many years as a dramatic critic had given him a sixth sense when it came to arriving at the theater in time for the first curtain; that exhausted his stock of punctuality. But this time his entrance might have been planned. Bess and he "took the stage"; while they did so, Bess gave Alice a nod and shaped with her lips the words, "We're all set."

The Martins served double dry Martinis, but only one to each guest; they calculated that that would whet appetites, not destroy them. Then came the traditional feast. After second helpings and both mince and pumpkin pie for dessert, large cups of coffee were very much in order. Then came an interval of lethargy, devoted largely to the simple pleasures of digestion.

Naturally enough the conversation presently turned to reminiscence. Then presently Ben Johnson went into that spiel about the old days in Greenwich Village and the amateur psychoanalysts.

"Oh, but it's different now!" Bess assured him.

Ben rose and took a step toward her. Obviously he was now well into his act. "Yes, my darling, in what way is it different?"

"I got to thinking along those lines the other day, and I wrote a little poem."

"May we have it, fair Sappho?"

"No one here cares to listen to poetry," she demurred.

They all assured her they did care, and Emil Koenig led a round of applause. Bess rose and swept them a curtsey. "I call it 'A Case History,'" she began. Then she went on to declaim:

A cranky old lady whose name was Jane Hastings
Spent most of her daylight hours pulling out bastings.
Then, so she could keep herself busy as sin,
She sat up at night to put them back in.

To my way of thinking, her conduct was dense.
It didn't make money, not even ten cents.
It didn't make clothing, or darn or mend rents.
I suppose it was poor old Jane's "psychic defense."

That's modern big words for old-fashioned "plain crazy";
It's used nowadays when our thinking is lazy.
Jane didn't hurt anyone with her strange dizziness.
Suppose you and I just mind our own business.

There was a patter of applause after that. Bess was still bowing acknowledgments when Alice caught Walter Ferrar's eye. She gulped audibly. She had completely forgotten that he was a magazine editor. But he must think that Alice had done this on purpose—or that Bess had talked her into it.

Alice was about to swing the discussion to Little Red Riding Hood and her grandmother when Walter Ferrar spoke up. "I don't know why people think that poetry has to be printed in order to reach an audience. The spoken word is still available, even if it isn't quite so permanent. In your case it's wonderfully effective, Mrs. Johnson."

Bess beamed at him. "Ben and I do ham it up somtimes. But we're not an awful lot worse than some people who get paid for their histrionics. Some of the shows I have seen with him—!"

The conversation switched naturally to the theater. Alice turned to watch Nina for a minute or two. Some of this conversation might be over her head; but it could scarcely do her any harm. Where was Anita De Byles spending Thanksgiving Day? Alice wondered in passing. Did she ever regret giving up the child, who was so much better off without her? Queer, the way lots of people spent this great family holiday. Queer even the collection of souls who were spending it here with the Martins in their old Brooklyn home.

Carrie had been on duty for the one-o'clock dinner and remained through the afternoon; for the supper shift, her daughter Phyllis took over. Her faithful helpers had been with her for years; if it hadn't been for them, Alice Martin wouldn't have been freed to do her big job in Waverley Book Shop.

Cold turkey and cider cup were, if possible, better than hot turkey and Martinis had been. In that evening relaxation, even Walter Ferrar got completely to a front-name basis. He and his Peggy stayed late, as did the nighthawk Johnsons. The old neighbor offered to help the Thayers find a taxi. No, he wouldn't be back; it had been a lovely party, and he hoped the Martins were around here more this winter than they had been lately. The Koenigs left at the same time.

Bill Thayer had to open the shop Friday, to be sure; Nina was already rubbing her eyes and trying to suppress her yawns, though she was thrilled at getting to stay up with the grown people. She could go to sleep in the taxi, of course. What joy to undress a sleeping child and get her into her own bed! Those were actually the richest years of a person's life: the years spent ministering to young children, yes, and fearing for them and hoping against fear, and making mistakes and regretting them. Those were the years that Jim and his wife were living through now out there in Chicago, the years that Jean was now looking forward to so blissfully.

Walter Ferrar stayed late for other reasons besides having one more sip of cider cup and a final cigarette. Alice did not suspect it at the time. She was in her usual after-party mood of fatigue and wakefulness; she lay down in Jean's old room for a time to let her nerves come unstrung. It was very late indeed when she moved into the connubial bedroom, and Harry was sound, though not quite silently, asleep.

It was the middle of Friday afternoon when an excited Bess Johnson came rushing into Waverley Book Shop and demanded Alice's immediate attention. "Alice, darling, you never told me that nice Mr. Ferrar was an editor! He says if I want to submit some of my poems to his magazine, I must send them to his secretary with an enclosing letter, and he will see to it that they get his personal attention. That is so different from a printed slip!"

"He didn't ask you for the poem he had already heard?"

Alice regretted the words as soon as they were out; but Bess began to laugh. "He doesn't have to. He's going to get that one as soon as I've done some more work on it and written a few more to go with it. Or maybe I could hunt up a few of my old ones and polish them up. Alice, will you help me with my Christmas list? Books are the best present I can give Ben. You prompt him, too, in case he comes looking up something to give me."

Harry Martin's birthday was late in November. His dutiful children never forgot it. This year Alice gave him a new billfold. His wardrobe had already been replenished. But he protested in vain that no special celebration was required this close to Christmas; Harry himself said he didn't need to be reminded how confounded old he was getting. He simply gave Alice another idea.

"Why not give yourself a trip down to Washington to see the Inauguration?" she demanded. "You've lived this close all these years, and have never seen one yet."

"Would *you* like it?" he demanded.

That left the question nicely up in the air, which was where a good many questions between them seemed to take refuge these days.

Then the Christmas rush descended on them. Alice and Harry did a terrific business. They not only gift-wrapped; on request they also mailed gift packages and made their prices "postage included." None of the younger generation of their own family would be with them this year. But there must be a bangup celebration anyhow. A few shifts in policy would help. Custom must never be allowed to deteriorate into routine.

Alice and Harry had for years started off their own Christmas celebration by attending the carol singing at Wanamaker's. They used to take Jim and Jean there as little children. Wanamaker's "Old Store," which had been the site of the A. T. Stewart business before John Wanamaker ever invaded from Philadelphia, was a suitable setting for the traditional rite. A branching staircase led down from the second story. An organ was already playing when the spectators assembled. At the appointed hour, a platform containing Santa Claus and a clown was wheeled in. It all connected up so beautifully: the clown with the Roman Saturnalia, Santa Claus with northern mythology; then the winter solstice, and the coming of the Christ Child. The pages sang, entering in solemn procession. It was all very touching, and somehow fresh each time.

This year the Martins decided without argument that Bill and Marion Thayer must attend and take small Nina with them. But when Alice decreed that Harry must go with them while she took her solitary way to Brooklyn and got things started there, Harry flatly refused. She could come with him and the Thayers, or he would stay with her and let the Thayers proceed by themselves. The subway would get them to Brooklyn just as well from either the carol singing or their own shop.

Eventually, of course, Alice gave in. She went along and enjoyed Nina's thrill when the pages, with white cassocks over their best blue uniforms, started down the stairs two and two, the girls on one side, the boys on the other. The carols just suited those fresh young voices. They went through all the standard numbers. To the soft strains of the special recessional, which wished everybody "A merry, merry Christmas and a brand New Year," the platform was finally wheeled out, with Santa Claus swinging his sleigh bells and the clown waving good-bye.

The Martins watched Nina's radiant little face there at the final moment. Right now she was as happy as it was possible for any human being to be. Happy in one of the many ways that people can be happy; the Martins as well as Bill and Marion rejoiced in her joy. They bade her good-bye at the door of the store. The trio would journey to Brooklyn for their Christmas dinner; but parting from them was just a little lonesome.

Harry and Alice sat down alone to oyster stew and coleslaw. They had omitted their afternoon snack; but neither of them had much appetite. Not only were they tired physically, a certain spiritual weariness had come over them both. They had gone through the motions so many, many times. "A brand New Year," indeed! What was so exciting about that word "new"? All too soon it would become the old, the worn-out, the discarded. Things kept happening; but they were so much like the things that had happened before. In the end, it all turned flat and stale.

The Martins were closer together right now that they had been for months; but it was the closeness of satiety, which had only to take a step to land them in quiet despair. Harry shivered in the warmth of the old railroad flat. Alice rose hastily and turned on the radio.

23

THE SECRETARY OF STATE MADE IT OFFICIAL ON THE SIXTH OF February, 1933, when he announced that the Twentieth Amendment to the Constitution of the United States was now in effect. From now on, Presidential Inauguration Day would be the twentieth of January.

"How many more amendments will it take to close that gap a little farther?" Alice Martin demanded. "I'm sure two weeks would give any man time enough to clear out his desk. Any family ought to be able to pack in a month, too, even if it's for a move into the White House."

"If I should be elected President, which is most unlikely," Harry Martin argued, "you couldn't possibly clear out that Brooklyn flat in a month."

"If you should be elected President, I'd continue to store some of our choicest books there. I shouldn't dream of trying to clear it out. You'd need some place to retire to when your term of office was over."

"You're never without an answer, Mrs. Martin. But this argument is academic. The important amendment will be

Repeal. Pending that, are you going to Washington for Inauguration?"

"Somebody has to stay in New York," Alice assured him. "You're free to go if you like, but I'm staying right here."

He shied away from the implication. There was nothing that he would have liked better than to take her to Washington, not only for the Inauguration but for a second honeymoon. Without her, what would the Big Show amount to?

Actually by the time March blew in, Harry was swamped with labor on his own undertaking. Very low-down labor it turned out to be, too. The galley proofs of his anthology were beginning to come in. There would be page proofs after that; and even if the printer's proofreader had been over them, the chances for error were numberless. When the finished book slid smoothly into the shop, it looked so easy; even Harry Martin, long as he had been associated with this business, had not realized quite how much lay behind the scenes. *Reader's Choice* was scheduled for August publication. In July Messrs. Knowles and Wingate were bringing out another whodunit by that chronic contriver of such, Donald Burgess.

The Martins had offered to let Bill Thayer have the time off. "He ought to go down to Washington and let Nina see the spectacle. It should mean a lot to Young America," Harry told Alice.

"If they can get some kind of decent hotel accommodations," Alice demurred. "Or wait a minute! Suppose we put the idea up to him and let him do his own worrying."

It developed that Marion had an old school friend in Washington. Accommodations of a sort were arranged for all three Thayers. An unexpected dividend accrued to the Martins from Bill's firsthand report.

"I'm a Republican by principle, a Republican even in defeat," Bill said. "But I'm an American before I'm a Republican. Honestly, the whole thing was so impressive it made me proud of my country. Roosevelt actually looked as if he was touched by his high mission; and in the parade to the Inauguration, Mrs. Roosevelt never took her eyes off him."

Marion contributed another touch. "Our seats were in front of the Treasury Building. Expensive, of course; but I figured that while we were doing it, we might as well do it up brown. It was a first for Nina and for Bill too. Some things never become an old story, though I had seen it before. There was a man near us; he came bringing his little boy and a big apple to keep the child happy if the proceedings got too lengthy. A workman by his looks; he was doing things properly. He and Bill got to talking. Just behind me sat two women, hardened Democrats by their talk. —I hope I'm not boring you."

Assured that she was not, Marion went on, "The state delegations marched in alphabetical order. New York is pretty far down the alphabet. When our delegation came along, there on foot, in the third rank and the second file came Al Smith, wearing his insignia as a Sachem of Tammany Hall. One of the Democratic ladies burst out crying and said, 'There he goes, and he ought to be riding at the head of this procession today!' We all began to cheer and holler, 'Al!' He looked around at us and smiled. Indeed he actually blushed. You would think that he had never received an ovation before."

"It came just when he needed it," said Alice quietly. Al Smith, perhaps the best governor New York State had ever had; unsuccessful candidate for President four years before; a man who had conquered his own spirit. For the first time, Alice wished she had been there in Washington to see for herself.

Ben Johnson had covered the Inauguration for his paper. He still pulled down a news assignment every now and then, though it was always under his byline. He was ever the dramatic critic, though; he wrote the whole thing up as if it were a show.

He was working on another article for his high-brow magazine, too. "They are fun to do, and I can take my time," he confided. "In print I look so convincing! If I didn't know I'd written that stuff myself, I'd honestly believe that the writer knew what he was talking about."

"You do know," Harry Martin assured him. "That's something you can go back over and reread sometimes, too. You'll make that lecture tour yet."

Ben smiled and shook his head. "My free evenings I can now stay home and read. I don't set Bess a very good example, do I? But it all makes business for Waverley Book Shop. Have you anything on hand that Alice would honestly recommend?"

Bess Johnson was another story. A contradictory story, too, in Alice Martin's opinion. Those anonymous cards of hers brought her a little money and were fun to do in their way, no doubt; but from the chance of recognition she seemed to be shrinking.

She had been looking over some of her old poems with an eye to submitting them to Walter Ferrar. A little more work would help certain ones; others were as good as she could hope to make them. After all, the worst Walter's magazine could do to her was to say "No." But she was by temperament both a perfectionist and a procrastinator. It was March now, and she had still taken no action on his Thanksgiving offer.

Then there descended on her out of nowhere a line that struck her as memorable beyond any other line which had ever come into her mind. So good did it seem that at first blush she was afraid it was something she had remembered. But Ben had never heard it, nor had either of the Martins. It must be what old-fashioned writers called "inspiration." It ran:

And so she slept, and sleeping dreamed, and in her dream she died.

There it was. It haunted her. But where was the poem to go with it? "Find it," said Ben. "Wait, and the rest will come," said Alice Martin. "You have this much. Be thankful for it," said good old Harry.

It stirred her into action. She selected three poems for Walter Ferrar, directed the missive as he had told her to direct it, and at the last moment changed her mind and thrust the communication back into her desk. So there went Elizabeth Davis Johnson, well on her way toward getting nowhere.

Ben, reminiscing one evening when he felt more like talking than reading, suddenly remembered the episode at the Martins' when "that fellow told you to send him something. You know, the bird who had just married that young friend of the Martins'."

Bess protested that she couldn't remember. He went ahead and nailed down Walter Ferrar's name and that of his magazine, which was one of the standard monthlies. Ben hadn't forgotten the man or the magazine, of course; he was just now getting around to the episode, and was giving her a chance to tell her own story.

Bess did not tell quite all of it. She did confess however that she had one poem which she figured was good enough for submission. He made her dig it out then and there and read it aloud to him. Next day he nagged her into mailing it.

There was an agonizing wait, tempered for Bess by thankfulness that she hadn't sent all three poems. Any one rejection would be bad enough; but to have so much of her output spurned would be very deep humiliation.

What actually ensued was a polite letter of acceptance accompanied by a small check. "Why, I'm in!" she gasped.

She was not only in but alibied against the future. She couldn't very well make another submission until after her first lyric had appeared. Bess almost wore out Mr. Ferrar's letter rereading it. The check she deposited in the small but growing account which she had started with the proceeds of her greeting cards.

Relaying the good news to Alice Martin in the book shop, Bess Johnson wound up, "Ben has so much more confidence in me than I have in myself. Sometimes I wonder how he ever stands me."

All this because an editor had accepted a poem which he had certainly asked for. He had asked for it because he was the Martins' Thanksgiving guest and was in a mellow mood. He was the Martins' Thanksgiving guest because Alice thought that a bride should make up the couple's social schedule. But it had not been pure benevolence on Walter Ferrar's part. A magazine could not very well appear with any of its pages blank.

Walter had by this time got into the habit of taking each new issue home to Peggy and demanding that she read it carefully and comment on it. That was getting reader reaction in a very small way to begin with; but it began to help him build up his standards. Also it contributed greatly toward their companionship. There was a current school of thought which held that American marriages were very much the wife's doing. Probably just a rehash of an ancient notion; anyhow, much too broad a generalization. Here were two instances where the husband obviously did a generous share.

One change in the Martins' old circle was primarily the wife's decision, though her husband had soon seen the wisdom of it. Virginia Daly Burgess was closing the small Village apartment where she had dwelt while she was still single, and had since retained as a *pied-à-terre*. It had become an unnecessary extravagance. "A necessary extravagance is where you let yourself go and enjoy being a prodigal," she said in explanation of her phrase. "Some extravagances are just a bad habit."

"You think self-indulgence is an art?" asked Alice.

"I like to dress up a mediocre idea in highfalutin language. It's the writer in me. It's a cheap pleasure, too, and especially suitable right here at the heart of the Village."

"You're going to miss the Village if you do give us up."

"I'm attached in a way to my little old place. I could always doss down there, too, if I felt like working until the New York Public Library closes for the night. But if I really have to do research work there I can commute. Anyhow I can pay Waverley Book Shop for a lot of source books and still be money ahead if I get rid of my Horatio Street place. Phone and utilities bills as well as rent, you know."

Harry Martin now entered the discussion. "But it gives you such a nice change if you spend a night in town sometimes. You can trust George and Daisy with the chee-ild, can't you?"

"Nothing pleases them better. Or Joan either, for that matter. But as for needing a place to stay when we go on the town, that just isn't a part of our lives anymore. Next winter, if by any chance we should take it into our heads to see a show, we could do it on the cheap. Have sandwiches and coffee beforehand, occupy balcony seats in the theater, go home afterward for a bite and a drink. Babies come high, but they're worth it. Ours is, anyhow."

Galley proofs for Harry's anthology had been succeeded by page proofs. That second task too was completed without his succumbing either to boredom or to eyestrain. So far too he had kept the dedication a secret from Alice. Officially a secret, that is. She must certainly have her suspicions.

The Thayers had decided to send Nina to camp again this summer. "I'm going to miss her—God, how we'll both miss her!" Bill confided. "But it's for her own good. Not only will she enjoy camp; having her away will keep us from becoming too possessive."

Harry struck an attitude. "I declare, modern parents have a lot of worries that have been dreamed up for them by modern psychology. Nina is as happy a child as I ever saw; so it won't do to go ahead and let her be happy. That might give her a fixation about walking under stepladders."

Bill grinned sheepishly. "I do sound rather like that poem of Bess Johnson's about mental ailments, don't I? But it gets hot in New York in summer, and Nina did enjoy camp last year."

"Simple common-sense reasons those for sending her away. Mind you, I'm not advocating a return to the 'good old days' of the old woman who lives in a shoe. But at least, if she had so many children she didn't know what to do, the children could keep each other company in their misery. An only child can be too much alone, or spend too much time with grown people."

"Besides, maybe the broth was good rich stew, and maybe the children didn't care too much for bread anyhow," put in Alice.

The two men laughed. "Maybe the stew had dumplings in it," suggested Bill. "But trust Alice Martin always to say a good word for everybody. Give the Devil his due, you know; a lot of his clients simply asked for it."

Alice smiled, but went on thoughtfully, "Those things in the Mother Goose rhymes don't seem to bother children. Perhaps they regard it all simply as a part of the passing show."

"That's better than to regard it as scum turned up from the lowest depths of a person's subconscious mind," Bill conceded. "People do sometimes act from decent motives."

"It has been known to happen," Harry agreed. "Marion and you have earned a little respite from being parents, too. It's a great privilege; but it's also something of a strain."

"We can arrange for you to have some weekends off to visit Nina at camp," Alice offered. "Just let us know in advance."

"Indeed we can," said Harry. Alice's speaking thus in their

[293]

joint names sent a warm glow to his heart. It faded again when he realized that she could scarcely say less to a faithful employee.

It promised indeed to be a quiet summer. Jean had already written that she was staying on in Minneapolis until Earl finished teaching in summer session; then the two of them would take their vacation together. "Possibly at a lake resort; possibly in Chicago; more probably giving each a turn. I'll be sorry not to see New York and the parents. It's just the old difficulty of not being able to be in two different places at the same time."

"Do you suppose they have started a family?" asked Harry.

Alice shook her head. If Jean were expecting a baby, she would have shared the sweet news with her parents just the way Jim always had. Perhaps she felt that a quiet connubial summer might be fruitful in that respect as well as others. Harry, looking back at the loveliness which had been his a year ago, decided that for once he would write his daughter a long letter. Generally he left the family correspondence to Alice: "a true manly gesture," he had once explained in a postscript, which was his ordinary contribution.

He made the exertion, and felt all the better for it. While he was in the mood, he wrote to Jim, too. By telling of the pleasant things a person enjoyed them afresh. Loneliness was mitigated, too: not only loneliness for the object of the letter, but pervasive longing for absent friends. That was a good line; Harry made a note of it with a view to subsequent letters.

Another absentee, however, brought the Martins added company. Emil Koenig came into the shop to report that Katherine, his wife, was taking her vacation from the office the second two weeks in July. She was going to Cape Cod with two other women from the same office. Originally she had wanted Emil to go with her; but he didn't wish to dip into his shrinking savings for any such purpose, and he certainly would not let her pay his vacation expenses.

"So I'm a bachelor again for two weeks, and I rely on you good Martins to come over sometimes and eat dinner with me. Say Tuesday of the first week for a starter. What time can you get away from that shop of yours?"

So there you had it. He didn't say, "Will you or won't you?" He simply ordered, "set the hour."

But at that, Harry Martin paid his way in. His advance copies of his anthology arrived that afternoon; Harry autographed one and took it with him.

Alice was not too much surprised by the dedication; but she was intensely pleased. It hadn't been at all certain that he would dedicate *Reader's Choice.* An original work was generally inscribed in that fashion; an anthology was different. Anyhow Harry might have dedicated to his son or his daughter or to them both jointly. Instead he had chosen to honor his wife both by name and by setting forth the nature of the relationship.

He explained the nature of that dedication to Emil Koenig. Explained it too much in detail and too repetitiously. He was erecting a "Keep Off the Grass" sign. Harry had sometimes betrayed a certain jealousy of the feeling between Alice and Emil. It was a feeling on a high plane, and Harry must know that. Perhaps in a way, it made his resentment only the more bitter.

It was a gala evening anyhow. By the time they came again on Thursday, Harry had mailed advance copies of *Reader's Choice* to Jim and Jean, and had had Alice autograph them on the dedication page. Bill Thayer was similarly honored. A copy was mailed to Virginia and Don Burgess in their Long Island retreat; being in the business themselves, they could be trusted not to break publication date.

Alice laid aside a copy for the Johnsons. For the Great Day itself she would arrange a special display. The anthologist autographed several copies in advance; others he planned to sign on request. This is, of course, if he had any requests. These were early days yet; he must let the sight of his name in print go to his head.

Just before Publication Day (capital letters for that in the Martins' estimation), Bess Johnson came in highly excited about a matter which concerned her professional self. "I have the idea at last!" she announced. "The idea did come, just as you predicted that it would, Alice."

"The idea?" Alice was puzzled.

"The idea for the poem. You know, the poem of which I had only the last line," Bess reminded her impatiently.

"I hadn't forgotten. That lovely line, 'And so she slept, and sleeping dreamed, and in her dream she died.' You have the whole poem now?"

"Oh, no!" Bess smiled. "I myself didn't realize that there would be a second step, a step in between. It's the idea that I have."

"All the better," Alice encouraged. "A great deal of so-called poetry is simply a very elaborate way of saying nothing."

"I suddenly realized what happened to the lady earlier in that evening," Bess went on. "She was looking at herself in a mirror. A triple mirror. You don't see so many of those around any more; but when I was a girl down South there were lots of them. Three mirrors, hinged together so that a woman could see herself in profile on both sides as well as full face. A great advantage if you wanted to be sure your hair and your face powder and all the rest of it was exactly right."

"I used to have one of them when I was a girl in upstate New York," Alice remembered. "It's still around somewhere, I suppose, in the depths of the old Brooklyn flat."

"An explanation of how the three mirrors swing on hinges will have to come in somehow," Bess went on. "The lovely lady is there alone in her boudoir at bedtime. Gazing at herself she almost goes into a trance. Look, that much is right,

And half entranced, a vision saw, and seeing smiled and sighed.

Give me a pencil and paper quick and let me write that down." She wrote, then went on, "The lady Geraldine—call her that for the present—" again she scribbled, then resumed, "sees past, and present, and future, in the three aspects of her own head. She shivers away from that last one, the future, in a line that ends, 'with a nameless dread.' I hope I'm not boring you, darling Alice. I can't talk to anyone but you or Harry about this. Ben is hopeless. He thinks I can do anything in the writing line. He's *hopeless*."

That was, of course, an inverted form of bragging. Alice smiled and agreed, "It must be exasperating. From greeting cards to poetry of this nature is quite a span. The next thing you know he'll be suggesting that he'll change places with you and let you write the dramatic criticisms for the newspaper."

"He asks my opinions after the acts and sometimes during them. The actual writing I'm glad to leave to him. He has to go back to the office afterward to write his review, while I go home to make the sandwiches and be sure there is enough liquor on hand. Now about that triple mirror idea, Alice, the idea of threes must run all through the poem." Bess talked some more, scribbled some more, finally remembered to ask about *Reader's Choice.*

"Harry has your copy ready for you," Alice assured her. "He wants you to autograph your poem in my copy and his, too. He has taken a mail order to the post office. You'll wait for him, won't you? He should be back any minute now."

Bess didn't wait; she was in a fine fever of composition. But she promised she would be back on Publication Day.

That glad afternoon, Waverley Book Shop held open house. There was a special display of Harry's anthology. Punch and cookies were served to all comers, whether they bought or not. The punch was nonalcoholic, of course; but with judicious mixing and enough ice, it went down very well. Ginger ale could give a beverage a decided tang. Wouldn't it be nice when the Repeal Amendment became a fact, and a person could actually go on the water wagon without any risk of being considered a poor sport or a sissy?

Both the Burgesses came in for the party, and brought an armful of garden flowers. The Johnsons were there, and Walter Ferrar and his Peggy, just about to leave for Walter's vacation in Maine. Emil's Kitty was back in New York, too. Mr. Herbert Knowles represented the publishing firm; Sylvia Norton, the typist, was there, taking a good deal of credit to herself and very much on the alert for a complimentary copy. Jim and Jean telegraphed congratulations. Curiosity seekers, customers, idlers, all kept the place humming.

It was as great an occasion as it had promised to be. When the blowout at the shop came to an end, there was a small private party at the Commerce Street apartment, with solid food and long drinks of Scotch. After all, Prohibition was still fun.

The afterparty ended only too soon. The commuters had their train to catch. Emil's Kitty must get up tomorrow morning and get back to her job. Even the nighthawk Johnsons finally took their leave. Harry and Alice were left alone in the midst of the party flowers and the party lights. The ash trays had been emptied and the last of the bottles put away.

"It's all over," said Harry sadly. "You have a beautiful bright idea to begin with. You work so hard and so long. The thing becomes a solid fact. Then—now—it's only a done-for fact, a has-been, a stale something to be forgotten as soon as possible."

Alice wrinkled her nose at him. "Don't make me cry. You

still have to install your private copy of *Reader's Choice* in your study. Give it a place of honor on a shelf, instead of letting it lie on your desk as a newcomer. I'm going to take my copy to bed with me and begin to reread it there."

"You think you can read it as you would any other book?"

"As I would any other new book, partner. I'll be thinking up arguments to use in its favor when I recommend it for the Christmas trade."

"You're right. It's no longer a project; it is a trade item. A good book to take to bed with you on a winter night, Mrs. Martin?"

"You see, you can think of them too, Mr. Martin. All right, then, let's install your copy and perhaps take one more small drink to wish it luck."

That was really a pretty thought on her part. Alice had so many pretty thoughts, gentle thoughts, considerate thoughts. But when Harry Martin began to undress that night, the anthology was already lying purposefully there on Alice's pillow.

24

Ben Johnson's paper carried a news item about the Publication Day party at Waverley Book Shop, "a popular Greenwich Village rendezvous." The other gazettes would review *Reader's Choice* in the regular course of business— provided they noticed it at all.

Alice was again busy reading the cream of the new books. Those she liked best she handed over to Harry for his perusal. "You're doubly spoiled, you know," she pointed out. "When it's a question of what we'll offer in the shop, I skim off the cream and hand it to you. When you yourself do a book, the material has already been tried and proved for you."

Harry Martin was indeed a lucky man. If as an undergraduate he could have pictured his present state of reasonable prosperity, he would have thought it well worth any struggle it might cost. As for seeing his own name in print, and being in a position to help circulate his own published work, well, that was just too good to come true. But it *had* come true. On every copy of *Reader's Choice* which was disposed of at Waverley, too, he would earn not only his royalty but also a bookseller's profit. Warming both to the ego and the pocket-book.

Why then this "letdown" feeling of his? Just that the woman Alice was holding out against him. And that what with one thing and another he never did manage to get enough sleep. And that his children were a long distance away and doing very nicely without him.

Schools reopened now. The theatrical season was on. "Everybody" was back in New York. The Twenty-first Amendment to the Constitution was just around the corner; the next thing anybody knew, Repeal would be the law of the land.

Then a really wild thing happened. The Metropolitan Museum of Art, greatest repository in the country and one of the greatest in the world, bought one of Emil Koenig's works: his new marble portrait bust of Alice Martin, now officially entitled "Portrait of Madame X." All very discreet and impersonal, to be sure. One more proof that Emil Koenig and Alice Martin had kept their whole affair on a high plane. Still, one more proof that Harry Martin had been generous with his wife.

Harry had a vision of his grandchildren, years from now, trailing through the Metropolitan without ever giving that piece of sculpture so much as a glance; at the same time Grandpa's book would occupy a place of honor on all their home bookshelves. It would gather dust on the shelves, maybe, but at least it would help to perpetuate the name which they were so grandly carrying on.

Carrying on, all right. Their third grandchild, arriving out there in Chicago, was one more boy. "I am a little disappointed, but I won't take it out on Richard Carter Martin," Jim wrote them. "The next one has to be a little girl, if only so that we can name her Harriet. None of this about Old Harry and Young Harry. No mixup about Junior and Second. No giving girls their mother's and grandmothers' names.

But let that go for the present. It's just too long a look ahead."

So there went the junior Martins; and here were the seniors.

Harry, half waking in the dull light of an autumn dawn, would turn away from the wall sometimes to watch Alice on her side of the bed they still occupied together but no longer shared. He yearned to draw her to him, even if it was only to feel her warm body touching his in the most casual way. More than once he half stretched out toward her; but then he paused and drew back. Alice would think he meant only that one thing. He meant it all right. He still desired it. But it was not an end in itself. It hadn't been since— Not since—

He wondered sometimes what had happened to Gloria Gregory. He went so far as to look her up in the phone book. Suddenly he remembered that she had not appeared at the coming-out party for his anthology. If she was avoiding the neighborhood of Waverley Book Shop, all the better. Of course she might not have known about that festivity; large hand-lettered posters in the windows and much word-of-mouth advertising for a week beforehand might not have told the whole story. Greenwich Village was a world unto itself in a way; and it was a small world, but not that small.

Just ahead of Alice now was an extremely pleasant task. She hadn't seen George Scudder for some time; now she could see him with an end in view. He had been wonderful about straightening out the matter of Nina's custody and adoption. The Thayers had thanked him for it, no doubt; but Alice Martin could make a very special acknowledgment.

It took a little arranging. First Harry must autograph *Reader's Choice*. Then Bess Johnson must sign her own special page. Finally Alice signed the dedication page; under her name she wrote, "who joins an anthologist and a poet in thanks to George Scudder for a very great favor." Finally she called George's downtown firm and made an appointment to visit him in his office. "At his convenience, please," she stressed. "It's nothing urgent."

George was very much pleased with the book, though he protested politely, "You didn't need to do this, you know. I like to think I'm of a little use in the world sometimes, and I should never even have heard of this case if you hadn't called it to my attention." He paged over the anthology, made various admiring remarks, finally closed the book and made a reference to the subject of its bestowal. "The Thayers are perfectly satisfied with their bargain?"

"Indeed they are. Adopted children are generally adored, aren't they? They should be. After all, adoptive parents undertake the responsibility with their eyes open. Most of us just find ourselves involved, and go on from there."

"Of course an adopted child is not taken over sight unseen," he said slowly. "Queer, we try to keep everything smooth on the surface. But not far below the surface the going gets awfully rough."

There you had it: Harvard man or subway guard, Mrs. Martin of Waverley Book Shop or Carrie frying chicken back in Brooklyn, we all came out of a moment of aberration on somebody's part. Alice remarked that fact aloud. They laughed together over it. She felt closer to George Scudder at that moment than she had ever felt before.

"The Thayers don't seem to feel afraid that there is bad blood in Nina?" he went on.

"That's a risk they took," Alice said rather sharply. The time for misgivings was long since past. One person to have had misgivings, if there were any due earlier, was that born General Manager and Meddlesome Mattie, Alice Frederickson Martin.

George Scudder grinned. "There is bad blood in all of us. It's seldom mentioned, though. People brag about their lofty ancestors. They suppress the ones who may have gone upwards at the end of an executioner's rope."

"You sound as if you had a specific instance in mind."

"I have. In dear old Harvard I used to room with a bird who bore a good old Plymouth Rock and Boston name. A Mayflower descendant he was and all that. But late one evening, in a burst of resentment at some fresh instance of paternal stupidity, he confided that the Mayflower and Governor Bradford were not the whole story. Another of his ancestors had been arrested by the authorities on a charge of counterfeiting wampum."

"Counterfeiting *wampum?*" Alice echoed. "But wampum was what the Indians used for money. Shells, wasn't it?"

"Beads made from shells, I believe. The dark beads were worth at least twice as much as the white, too. Yes, I can see there would be temptation there for a certain type of mind."

"What ever became of him, do you know?"

"One feels a little delicate about asking some questions. But since he was included in the family annals, the inference is that some arrangement was reached."

"Perhaps he had a good lawyer," Alice suggested.

George grinned. "Corporation law legitimizes a lot of things. But it legitimizes them in advance."

"Perhaps the culprit paid off in good wampum," Alice went on. "But more likely he found something else to use for money."

"That is a field for conjecture. You might suggest the idea to that mystery-monger husband of Virginia's. You still see a good deal of the Burgesses, don't you?" George Scudder had been a devoted suitor of Virginia Daly; but she had gone ahead and married the other fellow.

"Not so much any more. They like the country in summer, and she has given up her Greenwich Village apartment," Alice reported.

"Wedded bliss on Long Island, eh? I was hoping that he would choke on one of his own implausibilities and the field would again be left clear for me. There, that's a statement he could use in one of his stories: I've been heard to offer threats, and when he dies of eating poisoned chocolates that were sent him anonymously through the mail, I'll come under immediate suspicion."

Alice shook her head. "No good. Too implausible. I remember when the head of New Scotland Yard actually did eat some poisoned chocolates which had come to him anonymously through the mail. But Don couldn't use that in one of his stories. It's much too far fetched."

"Don's readers must suspend disbelief, surely."

"So must any reader. Virginia writes about facts. But she works from facts as they are reported by other people. She has threatened lately to write a novel. Oh, perhaps I shouldn't have said that!"

"That's a harmless threat. I hear from her at Christmas. Speaking of which, your anthology will solve the problem of my Christmas list. Keep up my file of Burgesses and Dalys, too. She still writes under her maiden name, doesn't she?"

Alice allowed that statement to go unanswered. Gathering her bag and gloves, she said, "Let me know how many copies of the anthology you'll need. And George, that one about the wampum—you won't mind if I tell it to people, will you? It's the funniest thing I've heard in a long time."

George rose when she did; but before she could turn toward the door, he put out a detaining hand. "Don't wait until you have another anthology you can bestow on me, or find another semiorphan deserted on your hands. Won't you and your husband dine with me some evening when you can arrange to get away from the shop?"

"Our fall busy season is starting in right now," Alice informed him. "But we have our off days almost any week until after Thanksgiving, when our Christmas rush starts."

They left it at that. Alice repeated most of the details of her visit when she talked it over with Harry. The episode of the counterfeit wampum, however, she reserved for Don

Burgess, whenever she should see him next. He might be able to use it, either as an episode or as conversation in one of his books; in any case, it was too good to be wasted as idle chatter around the Village.

Remembering Don Burgess and that discussion of nomenclature and changes in names for purposes of disguise, she remarked to Harry, "Couldn't Don do something with the idea of a person who simply reversed his names when he took to a career of crime? For instance, suppose his name was originally Harry Martin—"

"Wait a minute! The wrong Harry Martin might get his mail. That would include the letter which might have cleared the fugitive."

"We'll tell Don that for what it's worth," Alice decided. "Or rather you can tell him. I want you to get full credit for the idea."

"You want me to take the blame, you mean. But what were you saying when I was rude enough to interrupt you?"

"If the man's name was originally Harry Martin, he could reverse it and put in a middle initial. Harry Martin could then become Martin K. Harrison. That would give a clue of sorts. It might even provide a new twist to that old situation of the initials on the bags."

"Leave out the middle initial and the name sounds less authentically American somehow. Not Dickensian, though, does it? Dickens generally had ordinary-enough given names for his characters; it was the surnames which were strange."

"Chuzzlewit, Scrooge, Pinch. Harry, you ought to write down your random reflections," Alice admonished. "You might work them up into a magazine article some time. Or they might come in handy when you write the running commentary for your next—"

Harry laid his hand over her mouth. "Bad luck to say it! I haven't yet recovered from the first one, anyhow. I need a little time for recovery."

"Time to sing 'Forty-Nine Bottles,' some afternoon when you're on your way back from the post office and stop in at the apartment instead of returning to the shop."

It was on the tip of Alice's tongue then to say, 'She came looking for you one day when you weren't in the shop. That trollop, all scented up to catch a man in spring.' But before the words were actually out, Harry commented, "My singing is too bad even for me to listen to. We've canvassed that subject anyhow, haven't we? Another ditty occurs to me. One that's much shorter." He closed his eyes and hummed,

You may push the damper in,
You may pull the damper out,
But the smoke goes up the chimney just the same.

"Oh, but that's for Bess Johnson!" cried Alice. "She really might make something of it. Not that I'm sure the smoke does any such a thing. Even if it did, that's the philosophy of defeatism."

"It does sound like an unsuccessful candidate after Election Day. Better at that than combing over one's past mistakes."

"One's *past* mistakes?" Alice picked him up. "How can a person comb over his future mistakes?"

"How dismal you make that sound! You drive me back on the damper and the smoke. That way I can blame it all on fate."

"We're telling Don Burgess, and we're telling Bess Johnson. We really have plenty of business of our own to mind without trying to run their lives for them. You must give the anthology a big play in your mail-order lists. That part of the business still hasn't picked up much."

"It has picked up. The anthology should do well by it, and it by the anthology. Are we going back to Brooklyn for a weekend soon?"

[307]

"Almost any time, so far as I'm concerned. You like the change, don't you, Harry?"

"The change I would like—" began Harry, and checked himself halfway.

After a perceptible pause, she answered, "—would be what, Harry?"

She had hesitated just too long. He answered, "Oh, nothing!"

A dozen times later in the evening she wished she had been a little more receptive. Yet each time she hesitated to make a fresh opening. That hesitancy returned to plague her later. The very next day Alice's high horse came tumbling down; it was a very high horse, and gave her a long distance to fall.

Harry had gone off with a mail order. Bill Thayer and Alice alternately waited on customers; it was before the busy hour of the afternoon, and things were drifting along nicely enough for a pleasant autumn afternoon. But presently Alice's thoughts returned to Harry. It was almost time for him to come back from his errand. Just for once, it would do no harm if she were caught actively watching for his return.

She took up her station at one of the show windows. Then, catching sight of a familiar figure on the other side of Seventh Avenue, she moved toward the door of the shop just as the traffic lights changed and the sweep of city travel along a north-and-south highway began again.

To her horror, she saw a pedestrian breasting the stream of traffic. He took advantage of a momentary lull, darted halfway, stood there in the center of the fracas. Stood there while horns tooted and cars swerved, then did the worst thing possible: he again took up his eastward progress, then ducked back toward his former stand, then again ducked east. Finally he was brushed by a fender. Just then traffic lights again changed.

Alice had heard somebody shriek. She didn't know who it

was. But now Bill Thayer was beside her. A man got out of the offending car and asked her to give her name as a witness. A policeman appeared out of nowhere. There on her other side stood Harry Martin, who had crossed the next time he got the light. The injured man was a total stranger.

"I heard you scream," Harry said. "That was an awful thing for you to see. The buzzard's own fault, of course. I'll give my name as a witness, too, though I don't think I saw it quite as clearly as you did."

"Saw it clearly?" Alice gasped. "I—I didn't know what I was seeing. I thought—" She turned sick and giddy, between postponed shock and sudden relief. The two men helped her into the shop.

Alice sat there with her back to the street. They gave her a shot of liquor; but she refused a second drink. She had a bad hour to face right now. A bad person to face, too: an aggrieved wife, taking it out on her husband for his folly. His one season of folly, surely, in all these years. Harry had always been so generous with her, too.

She had razzed and tortured him. Yes, and tortured herself as well; she had missed the dear deep intimacy they had shared for so many years. She had rebuffed his attempts at reconciliation. The cheapness of his affair had been her great grievance. Actually that made it rather pathetic. Alice, you Pharisee! You have spent all this time thanking God that you were not as other people were. Perhaps the others were the ones who had reason to pride themselves.

It had taken a perfectly fortuitous happening to reveal Alice to herself. Scores, possibly hundreds, of just such accidents occurred in New York every day. If she hadn't happened to witness this one, she might have gone on indefinitely persisting in her folly.

The fact that she had mistaken a stranger for her own husband might reveal something dire about her subconscious. The Greenwich Village amateur psychoanalysts would certainly have opined that somewhere deep down Alice Martin wished her husband out of the way. The amateur psychoanalysts would have picked up the poker by the wrong end, as usual. What actually came home to Alice now was that sooner or later either she or Harry would have to die and leave the other.

She simply could not imagine life without Harry. The sword down the middle of the bed would be cold comfort indeed if the other side of the bed were sadly and permanently vacant.

Alice had been thrown off her high horse. No question any longer of climbing down; the best she could do now was pick herself up and brush off the dust.

The question was how. There was danger of saying too much; that would sound as if she were seeking grounds for a fresh quarrel. There was danger of saying too little; Harry deserved something explicit, if only to clear up the fog. There was very little question of when. The misunderstanding had already gone on much too long; it must be cleared up as soon as possible.

Alice turned to face the shop. Both Harry and Bill were waiting on customers in the casual Waverley way; but Harry was keeping one eye on her. The instant that it caught hers, he said, "Feeling better now?"

"Feeling all right. Get me a glass of water, will you please, Harry?—Oh, thank you!"

"Wouldn't you like to go home and rest for a while?"

"Later, perhaps. Not just now. I'll stay here a while and get my breath back."

Alice sat there looking out at Seventh Avenue. Now it was simply the passing scene, interesting to watch, but concerning her only as everything human must concern her. "I am a man, and consider nothing human alien to myself." That was one of Harry's Latin aphorisms, and very difficult to render into English. Either you sacrificed the play on words, as Alice had just done, or you used the word "human" twice. Blessed anthology, so lovingly and so fully dedicated to her! Blessed atmosphere of the shop, their beloved joint undertaking!

Carrie was on duty at the apartment today. She phoned presently to report that the casserole was in the oven, the salad made and the table set. Was there anything else Miss Alice wanted her to do before she left?

"Help yourself to whatever is on hand," Alice invited. "I'll be along later."

She sent Bill Thayer home then. At closing time she and Harry put the shop to bed. Then they went together to the tidy home where a light had been left burning for them. A real homecoming this was, not just a return from work. Alice felt that now she had the situation in hand.

"Let's change to our holiday house clothes," she suggested. "Make us a good stiff drink, too. I can feel for one now."

"You make the occasion; that's your 50 per cent. I'll make the drinks, with pleasure. Is this a case of celebration, the way you make it sound?"

"It's a case for confession on my part," said Alice. It wasn't until they were sociably seated together that she elaborated, "That woman came looking for you in the spring." She watched the color come up in his cheeks: an old man's slow, ugly flush. Then she went on, "She was scented for spring, but pretended it was just a casual errand. I didn't report it to you at the time, because that would have sounded too much like an accusation."

"She had phoned a few times; but I supposed she was discouraged," Harry muttered.

"I know. She threw herself at you. Women do these days and hereabouts."

"It's the Village, eh?"

"Call it that."

Harry sipped his drink, but with an air of not really tasting it. "I suppose she thought that I had money."

[311]

"No need to abase yourself too much," Alice said dryly. "You're a man as well as a meal ticket."

"You're in a position to know, Mrs. Martin. You've put up with me for a good many years. A good many years!" Harry repeated sourly. "I suppose this just shows the truth of the adage, 'There's no fool like an old fool.' "

"You said that, not I," Alice reminded him.

"It's a brutal saying; but it's fatally true. There *is* no fool like an old fool." But Harry could smile again now; and when he resumed his glass, he lifted it to her.

Alice drained her glass and extended it for a refill. Then she said softly, "Those years with you haven't been too bad, Harry, until this last one, which hasn't been too good. But that was as much my fault as it was yours."

He stared at her with his mouth open. "You mean you're forgiving me for that ghastly folly? Things between us will be the same as they used to be?"

"See *Reader's Choice*, the section on 'Latin Aphorisms,' the aphorism which runs, 'Amantium irae redintegratio amoris,' which Mr. Harry Martin renders, 'Lovers' quarrels are the renewals of love.' In simpler English, 'Let's kiss and make up.' "

"Alice, you mean it? You really mean it?"

Alice lifted her left hand in a gesture of fending off; but in her right she held her glass. "All in good time, friend husband. The night is yet young. But I somehow feel that this is one occasion when I won't have any need for a pillow book."

Harry in turn lifted his glass. "Here's to more and better pillow books for everybody else! But for Harry Martin, Esquire, and Alice his wife, here's to only one pillow tonight!"

"Only one pillow!" echoed Alice. This time she was the one who reddened. But it was a soft, becoming blush like a bride's. For her, indeed, love was beginning all over.